A Latte Like Love

MICHELLE C. HARRIS

BERKLEY ROMANCE
NEW YORK

BERKLEY ROMANCE
Published by Berkley
An imprint of Penguin Random House LLC
1745 Broadway, New York, NY 10019
penguinrandomhouse.com

Copyright © 2026 by Michelle C. Harris
Penguin Random House values and supports copyright. Copyright fuels creativity, encourages diverse voices, promotes free speech, and creates a vibrant culture. Thank you for buying an authorized edition of this book and for complying with copyright laws by not reproducing, scanning, or distributing any part of it in any form without permission. You are supporting writers and allowing Penguin Random House to continue to publish books for every reader. Please note that no part of this book may be used or reproduced in any manner for the purpose of training artificial intelligence technologies or systems.

BERKLEY and the BERKLEY & B colophon are registered trademarks of Penguin Random House LLC.

Book design by Alison Cnockaert

Library of Congress Cataloging-in-Publication Data

Names: Harris, Michelle C., author.
Title: A latte like love / Michelle C. Harris.
Description: New York: Berkley Romance, 2026.
Identifiers: LCCN 2025030401 (print) | LCCN 2025030402 (ebook) |
ISBN 9798217188673 trade paperback | ISBN 9798217188680 ebook
Subjects: LCGFT: Romance fiction | Novels
Classification: LCC PS3608.A7832626 L38 2026 (print) |
LCC PS3608.A7832626 (ebook) | DDC 813/.6—dc23/eng/20250918
LC record available at https://lccn.loc.gov/2025030401
LC ebook record available at https://lccn.loc.gov/2025030402

First Edition: March 2026

Printed in the United States of America
1st Printing

The authorized representative in the EU for product safety and compliance is Penguin Random House Ireland, Morrison Chambers, 32 Nassau Street, Dublin D02 YH68, Ireland, https://eu-contact.penguin.ie.

To anyone who has ever felt like they've lost themselves, just know:
You can always find your way back.
You're so much more than the scars you carry.

And to Katy.
You were right.

Author's Note

Dear reader,

A Latte Like Love contains depictions of anxiety; depression; PTSD and panic attacks; suicidal ideation; internalized ableism; negative self-talk; self-harm; body dysmorphia; disfigurement; surgical recovery; dysfunctional family dynamics; physical violence; gore; the death of a parent; explorations of grief; discussions of drug use, abuse, and overdose; abandonment; food insecurity; explicit language; and explicit sexual content.

I know. That's a lot for a coffee shop romance.

However.

Despite all that, or perhaps even because of it, *Latte* is the sweetest, coziest love story I could possibly imagine—and it has the happiest of endings.

I can promise you that the destination is worth the journey.

Ultimately, I like to think that it always is, in the end.

All my love,
Michelle

A Latte Like Love

One

THE FIRST TIME he came to the coffee shop was on a Tuesday at exactly 8:17 a.m.

Audrey knew the precise time he walked through the door because their resident Karen (whose name was actually Patricia) had just gotten done berating her for the fifth time in as many shifts, and she always came in at 8:10 a.m. on her way to work—and because after dealing with Patricia, Audrey always had exactly thirteen minutes before she could go on break.

It was the same thing, the same routine, with the same regulars nearly every day she'd worked at Déjà Brew. She'd gotten a job at the little industrial-chic coffeehouse about five years ago, when she first set foot in New York City for college, and she learned pretty quickly that the clientele was definitely local. And they were definitely set in their ways.

But this guy was new. They didn't often get new customers, being so far off the beaten tourist path, and besides, she knew she'd never seen him before because she definitely would have remembered him if he'd ever come in during one of her shifts.

Audrey never forgot a face, after all.

But *this* man's face was almost completely hidden from her.

He was both enormously tall and wide, which would have made him plenty distinctive already, but he also wore a black KN95 mask over his mouth and nose. Not that it was terribly uncommon in New York, especially with the approaching fall and winter flu season, but still.

He stood out.

The new guy stepped up to the register, the hood of his black sweatshirt pulled over an equally black baseball cap tucked low over his eyes. A curtain of thick, dark hair covered the right one, hiding it from view, and the other peered down at Audrey, dark and wide and seemingly nervous—inasmuch as she could tell, anyway. So much of his face was covered, but she'd gotten fairly good at reading the nuances of eye crinkles over the last few years.

"Hi! Welcome to Déjà Brew. What can I get started for you?" she asked brightly, plastering on what she hoped was a dazzling smile.

Tips. She needed tips this month if she wanted to spread her loans further than they usually went.

Why were groceries so expensive?

The pile of debt she had to contend with didn't help either.

"Um . . ." His eye darted up to the menu and back down to her face before dodging away again. "One . . . l-large Americano." His voice was deep, but he said it so quietly, Audrey almost didn't catch it. She leaned over the counter slightly, a brow raised and her head tilted to hear him better.

"A large Americano?" He nodded. "For here or to go?"

"To go." He said it a little more loudly this time, though only barely.

Audrey grabbed a paper cup and scribbled the order on the side. "Room for cream?" He shook his head. "Name?"

"Theo."

She wrote that on the cup too and was just about to pass it off to Josh to make when Theo held up a hand to stop her, his single visible eye wide and worried. His hand trembled slightly.

"Wait! Uh . . . c-can I get that extra hot, please?"

"Of course you can." Audrey noted it and smiled softly at him, a real one this time. She'd never seen someone so obviously terrified to order a plain black coffee before, but how hard he was trying was endearing. When she rang him up, he silently passed her a twenty-dollar bill—and then promptly dropped all of his nearly sixteen dollars of change into their tip jar, immediately shoving his hand back into his pocket as soon as the coins clinked on the glass bottom.

"*Whoa.*" It was Audrey's turn for her eyes to widen. "Wow. Thank you, sir! That's—"

But before she could finish, he turned his back and retreated to an empty table in the corner. Josh called out his name, and Theo practically sprinted over to grab his coffee before hiding again, drawing his cap lower over his face as he sat and hunching his shoulders as though he were trying to make himself smaller. A futile attempt, to be sure, but she commended him for the effort.

Audrey took her break. When she came back, he was still sitting there, his mask still concealing his mouth, writing diligently in a little black leather notebook and not making eye contact with anyone.

He left at exactly 9:00 a.m.

He never took a single sip of coffee.

THE NEW GUY didn't come back until the following Tuesday.

Audrey didn't know why, but for the rest of that week, every time someone walked in wearing a black hoodie, she searched their face to see if it was him. But she was disappointed every time—not a mask in sight. Perhaps he hadn't liked their café or their coffee after all. Perhaps he was just visiting.

Was it because of how nervous he'd seemed? He'd barely been able to order from her. And then he'd left such a large tip.

Why?

Well, she supposed it didn't matter in the end. So many people came through their doors.

Easy come, easy go.

But on Tuesday at 8:17 a.m. on the dot, the door opened and he lumbered inside, his right leg hitching slightly as he squeezed his large frame through the gathered crowd lined up in front of the register, clearly trying to make himself as inconspicuous as possible while he waited his turn.

"I just don't understand why it's so hard to make me a mocha Frappuccino with extra caramel drizzle." Angry fingers tipped in long, fire-engine-red acrylics snapped in Audrey's face. "Hey, are you listening to me?"

She hid a scowl behind an expertly crafted customer service mask. "Patricia, I'm really sorry, but like I tell you every week, we're not a Starbucks. We don't have Frappuccinos."

"You could. I know you have blenders, I can see them in the back."

"Those are for our smoothie selection. I can make you a smoothie, or if you still want coffee, I can get you an iced mocha with some cold foam and a caramel drizzle. Does that work?"

Patricia rolled her eyes and tossed her frizzy bleach-blond hair over her shoulder. Her brow would have been furrowed if she were capable of it, but it looked like she'd just gotten a fresh round of Botox injections. "Fine. I'll take a grande iced mocha. Extra caramel. And I want that on the house."

Audrey's eye twitched, but she rang her up for a large, just like she did every time. She did not put the drink or the caramel on the house, and she ignored Patricia's irritated huff when she handed her the receipt.

A few more customers, and then it was the new guy's turn to step up to the register.

"Hey, Large Extra-Hot Americano! Welcome back." Audrey

gave him another brilliant smile, this time every bit as genuine as the first one she'd given him was not. He was dressed more or less the same as he had been the week before—black hoodie, black KN95, dark jeans, Air Jordans, well-worn black leather satchel slung over his shoulder—and still only one eye peeked out from beneath the pulled-low brim of his cap. But Audrey liked the way it crinkled around the edge when he looked at her, if only the slightest bit. "I was wondering if I'd see you again."

His gaze rested on her slightly longer than it did last week, and she could have sworn she heard a soft, bemused snort from beneath the mask. "You remembered me?"

"'Course. I never forget a face. Especially not one like yours."

The crinkles faded.

Audrey's stomach dipped. There was something about him that made her want to make him smile, but now she had the sense she'd done something terribly wrong. He shifted awkwardly on his feet and glanced up at their menu without responding.

"Did you like the coffee you got last time, or would you like to try something new?" she prompted. Déjà Brew prided themselves on their small-batch craft coffee roasting and careful brewing, and it bothered her that he didn't drink what Josh made him last week, even if he *had* taken it with him to go. It had to have been ice-cold by the time he'd left. She'd already resolved to step away from the register and do it herself this time, even though Josh was a fabulous barista and he knew his way around the Marzocco almost as well as she did. "I could make you a latte if you'd like." She leaned forward and cupped her hand over her mouth. "I'll even draw you something nice in the foam," she whispered conspiratorially.

"N-no, no, that's . . . that's all right." He waved her suggestion away. "You don't have to go through the trouble."

Oh.

Oh . . . wow.

Audrey stared. She hadn't noticed last week, but his hands were huge, with thick, strong fingers. They were covered in calluses and dotted with what looked like burn scars, little starbursts of long-healed white sparks and splashes and dots. An expensive-looking watch wrapped around his left wrist and flashed silver in the daylight streaming from the windows.

Theo raised a hand as if he was going to run it through his dark hair, but he stopped when he touched the fabric of his hood, almost like he'd forgotten he was still wearing it. His hand began to tremble, and he quickly clenched his fingers and swept them into a hoodie pocket as soon as her eyes landed on them.

"I'll get you another large black Americano, no room for cream and extra hot, then, if that's okay?" He nodded and she scribbled the order on the cup, just like she'd done last week. "For Theo, right?"

"Yeah. Th-Theo."

"Hi, Theo." Her smile widened. "I'm Audrey."

"Audrey? Like . . . Audrey Hepburn?" The way he said it with such hopeful interest made her tilt her head at him curiously. "You . . . look a little like her." Red emerged from beneath his mask, creeping into the tops of his cheeks, and he rubbed the back of his neck awkwardly with his unhidden hand.

"Oh, I don't know about that. Maybe." She shrugged. Why were her cheeks so warm all of a sudden? "She was lovely, though, wasn't she?"

"Yeah." What little she could see of his face softened. "Lovely."

She smiled at him again and stepped behind the machine, nodding at Josh to switch places with her. Luckily, they weren't as busy today as they normally were, and her hands swept with expert ease across the machine as she pulled a few fresh shots of espresso and poured them into extra-hot water. Technically, this was a long black and not an Americano, but she wanted to give him a nicer, richer crema without breaking the espresso.

All right, fine. She was an *excellent* barista. Maybe she wanted to show off a bit.

Maybe she could tempt him to drink it this time.

"Here you go, Theo. Just for you."

"Thank you," he mumbled, his fingers just barely grazing hers as he took the coffee in his hand. At her touch, he nearly dropped the drink and yanked his arm away as if he'd been electrocuted.

"Oh, s-sorry," he stammered, reaching forward again. "So sorry."

She pushed the coffee across the counter to him and drew her hand back, stifling a look of concern and replacing it with a soft smile. "It's fine. Don't worry about it."

"Thank you, Audrey," he muttered, retreating to the same corner as last time.

She postponed her break in favor of keeping an eye on him. Once again, he took a small black leather notebook out from his pocket and scribbled into it with a gold-tipped fountain pen. Once again, he pulled the brim of his baseball cap low over his face. And once again, he never removed his mask and never took a single sip of coffee.

At precisely 9:00 a.m., he gathered up his things, took his coffee cup, and left in a rush, without giving her so much as a backward glance.

Audrey checked the tip jar.

Just like last week, he'd left all of his change inside.

SHE STARTED LOOKING for Theo every day that summer.

The third week, he came in on Tuesday at exactly 8:17 a.m., just like the previous two weeks.

But then he also came in on Thursday.

And Friday.

Always at 8:17 a.m.

He always paid in cash.

And he always left the remainder of his broken twenty-dollar bills in their tip jar.

Theo began coming in three times a week, but little else changed. He barely spoke, struggled to order the same coffee every time, and never once removed his mask to drink it in the café. Instead, he claimed the same table for exactly forty minutes, clutched the warm cup in one hand, and wrote in his little notebook with the other, his leather satchel resting faithfully against his long legs. He always wore black, and Audrey could only ever see the upper left corner of his face.

No matter how hard she tried, no matter what she said at the register, she never got him to laugh.

It was hard not to fixate on such a goal.

He looked like he could use a laugh.

He was so sweet, Audrey ached to give him one.

He'd been coming in regularly three times a week for a month when the fall semester started at the tail end of August and time went strange. It was always like that when she shifted mindsets from just work to work *and* school, but she only had to do this one more time.

The Tuesday of her second week of classes was already an odd day. Monday had been so crazy, she was almost late for her capstone course after her shift, but this morning was practically dead.

"We haven't seen Pattycakes yet, have we?" Josh tamped freshly ground beans into the group head and clicked it into place. "Think she died?"

Audrey snorted at the nickname and shook her head. "Fat chance."

The lack of Patricia meant one of three things: she was running late (unusual, but most likely), she'd taken a vacation (god, Audrey hoped so), or she'd finally chosen to go get her goddamn Frappuccino at an actual Starbucks for once (wholly wishful thinking, but a girl could dream). A few of the usual suspects sat with their ceramic cups over in the lounge area, typing quietly away to the inoffensive lo-fi playing over the café's sound system, and Audrey drummed her fingers against the counter while Josh experimented with perfecting a ristretto.

"Hey, Auds." She glanced over her shoulder as he slid a shot to her. "Taste this, will you?"

"Sure." She sipped and thought for a moment as she rolled the coffee around on her palate. "You waited too long on that pull—it's a touch bitter."

"*Damnit.*" Josh turned back to the machine to try again, and that's when Theo finally slid into the café, looking mostly like he normally did. But this time, his cap wasn't pulled quite so low, and Audrey could see a bit more of his face and eye than usual as he stepped up to the counter.

"Hey, Theo! Happy Tuesday."

She leaned forward on an elbow and bit her lip as she grinned even wider at him. Now that she was getting a better look in better light, she could see his skin was speckled with freckles, dotting across his face like stars in the night sky. His eye also wasn't exactly brown, like she'd initially thought it was, but rather a more mottled hazel with dark brown clustered around his pupil and a lighter, greener color hovering around the edges.

Well.

That was interesting.

He was striking.

"Hi, Audrey," Theo replied softly, glancing around at the rest of the shop and looking even more nervous now that there were fewer people around. Perhaps it was because it might be harder for him to try to meld into the wall. "Slow day?"

"Yeah, you came at a good time. It's weird, but I'm not sad about it."

His eye caught on the shot of coffee she was still clutching between her fingers. "Wh-what are you, uh, dri-drinking?" he asked hesitantly, almost as if he was unsure if he should even try. His throat bobbed as he swallowed and tried again. "Well, I mean, what's—what's *your* favorite drink?"

Oh, so he was chatty today?

This was more words than she'd ever been able to wheedle out of him before.

How cute.

A slow smile crept across her lips while Theo fidgeted in front of her. He was about to wring those large, anxious hands together, and if she didn't know better, he might have even been sweating under that hoodie.

Actually, he *might* have been. It was a lot to wear out in the city in September when it was still this hot.

She folded her hands on the counter. "I'm drinking Josh's awful failed attempt at a ristretto."

"*I heard that!*" Josh snapped at her from the machine, and she giggled. Theo's eye crinkled, and his mask tilted upward over his cheeks.

There it was.

Finally, a smile.

Audrey beamed even wider at her victory.

"What's that?" Theo asked. "I've never heard of a ristretto." He winced and his mask shifted back down over his face, but it was so quick Audrey almost didn't notice. The door opened again behind him and another customer stepped up in line, but she couldn't see who it was. Theo was far too broad, and she was far too pleased at having made him smile to care. Whoever it was could wait.

"It's like an espresso, but 'restricted.' Pulled for less time, so it's sweeter, lighter. I like to put mine in a flat white. You can make some nice designs in the foam of a flat white." She rolled the glass between her hands. "I don't always have time to do it, but when it's slow, we like to practice that sort of thing. It's really fun, and a nice change of pace from the kind of stuff I study in my classes. I like the art of it."

"Oh, are you in school?" He raised a dark eyebrow. "Do you study art?"

"No, I'm an electrical engineering major. A super senior, actually."

"Don't sell yourself short, Audsbodkins," Josh shot from the Marzocco as he worked on another ristretto. "You're graduating this December from NYU. That's nothing to sneeze at."

"'Oddsbodkins'?" Theo's brow furrowed.

She jabbed a thumb over her shoulder. "Yeah, theater nerd over here's auditioning for the Scottish play, so he's working in Shakespeare puns wherever he can."

Josh lifted the fresh ristretto and struck a pose, holding it aloft as though it were a skull. "'*Tomorrow, and tomorrow, and tomorrow!*'" He clenched his free hand into a fist and sighed dramatically before opening one wry eye and straightening. "The audition is tomorrow and I'm hoping I at least get cast as the Porter this time. Hell, I'd even take Background Player Number Three if I could."

"Oh. Uh . . . break a leg, I suppose?" Theo huffed a laugh and turned his attention back to her. "That sounds like a nightmare to me. Acting, I mean."

Audrey's grin widened. "Me too. I could never. Too much attention. I don't think I'd like that, all those people looking at me."

"Exactly." What little she could see of Theo's expression softened. "I'm glad I'm not the only one who—"

An impatient finger jabbed at Theo's shoulder, and he nearly jumped out of his skin at the contact. "You can flirt with her some other time, *sir*," snapped Patricia as she shoved forward to the head of the line, obviously running late (the worst of the three options), and obviously salty about it. "I need to get my coffee and I need to get it *now.*"

"I'm sorry, ma'am." Theo's shoulders slumped and he started to shuffle aside to make room for her. "You can go ahe—"

"No, Theo, you were here first." Audrey let her usual mask fall and glared at the woman before turning back to him. "What would *you* like?"

He held up a trembling hand. "No, it's fine, I can wait, I've got time. I—"

Patricia shoved him fully out of the way and stepped up to the register, and Theo stumbled back with an anguished grunt, grabbing on to the counter with his left hand and barely managing to stay on his feet. His right leg buckled. "I want my usual." She jammed her finger onto the counter. Demanding.

No.

Absolutely not.

"You don't have a usual, *Patricia,*" Audrey snarled, "you order something different every time. And it's not your turn."

"Then I want a venti caramel macchiato Frappuccino, upside down, extra shot, three extra pumps of vanilla, and made with heavy whipping cream."

"It's not your turn and this is not a Starbucks, *we don't have ventis or make Frappuccinos,*" she hissed.

"Well, I'm friends with the owner and *you need to make me the fucking coffee I ordered, you little bitch*!" Patricia shouted.

"HEY."

Theo rested a hand softly on Patricia's shoulder. "Don't talk to her that way," he growled. "I think you need to leave before—"

"Is that a threat?!" Patricia shrieked as she whirled around and pointed a finger in his face. "How *dare* you touch me! And why are you still wearing a goddamn mask? Get that off your face so I can see who you are to report you!" She reached up, grabbed his mask, and yanked.

"Hey, don't you touch him! That's assault!" Audrey cried, running for the gap in the counter to get to the front of the café. Josh was already in the back calling the police.

Theo jerked away from Patricia's hand, but she had too good of a grip on the mask between her clawed fingers. The elastic ear loops snapped, and it fell away from his face. His eye widened in horror and he scrambled to catch it, but it was too late. It dropped on the floor and everyone froze.

And Audrey finally got a good long look at him.

He was handsome. *Really* handsome. He had a wide mouth, and full, plush lips, with deep indents carved around it where dimples might appear if he smiled. Large moles intermingled with the delicate freckles skipping across his cheeks, more constellations of beauty marks contrasting brightly against his pale skin and high cheekbones.

But those features were all overshadowed, all marred by the thick, red, vicious scar crackling violently across his face, not quite healed and obviously devastatingly fresh. Whatever had wounded him had cut deep—*very* deep. His skin was still puckered around the edges of the scar where some of the dozens—no, *hundreds*—of stitches had only recently been removed, and parts of it were still scabbed over.

It crept up from under his collar along his neck, and her eyes traced the length of it. The part that disappeared under the thick, dark waves covering his right eye was still stitched closed with black sutures twisting deep into his skin. He must have been split open to the bone.

Whatever happened had hurt, in more ways than one, and that hurt was reflected now in the way his lovely mouth dropped open in fear and how horror darkened the one eye fixated on Audrey's face.

"Theo—" She stepped up to him and tried to put her hand on his shoulder, but he stumbled away from her touch. Patricia stayed silent and rooted in place, gaping openly at him as if he were some sort of freak. As if he were a monster. The look of disgust on that woman's face made Audrey feel sick. "Theo, are you okay? I—"

He couldn't look at her. He covered his face with his arm and bolted for the door, shoving it open with his free hand and disappearing out into the street.

The café was completely silent. Everyone had seen.

Audrey looked down at her feet. He'd dropped his little black notebook. It must have fallen out of his pocket when he'd leapt away from Patricia, and she picked it up and clutched it to her chest, fighting back tears for him.

Josh had Patricia arrested for assault. The whole thing was caught on the café's security cameras and by the customers working in the lounge on their phones. At least one of them posted it on social media, and it caught like wildfire. The incident even briefly went viral on TikTok.

Tim, the owner of Déjà Brew, called both Audrey and Josh into the admin office in the back the next day. He was mortified by the kind of attention the café was getting online and had already written a scathing response to someone on Reddit about it—particularly since Patricia was, predictably, a liar. They weren't friends, he had no idea who she was, and while he wasn't thrilled with how Audrey had escalated the situation, he wasn't going to hold it against her. He permanently banned Patricia from the premises for the assault. She didn't try to come back to Déjà Brew after that.

But neither did Theo.

He didn't return to the café the next Tuesday.

Or the Tuesday after that.

Or the Tuesday after that.

Or the Tuesday after that.

Two

YOU'RE STILL LOOKING at that thing? Auds, it's been a month."

Violet shut their apartment door and tossed her keys onto the rickety old table near the entryway. They'd found it in the street and painted it a bright mint green once they'd determined it wasn't infested with bedbugs or termites. Their whole apartment was decorated that way: filled with secondhand inheritances, thrift shop treasures, IKEA clearance items, found objects, and donations from family.

Well, from Violet's, anyway.

"I know, but you weren't there and you didn't see his face, Vi. It was heartbreaking. I can't get him out of my head."

"You never figured out his last name? It wasn't on his credit card? You would've run it every time he came in."

"He always paid in cash."

Audrey ran her hands over the cover of the little leather notebook Theo had left behind at the coffeehouse. She'd taken to looking at it in her spare moments, flipping idly through its pages while searching for clues to its owner's whereabouts.

When she first picked it up, she'd expected it to be a journal, given the way he'd seemed to be writing in it. But it wasn't at all. It was actually a tiny sketchbook, covered in rich, hand-lettered art drawn in black ink. Odd, incongruous words and phrases snaked along its pages, all in different styles, some calligraphic, some gothic, some blocky, others more sleek and modern or funky and futuristic. Sometimes there were little numbers scratched beneath the lettered designs—some that were definitely dimensions, and others mixed with letters and paired with a hashtag. She'd Googled them, and a few were either hexadecimal color codes or codes for Pantone colors, depending on the combination. The rest she couldn't decipher.

Every so often, the word art was interrupted by a page full of abstract lines or curves, idle squiggles and incomprehensible doodles. More often than not, there were full sketches. Landscapes of Central Park in the spring, views of the Brooklyn Bridge, studies of architecture, pensive portraits of people on the subway. Sometimes they were only rendered in black and white, messy and haphazard and experimental. Other times, they were painted with layers of watercolors or filled in with pastels or inks.

All of them were beautiful.

Even the more recent ones at the back—despite the way the lines twisted and trembled.

They shook like his hands.

There was a marked difference between those and the ones at the front.

"He's gotta be an artist or a designer or something, right?" she muttered to herself, turning a page and tilting the journal to look at the design there. This one was another hand-lettered piece, and it took up an entire sheet, curling along it horizontally in a smooth, sweeping cursive. It read "The Cherry Stem," and it incorporated a little photorealistic sketch of a pair of cherries with their stems twisted into a heart shape around the words. "If he is, I should be able to find his portfolio."

"Yeah, but how long have you been looking?" Violet plopped down on the couch next to her and rested her head on Audrey's shoulder with a sigh. "I think you've sorted through half of the Theos in New York on Facebook and Instagram, and still you haven't found a trace of him. I'm betting he's one of those guys without social media. If he's as skittish as you say, I don't think he's going to like attention." She peered at the design. "And it could be a hobby. Not every creative pursuit has to be monetized."

"You're probably right." She picked at the edges of the notebook with her nail. "Do you think he's local to the coffeehouse? Maybe he lives nearby. Maybe I've been casting too wide a net."

"Didn't he always come in at the same time?"

"Yeah. Eight seventeen, every morning."

"That's awfully specific." Violet hummed. "Maybe he does live close by—maybe that's how long it takes him to walk there from his building? Or ride the train? Seems too exact to be anything random."

"That gives me hope, then. I should start looking at property records in the area, see what I can find."

"Way to be a stalker."

"It's important, Vi. Trust me. I feel it."

Audrey rested her head on Violet's and closed her eyes. They'd lived together all throughout college after being randomly paired by their university's roommate-matching system when they were freshmen, and it was the luckiest thing either of them could imagine. They'd melded together immediately like peanut butter and jelly and had become almost instant best friends, even though Violet was at the Gallatin School of Individualized Study pursuing a custom degree in sustainable fashion and business, something Audrey couldn't even come close to understanding. Violet had graduated on time over a year ago, though, and she'd gotten an admin job at some fancy department store in Midtown. Not the real dream of being a designer, but it was something in the industry, at least. And it paid the bills.

Audrey still felt odd sometimes about how different their lives—

and their paychecks—were now. It was hard not to feel left behind by all of her friends. But she was thankful they could at least still afford to live together in their tiny, cramped apartment while she plugged diligently away at the last remaining dregs of her undergraduate degree.

She flipped another page in the book and stared at the graphic word art there for the umpteenth time. "I really hope he comes back."

"You barely talked with him, though. He just ordered coffee and sat there. What makes him so special?" Violet stood with a sigh and went to stare blankly in the fridge. "I've never seen you fixate on someone like this before, much less a customer."

"He's really sweet, and *so* shy. You haven't met him, but if you did, you'd get it." She drew in a deep breath and let it out slowly. "He was just . . . so different than my other regulars, and he was trying really hard to talk to me. I like him." And then she scoffed and raised an eyebrow. "And besides, don't tell me you *don't* know what it's like to have a crush on someone at work, not with the way you talk about that Alastair guy."

Violet's face darkened. "Don't you *dare* mention that asshole," she hissed. "That ginger twat won't even give me the time of day."

"And yet I somehow hear about him constantly." She tapped her finger pensively across her lips. "Almost like how I talk about Theo."

"Shut up, Audness," Violet shot over her shoulder. "That's not at all the same and you know it."

"Oh, so you *do* get it, then?" Audrey purred, taking pleasure in needling her bestie. "Are you going to admit that I can read someone like a book at first glance and I know the sweet ones when I see them?"

Violet grabbed some leftover Chinese food and opened the container, plunging chopsticks straight into the cold noodles. "Fine,

fine," she mumbled between bites. "You see the best and the worst of humanity in that damn café. When are you going to quit? You're too good for Déjà Brew, and that coffeehouse is way too cool for half of that clientele."

Audrey sighed and sank back onto the couch cushions. "I'll leave it behind when I graduate and get a big-girl job. And besides, at least my boss is never around. Tim pretty much lets us do whatever we want during our shifts as long as we make good coffee and make him money. It's not so bad."

She turned back to the notebook and ran her fingers over the pages again. She'd already done it a thousand times this month, but maybe once more would finally unlock some information she could use. Maybe she could simply magically absorb information from it through her fingertips.

"Actually, that's a good point," Violet said with a jab of the chopsticks. "Where are you going to start applying for jobs? You're not going to leave me, are you?" Violet threw herself into their ratty armchair across from her, one so well used and well-worn that it was a sight to behold but also easily the most comfortable piece of furniture either of them owned. Sometimes it wasn't just about looks; it was something's character that mattered most. "You can't leave New York."

"I don't want to ever leave you, don't worry. And I love New York. This city was always my dream." Audrey turned to the last page. It was blank, just as it always was. Theo hadn't quite filled up this notebook, which was at least half of why she wanted to get it back to him. He probably had so many more beautiful things to draw in it.

But today, she noticed something different, and she raised an eyebrow as she ran the paper between her fingers. It was thicker than it should have been compared to all the other pages. How had she never realized that before?

She rubbed the corner of the page between her thumb and forefinger. It loosened and cracked, finally coming apart to reveal that two pages had been stuck together. She turned to the actual last page in the journal and then held a hand to her mouth as she gasped.

It was a sketch of her in black ink, facing the viewer from behind the café's register. Loose pen strokes curved and twisted in the way her hair was always falling out of her messy bun to frame her face, and she plucked absently at the real strands, perfectly replicated on the page before her—not quite straight, but not quite wavy either. Her expression was soft, the corners of her mouth only just tilted up at the beginning of the smile she usually gave Theo, and he'd somehow managed not only to faithfully capture her looks but also to infuse an added radiance all the way into her eyes, which were wide and luminous. Audrey had never seen herself portrayed in such a way. No photo had ever made her look like *this*.

Was this how he saw her?

She was *beautiful*.

She'd never really thought of herself as beautiful before. She'd always assumed she was kind of plain: medium brown hair, mottled green eyes, entirely too many freckles that just sort of looked like she was perpetually flecked with stray coffee grounds. Nothing exceptional. Nothing extraordinary.

She wasn't anything special.

Was she?

Her eyes trailed down the rest of the drawing. Everything about the coffeehouse had been lovingly and accurately rendered around her, down to their tip jar sign and the Marzocco espresso machine and the pastries in the cooler to her right. Each shape was outlined in rich black ink, but the rest of the sketch had been shaded in layers of light, flowing sepia reminiscent of watercolors.

But there was something especially odd about that paint. There was a scent to it—one she knew intimately.

When Audrey lifted the notebook to her nose, a wave of emotion washed over her and she fought back the tears pricking at her eyes.

Because it smelled like coffee.

BY THE TIME mid-October rolled around, the air was finally beginning to turn crisp and the leaves swirled around in the streets, their once-verdant color now burning in the fiery shades of autumn.

Audrey kicked some across her combat boots as she made her way home from class, relishing the dry crunch and the musty fall scent in the air. Autumn was her favorite time of the year, when flavors became spiced and warm, when you could start lighting fires to combat the tentative nip of a wilder, cooler wind, and when jack-o'-lanterns began grinning in windows out at the street.

Midterms were only a few weeks away, and Audrey was getting nervous. She was almost ready to graduate, but her senior capstone course was proving harder than she'd wanted it to be. Choosing to work on designing a more sustainable, eco-friendly industrial battery had seemed a worthwhile endeavor at the time, but she was running into roadblocks in the lab, and she wasn't at all sure how her final project showcase was going to go in December. Failure was looking exceedingly likely, and even though that might not actually result in an F, it would still be devastating to her pride all the same. She'd worked so hard to get here.

Losing her scholarships that first year had been difficult enough.

She was so preoccupied with her thoughts that she almost missed him. But it was the unmistakable way he walked that jolted her back to reality.

She'd know that gait anywhere.

She'd been looking for it for well over a month now.

"*Theo,*" she gasped.

He turned a corner down the street, but it had to be him—same dark hoodie over a black ball cap, same mask worn tightly over his face, same painfully anxious waddle. Audrey took off at a sprint to try to catch him, her book bag slapping against her thigh and making her dress ride up. She yanked it down angrily and lost precious seconds, but turned the corner just in time to watch him enter an unassuming brownstone, the door still swinging shut after him.

She waited a minute and trotted up the steps. It wasn't a residence, but a commercial building, and the frosted letters on the window read: Dr. Amelia Harper, MD, PsyD, LPC, CCTP, DBT-LBC. She did a quick Google search.

Oh.

Pain shot through her chest when she opened the link for the top result.

Dr. Harper was a trauma therapist.

Audrey bit her lip. It felt wholly inappropriate to wait for him here while he was in a therapy session. She'd had to go through state-mandated counseling herself after an incident in high school, and she knew how raw it could feel after one of those visits.

But she also couldn't leave without letting Theo know how to contact her. Odds were she'd never find him again if she did.

She hesitated long enough on the stoop for a squat, middle-aged woman with a kindly face to approach from the inside and unlock the door.

"Can I help you, honey?" the woman asked. "I was watching you hover on camera." She pointed to the doorbell and Audrey blushed. "Are you lost? Or do you need an appointment?"

"Well, I don't know. Maybe I do," she muttered. "You're not Dr. Harper, are you?"

"No, sweetie, she's in a session right now. I'm her receptionist."

An idea crept into her head. "Oh that's—that's perfect, actually. Can you give the man who just came in a message for me? He's a friend of mine, but I haven't gotten to talk to him in a while. I've been worried about him, and I saw him come in here from the street. I thought—"

"Oh, uh . . . well . . ." The woman hesitated. "I suppose so. What do you need to tell him?"

"Can I come inside for a minute? I just need to write a note."

The receptionist looked her up and down, probably noting her windswept hair, ragged tights, and NYU book bag, and decided she looked harmless enough before finally nodding and motioning her over to a desk in what might have been the sitting room when the house was still used as a home. Audrey pulled a notebook out from her bag and scribbled a quick message before tearing it out, sending a few scraps of paper flying.

"You can read it, I swear there's nothing that might upset him in it," she said, handing it over. "At least, I should hope not. And I hope you're not violating anything by giving it to him. I really just wanted to check on him, and—"

The woman put on a pair of readers and glanced at the note. She gave Audrey a soft smile. "I'll make sure he gets it before he leaves, dear."

She breathed out a sigh of relief. "Thank you. I really appreciate it."

Audrey turned and left, shutting the door carefully behind her and glancing up at the charming brownstone before striding back down the way she came.

Maybe he'd come back.

Maybe she'd see him again after all.

HE CAME BACK to the café the next day, a Thursday, at 8:17 a.m.

Audrey's heart skipped a beat when Theo walked in, squeezing himself through the narrow doorway with a vaguely terrified look in his eye, and she motioned to his usual table. He hesitated, shifting awkwardly on his feet before finally taking her hint and limping over to sit with his back against the wall. She turned to Josh and jerked her head in Theo's direction.

"Hey, can you switch with me for a second? And then I'm taking my break a little early. And a little longer."

"Sure, I got you, boo. I can cover."

"You're the best."

He snorted as he took her place behind the register. "Yes, I am. And you can make it up to me later when I have to leave a little early for rehearsal."

"You don't have rehearsal, you didn't get that part. It's a date, isn't it?"

"Excuse you, Audball!" he gasped, clutching nonexistent pearls. "Cutting straight to the quick. Rude to call me out like that!"

"You'll get the next one." She waved him off with a smirk. "And I've got your back, don't worry."

Audrey fired up the machine and made two coffees, one in a to-go cup and one in a thick ceramic mug, before undoing her apron and sliding through the gap in the counter to the lounge area.

Theo was waiting for her, his hands folded on top of the table and his leg bouncing anxiously up and down beneath it.

"Hi." Audrey beamed as she set down his usual order in front of him. "Can I sit with you today?"

"Uh . . ." His eye darted between the coffee and her face. She waited patiently with her cup in hand. "Sure, if you want to."

"Great." She slid into the seat across from him and took a sip of her flat white. "I'm sorry about the note, I—"

"You didn't need to get me anything. I didn't pay for this." What little she could see of his brow furrowed, and she bit the inside of her cheek.

She'd expected this much. She didn't need to know him well to have guessed he'd have a hard time accepting something for free.

"Of course I did, Theo. I wanted to. I owed you a thank-you for standing up for me that day. It's on the house."

"Oh."

He took it between his large palms and slid it closer to his chest. Even if he wasn't going to drink it, she'd wanted to give him something to do with his hands, especially since he'd lost what usually kept them occupied.

"Well, it was nothing." His neck turned pink. "But thank you."

"It wasn't nothing. And Patricia's not allowed here anymore, by the way," she said, taking another casual sip of her drink. "I mean, she's always been a nasty piece of work, and I should've kept my cool. The whole thing was my fault, but I didn't like her pushing you around like that. I don't do well with bullies."

That got him to huff. "Yeah, me neither." He plucked absently at the cardboard sleeve around his cup. "And it wasn't your fault."

"I'm really sorry about the whole thing. I get it if you haven't wanted to come back since then." She grasped her own cup between her hands, grateful for its warmth. "You didn't have to come here if you didn't want to. You could have just texted me like I said in the note. You have my number now."

"No, no, it's all right. I—I wanted to see you." He finally looked at her head-on, gazing steadily into her eyes. "You said you had something of mine?"

"Yeah, I do." She pulled his notebook out from her pocket and slid it across the table to him. His eye widened and he gasped beneath his mask.

"*Oh my god.* I thought I lost that." He snatched it up and flipped through it eagerly. "I've been looking everywhere for it. I tore my whole house apart."

"You dropped it that day and I picked it up right after you left. I've been trying to find you to give it back ever since."

"That's so sweet of you, thank you. You have no idea what you've just returned to me. You've really saved my ass, here. I thought I'd have to—" He suddenly froze, a hint of redness coloring what little she could see of his cheeks above the mask. He looked back up at her slowly. "You, uh . . . you didn't happen to look through this, did you?"

"Yeah. I did." Audrey bit her lip. "I was trying to find clues as to who you were other than Theo-who-orders-large-extra-hot-Americanos-to-go, so I went through the whole thing. Turns out there are a lot of Theos in New York and none of the ones I found online were you."

He swore under his breath and ran a trembling hand over his face before wincing and jerking it away, only to rest his forehead carefully in his palm. He seemed to be having some trouble breathing.

"Audrey, uh . . . look. I—I'm sorry about the drawing. You were *never* supposed to see that. I was just—"

"I liked it." When she spoke, he stilled and slowly glanced up at her again through his fingers. "The portrait of me? I thought it was stunning."

"You—you *did*?" He sounded surprised. "Are you sure? I . . ." He hesitated. "I didn't ask permission to draw you. I don't want you to think I'm creepy or anything, I just—" He drew in a deep breath and closed his eye, as if he couldn't bear to see her reaction. "I just like to draw what I think is beautiful," he muttered.

Audrey reached across the table and slowly slid her right hand over his left. He'd jerked away from her every other time they'd so much as barely grazed each other, but this time, he didn't. His hands dwarfed her own, and his skin was rough and calloused, but warm. When she touched him, his eye flew open and he stared at their hands in disbelief before meeting her gaze.

"I've never seen myself the way you drew me. It was nice." She rubbed her thumb over the back of his hand, feeling the bumps of his tiny starburst scars beneath the pad of her finger and trying to read them like braille. They were such curious markings, and she really wanted to know what she could divine from them. "I'd like to get to know someone who sees me like that—and stands up for me like that. He seems worth knowing." She squeezed his hand. "He's a mystery I'd like to unravel. Would that be okay?"

"Are you serious?" He raised an eyebrow. "*You* want to get to know *me*?"

"Yeah."

"Why?!"

Bemused.

Theo was completely bemused.

It was adorable.

"Because I think you're really sweet and cute and I can't stop thinking about you. Do I need another reason?" She shrugged.

"Wait. '*Cute*'?!" A crease formed between his brows. "No. But you . . . y-you saw my face. You saw what's under the mask."

"I did, yeah."

"And you still think—?"

"I couldn't *stop* thinking about that day—when you finally started talking to me and we were so rudely interrupted." She gave him a serious look. "Is it a problem if I want to get to know you? You don't have a girlfriend or anything, do you?"

He barked a sardonic laugh and then coughed. "Uh—*no.* No, I definitely don't."

"Well then, are you interested in me?"

"*God yes,*" he whispered, his voice so low she almost didn't hear him.

"Then why is this so shocking?"

Theo drew in a deep breath and blew it out, running his free hand along the back of his neck beneath the hoodie. The mask puffed over his cheeks, and she bit her lip again to hide a smile.

"How can you just be so . . ." he muttered to himself before shaking his head. "Audrey, I, uh . . . I don't get out much these days, you know. You already saw one of the few places I go. And . . . you already saw why." The red in his face deepened and he looked away from her again.

"That's all right. I don't get out a lot either. It's pretty much here and school and home."

"Are—are you *sure*?" He seemed wholly uncertain if what was happening to him was real.

"Yeah. I like you." She beamed at him and his eye grew even wider.

"You do? Just like that? Even with—with *this*?" He pointed nervously to his right cheek.

"Yeah. I do." She tightened her fingers around his palm. "It's just a scar, Theo. We all have them."

"No." He shook his head. "Not many people have them like I do."

He'd murmured that last part while he searched her face, almost as if he thought she might be lying. Panic briefly flashed across what little of his expression she could see, but when she didn't contradict herself or withdraw, he seemed to realize she was serious.

And he calmed.

"Okay." Theo stared down at their hands. "Okay. I'd . . . I'd like that, if you have some time to spend. I have—well, I have plenty of time these days, if I'm being honest."

"Great. I'm glad we're in agreement." She withdrew her hand and took another sip of her flat white. "Let me ask you something: Do you ever drink the coffee we make for you?"

"Of course I do." He looked at her like she was crazy. "Why wouldn't I? It's great coffee. Yours is particularly good."

"Do you drink it cold?"

He shook his head. "I try not to. It's usually cooled down a lot by the time I drink it, but it's warm enough. I put it in an insulated mug when I leave and take it home with me." He pointed to the worn leather satchel he carried. "I keep one in there."

"You do know we can make coffee directly in your own mug, right?" Audrey gave him a wry smile. "Josh and I implemented a sustainable cup policy a while back. And that will keep it hotter for you." She leaned across the table and gave him another stern look. "It's better when it's fresh."

He chuckled under the mask and then winced. "Fair point. And no, I didn't know about the cup policy. That's cool." He bent and rummaged around in his bag, eventually emerging with a fancy black-and-silver insulated coffee tumbler. He pulled the top off the coffee she'd made him and poured it inside before screwing the tumbler lid on tightly. "Thank you."

"You're welcome." Audrey checked her phone. Her break was over. "All right, Theo, I've got to get back behind the counter, but you're going to text me, right?" She pointed at his phone. "You put me in your contacts yesterday like I told you to, yes?"

"I didn't, but I will. I promise I'll text you tonight." He hesitated for a moment before steeling himself, squaring his shoulders and sitting up straight in his chair for once. "You'll get one from Theo Sullivan."

Finally: a last name.

"Okay, Theo Sullivan." She held out a hand and waited. "I'm Audrey Adams. It's nice to finally, truly meet you."

He stared at her hand before slowly pulling his right one out of his hoodie pocket. It trembled while his palm swallowed hers whole, and he seemed to have some trouble gripping, but he still held her firm as he shook her hand.

"It's nice to meet you too."

Her smile widened.

When he pulled away and hid his hand in his pocket again, his warmth lingered on her skin.

"You know I'll text you back, right? You don't have to wonder if I will or not." She tilted her head at him. "Are you going to come and see me? I can have coffee with you during my breaks, and I'd like that. I'm here every weekday morning until ten."

His eye crinkled. "Yeah, I'll come back. I've missed you, I was just worried about . . . about what you thought."

"You didn't have any reason to worry."

The crinkles faded. "Actually, yes. I did. I saw the video from TikTok. The one that went viral."

Audrey paled. "Oh." The video wasn't very long, but there was a part of it that had captured Theo's face during the altercation. Some of the comments she'd seen were reason enough for her to hope he didn't have social media, even though she'd been searching so hard for him there.

"But Theo, so many of the responses talked about how you were doing the right thing by standing up for me and trying to stop Patricia. They weren't—"

"Freeze frames of my uncovered face were posted on Reddit and Twitter, Audrey." He shook his head. "A few reporters even found me. I don't know how they got my contact info, but they tried to interview me, and the last thing I wanted to do was talk about it with them. I had to get my lawyer involved for them to leave me alone and not publish anything." He closed his eye. "Not everyone was kind."

"Those people can go fuck themselves." Her voice shook, and she bit the inside of her lip so hard, she thought she might bleed. She drew in a deep, steadying breath, trying to still her shaking hands. Her anger over the whole thing still simmered so close to the surface, it was hard to hold back.

Theo looked at her for a long moment before finally nodding. "All right," he murmured. "I'll come back and see you tomorrow."

She let out a long, relieved sigh and beamed at him. "Okay then. It's a date." She gave his shoulder a squeeze and grabbed her cup, slipping behind the counter and pulling her apron back over her head while she placed the mug in the dirty bin.

"All right, Au*dacity*," Josh muttered in her ear as she crossed him. "That was smooth. Real smooth. And you're getting on *me* about a date? You sure you should mix business and pleasure?"

"Shut up, you creeper." She punched his shoulder and grinned impishly. "But that was good, right? Could've gone south really fast."

She got back to her work, taking over making orders at the Marzocco while Josh worked the register. Theo stayed until 9:30 this time, drawing quietly at his table in his recovered notebook. Every once in a while, Audrey would glance up and catch him watching her, and he'd look away in embarrassment.

But every time he did, it made her smile.

Three

UNKNOWN | Hi, Audrey. This is Theo.

"Oh my god, he followed through," she muttered in frank disbelief, jolting up so fast from her almost-nap on the couch that her vision went fuzzy and she nearly passed out. Her fingers flew to save his contact information. Even though he'd promised to text her, you never knew with men. She'd been ghosted enough to hope for the best but expect the worst.

Though he did admit he was interested.

And he wouldn't have drawn her that way if he wasn't.

Violet poked her head curiously through her top bunk bed curtains. "Your cryptid? He actually came out of his cave to text you?"

New York was expensive, and they saved money by sharing a studio apartment rather than having separate bedrooms. They'd already spent so much time living in close quarters in a dorm that the tiny apartment with a kitchenette and a living area felt positively luxurious by comparison. Plus, it was helping Violet save enough money to make her student loan payments and giving Audrey enough financial leeway to buy some decent groceries. Sometimes. On occasion. Twin bunk beds with makeshift privacy curtains and a rule never to let dates stay over was a small price to pay.

Not that Audrey ever had any dates to bring here.

"Shut up, Violet. And yes, he did." Full punctuation and everything. Of course he'd use proper grammar.

AUDREY | Hi Theo! What are you up to this evening?

He seemed like he was probably a little older than her, so she upped her game. Didn't want to come across as juvenile with all lowercase and too many emojis or something.

THEO☕ | Nothing. Just watching a movie.

AUDREY | Which one?

THEO☕ | John Wick—the first one.

AUDREY | The best one, you mean

Violet groaned as she watched Audrey frantically type her responses. "You're going to go off and get yourself a boyfriend who worships the ground you walk on and then never spend time with me again, aren't you?"

"I am not going to abandon you and you know it," Audrey shot back while still staring at her phone screen. God, what a rush. Theo had said more words to her today than he had in the six weeks he'd been a regular at the café. Was this what being high felt like? Had she actually managed to crack him open a little? "But you do need to let me have this. You know how chronically single I've been."

"Understatement of the century."

Her phone buzzed again. Theo had sent her a photo of a new drawing in his little black notebook. She expanded it and a sketch of a tree-lined street filled with leaves soaked in blazing, fluid watercolors of red, orange, and gold filled her screen.

THEO☕ | I drew this one today. Fall in the city's my favorite season.

THEO☕ | What's yours?

Her heart beat faster.

"All right, fine." Violet pulled herself back inside her makeshift bedroom and started to close the curtains. "Have fun texting your new mystery man."

She flashed her roommate a smug look as her face disappeared in the seams of the fabric. "I am and I will." Violet shut herself inside for the night, and Audrey turned back to her messages.

AUDREY | What a gorgeous sketch.

AUDREY | Fall's my favorite too.

JUST LIKE ALWAYS, Theo slid inside the café at 8:17 a.m.

Fridays were magnificent, if only because Audrey didn't have class and she actually had weekends off these days. She was missing out on the extra income from those shifts, but she'd wanted to dedicate herself to adjusting to a more typical workweek schedule in anticipation of finally graduating, not to mention needing to catch up on homework and reading for school. So for the first time in years, Fridays actually were the beginning of her weekends. And this one was even better than they normally were.

He waited in line and sidled up to the register like he always did. But rather than hesitating this time, his eye had already crinkled beneath the shadow of his hat.

"Hi."

"Hi." Audrey grinned so wide, it was almost painful. But she couldn't help it. The thrill of seeing him again in front of her now was too intoxicating, and the way his gaze seemed to brighten when he looked at her only made it worse.

It was a delicious sort of ache, one to linger on and savor.

He had to have been grinning just as widely under that mask as she was now. But the suspense of not knowing for sure was killing her.

Josh banged some packed espresso on the counter a little more aggressively than strictly necessary, jerking her back to reality. Audrey cleared her throat.

"Would you like something different today, or just the usual?"

Theo thought for a moment before reaching into his satchel and pulling out his travel mug. "Can I have what you like? I want to try your drink."

"A flat white? You got it."

She took his mug from him and rang him up, but she didn't even need to signal to Josh to switch this time. He was already hovering behind her at the register. Theo dumped the rest of his change in their tip jar like he usually did, plus an extra twenty, while Audrey stepped over to the espresso machine. He waited quietly at his usual table for her to join him, tapping his hand on his leg anxiously.

Same time, different drink, same nervousness.

She hung her apron on a hook and slipped out to the lounge, setting his mug down in front of him while she slid into the empty seat across.

"You know, you're going to have to let me show you some latte art sometime. I can make you a good coffee in your tumbler, but I can't make it pretty. The foam's too delicate, and there's not enough room." She gave him a wry look over her cup, and a blush crept up his cheeks from under the mask.

"You don't have to go to the trouble to—"

"Theo, I'm asking you to let me show off for you."

He quieted, and his blush deepened. "Oh. Well, okay then. I'd love to see your art."

"Thank you." She took a sip of her coffee. "What do you do, anyway? Are *you* an artist? Professionally, I mean." She'd been dying to know for a few months now.

He tilted his head from side to side. "Yeah, normally I'm kind of an artist."

"'Kind of an artist'?" She raised an eyebrow. "You seem like you're very *definitely* an artist to me. Your work's beautiful."

He huffed. "Well, you haven't actually seen it—not the real stuff. You've only seen scribbles, and not even the good ones at that. But thank you all the same." Theo rubbed the back of his neck. She could see that it too had gone red from the front. His throat bobbed as he swallowed. "And okay, yes. I am—I *was*—an artist and a designer. Professionally. But I'm not sure I am anymore."

"Why not?"

He raised his right hand. It shook as he held it in the air, and even resting his elbow on the table didn't seem to help with the trembling. "Nerve and muscle damage."

Oh.

That wasn't from shyness like she'd thought, then.

He closed his eye and sighed before making a fist and hiding his hand in his lap, and she felt his despair sour in the pit of her own stomach. From what she could tell, he seemed devastated. "Sketching is mostly fine, watercolors are fine," he murmured. "You don't need to be precise for either of those. But my usual medium? It's a no-go. It'd be really dangerous to try if my hands shook like they do right now."

"What's your usual medium?"

"Glass."

They both grew quiet.

Audrey hadn't expected that. Everything she knew about blowing glass did seem like it would be far too dangerous to do if you were recovering from the type of injuries Theo must have sustained. "Wow. Glass? So what are you—"

"I do physical therapy and my doctors' appointments on Mondays, and—and the other kind of therapy on Wednesdays. It's getting better, but . . ." He trailed off and shook his head. "I don't know. I'm not really working right now. Mostly I'm just trying to piece myself back together, I guess. It's—" Theo shook his head again. "No, never mind. I don't really want to talk about it right now, if that's all right. I'm sick of talking about it. It's all I ever do."

He withdrew. Audrey saw it happen in real time when he folded in on himself, quieted, hunched his shoulders. He tried to make himself smaller, less conspicuous, less noticeable.

That wouldn't do at all.

"It's okay with me if you want to talk about something else." She reached out and rested her hand on the top of his left one like she'd done the day before, only now Theo seemed far less shocked about the contact. Though the way he eyed her hand suggested he still didn't entirely trust any of this to be real.

"I'm really enjoying sitting here with you, Audrey." He dipped his head apologetically and lowered his voice. "It's not that I don't want to tell you stuff like this, it's just that I don't—well, I want to *keep* enjoying this. I'd rather just be with you here right now and not think about everything else."

"I get it, don't worry," she whispered. "Just be with me, then."

His gaze softened as he looked at her, and he drew in a slow, deep breath while he searched her face.

Audrey didn't say anything. She only watched.

Everything about Theo was a puzzle: fragmented, scattered, broken, but just waiting to be pieced together. She wanted to lay him out on a table, all the scraps of him separate, and work out how best to make the picture of him whole. She wanted to know what the image of him amounted to, all of him, every disparate, quiet bit of him as a fraction of an entirety.

But he was clearly broken into so many pieces. It would take so much time.

Good thing she loved puzzles.

She waited. And the longer she sat with him quietly, not saying anything, not demanding anything of him, the more he calmed. Theo stilled and he raised his trembling right hand again, turning his left one over and picking hers up, softly cradling it between both of his. His palms were truly massive; they dwarfed her own, drowning her hand in warmth, and that same warmth rose slowly up through her arm and spread all the way up into her neck, finally landing in her cheeks when he drew a calloused thumb across her life line.

The more he explored what was written there, tracing the lines of her palm like the grid on a globe, looking at her as though he were searching for how he might find who she was through where she'd been, the longer he held her and the longer he seemed to concentrate, the more the trembling subsided—at least slightly.

After a while, he blinked and drew in another slow breath. "Thank you," he whispered. "I'm sorry if I'm a weirdo."

She hummed and smiled softly. "I don't mind weird. Josh calls me Audball for a reason, you know."

"I thought it was Audsbodkins?"

"Not since he didn't get the part. Too painful, he says. He's been searching *for* a bodkin to make his quietus ever since."

Theo finally laughed.

It was low and deep, his eye crinkling so much that it closed before the laugh was suddenly stifled with a grunt and a wince. But after a second, his gaze traveled back up to her face, and he gave her hand a light squeeze before returning his grasp to his coffee mug.

"How about you tell me what you're working on at school? I'm really interested in hearing more about this whole electrical engineering thing."

"You remembered?"

"Of course I did. I never forget anything you tell me."

So she did. Audrey prattled on and told him all about her classes, her classmates, her capstone project, and her goals for graduation and beyond. Theo listened, nodding attentively when warranted and asking intelligent, incisive questions when he had them. Her break time flew by, and before she knew it, the timer went off on her phone and her heart sank to the bottom of her stomach.

"Over already?" Theo's one visible eyebrow dipped into a disappointed frown.

"I'm afraid so." Audrey gathered her mug and stood. "What are you doing tomorrow?"

He lifted a shoulder in a careless half-shrug. "Same thing as usual. Nothing."

"Do you want to change that?"

He straightened so quickly in his seat that Audrey stifled a laugh. "*Yes.*"

"Okay, great. Then I'll text you later and we'll figure something out."

His eye widened and panic flashed across it. "Oh, uh, I—I haven't—I h-haven't been out in so long, I don't even know what to—"

She rested her hand on his shoulder. "Don't worry, Theo, it's all right. Don't stress about it. We can always just take a walk in Central Park and look at the trees." She leaned down and swept part of his sweatshirt hood carefully out of the way of his right ear with her free hand.

He froze as soon as he felt the subtle movement of the fabric. His breathing quickened and he stared straight ahead.

She leaned down. Theo was so tall even sitting that she didn't have far to go. "Does that sound okay to you?" she murmured. "A walk—with me?"

It was a chance she was taking, she knew that, but she wanted to see how he might react to stripping away part of his public armor.

For the first time, she could see one of his ears. It was huge and adorable, and while it was partially buried in the depths of his thick, dark waves, the tip of it poked through beneath his cap. The tiniest freckles dotted along it like the delicate speckles of a quail egg.

It flushed bright red, the scarlet creeping swiftly along the visible curve of the shell and settling fiery-hot at the apex.

But Theo didn't say anything. He didn't even turn to look at her. He only nodded once—a tiny movement, barely perceptible—and then again slowly, more assuredly.

A wicked grin spread across Audrey's lips as she gently tugged his hood back into place and straightened it over his cap for him, running a hand along the fabric to smooth it down and tuck him safely back in. She squeezed his shoulder fondly before pulling away.

"See you tomorrow, Theo."

For the rest of the time he stayed in the café, he didn't draw. He didn't pull out his phone. He didn't even so much as shift his posture or move.

Instead, for almost the next hour, he alternated between clutching his tumbler to his chest with his eye closed and glancing quickly up at her over the counter to catch her gaze while she worked.

This time, he was never the one to look away first.

> **THEO☕** | Are you sure all you want to do is take a walk tomorrow?

Audrey grinned at her phone as she walked home from the coffeehouse, tired and spent and with a pocket full of tips in cash. A not-insignificant portion of it was from Theo, and the message from him lit up her screen just as she was turning onto her block on the way home to go take a nap.

> **AUDREY** | What, did you have a better idea or something?

Was he getting a bit bolder?

Three dots danced across her screen and another message bubble slid through.

> **THEO☕** | I could buy you dinner.

She blinked in surprise. Okay, that was a *lot* bolder. She bit her lip in amusement.

Guess he'd had a good time today.

> **AUDREY** | Do you have any idea how many dinners you've already bought me?

> **AUDREY** | You always tip way too much.

She wanted to give him an out. Imagining him in a restaurant trying to order an actual meal when he could barely order coffee seemed a bit ambitious, but she appreciated the gesture all the same.

Three dots appeared, then disappeared. They popped up again, faded, leapt onto the screen once more, and then promptly left.

She snorted.

He was having a right conniption on the other side of her messages, that was sure.

Finally, something concrete pinged through.

THEO☕ | No, I tip just the right amount, especially if I've been feeding you all this time.

THEO☕ | That's more than worth it.

THEO☕ | I'm sure you're not paid enough.

Her grin widened. Look at him, trying so hard to be smooth. It was really cute.

Another bubble jumped into the conversation.

THEO☕ | If you don't want to do dinner, we could do a movie instead.

Ah. That seemed more his speed. Maybe he'd thought better of the dinner plans after all. Or maybe . . .

She chewed on the inside of her cheek, hoping she hadn't been too quick to shut him down and immediately regretting her initial quip about the tips. Maybe it was a mistake not taking him up on his first suggestion. She could only imagine the courage he'd had to screw up to send it at all.

AUDREY | I'd love to do a movie. What do you wanna see?

That response took no time whatsoever.

THEO☕ | They're showing Casablanca in 35mm at my favorite classic movie theater this weekend.

THEO☕ | Have you ever seen it?

AUDREY | No. But I'd love to go with you

THEO☕ | Great. We could go for a walk and then see a movie.

She smiled to herself, hardly able to contain the warmth swelling in her chest.

AUDREY | Sounds perfect.

She reached her stoop and paused, resting a hand on the iron rail before heading inside. She typed another text and sent it off before she second-guessed herself.

AUDREY | And just so you know, it wasn't a no to dinner.

AUDREY | But we can play it by ear.

She was just about to let herself into the building when her phone buzzed one more time, stopping her in her tracks.

THEO☕ | "Play it by ear," huh?

More dots. The cool autumn air swept past her cheeks while she stared at that last message and waited, wondering what on earth could be taking him so long to type.

Finally, she had her answer.

And she blushed.

THEO☕ | I did enjoy the last time you played it by one of MY ears, Miss Adams—as big and dumb as they are.

THEO☕ | You can do that anytime you like.

Her face burned as she raced inside and up the stairs to hide in her apartment.

She'd learned something new about him today.

Snapped another puzzle piece into the edges of him.

Theo Sullivan was a lot more audacious in writing than he was face-to-face.

Four

THEO WAITED FOR her by the subway stop near Central Park.

He came more into focus once Audrey's eyes adjusted to the onslaught of early-afternoon autumn light, and she blinked as she mounted the stairs, a slow smile spreading across her lips.

Because he wasn't wearing his hoodie.

He was still wearing a baseball cap, his thick waves pressed down against the sides of his head, tumbling and licking at his cheeks and his jaw, which were still covered by a black mask. His right eye was also still concealed within the shadowy depths of those waves and by the shade from the brim of his hat, but this was the first time she'd seen him wear anything other than that hoodie zipped all the way up to his neck. Instead, he'd traded it for a thick, dark blue cable-knit sweater, nice jeans, and a pair of well-worn brown leather shoes. And while his usual satchel was still slung across his broad chest, today he clutched something new in his right hand.

A bouquet.

His fingers twitched nervously against the brown wrapping paper surrounding the flowers, and his tremor intensified while he shifted on his feet at her approach.

"H-hi, Audrey," he stuttered, and his throat bobbed as she stepped up to him. A touch of his red scar slashed across his neck and disappeared under the collar of his sweater. It was usually hidden by his hoodie, but she didn't let her eyes linger there. She looked back up at his face quickly.

His gaze was fixed on her, one brow bent in concern.

"Are those for me?" She pointed at the flowers, and he nodded.

"I wanted to get them for you because I saw them and thought of you, but then I got nervous that they'd wilt before you could get them in water, so they put some in a plastic baggie for me at the florist and tied it to the base of the stems, but then I worried it'd be too messy if I spilled it with my hand being so shaky, and then I thought maybe I'd gotten them for you too early in the day, so you don't have to carry these around or anything if you don't want to, I can—"

He quieted when Audrey gently peeled the arrangement away from him. It was a mix of roses and other flowers matching the spectacular fiery colors of the fall leaves, their delicate, silken petals bursting into blooms of deep reds and oranges and golds. Warmth swept up from the bases of some of them, lightening at the edges and reminding her of crackling flames licking through logs. Others were a deep red, like the horizon melded with the last light of a setting winter sun. She held them to her nose and took a deep drag of their sweet scent, closing her eyes as she let it wash over her.

He'd matched them with her favorite season.

"I love them. That's really thoughtful of you, thank you." She clutched them to her chest. "They're beautiful."

"Oh. Good." His eye crinkled as he looked down at her, and he took a deep breath under his mask. "I'm really glad you like them."

Audrey plucked softly at his sweater. "I also like this look. No hoodie today, huh?" She raised an eyebrow and grinned wickedly when his throat and the tops of his cheeks burned a deep red nearly matching some of the roses he'd just given her. He rubbed the back of his neck.

"My friend Diego told me I couldn't wear that on a date. He also tried to get me not to wear the hat, but . . ." Theo looked down at her apologetically and hid his right hand in his jeans pocket. "It's been a long time since I've been out with anyone. Sorry if it takes me some time to remember how."

"Do you feel comfortable without the hood?"

His blush deepened and he glanced away from her. "I feel a little naked, if I'm being perfectly honest," he muttered.

"Then hold these again for a second." She shoved the bouquet back into his hands and unwound the scarf from her own neck. "Bend down a little so I can reach." His brow twitched into half of a bewildered frown, but he did what he was told, his eye widening in surprise when Audrey stood on her tiptoes and tied the scarf around his neck, hiding it and his scar from view. She straightened it for him and patted it down gently with satisfaction. "Now give me my flowers back."

She could have sworn his mask lifted over his cheeks, concealing what could only be a grin. He winced and it dropped again, but what was left behind was unmistakable: the part of his face she could see had definitely lit up.

Theo passed her the flowers again, and she took them and slid her free hand in his, clasping her fingers as much as she could around his enormous, warm palm before they crossed the street and set off for the park together.

It was crowded today, filled with playing children and chattering couples and friend groups picnicking in the sun or throwing Frisbees in the perfect fall temperatures. They wove through the crowds and wandered through the trees, not really needing to talk, simply enjoying each other's company. While it was warmer in the sun, it was chilly in the shade, and Audrey clutched her cardigan around her bare neck, drawing it in closer.

"I shouldn't have let you give me your scarf," Theo said, finally breaking their silence. He'd been watching her intently as they meandered and tried to find a quiet place to sit. "I don't want you to get cold."

She beamed at him. "I'm fine, don't worry. I'm plenty warm." But her gaze dropped to his right hip. She'd noticed that his limp had become more pronounced the longer they walked around the park, and he was rubbing absently at it now. She nodded at a nearby bench. "Let's sit in the sun for a bit."

She interlaced their fingers to pull him over to it, and he sat heavily beside her, stretching his leg out and setting his bag between them.

"So who's your friend Diego? Tell me about him."

"He's, uh . . . well, yeah, I guess he's my best friend. I don't have many in general, but I grew up with him. We've known each other since we were kids. He's maybe more like my brother than a friend." He flipped the top of his bag open and rummaged around. "Played lacrosse together in high school and were roommates when we went to college."

Audrey peered curiously inside the satchel. It was filled with sketchbooks and art supplies, little tins of pencils and erasers, charcoal sticks and pastels and packs of fancy, well-used colored pencils. The back camera of an iPad Pro glinted from a tablet pocket, safely covered and surrounded with generous padding, the pencil stylus held close in a loop built into its leather case. His coffee mug was there too, tucked next to a few bright blue paper bags.

Theo plucked out his little black sketchbook and flipped it open to a blank page, reaching for his fountain pen next before pulling out one of the little blue paper bags. He handed it to her and then unscrewed the pen cap, fixing it firmly on the end and pressing the nib to the paper.

"Oh yeah, I got you that too. In case you were hungry."

Audrey opened it up and was immediately struck with the intense aroma of browned butter and sugar and chocolate.

She knew that logo.

"Did you get me Levain cookies?!" she cried before biting into one. She closed her eyes and moaned while she chewed, tilting her head back in the sun and sobbing a little as she crunched through the crisp edges, letting the gooey, doughlike center and chocolate chips melt in her mouth and coat her tongue. "Oh my god, Theo," she groaned again between bites. "You're going to spoil me."

"That's the plan."

She glanced at him again. His eye was fixed on her, but his hand was flying across the page of his sketchbook, the dark black strokes gradually taking shape. His fingers spasmed as he struggled to grip the pen, but he kept at it, and when she tried to peek at what he was drawing, he shook his head and tilted the sketchbook away to hide it from view.

"No. You don't get to see yet."

She slowed her chewing and scowled at him before holding the cookie out as an offering. "Do you want some? It's so good, and we should both get to enjoy it."

His sketching hand slowed and came to a stop. The mask shifted over his mouth. "Maybe later. I'm not hungry. But thank you." He pointed toward his bag with his pen and went back to drawing, dropping his gaze down to his work. "I didn't know what kind you might like best, so I got three. There's a dark chocolate peanut butter one, and a chocolate walnut one too, but I wasn't sure if you might be allergic to nuts or something, so I went with the classic double chip first, and—"

"Theo, it's all right with me if you take your mask off, you know."

He froze.

"I really don't mind your scar." Audrey leaned over and put her hand on his arm. "Promise."

"Maybe you don't. But I do."

Her face dropped and she lowered the outstretched cookie.

Theo still didn't look at her. Instead, his eye skipped between the clusters of people sitting in the grass nearby. It followed the couple walking past their bench, arm in arm and deep in conversation, before traveling over to the group of runners just traversing the bend in the path down the way. He shook his head.

"It's not you I'm worried about. It's everyone else." He reached over, pen still gripped between his now ink-stained fingers, and covered her hand with his. Audrey continued to stare at him, one brow slowly raising, and he sighed. "All right, fine, I guess I'm still a little worried about showing you. I don't like it. Or the way it makes me feel about myself."

"But I've already seen it."

"And I wish every day I could go back to that moment and take the memory of my face away from you."

He'd whispered it quietly before withdrawing his hand and going back to his sketch, his gaze darting up periodically to study her eyes, but refusing to linger on her expression.

The pain in his own broke her heart.

"Theo—"

"When I look in the mirror, the face I see staring back at me isn't mine. It doesn't belong to me. It's something—some*one*—else." He shook his head. "The face you saw when that woman ripped my mask off? That's a stranger's face. I don't know that man. I don't know yet if I want *you* to know that man." He tapped at the mask with his left hand. "When I wear this, I can almost forget that I don't have my own face anymore." Theo screwed the cap back onto the pen and tucked it back into his bag before reaching for a tin of watercolor pencils next. "At least until I take it off and catch sight of myself again." He opened it up and chose a color, shading parts of whatever drawing he was making with it before switching to another.

"What happened?" Audrey picked idly at the blue cookie bag, tearing at the edges of it. The breeze picked up some of the tendrils of hair that had escaped from her messy bun and whirled them around her face, sending cool shivers skittering down her spine and dry leaves curling around her boots. "Was it some sort of accident?"

Theo paused his shading and stared at her quietly before leaning over and tucking some of the stray hair behind her ear, carefully smoothing it back down against the side of her head. "I'll tell you some other time, sweetheart."

"You know I'll listen, right? And that you can tell me anything? You don't have to wait or hold back."

His eye softened on her face, his calloused fingertips grazing briefly beneath her chin as he pulled his hand back. "I know. I already know you're kind—I figured that out a long time ago. But I only want today to be filled with good, happy things. And it's not a happy story."

He asked her next about where she was from, and she told him about growing up in Florida with a bunch of foster families until she finally landed with Gladys Kane, who loved her like her own daughter, even if she couldn't adopt her. Audrey had been one of her many charges, but none of them wanted for love and attention while they were under Gladys's roof, and she lived there during high school until she got into her engineering program at NYU and came to New York.

Theo colored his drawing while he listened, alternating between using his pencils and his fountain pen, and after a while, he took out a paintbrush and a tiny jar with a screw top. He poured some water into the jar from his mug and skated the brush across the page after tucking a sheet of blotting paper behind it, working the water carefully into parts of the piece. Audrey slowly ate the other two cookies until she was stuffed, mopping the crumbs off the blue parchment paper with her fingertips and licking them clean with relish while they talked.

He told her all about growing up in New York. His mother was a lawyer from a rich family with houses in the Hamptons who'd fallen in love with a mechanic, and he was their only child. They fought frequently, and his mother was almost never around—until his parents finally got a divorce when he was eight. She got primary custody and Theo moved with her into one of the properties her family owned on the Upper East Side, where he was shepherded to private schools by nannies and got the best education his mother could provide. Weekends were spent with his dad at the apartment above the old auto shop he owned in Brooklyn, the borough where he and Audrey both lived now.

Theo replaced the lid on the jar with his dirtied water and snapped his case of pencils shut. "All right, are you ready?" His eyebrow quirked up with intrigue, and Audrey bit her lip to hide a grin.

"Show me."

"Still not my best work, mind you, so don't judge too harshly. But—" He turned his sketchbook around and tapped the page. "I told you I like to draw what I think is beautiful."

It was a portrait of her, with her head tilted back and eyes closed after she'd taken that first heavenly bite of cookie. The sun shimmered in her brown hair and scattered golden highlights through the loose, windswept strands. Dark sweeps of her lashes curved across her chilled, rosy cheeks, and the autumnal fire of the park's trees blazed behind her, contrasting with the green of the baggy cardigan she wore over her long-sleeved shirt and plaid skirt. He'd even managed to capture the swath of tiny freckles dancing across her cheeks.

She looked happy.

No, it was more than that.

She looked *radiant*.

Her heart pounded as she took the sketchbook from him and held it reverently in her hands.

"You're beautiful, Audrey," he murmured, his eye never leaving her face as he gazed down at her from beneath long, dark lashes of his own. "I mean that."

"Thank you, Theo."

"I genuinely don't know why you're going out with me."

"I think the answer is pretty obvious, given everything you've handed me so far today. And—" She leaned over and did something she knew might scare him, but she could hardly help herself. She set the sketchbook back onto his lap and very gently cupped his right cheek to press her lips just beneath the only eye he ever let her see.

He straightened on the bench where they sat, startled and blinking at her, and what she could see of his expression made her laugh. Red crept up to the tips of his ears poking through his dark hair again, and she rubbed the right one fondly before pulling away and letting him compose himself.

"You're going to give me that too, right?" she asked, pointing to the drawing.

Theo reached into his bag and pulled out another sheet of blotting paper, laying it carefully over the freshly watercolored portrait. "Absolutely not. Did you think this was for you?" He snorted. "This was for *me*. I already got you cookies and flowers." He lifted a hand. "And speaking of the cookies . . ."

He swept his thumb along the corner of her mouth, and Audrey spotted a streak of chocolate trailing along its pad when he pulled it away. Theo lifted his mask slightly and popped his thumb into his mouth, licking it clean with an amused huff. She caught the barest glimpse of those plush pink lips of his, their edges tilted up in amusement before he lowered his mask back down again.

"You're right: I missed out. Should've taken you up on your offer to share."

That made her laugh even harder, and he clapped his sketchbook shut and secured it with elastic before packing up his things and standing, extending a hand to help her off of the bench.

"Let's go. Movie starts at four, and we don't want to miss out on the good seats."

THEY WERE THE first ones in the theater, and Theo let her pick their seats.

Of course she chose as close to dead center as she could, and the old, decades-worn padding squeaked under Theo's weight when he wedged himself next to her, his long legs butting up against the metal back of the seat in front of them. He passed her the soda and bucket of popcorn he'd bought, and they settled into the dim lights while a smattering of other classic movie enthusiasts shuffled in and took their places in the theater around them.

"Are you sure you've never seen *Casablanca*?" Theo glanced at her suspiciously out of the corner of his eye.

Audrey grinned and shook her head. "None of the households I was placed in were into black-and-white films. There was a lot of wrestling and reality shows, though." She waggled her eyebrows at him. "Tell me, Theodore: How much do you know about *Teen Mom*? Because oh *boy*, could I write a dissertation on those girls."

He snorted. "Oh god, please don't." His mask puffed away from his face as he chuckled. "I guess I'll just have to get you caught up on some of the classics. Tell me what you think of this one."

"Okay. But then you have to watch an episode of *Love Is Blind* with me." When he covered his eye with his palm and groaned, Audrey held up an indignant finger. "*One episode*, Theo."

"Fine. I'll suffer through whatever terrible reality trash you want if you make it through this movie."

"Deal." She grinned up at him. "So how many times have you seen this?"

He grew quiet for a moment. "A lot," he finally murmured. "My dad and I used to watch old movies all the time. On rainy Saturdays, we'd take the couch cushions off and throw them on the floor, put pillows everywhere, make a big bed, and pop popcorn while we watched something in black and white. The whole day, spent watching movies. It was my favorite thing to do with him."

"That sounds so nice."

"Yeah. It—it really was." His voice hitched a little, and he suddenly reached over and squeezed her hand before letting his own fall back into his lap. "But now I'm glad I'm getting to do this with you today."

Something about the way he looked at her and said that made her ache. But before she could respond, the theater completely darkened and the film began to roll.

The theater was only about half full, and everyone had largely opted to spread themselves out, so Audrey and Theo were left well enough alone. His eye was glued to the screen, the black-and-white movements of the actors reflected in his oddly colored dark iris.

Audrey moved her soda to her left and lifted the cupholder armrest on her right, removing the barrier between her and Theo and wedging it between their seat backs. He broke his trance and looked down at the movement, but as soon as he did, she wriggled against his side, resting her head on his shoulder while she munched on popcorn.

Just when she was beginning to wonder if he'd get the hint, he finally did. Theo lifted his arm and wrapped it around her, pressing her into his left side. Audrey snuggled closer, burrowing into his soft sweater, and she lost all track of the story. She was far too distracted by the way his large hand trailed softly along her arm, his fingertips gently caressing the cardigan she wore. His cologne reminded her of cedarwood and juniper, and it mixed with the lingering aroma of dry leaves and sunshine from the park. He was warm, absolutely radiating heat in the cold theater, and she closed her eyes for a moment and allowed herself to melt into him.

She'd always wanted someone to hold her close like this.

No one ever really had.

Audrey looked up at him, and when she did, he glanced back down at her, apparently acutely aware of every one of her movements. She took the opportunity to do what she'd been planning since the park: she held up the popcorn bucket to him and gave it a tempting shake. His eye rested on it for a moment before it scanned the scattered theater crowd, his gaze skipping across the faces of the people closest to them. None of them paid him any mind.

So wonder of all wonders, Theo Sullivan lifted his right hand—and finally removed his mask.

His fingers trembled as they tugged the black elastic loop free of his left ear and let it hang from the right one, fully freeing his mouth.

Audrey could hardly contain herself at the sight of his lips in the flashing light from the film. It was the longest look she'd had of them thus far, and she beamed victoriously at him as she offered him the popcorn again. That smile only grew larger once his shaking fingers tentatively scooped up a few buttery popcorn kernels and *the man actually consumed something*.

He peered down at her out of the corner of his eye again with a huff, and she knew he was steadfastly refusing to show her the right side of his face. There was no way he'd turn and look at her head-on.

But that was all right. She'd make do with his profile for now, especially once his mouth finally cracked into half a crooked grin as he gazed at her.

My god, what a smile.

His eye slowly crinkled, and at last she could see part of what the mask had long been hiding.

Audrey had thought him handsome when she only knew a quarter of his face and the briefest flash of the rest of it. Now that she had an extended look at half, her attraction to him only increased exponentially.

Her heart thundered in her chest at the slow blooming of that lopsided grin across the part of himself he'd decided to show to her. Two dark moles dotted the side of his large, distinguished nose, and Audrey had to suppress the urge to run a finger down its perfect slope, if only to finally trace the curves of it, to try to read him the same way she'd wanted to interpret the tiny scars dotting the landscape of his hands under her fingertips.

But the light of the smile flashing across his face was short-lived. As soon as it was wide enough to stretch up and across his cheeks, he winced and shuddered forward slightly, closing his eye as though he were in sudden pain. But that too was gone in a flash, and he pressed his lips together in a softer, smaller smile before grabbing more popcorn. He turned his attention back to the film, crunching contentedly on their shared snack, and the spell was broken.

Audrey tried to turn back to the movie.

She did her best to focus on Ingrid Bergman and Humphrey Bogart, she really did.

But it was hard when someone so much sweeter and so much more interesting still had her attention.

Especially since his fingers were still gently caressing her sleeve, his strong arm still pressing her into his side, and his warmth still sending sparks skipping all across her skin and straight into her heart.

"BOGART IS HOT, isn't he? The way you could tell how much Ilsa wanted to leave her husband for him? I mean, I would too." Theo held her hand as they walked out of the theater, gesticulating wildly with the other while they discussed the film. It was the most animated she'd ever seen him.

"I can't believe you're commenting on how attractive another man is."

"Well, I appreciate how smooth he is in this—and in every movie, really. I'm secure enough in my masculinity to admit when someone else is attractive. Jimmy Stewart, Clark Gable, Humphrey Bogart, Gregory Peck, Cary Grant?" He ticked the list off on his fingers. "You can't beat old Hollywood charm. And game recognizes game," he added smugly.

"I'm not sure you actually have any game to recognize."

He stopped in his tracks and stared at her before scoffing as if affronted. He shook his head and dropped her hand, then immediately changed directions and started walking the other way, abandoning her on the sidewalk. Audrey yelped and ran after him but easily caught up, grabbing his hand again and whirling him back around to face her. She wouldn't have been able to do that if he hadn't wanted her to, of course. He was far too large, and the playful crinkles around his eye betrayed any sort of pretense at guile.

Which proved her point exactly.

"I'm very sorry, Theo," she said, struggling to keep a straight face. "I meant to say that you have tons of game. Scads of it. You're dripping with charm and charisma—just as much as, if not *more* than, Humphrey Bogart himself."

"That's better." He threaded his fingers through hers again and adjusted his bag over his shoulder with an indignant snort. "But you owe me some more compliments to make up for that dig."

"I'll see what I can do."

It was dark when they'd gotten out of the movie and the streetlights had already popped on, joining the millions of lights twinkling across the expansive Manhattan skyline. Despite the steady stream of snacks he'd been feeding her all day, Theo still insisted on treating her to dinner too, and even though she wasn't sure she could fit one more thing in her stomach after those Levain cookies and half the tub of popcorn, she went along with it. He had to have been starving, and she was far too curious to see what he might have up his sleeve at this point to tell him no.

They wound their way through the streets, continuing to discuss the movie at length. He really, *really* loved film, and he filled her in on all of the historical context of the movie, how it was received, how it fit in with the backdrop of World War II, why it became so important even though it wasn't exactly a blockbuster hit at the time it released. Audrey completely lost track of where they were wandering, but Theo seemed to know exactly where he was going, and she let him lead the way.

But more than anything, she was really enjoying how much he'd started to come out of his shell today. When she'd first schemed to take him out of the café, she was resigned to the fact that he was so skittish, she might not actually succeed in coaxing him out of his own head for long. She'd been fully prepared to take a walk and then call it a day to head home the second he'd gotten overwhelmed. She'd been prepared to take things incredibly slowly with Theo.

But instead, they'd met up in the park nearly five hours ago now—and she found herself never wanting it to end.

It was already the best date she'd ever been on.

Theo guided them to a street just off one of the main thoroughfares where the bright lights of a food truck cut through the growing darkness. A long line of people waiting for dinner wrapped around the block and music blared into the night. But when Audrey made to join the throng at the end of the line, Theo shook his head and squeezed her hand.

"Nope. I have an in," he shouted through his mask over the noise of the crowd. "A backdoor contact."

She trotted behind him as he wound through the long line of people, eventually leading her around the back of the blazing orange food truck with an enormous matching neon sign mounted onto the top of it, emblazoned with stylized text that read Y TU BIRRIA

TAMBIÉN and featured a glowing icon of an orange taco. Theo knocked twice, waited, knocked four times, waited once more, and then knocked twice again before stepping back. The metal door swung open, and a short, squat man stood in the lights. His face brightened when he saw Theo, and he guffawed and extended a hand, pounding his fist together with Theo's before they did some sort of intricate handshake so fast, Audrey could hardly catch all the movements.

"*Hey, papí!*" said the man, taking a handkerchief out from a pocket and wiping the sweat from his shiny brow. He looked to be about in his fifties or sixties, with copious silver threads running through what little of his once-dark hair remained on the sides of his head. The rest of his bald dome was so shiny, it reflected the light spilling through the door from inside the truck. "Damn, you're looking *good* tonight. You got a—*ah*." His eyes fell on Audrey, and he grinned even wider and patted his round belly. "Ah, I see. You didn't come to shoot the shit with *me* now, did you, Teddy? Totally fair, man. You want the hookup?"

"You've got the best birria in the city, Tío. If I was gonna call in a favor on a busy Saturday night, it was going to be for a good reason." Theo stepped back and put his arm around Audrey's waist. She glanced down at his hand resting featherlight against her side and raised an eyebrow, unable to suppress a smile this time.

Someone had gotten more comfortable after all.

"You got it, mijo. Hang here for a few minutes. You want some margs with that too?"

Theo's eye went wide. He bent down. "Uh, Audrey?" he whispered. "How old are you?" His cheeks above the mask burned in the light spilling through from the food truck's door.

She bit her lip and swept some of his hair away from his ear, doing her best to strangle a laugh. "Twenty-four," she whispered back, standing on her tiptoes to reach him. "I'd love a margarita."

He blew out a sigh of relief from beneath his mask. “Oh, thank god. I panicked for a second.” He turned back to Tío. “Definitely want some, thanks, man.”

Tío winked and shut the door behind him, and Theo winced as he turned back to Audrey.

“I was, uh . . . *shit*,” he swore and rubbed the back of his neck. “I worried you might be a little, um . . .”

“Young for you?” Audrey pressed her lips together even harder to keep from bursting out laughing. He looked *so* flustered.

“Well, yeah. If you were any younger, I would’ve pitched myself straight off the Brooklyn Bridge for being a total creep.”

“How old are you? You can’t be *that* much older than me.”

“I’m thirty-two.” He closed his eye, and she didn’t need to be able to see it to know he’d scrunched his face up in shame.

“I think eight years is fine, Theo. I’ll only give you a little bit of grief for being an old man. It explains why you think Humphrey Bogart had such good game, though: turns out he’s your contemporary.”

He groaned and she continued to needle him for a few minutes, but he was saved additional teasing by the door bursting open again and Tío descending the truck’s steps, carrying a heavy paper bag and two drinks nestled into a cardboard carrier. Theo pulled out his wallet when the older man approached, but he only laughed and shook his head.

“Nah, Teds, put that shit away. Your money’s no good here. It’s on the house.”

“Thanks. And tell Ricky I said hi.”

Tío motioned over his shoulder. “He’s too busy stressing at the plancha to come out right now, but swing by when it’s slow and he’ll want you to test the new recipes.” Audrey peered around him and spied a tall, lanky blond man frantically slinging steaming tacos on the grill back in the truck. He did, in fact, look fairly stressed, but she could hardly blame him—the line on the other side of the truck was *long*.

Tío handed them the food and drinks before fist-bumping Theo again. "*Ahí las ves*, eh? Don't be a stranger."

"Yeah, definitely. Catch you later, Tío."

Theo waved and led Audrey away from the food truck, turning the corner onto a quieter neighboring street. There was a little alcove behind one of the restaurants with an empty picnic table and benches tucked into it, and he sat down and began spreading the food out on the table.

"This is where the restaurant employees eat sometimes," he explained as he removed what seemed like box after box of food. "The owner is a frequent patron of the food truck himself, so he's cool with it. Jesus, Tío went nuts tonight, didn't he?" he muttered to himself as he sorted through all the boxes. "Did he give us the whole menu? He must've raided some already cooked orders to get us all this so quick."

"How do you know him?"

Theo opened one of the boxes to check inside and slid it over to her. "He's Diego's uncle—I grew up with him. And I also did branding work for him and his partner awhile back when they first launched the truck. They've since been featured in a whole helluva lot of magazines and blogs and food write-ups for the city, so my secret spot got outed, but they still like to feed me from time to time." He pointed at the box. "Try those first."

For the second time that night, he unhooked his mask and this time removed it completely, tucking it into his jeans pocket before greedily turning to a box of his own. The lighting behind the restaurant was dim enough to obscure his face, partially bathing him and his scar in shadow. But Audrey was just glad he felt this comfortable around her after today. They tapped their plastic margarita cups together and dug in.

They were the best tacos she'd ever had.

Every bit of that food was incredible.

They stuffed themselves on birria tacos and flautas, chips and salsas, elotes and quesadillas. Tío had also included some flan for dessert, and despite the fact that Theo inhaled enough food to feed four Audreys (she knew it, he'd been *starving*, popcorn aside), neither of them even managed to touch the tortas. When they were finally defeated, he packed up the rest of the food and tucked the leftovers and her bouquet neatly back into the bag, tossing their trash in a nearby bin before replacing his mask and taking her hand in his. She was so full, she was suddenly having trouble keeping her eyes open.

"Food coma, huh?" Theo snorted. He must've noticed her sway on her feet when she tried to get up.

"Oh my god, I'm going to sleep for three days," she moaned. "Just roll me down the subway stairs. I'll tumble onto a train headed home eventually."

"I could never. I'd rather carry you home if I needed to." He paused and considered her for a moment before reaching up and untying the scarf from around his neck. "And it's getting chilly." He wrapped it back around her, looping the ends through and tucking it carefully around her neck to lend her maximum warmth. "Let's get you home."

Her scarf still radiated his heat, and Audrey closed her eyes and breathed in deeply. It smelled like him too, warm and clean, spiced and woodsy, like a sun-kissed pine forest in autumn. She could burrow into that scent and never leave. The urge to bathe in it was overwhelming.

"All right."

They made their way to the train and rode back to Brooklyn. Theo wouldn't hear of her walking home alone, despite the fact that she did it nearly every day herself and had done it even later than this plenty of times. He walked her all the way up to her stoop and shifted awkwardly on his feet while she searched her bag for her keys.

"Theo, that was—"

"That was the best day I've had in a long time," he blurted at the same time.

"Yeah." Audrey beamed up at him. "It was for me too." She found her keys and wound them between her fingers, trying to delay actually putting them in the lock.

"No, Audrey, you—" He drew in a deep breath. "You don't understand how good of a day this was for me." He set the bag of leftovers down on the stoop and buried his face in one wide palm. "I don't get days like this anymore."

"Well, maybe you should. We can have more, you know."

He uncovered his eye slowly and gazed down at her before stepping closer. "Yeah? You want to do this again?"

"Of course I do."

"Really?"

She hummed with pleasure. "This was wonderful. I'd do this every day with you if I could." Audrey took a step forward too, bridging the gap between them and running a hand along his broad chest, feeling the soft knit of his sweater beneath her fingertips. "Thank you for planning it so well—and for showing me some of the things you like." She kept her hand there and waited, wondering what he might do if she lingered.

He answered that question by drawing her into a tight hug, tucking her under his chin and resting his head on top of hers while he enveloped her in his warmth and his scent, more concentrated than what clung to her scarf. His palm practically covered the entire back of her head, and Audrey closed her eyes as she wrapped her own arms around him, pressing her ear to his chest. His heart raced through his sweater just as fast as her own—if not faster—and she dug her fingers into his back, unwilling to let him go.

"Theo," she whispered. "I want you to kiss me."

He'd been gently combing his fingers through her hair, but when she spoke, they stilled. His chest rose and fell faster, but he didn't say anything for a long moment—until he shifted his hands, drew away slightly, and placed them on either side of her face, tilting her head up to match his gaze.

"Close your eyes," he finally murmured, his voice rumbling low in his chest. "Don't open them. No peeking."

Audrey did as she was told. There was a rush of cool air as he moved, and she heard the elastic release from the mask loops. His right hand still trembled at her left ear, the tremors tapping softly against her cheek. There was nothing else but the silence humming in the air and the latent sounds of the New York cityscape permeating the stillness. She waited.

And just when she thought that Theo might have changed his mind, that perhaps she might have scared him off, that her request had been too much, his lips and nose swept across her cheeks.

He drew them so softly against her skin, for a moment she thought it was a petal from one of the roses he'd given her earlier. But then he pressed them more assuredly, more firmly first to one eyebrow, then the other, before moving them gently across both of her eyelids. Her mouth went dry, and it dropped open of its own accord as Theo took his time exploring the curves of her face with his lips and his nose, his hands still cradling her head and tilting it softly this way and that. Shivers ran up and down her spine, and heat grew in the pit of her stomach as her heart raced and her breathing quickened to the point where she thought she might pass out.

No, it was more than that.

She might die if he didn't properly kiss her.

His lips finally found hers, and as soon as they touched, a wave of sensation burst from the point of contact and rushed through her entire body, tingling all the way from the tips of her fingers down to her toes. With her eyes still closed, Audrey's hands searched out his neck, and once she found it, she wrapped her arms around him and stood on the balls of her feet, drawing him closer and deeper. Her fingers knocked his hat off his head and she buried them in his hair.

Oh no.

It was so much softer and thicker than she'd thought it'd be, and it shifted luxuriously like silk between her fingers.

Suddenly, she was starving again.

Theo pulled away, and Audrey knew he was trying to be sweet. She knew he was being cautious, knew he wouldn't want to push his luck, knew he probably couldn't even believe she'd wanted to kiss him in the first place.

But she wasn't done with him yet.

Audrey yanked his face back down to hers, and as soon as their mouths met again, their cadence increased in intensity, both of them trembling as they moved together as one, broke apart, and then crashed together like waves against a rocky shoreline. One of Theo's hands migrated to the back of her neck, pulling her closer to him when he deepened the kiss. She opened her mouth for him, hoping, inviting, *pleading* with him to give her what she wanted, and he finally slid his tongue inside, tentatively, questioningly, tasting her and exploring her in the deliberate way he seemed to approach everything.

"*Theo*," she gasped when he stopped to catch his breath. The space between them in that second was too much, and she wrenched her fingers in his hair to pull him back to her, to claim his warmth for her own, nipping at his lips in her determination to devour him. He made a low, strained noise in his throat, something halfway between a grunt and a growl before he took her mouth with his again, kissing her until their lips were raw and inflamed, swollen and sore.

It was Theo who finally drew definitively away, panting and gasping, his breath ragged and his hands shaking far more than usual. But before Audrey could open her eyes to look at him and get a glimpse of her handiwork, he covered them with one wide palm.

"Eyes still closed, Miss Adams." He still sounded strained, but resolute.

She huffed indignantly, but kept them shut. "Theodore Sullivan, I think I've just made myself pretty clear that I like your face no matter how *you* feel about it."

He cupped her chin with his fingertips. "I know. But I need a little more time." A few seconds later, he was smoothing her hair away from her face and tucking it behind her ears with both hands. "All right: open."

She did.

He'd retrieved his hat and replaced his mask.

Well, *fine*.

Audrey supposed Rome couldn't be built in a day. She shoved the disappointment down and chose to focus on the fact that the man standing before her and wholly intent on hiding his face had just ruined her for any other first kisses. Completely and utterly *ruined* her.

There would never be another who could compare to what he'd just done.

He bent and pressed his forehead to hers, closing his eye and breathing slowly with her for a moment. "Thank you, Audrey," he finally murmured, running his hands along her arms to keep her warm. "See you soon?"

"You'd better."

His eye crinkled, and he stepped back and pressed the bag of leftovers into her hands.

"Good night, sweetheart."

She took it from him and he stood on the stoop while she unlocked her building's door and made her way upstairs, only leaving once she'd entered her apartment and turned the light on.

She knew, because she looked for him out the window.

She knew, because she watched him walk back down the street the way they'd come, though one thing was vastly different about his gait.

His now-familiar limp looked rather more like a skip as he turned the corner and disappeared from view.

Five

AUDREY WAITED ALL day on Sunday to hear from Theo again.

Every minute her phone screen stayed dark was another she spent fidgeting on her couch. Every piece of her had been vibrating since their date yesterday, and she couldn't stop thinking about how softly his lips had grazed against her skin, warm and careful and hesitant, as though she were something he was terrified to hold, to break, to shatter if he so much as *breathed* on her.

Until they'd finally kissed.

Every time she thought about it, an odd feeling settled into her stomach, sending it churning and roiling in a way that made her want to strip away her own skin simply because he wasn't touching it right now. Now that she'd had so much of him and knew what it was actually like to have him by her side rather than imagining it, she needed more.

And not having it, not having *him*, was maddening.

Imagination had sufficed before she'd gone out with Theo. He was a mystery she could puzzle through, turn over in her mind, analyze and savor every minute of the wondering.

But now? Now he was so much more. He was so much more of a sum than parts, so much more real than ephemeral, so much more of a totality than a construct.

Her imagination paled in comparison to the real thing.

It was the difference between a sketch and a painting.

And she still needed to add the shades of it, the highlights and the lowlights, the contrast and the shadows, just so she could see him whole.

She checked her phone again.

Nothing.

When no text from him had come through by 5:00 p.m., she took matters into her own hands.

> AUDREY | Okay, Mr. Sullivan: you surprised me last night.
>
> AUDREY | I take back what I said about you not having any game.
>
> AUDREY | I was wrong.

His response came immediately and without hesitation.

> THEO☕ | I told you: game recognizes game.
>
> THEO☕ | I have SOME skills.

More dots appeared on her phone screen and another message popped through.

> THEO☕ | It's just that most of them aren't exactly social.

Okay. That made Audrey laugh, and the butterflies in her stomach calmed a little. Maybe Theo had been waiting by his phone too, anxiously hoping she'd text him. Honestly, that did seem likely. And at least he was self-aware. Probably *too* self-aware, if she had to guess. She bit her lip while she wrote her response.

AUDREY | Oh yeah? So what other skills are you hiding under that mask? 👀

THEO☕ | Plenty.

THEO☕ | What are you doing tonight?

Oh. She wrinkled her nose at the pile of books and notes she had stacked by her laptop next to her on the couch.

AUDREY | Homework, unfortunately.

AUDREY | Midterms are coming up and I'm buried.

AUDREY | Plus, my capstone project isn't going well and I have to open the café tomorrow.

AUDREY | Early night for me, I'm afraid. 🫠

It took him a minute to respond.

THEO☕ | Ah. I thought you might be working today.

THEO☕ | didn't want to bother you.

"You're not bothering me, Theo," she mumbled as she typed the words onto the screen. "You can text me whenever you want. I spent all day hoping you would."

THEO☕ | You did?

She shook her head. Still so unsure.

AUDREY | Yeah, you dummy.

AUDREY | I told you I had fun yesterday, and now I miss you.

AUDREY | Look at what you did—it's all your fault, making me think about you all day and not texting me.

Dots, no dots, dots again—then they were gone.

There it was, the hesitation she'd been expecting. She could feel him sputtering on the other end of their messages.

God, it was so refreshing.

God, how she'd missed him.

His response finally arrived.

THEO☕ | Then you'll have to let me make it up to you, Miss Adams.

That got her to raise an eyebrow.

That was flirtier than she was expecting. Maybe he wasn't as flustered as she thought he was.

AUDREY | Oh yeah? What do you propose, Mr. Sullivan?

She waited. But he didn't respond, or at least nowhere near as fast as he had been texting her today. And when not even any dancing dots appeared on her screen, her stomach dropped and her nerves came crashing back with a vengeance. Was she too forward? Did she scare him off? She typed another message.

AUDREY | Are you coming to the café tomorrow?

AUDREY | Seeing you during my shift would be a great start. 😘

She tapped her pen against a textbook while she waited. Finally, a message slid through.

THEO☕ | I can't tomorrow.

THEO☕ | I have physical therapy in the morning and I won't be done until after 10.

THEO☕ | I won't catch you in time before you go to class, and I don't want you to be late on my account.

Oh.

Her heart sank. That's right—he'd mentioned that earlier, and that must've been why she'd never seen him on Mondays, even though he'd started coming in much more often and staying longer than he used to.

She was about to respond to him when he texted again.

THEO☕ | So I'll just have to keep thinking about you—and missing you—until I can come see you.

THEO LIMPED INTO the coffeehouse at 8:27 a.m. on Tuesday.

He didn't even have a chance to limp up to the register with his mug before Audrey shoved Josh in front of it and got behind the machine, making them both their coffee and ripping her apron over her head while Theo paid and dumped the rest of his change in the tip jar like he always did. His bag had barely hit the ground at their usual table by the time she was sliding their drinks onto its surface so she could throw her arms around his neck.

He blinked in shock for a moment before his eye crinkled and he wrapped his arms around her, lifting her off the ground and enveloping her in a big, warm hug.

His hood was still down today.

"Hi, sweetheart," he whispered. His voice only betrayed the slightest bit of bemusement, but he sounded pleased, and she could practically sense his smile bloom under the mask when she held him tighter and nuzzled into his neck. His fingers shook as he gently stroked her hair before setting her carefully back down.

"I missed you."

"I missed you too."

She beamed up at him, and her grin grew wider when she realized how he'd picked her up as if she weighed nothing. He was really strong, despite the tremble and the limp.

Speaking of which . . .

Her eyes darted down to his hip, and she frowned. "Are you doing okay? You're a little late today."

He grunted and slid into his seat, stretching his leg out and rubbing absently at his thigh. "Rough day of PT yesterday. I'm really sore, and my hip's giving me trouble again." His brow furrowed and he held up an apologetic hand. "I had to have screws put in it, you see. Not a fun experience, let me tell you. But at least I'm not using a walker anymore."

"Oh my god, Theo." Audrey's frown deepened as she sat and took her coffee between her hands. "Why didn't you say anything when I suggested a walk for Saturday? Should we not have done that?"

He shook his head and waved her worry away. "No, I'm supposed to, actually. I have a minimum number of steps I have to hit every day for my physical therapy homework, so it was helpful. And it's one of the reasons I started coming to this coffee shop in the first place—I walk here, and it was the right distance away from home for what I could do in one stretch at the time."

So he did live in the neighborhood.

"One of the reasons?" She raised an eyebrow. "What are the others?"

The tips of Theo's ears reddened, and he fiddled absently with the lid of his coffee tumbler. "I . . . stopped leaving the house after—after a while. It got really easy, you know, with all the delivery services available. I could order anything I needed from my phone: groceries, supplies, films, you name it." He looked down at his hands. "My therapist said she'd stop doing Zoom visits with me once I was mobile after"—he stopped himself and changed direction quickly—"a couple of months ago, and she made me come to her office instead. That was hard enough at first."

"Well, that's understandable."

Theo shifted his head from side to side. "Well, I—" He sighed deeply. "I used to be a little more social before all this, but I've always had trouble with anxiety. And talking to people. Especially new people."

"But you seemed to have an easy time talking to *me*."

Theo stared at her and then barked a laugh. "Oh, no. Audrey, uh . . ." He huffed again and then shook his head before running a hand along the back of his neck. Every last inch of his visible skin had flushed bright red. "I would have never talked to you—*ever*—if you hadn't said something first." His blush deepened, and he wasn't able to meet her eyes. "The only reason I'm maybe doing a halfway decent job is because you said you liked me, and I sort of . . . believed you. Or at least I really wanted to, anyway."

She leaned across the table and slid her hand under his left palm, and he curled his fingers around hers. "You're doing a great job. And you *should* believe me." She gave his hand a squeeze. "So you had to go see your therapist in person?"

He nodded and withdrew his hand, his fingers twitching slightly as he went back to flipping the lid of his coffee mug back and forth. "Yeah, I went to see her. And that was all for a while. Home, and her office. And then she recommended I start going out again to other places, and to try something low-stakes. Like a café. Especially since I really like coffee." Theo finally met Audrey's gaze. "I tried another place first, but it was awful. I had a panic attack, so I went home. And I stayed there. But Dr. Harper wanted me to sit at least thirty minutes out in public, even if I didn't do anything or talk to anyone, so she pushed me to try again. I felt so bad, my heart raced so fast, my hands shook so much that I wanted to die the first time I tried another café. Until I came here."

What little she could see of his face looked nervous, but Audrey only smiled softly and rested her chin in her hand. "Until you came here, huh? And what was so different about *this* café?"

He didn't say anything. He only looked at her, the little corner of his face finally softening more and more the longer he studied hers. His leg, which had a tendency to bounce under the table while they talked, stilled. Even his hand, which shook as he'd played with his coffee tumbler, stabilized slightly.

"I don't know," he finally murmured. "Must have been something about a very pretty barista who was very kind to me and very patient every time I came around. She didn't seem to mind that I had trouble ordering, or talking to her, and she also happened to make me very good coffee—and tried to make me laugh. Maybe that made me feel safe after a while." He shrugged. "But who am I to say?"

She grinned over the top of her cup. "I guess we'll never know."

His gaze warmed, the swirling colors in his eye more whiskey and amber today than they usually were. "I guess not."

They talked through her break like they normally did, with Audrey drinking her coffee while Theo simply clung to his like an anchor. When she went back to work, Theo stuck around this time instead of leaving. Whenever she looked up to check on him, he was busy with his iPad. He was hard at work on something, the pen stylus gliding relatively smoothly across the glass surface despite the tremor in his hand, his eye never straying from his design, and she found herself trying to catch glimpses of the screen from across the café.

Not only that, but when she hung up her apron and gathered her things in the back room at the end of her shift, he still hadn't left. She came out to find that he'd packed up as well and was waiting for her by the door, fidgeting back and forth on his feet and clutching the strap of his satchel across his chest.

"You waiting for me, Theo?"

His eye crinkled as he nodded. "You're heading to campus, right?"

"Yeah." Her face brightened. He'd paid attention when she talked about her schedule. "I've got an hour and a half before my next class."

"I thought maybe I could at least walk you to the subway? If that's okay?" He held his right hand out.

Audrey took it with a soft smile and marveled once again at how his entire palm engulfed her own. "Yes, please. You never have to ask."

It was another beautiful fall day outside, the air crisp while the sunshine was warm, and she took her time strolling down the Brooklyn sidewalks with Theo, enjoying the way he radiated heat at her side. She also savored the way he looked in the light. Hints of auburn glinted in the shadowy depths of his hair beneath his cap, subtle highlights brought out by the sun. It was another little thing, cataloged and filed away in her mind, every new detail she noticed about him only adding to the overall portrait that was coming more and more firmly into focus. Every stroke of the brush added depth, and she saw more of him than she had before.

Layer by layer, he was letting her see him. She still wondered what she might find as more details emerged in the viewing.

But if she knew one thing, it was this:

Theo Sullivan was a sweet man.

He walked her all the way to the station, stopping only at the stairs leading underground.

"What are you up to the rest of the day?" Audrey finally asked him, giving their interlaced fingers another squeeze. His hand shook harder when he squeezed hers back.

"I had signed up for a charity art auction before my accident." He had a hard time meeting her eyes. "I'm trying to come up with something for it, but I think I'll have to quit. I don't think I can execute on anything with my hand like this, and I can't handle failing the organization I was hoping to support. They need the money."

Her heart ached for him.

"Theo—"

"I'm not sure I can even call myself an artist anymore," he muttered. "I might just give up."

His eye was downcast.

"Don't say that. I've seen your work. I know it's beautiful." She cupped his cheek and glanced around the subway stop, eyeing the crowds. There were a lot of people around, and while she desperately wanted to kiss Theo goodbye, she knew he wouldn't want to take off his mask in public. Not in broad daylight, and not here.

She was about to turn back to him when he answered the question that must've been written on her face.

"I'm sorry, Audrey," he whispered.

A large hand slid up to the back of her neck, and he bent down and pressed his forehead to hers, closing his eye as he leaned in close. "I'm sorry. I'd like to kiss you, but—"

"It's all right." She put her hand gently on his left cheek over his mask and closed her eyes too. "I know. It's okay."

He drew in a deep breath and stood with her for a moment, his thumb gently stroking against the heated skin at the nape of her neck, his fingers twining in the base of her hair. Her heart thundered in her ears, and the longer they stood there, the more she realized how okay it *wasn't.*

It was, but it wasn't.

She desperately wanted him to hold her, to *really* hold her, to capture her mouth the way he had on Saturday, to taste him and feel him like she had then. It should have been so simple, so easy. Her lips and mouth ached for the want of him. All he had to do was lower his mask and kiss her, and she would have let him, a thousand times over.

But he didn't.

Instead, Theo pulled away and tucked her hair behind her ear before twisting his hand and smoothing his thumb softly along her jawline. What little of his expression she could see bordered on despair, hurt lurking just around the edges of his single, extraordinary eye, and when he made to drop his hand, she covered it with one of her own and pressed it against her heart.

"Later?" she murmured, and she knew he understood the question in her eyes. "When we're alone?"

He nodded, some of his concern smoothing away. "Yes, sweetheart. I promise." She let her hand fall and he stepped back. "Have a good day at school?"

Audrey snorted and turned down the stairs, waving over her shoulder as she disappeared underground. "You too, Theo!" she called back up at him. "Social school! You get an A plus on your skills today!"

He held up a hand and waved back at her from the top of the stairs. Every time she looked back over her shoulder, she saw him still standing up there, silhouetted against the sunshine—until she turned toward the turnstiles and lost sight of him.

~

THE ACHE SHE'D felt on the subway yesterday only grew when she didn't see Theo on Wednesday. It was quickly becoming a problem, how much she missed him when he wasn't around.

But perhaps even more than that, it was an enormous distraction. Concentrating on her work was getting more and more difficult when all her thoughts kept turning toward him—and the void she felt without him.

She didn't feel like a part of herself was missing, exactly, only that . . . well, his warmth was gone. She liked having him near her. He was intelligent, and interesting, and every day she saw him was an improvement on the day before.

He was *nice.*

Being with him was nice.

And she wanted more of that.

It just wasn't the same without him around now.

Audrey sat at her workbench in her capstone class lab, staring down at the circuit she was constructing to test her battery project with a grimace. She'd been having trouble with the voltage, and something about the design was off. But before she could pick up her pen to try to sketch out some ideas of how to solve it, her phone buzzed.

> THEO☕ | You're in the lab today, right? Any lightbulb moments?

Terrible dad joke. She snorted.

> AUDREY | Not so much—it's been more like a blackout.

AUDREY | The power load is giving me issues.

A dot bubble, and then an immediate message. Thank god he hadn't continued to maintain radio silence after their Sunday conversation, and he'd begun texting her more regularly throughout the day since then. It didn't do enough to fill the void, but it was something, at least. And she could always tell when he was thinking about her now.

It was frequent.

Maybe as much as she thought about him.

THEO☕ | Oh yeah? I know some things about circuitry and wiring.

THEO☕ | Want any help?

She raised an eyebrow. He knew about circuits? Well, he *had* grown up in a mechanic's shop. Maybe his dad taught him something. Cars did include the sort of battery she was working on.

AUDREY | I should probably struggle through this one myself, but I'll keep you in my back pocket.

Another quick message slid through from him.

THEO☕ | Oh, so that's where you'll keep me?

THEO☕ | What a spectacular location.

THEO☕ | I could happily live there.

She gaped at her phone. Did he just—?

AUDREY | THEODORE SULLIVAN

AUDREY | . . .

AUDREY | Does this mean you like my ass? 🍑

AUDREY | 👀

He completely ignored her.

THEO☕ | Are you free tonight?

She sighed. She'd left an English literature credit until the end like an idiot, and if she hung out with him tonight, she'd get nothing done. She chewed on the inside of her cheek while she typed, and that now-familiar ache in her chest started to grow again.

AUDREY | I'd like to see *you*, but I'm stuck in the lab until at least 5

AUDREY | I have piles of reading to do and a paper to draft

AUDREY | And then I have to open the coffeehouse tomorrow 😩

That grimace emoji didn't do her despair justice.

Three dots.

THEO☕ | You have to eat dinner, right?

She'd only barely started typing that yes, she did, but she was just going to eat at home when another message popped up.

THEO☕ | You're not just planning on having ramen or something boxed, are you?

That earned him a scowl this time. So what if she had a box of Kraft macaroni and cheese calling her name?

AUDREY | Do you have something against blue box mac and cheese?

AUDREY | All my friends who work in kitchens have that for dinner most nights

AUDREY | Noodles are a perfect food.

THEO☕ | You're not wrong, noodles ARE a perfect food, but you shouldn't eat actual cardboard.

THEO☕ | Those are shit.

THEO☕ | They might as well be made out of the blue box itself.

She wrinkled her nose, trying hard to stifle a laugh.

AUDREY | You going to take me out to a fancy Italian restaurant or something? 🍝

The dots were back, until they weren't.

THEO☕ | No. I'll do you one better.

Another message slid in on its heels.

THEO☕ | I'll bring it to you.

Six

THEO RANG HER buzzer exactly when he said he would: at 6:30 p.m. on the dot.

Luckily, Violet was out at happy hour with her colleagues from the office and likely wouldn't be home until late, so Audrey had a bit of time to tidy up their apartment in the twenty minutes between flying back through the door from the lab and when he'd promised to arrive.

She'd just shoved one of her stuffed animals under her comforter and swept the curtain over her bottom bunk closed when he knocked, and she could practically hear his hesitation through the door. Her hair was a mess, and she tried to smooth it back into some semblance of order before lunging for the door and yanking it open.

Theo's relief at seeing her was palpable. "Oh thank god, I got the right apartment," he breathed through his usual mask. The left corner of his face brightened when she grabbed his hand and dragged him inside, locking the door behind him. But then silence suddenly descended upon them both, and that's when it hit her:

This was the first time they'd ever been truly alone somewhere.

There were no crowds, no coffee shop regulars, no unobtrusive lo-fi playing in the background. Josh wasn't there behind any sort of register, and neither was Tío, potentially bursting through the door of his food truck at any given moment. There was no New York backdrop, no ever-present traffic noises, no other movie patrons or people packed like sardines around them on the subway.

It was just her—

—and Theo.

Audrey had never been nervous around him before. Not once. But now? Now, seeing him towering over her and feeling his warmth radiating inside her tiny studio, butterflies fluttered in her stomach. When she caught a whiff of his familiar woodsy scent of cedarwood and juniper, her nerves settled into her stomach in full force and the butterflies flipped over on themselves in the quiet of her apartment.

"This is my place." Her mouth went dry. "It's not much, but . . ."

His eye crinkled as he looked around with interest. He was dressed like he usually was at the coffeehouse, still wearing his hat, his mask, and his hoodie. His satchel was draped across his chest as always, and he wore the same dark jeans and his Air Jordans. But at least his hood was still down, and his fingers tightened around the handles of a brown paper bag he carried while his eye swept along her belongings, landing and lingering first on the art and photos they'd tacked up on their walls, and then on their meager collection of books and movies. His hand holding the brown paper bag trembled, and his throat bobbed as he shifted on his feet.

But the crinkles around his eyes deepened when he turned back to look at her. "I like it! It's really nice."

"Thanks." She beamed anxiously up at him. "Do you want to—"

"Oh! Oh yeah, uh . . . do you mind if I use your oven?" He held up the bag and waggled it enticingly. "You're hungry, right?"

"I'm starving, actually. But Theo—"

He'd already turned toward her kitchenette. Her studio was so small it only took him two or three of his long strides to reach it, and he was busy cranking up the temperature of her tiny oven in the corner. "I hope you like this. You don't have any food allergies or sensitivities, do you?" He paused as he rummaged around in the bag and started removing aluminum to-go containers before suddenly paling. “Oh shit, I should have checked sooner, I’m so sorry. Gluten and dairy are fine, right? Well, you did have cheese when we had the tacos, though, and I guess the cookies had gluten and nuts, so I thought—”

“It’s fine, I don’t have any allergies and I’ll eat almost anything, I’m a human garbage disposal. But Theo—”

“Thank god.” He sighed in relief and put the containers in the oven, closing the door carefully and setting a timer on his phone. “I just really wanted to make sure that—”

“*THEO.*” Audrey stepped forward and put both hands on his chest. He stilled at her touch, except for his hand. It was shaking harder than it usually did, and his heartbeat . . .

She stared at her hands.

His heart was *racing* beneath her palms.

Her eyes trailed up along his throat. He swallowed anxiously, and when she finally reached his eyes, the one she could see looked terrified.

Oh.

So he was nervous too.

“Come here.” She took his hands in hers and guided him over to the couch. “Sit.”

He did as he was told, trembling while he untangled himself from the strap of his satchel still slung across his chest. He placed it on the ground and sat, his gaze darting frantically all over her face while she lowered herself onto the cushion next to him. He looked almost comically large on their loveseat.

“You didn’t greet me when I let you in.”

“I know.” He closed his eye. “I panicked when I saw you.”

“Why?” She covered his right hand with her own in an attempt to calm him.

"You're overwhelmingly gorgeous," he muttered. "I don't know why you like me."

Audrey looked down at the ratty leggings and oversized sweatshirt she hadn't had time to change out of before he'd gotten there, but he kept talking before she could contradict him.

"I missed you. And—"

"And?"

"And I really want to kiss you, but—b-but . . . I—"

When he lifted his hand to the elastic loop of the mask curving around his right ear, she held her breath. His fingers hovered there for a moment, grasping at the air, but still he hesitated. Her heart dropped.

Theo still didn't want her to see his face.

Did he still not fully trust her?

Or was it just that he hated it that much?

"Do you want me to help you?" she murmured. He shook his head. "You don't have to take it off if you don't want to." She rubbed his arm. "If you're not ready, it's okay. I'll wait."

It seemed like something he needed to hear. And she *would* wait. She would, as much as she was impatient to rip the mask from his face and kiss him senseless, just like he'd done to her the other night. But that wouldn't be the right thing to do. Jeopardizing the progress they'd made together was the last thing she wanted.

Theo grimaced. "No, I want to take it off myself. I'm tired of it too. I'm so tired of it, Audrey."

But still he hesitated.

She leaned forward and lifted a hand to gently pluck his baseball cap away from his head. Theo's eye snapped open and he watched her place it next to her on the couch. His breathing quickened, but he didn't say anything. He hadn't stopped her. And then it was her turn to wait and watch.

Only the rapid rise and fall of his chest betrayed how scared he was just now.

But his eye never strayed from hers.

His hand shook when he gripped the left elastic loop between uncertain, reticent fingers, and Theo finally lifted it over his large ear. He peeled the mask away from his mouth and cheeks, slowly sweeping it from one side to the other.

Bit by bit, his face gradually came into view, the pale, dotted expanse of his skin breaking through the black mask like the light of the moon and the stars shining through the clouds at night. The lips that had kissed her so well, so thoroughly, so passionately on her stoop not even a week ago were finally fully revealed, and Audrey's own heart raced at the sight of them. They were beautiful, just as wide and plush and soft as she remembered. Pinker than she'd imagined, and parted now as he panted slightly for air, his chest fluttering anxiously.

But as soon as she saw his mouth in the soft golden glow of the fairy lights strung up around her apartment, her awareness of the scar followed.

It had been nearly two months since she'd caught a glimpse of it on that horrible day, wicked and jagged and torn, still held together with hundreds of black stitches pulling his skin painfully taut with the swelling and puckering at the edges of it. But looking at it now, it was clear that the wound had healed quite a bit. It was no longer so angry, or so red, or so deep. All the rest of the sutures were gone, and they'd been replaced with a thick, clear film running the length of his cheek.

But even though it was obviously healing well, it was still devastatingly extensive. The scar coursed all the way down the side of his face and dipped along his neck like a long bolt of lightning crackling through the sky, disappearing beneath his hoodie and running up into the dark hair still covering his right eye.

Theo let the mask drop onto her coffee table.

He waited while she looked at him, deep apprehension flickering at the edges of his expression, barely contained and tenuously controlled. He looked like he might break if she uttered a single word.

Only one piece of the puzzle remained now.

Audrey cupped his right cheek, softly sweeping her thumb across the skin next to his ear. She lifted her other hand and combed his hair away from his right eye with her fingertips, pushing his luxuriously thick, dark waves back and away to reveal his entire face to her for the very first time.

At long last, she could see him.

The wound cut across his eye too, slicing beneath it and slashing deep through his eyebrow. The skin around it was still slightly swollen and a little discolored, either from the trauma or from its more recent repair. It had been a narrow miss for his eye, and while he couldn't seem to open the right one as well or as fully as his left, both of them rested on her now, anxious and unable to look away. His beautiful lips formed soundless words, not quite pressing together, the air not quite making it all the way through his throat, and he closed his eyes and swallowed again.

"Au . . . Audrey?" he finally managed to breathe. There was a question there, filling his lungs and caught on the tip of his tongue. A tear escaped his newly revealed eye and spilled down his right cheek, coursing along the side of the tape covering his scar and landing at the corner of his mouth. It disappeared between his lips, which quivered as he swallowed thickly. "I—I didn't used to look like this." He sucked in a short, anguished breath. "I, um . . . my—m-my eye, it—"

But before he could say anything else, she broke into a smile.

"*There* you are," she whispered. She combed his hair back again and ran her hands through it while she gazed at him, savoring the silken feel of it between her fingers and drinking in her fill of his face. "Hi, Theo."

He sniffed and drew back in surprise before his lips cracked into an unsteady, lopsided smile. "Hi."

"You're *so* handsome."

His dark brows—both of them—knit together. "What?"

She meant it. She'd known he wouldn't believe her, but she meant those words with her whole heart.

He was so handsome.

So attractive.

Every piece of him.

Audrey leaned closer so she could look into his eyes. Both of them were the same, that interesting heterochromic combination of darkness surrounded by swirling light. In the soft glow of her apartment, they were liquid shades of mahogany and amber, whiskey and honey, molten and soulful and sad.

"Look at you." She trailed a finger down the perfect slope of his nose before tapping softly at the groove just above his top lip. "Your face is lovely. Why would you hide it from me?"

At those words, his lip quivered again—and his face fully broke. A sob wracked his chest and he surged forward to press his lips to hers.

She closed her eyes and let him take her mouth, let him tell her with his lips what he'd lost the words to say. She tasted salt from the hot tears coursing down his cheeks, and her body shuddered from the force when another sob tore through his. He buried a massive hand in her hair and rested the other on her back, drawing her into his warm, strong embrace, and she threw her arms around his neck to pull him close.

This was what she'd been needing. She'd been needing his warmth, the feeling of his hands along her skin, in her hair, the taste of him in her mouth. She'd missed his wide, soft lips, and having actually seen them now in the light and at her leisure only somehow enhanced the feeling of them against her skin. But that wasn't all.

She could hardly believe he'd finally let her see his face.

Theo pulled away from her mouth and dipped his head low, peppering the delicate skin just beneath her jawline with tiny, ravenous kisses. She gasped and shivered in surprise at the sensation, raking her nails through his hair again, and when he buried his face in her shoulder, she held him while he cried.

Eventually, his broad chest stopped heaving, and he stilled in her arms, aside from one hand gently massaging the nape of her neck.

"I'm sorry," he whispered.

"For what?"

"For doubting you. For hiding for so long. For missing out, even just when I first got here."

"It's all right. We're here now." Audrey combed through his hair, and he melted further into her, relaxing his shoulders and letting the tightly wound tension humming through his entire body ease with every stroke of her nails against his scalp. "Not so bad, was it?" He shook his head, and she laughed softly when his large nose burrowed deeper into her neck.

"You're the first new person I've voluntarily shown my face to since the accident. I was so worried you wouldn't like what you saw. Because *I* don't." He huffed a bitter laugh, and his breath tickled across her neck, sending shivers down her spine. "But you didn't run from me or flinch away like I was imagining, and I feel silly for thinking that now." A few more tears spilled from his eyes and soaked into her sweatshirt, and she pulled away slightly and wiped them from his cheeks with her sleeve before pressing his head back into her neck where it belonged.

"I told you I like your face. I wasn't lying." She smiled into his hair and breathed in deeply. She could get used to bathing in that scent of his, whether it was his shampoo or his cologne. She couldn't tell, but either way, it was intoxicating. "I *really* like it."

"I'll be honest, I'm still mystified by that," he muttered into her shoulder, his voice muffled by the damp fabric of her sweatshirt. "But I'll take your word for it from now on. Promise."

"You'd better, Theodore Sullivan. You're so much more than the scars you carry."

He grew silent for a moment before he tilted his head and looked into her eyes. "And for what it's worth, Audrey, I . . ." He drew in a deep breath and rolled his lips together. "I think *your* face is the most beautiful thing I've ever seen."

It was her turn to blink away tears. No one had ever really told her anything like that before. "Thank you, Theo."

Theo closed his eyes and they lay quietly on the couch together. He wrapped his arms around her and sighed, his breathing finally slowing and steadying while he lay partially draped over her, warm and solid and safe. He was so big, they barely managed to fit on her tiny loveseat. But Audrey closed her eyes too, relishing the way his weight and warmth settled over her while she continued to stroke his hair and massage his scalp. He was like the world's best weighted blanket, and she almost drifted off to sleep. Her exhaustion from the day was bone-deep, she was so comfortable like this, and it was sorely tempting.

Was this what life would be like with him?

Was it supposed to be this easy?

Could she have this all the time?

But studying him now unmasked and unguarded was so much more interesting than sleep. She traced her thumb along his dark, heavy brows and counted the moles and freckles that had been hidden by his hair and the mask. There were so many, like constellations spelling out the history of him in the sky, and she cataloged them with her fingertips, filing them away so she could turn them over in her mind later when she thought of him. Every once in a while, he glanced up to study her face the way she was his, perhaps waiting to see if she might change her mind or if she'd drop some act and look away. But she never did.

After a while, he ran a trembling hand through her hair, carefully teasing and twisting the elastic out of her bun so he could properly bury his fingers in it. Audrey had never thought her hair was anything particularly special: it was a plain chestnut brown, nothing more, nothing less, not quite wavy and not much longer than her shoulders. It wasn't particularly soft or luscious, thick or long, but the way Theo was looking at her and treating it, combing through it with such reverence and care, made her feel like it was the most exquisite thing on the planet.

They held each other in the silence of her apartment, simply content to be. But just when Audrey was relaxed enough to contemplate dozing off, Theo's phone timer went off in his pocket, jolting them both up from the couch. A heavenly aroma floated in the air.

"Oh *shit*, I almost forgot! Glad I set this," he said, wincing at their sudden movement and massaging his leg absently. But after unzipping his hoodie and tossing it over the back of the couch, he leaned down and gave Audrey another quick kiss before limping over to the kitchenette.

She couldn't help but smile as she watched him bend over her tiny oven and carefully use a towel to take out the trays he'd put in there to warm. He took up half her studio by himself, and his hands were so large, it looked like he was using an Easy-Bake Oven rather than a real one.

"What's the clear stuff on your scar?" She draped herself over the side of the couch while she watched him move around the kitchen.

Now that his hoodie was gone, she could see his back muscles rippling through his thin shirt.

Wait a second.

Was he . . .

Was he ripped?!

Her mouth dropped open. He *was*. But he was also too preoccupied to notice how red her face suddenly got. "It's silicone scar tape," he answered as he set the trays on top of the stove. "It's supposed to help with healing. My plastic surgeon wants me to wear it pretty much all the time now that I have my latest reconstruction stitches out and the wound is fully closed."

"I don't remember feeling that on Saturday. Wouldn't I have?"

"I . . . might have left it off that day. Just in case." He peeled the foil off the tops and glanced over his shoulder. The tips of his ears had turned pink and his cheeks and neck were rapidly following suit.

"Oh?" Audrey purred, leaning forward and resting her chin on her hand. "So you *did* have that kiss planned after all."

Theo's deepening blush was all she needed to confirm her suspicions. "Dishes and silverware?" His voice might have cracked a little while he rolled the sleeves of his shirt up to his elbows, revealing strong, sculpted forearms thickly corded with muscle and dusted with dark hair. A few more fresh pink scars twisted along his right arm. Audrey pointed to the correct cupboard and drawer with a wicked grin, and he quickly plated up dinner before striding back over to the couch with two bowls held in each wide hand. He passed her one set, and Audrey's stomach growled at the sight of it.

It was handmade ravioli drenched in fresh tomato sauce and melted cheese, paired with a slice of soft, crispy focaccia topped with flaky sea salt and dripping in olive oil. She took a bite and nearly died.

"Oh my god," she moaned through the creamy herbed ricotta filling. "This is heaven."

"Better than blue box?"

"Holy hell, *yes*. Where did you get this?"

He grinned crookedly at her, wide and luminous. *Grinned*, which was made so much better now that she could actually see his mouth, especially when two long, sweeping dimples appeared, carved deep into his cheeks alongside it.

God, he had *dimples*.

"My secret. I'm not telling you."

"Oh, come on."

He shook his head. "Nope. Gotta keep some things close to the chest."

"You've kept almost *everything* close to your chest."

He snorted and tapped at the other bowl he'd brought over for her and set on the coffee table. "And I brought you a salad too."

She glared at him. "What, are you trying to make sure I'm healthy or something?"

A wicked gleam glinted in his eye. The novelty of actually seeing him smirk would never go away now. "Eat your greens, Miss Adams."

Audrey punched his shoulder playfully, and he gave her an indignant look. But she was already reaching for the remote to get her revenge before he could stop her.

"Fine, I will. But I need *some* sort of trash with my dinner and you owe me an episode of *Love Is Blind*. Don't think I've forgotten."

He groaned dramatically but didn't protest when she fired up Netflix on the little TV across from them. Audrey couldn't believe how happy she was in that moment, tucked next to him on the couch, nestled into his warmth on the outside while the incredible pasta he'd brought her warmed her from within.

Having Theo here in her space alone with her was so much nicer than she'd expected. Given how he was when she'd first met him, she'd half wondered if it might have been extremely awkward with no buffer and nothing between them. But she was shocked at how utterly *right* everything felt. Even the fact that he'd actually taken the hoodie off to reveal a dark green Henley underneath, the low, unbuttoned collar displaying far more of the length of the scar than she'd seen before, showed how much he trusted her. Theo really did seem to feel safe with her now, and that was enormous.

Things had shifted.

There was no going back.

Not for her, anyway.

They made it through the first episode and got up from the couch to wash dishes together. "They can't really be serious about expecting people to go on these weird dates and get fully engaged without seeing each other's faces, can they?" Theo asked while he scrubbed one of the bowls. "That's crazy."

Audrey slowly reached over and turned off the water to stare pointedly at him, the bowl she was drying abandoned in her hands. She blinked and said nothing, only continuing to stare.

Even when his face went beet red, still she said nothing.

"Well, I wasn't going to, uh . . . I-I-mean, I—" he finally sputtered. "It's not like I was—"

"Uh-huh. Tell me more about your exact plans in regard to that mask." She raised an eyebrow. "I'd dearly love to know."

The red crept up to the tips of his ears and slunk down along his neck, and he rubbed the back of it awkwardly. "Okay, so I wasn't really planning on anything, much less keeping it on for this long. I didn't really know what I was going to do, I only knew I—"

She snorted and turned the water back on, rinsing the bowl he'd left in the sink and plucking it away to dry and stack next to the other one. "I'm just giving you a hard time." She grinned impishly up at him.

He buried his face in a wide palm. "I'm never going to live this down, am I?"

"No." She shook her head. "Never."

"Guess I shouldn't pull that tiramisu out of the bag, then?"

"*Tiramisu?!*" she cried. "You brought dessert too?"

After dessert (and only a slight protest from Theo, who insisted that he should probably leave so she could do some of her homework before Audrey shut him down), she shoved him back onto the couch and played another episode, situating herself comfortably beneath his arm. They talked through the contestants and agreed on which ones were the biggest assholes, and she laughed when Theo got riled up about how much he hated the star fuckboy on the show while they watched him gaslight multiple women. As the show went on, they moved closer and closer, until eventually Theo was sprawled out along the small loveseat with Audrey tugged tightly against his chest, her head tucked under his chin and his warm, strong arms firmly wrapped around her, as if he never wanted to let her go.

But two episodes were apparently all he had in him, and sometime around the beginning of the third, he fell deeply asleep.

His breathing slowed, and Audrey lowered the volume and snuggled up to his chest. His lips were slightly parted, his face completely soft and lax, and he was so far gone, he didn't even move when she brushed some of his long, shaggy hair away from his eyes so she could see them properly again.

She didn't think she'd ever tire of looking at him now.

She was just about to close her eyes and nap with him when her phone buzzed in her leggings pocket. She pulled it out and lowered the brightness so it wouldn't wake Theo while she read the message.

> VIOLET🌸 | Hey, is your cryptid still there, or has he run away yet?

Audrey suppressed a snort. Her roommate was probably wanting to know if she could come back or not.

AUDREY | He's still here

AUDREY | He fell asleep on the couch, actually

AUDREY | Want me to wake him up and kick him out?

VIOLET✿ | NO

VIOLET✿ | OH MY GOD DON'T MOVE

VIOLET✿ | I want to see him

VIOLET✿ | Think I can sneak in?

She bit her lip.

AUDREY | He might freak if he hears you

AUDREY | His mask is off

VIOLET✿ | YOU GOT HIM TO TAKE THE MASK OFF?!?1

VIOLET✿ | STAY THERE FOR THE LOVE OF GOD, I'M ALMOST HOME

VIOLET✿ | I'LL BE SO FUCKING QUIET I SWEAR

Audrey shook her head and reached for the black KN95 that had been lying forgotten for the last few hours on the coffee table. Violet might be insanely curious, but she wasn't going to betray Theo's trust or let them go backward. Not after today.

As soon as her roommate's keys quietly clicked and turned painfully slowly in the lock, Audrey spread the mask over Theo's face and slid the loops over his big ears, arranging his hair back over his right eye the way he always wore it out in public. His face twitched slightly at the change, but he didn't wake. He must have been really used to having the mask on—or he really was that exhausted.

Violet finally opened the door just enough to slide inside, her cheeks flushed red with alcohol as she closed it silently behind her. She carried her shoes in her hand and padded carefully over to peer at Theo over the back of the sofa, her mouth dropping open as she followed the length of his body. One of his long legs was draped over the arm of the loveseat and the other spilled down the side of it.

He's HUGE, she mouthed silently. Then she pointed indignantly at the mask. *You put that back, didn't you?*

Audrey nodded smugly at her.

Bitch, Violet mouthed, rolling her eyes and slinking over to the bathroom, shutting the door quietly behind her. Audrey suppressed a laugh and waited until she could hear the shower on in full force before finally turning back to Theo. She cupped his cheeks, tilting his head slightly before gently running her hands through his hair again.

"Theo?"

His eyes snapped open and his head jerked toward the bathroom in alarm when he realized it wasn't Audrey in the shower. He touched the mask on his face before looking back at her quizzically.

She pressed her forehead to his. "Violet's home," she whispered. "I put it on for you before she got here. Didn't think you'd want a stranger to see."

He wasn't something to be gawked at.

Theo blew out a deep breath and plucked at the strands of hair around her face. "Thank you, sweetheart," he murmured, carefully tucking some of them behind her ear. "Sorry I fell asleep. I guess I was more tired than I thought."

Audrey shook her head. "It was really nice. Don't apologize."

He grunted as he pushed himself up off the couch, rubbing his eyes while he straightened and yawned beneath the mask. His eye widened when he glanced at his watch. "Oh shit, no, I should. You have to open tomorrow and it's already after ten. I meant to leave a lot sooner than this." His satchel was near the couch, and he stood and slung it over his shoulder.

She scrambled to her feet and grabbed one of his hands. "I'm glad you didn't," she whispered, standing on her tiptoes and putting her other hand on his cheek. "I don't want you to go."

Theo eyed the bathroom door over his shoulder before lifting a hand to rip off his mask, so quickly and so easily this time.

"I don't want to go either. I'm going to head home anyway, but . . ." He leaned down and slid a hand along the back of her neck. "I'm not making the same mistake twice." His thumb softly stroked her cheek before he bent down and pressed his mouth to hers.

The second good-night kiss he gave her was every bit as good as the first. His hands left fire in their wake everywhere his fingertips grazed against her bare skin, and together they lingered there in front of her door, quietly exploring each other's cadence and the planes of their faces now that they could. Her heart attempted to pound through her chest, and Audrey desperately tried to sear the way he looked and felt into her mind.

Theo hadn't even left yet, and she already missed him.

When the shower shut off, he finally pulled away from her with a sigh and slipped his mask back over his mouth, his lips swollen and red, his cheeks flushed, and his breath heavy. After one more hug, he turned and let himself out of her apartment, only glancing once over his shoulder to make sure she'd locked the door behind him.

With him gone, her apartment suddenly felt so very strange and empty.

Too quiet.

And too cold.

Seven

IT WAS AN exceptionally busy morning when a customer Audrey had never seen before stumbled into the café at 7:42 a.m. on Friday.

That in and of itself wasn't unusual. They had plenty of new people and one-offs coming through their doors after Theo's altercation with Patricia went viral on TikTok, even though the fervor had died down in recent weeks. But still: gone were the days of being frequented mostly by regulars with their laptops. A lot more people had found out about Déjà Brew, and Audrey missed those slower, more familiar times, despite the increase in tips.

But it was the way this new customer was so twitchy that caught her attention. He fidgeted the entire time he waited in line to step up to the register, like he had so much pent-up energy, he was about to burst out of his own skin.

That, and the way he kept staring at Audrey.

It was as though he were trying to put her under a microscope.

She watched him suspiciously out of the corner of her eye.

He was ruggedly attractive, maybe around his midthirties, with dark, curly hair, dark eyes, and olive skin. His artfully stubbled jawline was sharp, and so was his gaze; it was piercing and intense, like a hawk tracking its prey. She had the uncanny sense that he wanted to grip her in razor-sharp talons.

It wasn't often they had someone come into the coffeehouse with this much restlessness—and even less often did she find it seemingly directed at *her*.

When it was his turn to order, he sauntered over to the counter, leaning his palms on it and looking her up and down with a slight furrow in his brow. She plastered a smile across her face and tried to make sure Josh was paying attention, just in case the man tried to rob them or something, even though he didn't look at all the type.

Bracing herself for a fight wasn't pleasant; it had been two months since Patricia had received her lifetime ban, and Audrey couldn't say she missed having to deal with her daily combativeness. And now there was *this* guy. Luckily, he wasn't much taller than her. Hopefully, they'd be able to handle it if he tried anything.

Maybe he'd be a one-off customer.

"Hi! Welcome to Déjà Brew! What would you—"

"You're Audrey? Audrey Adams?"

"Uh . . . yes?" A creeping sense of foreboding prickled at the back of her neck, though she had no earthly idea what she could have done wrong. But the way he was looking at her gave her that impression.

He hummed and rolled his jaw while he considered her. "Okay, fine. You're real cute. I get it." He pointed at her. "You normally take your break around eight thirty, right?"

"Yes." The prickling sensation increased. Was he stalking her?

"Can you take one now too?"

"Uh . . ." Audrey caught Josh's eye and motioned to him with a microscopic tilt of her head. He got the message, and he wiped his hands on his apron and stalked over from behind the espresso machine, massaging his knuckles and eyeing the newcomer suspiciously. "I don't know. Why?"

"Because you and me? We need to have a chat. And we need to have it before your boyfriend gets here."

"*Boyfriend?!*" That was news to her, but her mind immediately leapt to Theo, and she couldn't help the flutter of warmth she felt in the pit of her stomach at the title.

It was immediately followed by a wave of fear.

Wait. *Was* this guy stalking her if he knew about Theo?

The man waved dismissively at Josh. "You can calm down, I'm not going to do anything." He turned to Audrey again and opened his mouth before seeming to think better of whatever he was going to say. Instead, he turned back to Josh and gave him an appraising look up and down. Her friend raised an eyebrow, and they both waited for whatever was coming next. "What's your name? Are you Josh?"

"Yeah?" He frowned. "I'm Josh. Who are you?"

"Ah. I see." He didn't answer the question. "You make a good cappuccino here?"

"Sure, I guess so."

"Then I'll take one of those." He turned back to Audrey and pulled out his wallet. "Large cappuccino to go for Diego."

"Diego," Audrey repeated. And then it dawned on her. "OH. *Diego*," she gasped.

"So you *do* know who I am, then?" Diego drawled as he handed her his card. "If you know that, then you know why I'm here."

She swiped it, noting his full name (Diego Vargas—why did his last name sound so familiar?), and turned the terminal around so he could sign and tip. "I'm going to assume it has to do with Theo?"

"Bingo, kiddo. We need to have a chat, you and I."

She shook her head. "Look, I would've liked to meet you some other time in some other context, but I'm on the clock right now. I only get one break per shift and I'm saving it for Theo, not using it on you. No offense."

"Then how about you two switch, and I talk to you while you

make the coffee? I didn't know when else I could catch you without lover boy around."

Audrey and Josh exchanged a look. "Fine. That'll work." She stepped away from the register and took her place behind the machine while Diego sidled up to the counter and leaned around the Marzocco.

Learning that Theo's best friend had sought her out did nothing to calm Audrey's nerves, and a heavy sense of dread churned in her stomach while she wiped down the milk frother and grabbed a large paper cup printed with their café's logo. Diego struck her as extremely New York, even without the accent and the brusqueness and the fast-talking, all snapping fire, fury, and frenzy.

She had no idea what was going to come out of his mouth.

"What are your intentions with my buddy Theo?"

That definitely wasn't a question she could've anticipated.

"Excuse me?"

"I asked what your intentions are with him." Diego clasped his hands together and leaned forward on the polished counters. "What is it about him, huh? Is it just that he's tall? He's cute, right?" He pursed his lips together. "Is it that mysterious artist thing he has going on? I mean, that definitely works for him, generally and historically. He's extremely broody. Or maybe you're one of those women who like to chase after broken men. Are you just interested in his mo—"

She drowned him out by angrily flicking on the coffee grinder, gritting her teeth while the grounds tumbled into the portafilter. She tamped it harder than she strictly needed to before shoving it in the group head to pull the espresso shot and bending to grab the milk.

"Do you want me to make you a shit coffee?" she growled at Diego when she straightened. "Because you're being rude as all hell and I have half a mind to scald this milk into oblivion before I give it to you."

He snorted. "Fair enough. You're right: I'm being a dick."

"I'll say."

Audrey steamed the milk and genuinely thought about giving him the worst cappuccino she'd ever made. But her pride got in the way.

She wanted him to taste how damn good her coffee was purely out of spite.

He watched her pour the milk artfully into his cup, detailing a quick, complicated design in the foam before she shoved it and a plastic lid angrily at him. Only some of the coffee sloshed over the sides, and Diego huffed while he inspected her handiwork.

"Regular iced chai with oat milk," Josh shot over his shoulder while handing her the plastic cup, and Audrey sighed in relief as she grabbed the concentrate from the fridge. Iced chai people were godsends.

"It's none of your business what my intentions are with Theo. That's between us. He's a big boy, don't you think? He can do what he wants and date who he wants." She stirred oat milk into the iced black tea concentrate and capped off the drink before sliding it to the pickup side of the counter. "Not only that, but he spoke highly of you to me, and now I'm wondering what the hell he was thinking."

That earned her a fresh glare. "None of my business? Oh, it *is* my business, believe me." He eyed the coffee she'd made him and took a sip. His eyebrows shot up, but he shook his head and huffed. "Look, my intention isn't to pry too far into Theo's personal affairs, and God knows I'm not going to stand here and rehash all of his trauma for you behind his back. But I will say that man has been through *absolute hell*." He punctuated the words by tapping his finger firmly on the wooden counter. "The worst shit you can imagine. It broke him. That's obvious enough, especially now that he's shown you his face—which is *huge*, by the way. Monumental. I hope you appreciate that."

"I do. I do appreciate how big that was for him."

He quirked a skeptical eyebrow as though he didn't quite believe her and drew in a deep breath. "Whether he's talked about it or not is his business, and his story isn't for me to tell. But here's the thing: I'm also not going to sit back and watch him get heartbroken by some little girl who has no idea what she's getting herself into, especially not after his last girlfriend. I've spent months—*years*, really—trying to help patch him back together and I won't see him torn to shreds again. He's too good for that."

"'Little girl'?!" Her face burned. "I'm not some *little girl*. You have no idea what I've been through. You certainly don't know anything about me, and even less about how I feel about Theo."

"I know enough." Diego leaned forward and tilted his head at Audrey. "I know enough to see that he's head over heels for you, and you barely know each other. And don't get me wrong: while I will continue to encourage him when it comes to getting out of the goddamn house and actually socializing in any way he can, I draw the line at him rearranging his entire life after only a handful of dates."

"What are you talking about?" It was Audrey's turn to scowl.

He scoffed bitterly. "Yeah, of course you don't know, because Theo won't fucking talk about shit with anyone except his therapist, and that's why he has to go see her religiously." Diego took another sip of his coffee and glanced over his shoulder at the door. He seemed to be keeping a close eye on it. "He told me he's spending today rescheduling all of his doctor's appointments for the next several months. And what did he say when I asked him *why* he's doing that with the top doctors and physical therapists and acupuncturists and massage therapists and medical aestheticians and trauma psychologists that are all extremely in-demand, booked within an inch of their lives, and the hardest people to schedule with in all of fucking New York?" His gaze darkened. "He said it was for *you*. Because he wants to spend more time with you."

"*M-me?*" she stammered. "I didn't ask him to do that. He hasn't mentioned anything about that to me." She didn't even know he had that many appointments. He never wanted to talk about it.

"Yeah, well, he wouldn't, would he? He just does stuff without consulting anyone." Diego rolled his eyes. "He's done this shit his whole life. Once Theo makes a choice, he pursues it single-mindedly, and God forbid anyone try to convince him otherwise."

He sighed and rubbed his eyes tiredly. "Look, I know it's not your fault, but I needed you to know what he's up to. He's planning on coming here every weekday morning to see you on your breaks, and that means he'll be missing several weeks of PT and therapy, since they couldn't squeeze him in sooner once he changed his preset appointment times. And that's not even counting the follow-up exams with his teams of medical doctors, or all his pain management stuff. All of it, his whole routine, his whole care plan, his health—mental *and* physical? He's tossing it out the window. Blowing it up. For you."

Audrey's breath caught in her chest. Diego was right about one thing: this was huge. She hadn't meant for Theo to do that, and without even knowing exactly what had happened, she did understand how desperately he needed that support. Would it all fall to her in the interim, then? Or was he strong enough to bear it himself now?

"Large latte with almond milk and lavender syrup," Josh muttered, passing her another paper cup.

Audrey gathered herself enough to pluck it out of his hands. "He's doing all that for me?"

"Yeah." Diego huffed a laugh. "He's over the moon for you. Talks of nothing else. I haven't seen his face light up like this in *years*." He set his cappuccino down with a sigh. "Maybe ever, really, if I'm being honest."

This was a lot to take in so early in the morning, especially after Theo had come over. She'd spent the rest of the night lying in bed, ruminating on the ache throbbing in her chest, unable to sleep from the empty feeling he'd left behind. She wanted more of him, more of his warmth, more of his face, his laugh, his wit. There was still so much of him to get to know, still so many layers to peel away. They'd only just begun.

And it seemed like Theo felt the same way. He was trying to make so much more time for her. A thrill coursed through her at the idea.

But she hadn't known the extent of the professional care he was receiving. And she hadn't ever really considered the consequences of it.

Had *he*?

Audrey made the latte in silence while Diego watched her over his own coffee. He checked his watch and downed the rest of his cappuccino. "Look, I've got to get out of here. You make a damn good coffee, but I've got to go to work and I also don't want Theo to catch me encroaching on his territory." He shook his head. "But frankly, you needed to know. You seem sweet. That's good. But I swear to God, if you hurt him, *I will come for you*." He pointed directly in her face again. "And yes, that is a threat. *Capisce?*"

"Don't point at me like that." She shoved his finger away. "Come for me? What are you, mafia or something?"

"Mafia?" Diego gave her a disgusted look. "*No.* Come on, do I look like mafia to you?"

"I don't know, I'm not a native New Yorker, I don't—"

"Well, that's obvious."

"Okay, but—"

"So here's what we're gonna do." He straightened and smoothed the wrinkles from his jeans before adjusting the tan leather jacket he wore. "Theo's going to come in here on Monday during your break and you're going to act surprised. I was never here, we never had this conversation, he would kill me if he knew. Would wrap one of his gargantuan hands around my neck and pinch my windpipe shut like it was easy, tossing that whole 'gentle giant' schtick straight out the window."

Audrey glowered at him while she slid the next coffee onto the pickup counter. "First of all, Diego: you're obnoxious and I'm not helping you. Second of all: I've met Theo. I don't believe he'd actually hurt you for one minute." As much as she'd like to see Theo strangle his supposed best friend right now, she still couldn't imagine him hurting a fly.

Diego barked a laugh and shook a finger in her direction, his mouth twisting into a crooked smirk while his eyes lit up. He looked a lot less predatory, and his smile only grew the more he studied her.

"You know what, Audrey? Feel free to hate me, but I like you. You've got backbone." Then he snorted. "Theo may be as sweet as they come to you, but he was a beast when we played lacrosse together and it wasn't for nothing. Absolute tank on the field, and he's capable of doing plenty of damage even now, believe you me. And you probably don't know it yet because he'd never show it, and *especially* not to you, but he does have a temper. It takes a lot for him to boil over, but it happens on occasion. He's been very clear about not wanting any interference in this thing you two have going on, and I definitely went behind his back today."

"Regular mocha." Josh handed her another cup and Audrey turned back to the Marzocco.

"That's a you problem if you knew the consequences," she shot over her shoulder at Diego while she pumped chocolate syrup into the cup. "You came here and threatened me, and I'm absolutely not covering for you. I'm not lying about anything to Theo and I'll let him handle you however he sees fit."

Diego waved a dismissive hand in the air and flashed her a scathing look. "Hey, hey, hey: don't give me that. I don't want any of your logic or integrity, I don't care how sound it is." He leaned around the machine and held out a hand. "Now give me your phone."

"No." Audrey wiped down the steam wand and pumped it pointedly in his direction.

Diego yanked his hand away rather than be scalded. "Oh for fuck's sake . . ." He ripped the cardboard sleeve off his drink and pulled a Sharpie out of his jacket pocket while Audrey topped off the mocha she'd just made with foam. He scribbled on it and slid it over to her.

"Here's my number. If something happens with him and you don't know what to do, you text or call me, all right?"

"I don't want your number. You did not endear yourself to me today." Her scowl deepened. "And now you've also ruined Theo's surprise for me. I don't even get to enjoy *that*."

"*Jesus Christ.*" Diego sighed and muttered to himself in rapid Spanish while massaging the bridge of his nose again. "Fine. I'll take responsibility and deal with him later." He checked his watch and blanched. "Shit. All right, I've gotta run. I'm not facing him in person over this, not today. I might be dumb, but I'm not *that* stupid." He grabbed his satchel and tapped the sleeve again before pushing it closer to her. "You know, it was really nice to meet you, Audrey. Don't take me bristling at you as an insult—it's actually a huge compliment."

"Don't try to backpedal now, Diego. You've already dug yourself a hole with me." Josh passed her another plastic cup with a whispered, "*Large cold brew,*" and she shook her head while she filled it with iced coffee. "And you were doing so well, too, convincing Theo to wear that beautiful sweater on our first real date. He looked *so* sexy. Pity I have to dislike you now." She shoved the top on the cup. "Especially since I would *very* much like to be his girlfriend."

He chuckled. "Fine, kiddo. I'll figure out how to make it up to you. And I'm sure I'll see you around—if Theo doesn't kill me first."

He gave her and Josh one last look, lingering for the briefest of moments on Josh's face. "Catch you later," he said before spinning on his heel and striding confidently out of the café, trotting down the street at a quick clip in the direction of the subway.

Audrey eyed the sleeve he'd left behind and slid the cardboard into her back pocket.

Josh took the last customer's order and leaned over to Audrey while he passed her the mug. "That guy was really hot, if combative. Think he's single?" he muttered, flashing her a sheepish grin when she glared at him. "What the fuck was all that about?"

She hummed. "I might have myself a boyfriend."

THEO ARRIVED AT exactly 8:30 a.m.

But this time, he didn't slink into the café so much as he strode into it, his single visible eye bright and locked straight onto Audrey. He'd already texted her saying he'd be a little late, but he'd see her at her break time, and she already had their coffee made and ready to go. Josh had steeled himself enough to cover for her like he usually did, and when she brought their drinks over to their table, Theo put one hand around her waist, lowered his mask with the other, *and kissed her.*

Audrey gasped in surprise before throwing her arms around his neck and kissing him back.

"Good morning," he murmured while sliding his mask back over his mouth and nose, his eye crinkling as he gazed down at her. She got a quick glimpse of a mischievous, crooked grin before it disappeared beneath the black KN95, and she matched it with one of her own.

"Well, that's different. I like it."

"Me too."

"Feel better after yesterday?"

"Loads better. You have no idea." He caressed her cheek gently with only the slightest tremor before pulling away to sit. Some of his eye crinkles faded slightly. "You're not having second thoughts after last night or anything, are you? You weren't too embarrassed for Violet to see my face and that's why you put my mask back on while I was . . ." He trailed off when she scowled at him.

"*Theo.* I swear, if you question me one more time, I—"

He held up his hands and the tips of his ears turned bright red. "It was a joke?"

"No, it wasn't," Audrey said with a snort. "But nice try. You're not getting rid of me that easily."

"I'd never get rid of you. In fact, I'd never want to be parted from you if it were solely up to me."

She bit her lip in amusement. "You say that, but you've never tried my cooking."

"I'm sure it's wonderful."

"It's not. And I also kick in my sleep, according to Vi. Hard."

"I can take a few hits. I'm very sturdy." Theo paused and blinked for a moment. He frowned. "Well, okay, maybe with one *really* notable exception."

Audrey gaped at him. "Oh my god. Did you just make a joke about your accident?"

He blinked again, and then the crinkles very slowly deepened anew around his eye. His mask shifted across his face as he beamed beneath it, and his expression lit up. "You know what? I did. Dr. Harper would be so proud of me."

Audrey couldn't help but beam right back. "*I'm* so proud of you!" She grabbed his hand across the table. "You going to tell me what happened now?"

"Nope."

"Ugh, *fine*. But you need to tell me someday."

"Sure, but I'm not going to ruin this moment. Let me have this."

"All right." Her smile faded. "Speaking of ruining things, I met Diego today."

Theo's eye crinkles faded completely, gone twice as rapidly as they'd appeared. "What?"

Uh-oh.

"Did he come in here?" His voice dipped low and his entire body stilled.

"Yes." She gripped the handle of her mug and Theo's eye narrowed.

"Why?"

"For . . . a cappuccino."

"And?" His gaze darkened.

"And . . ." She winced. "And to tell me about how you moved all of your various doctors' appointments so you could come see me at work every day."

His left eye twitched.

"Excuse me for just a second."

His voice was tight, strained, and he reached into his pocket to pull out his phone, tapping a few times at the screen before holding it up to his ear. He waited, and there was a faint beep on the other end before he started speaking.

"*Come to my place when you get off work, you asshole,*" he growled. "And don't be a chickenshit and try to hide. I'll fucking find you. *I have time.*" He hung up and Audrey gulped.

He looked furious.

All right, so maybe Diego hadn't been kidding about his temper.

Theo set his phone facedown on the table and calmly folded his hands next to it. "I am so sorry about that. He is, very unfortunately, more like family than a friend. I'm going to have a talk with him about sticking his nose in other people's business—and overstepping boundaries."

"What if he doesn't come over?"

He huffed. "He shared his location with me when he was drunk one night and couldn't find his way home—and then completely forgot about it. I'm able to track him anywhere he goes, but I don't want him to realize that. I'd rather he continue to think I'm on Liam Neeson's level."

He turned his phone back over and unlocked it again to show her the Find My app. There he was: a little circular floating headshot simply labeled "Diego" hovering somewhere in Midtown.

"It's been four years and he still hasn't figured it out. For such a talented investigative reporter, he really has some truly idiotic moments." He tucked his phone back into his pocket. "I guess he can't use all of his brains all at once on all things."

Audrey laughed, and some of the light came back into the visible corner of Theo's face. She covered her mouth until her giggles subsided and considered him again. Okay, he was mad, but he didn't seem like he was going to completely kill his friend. Maybe Diego wasn't so bad.

Maybe he *was* just a little dumb.

"He cares about you," she finally ventured. "That's clear. He was concerned."

Theo buried his face in his hand with a sigh. "I know. And that's generous of you to point out. But frankly, I'm exhausted by it. I've had enough people fretting and hovering over me for the last several months. I don't need it anymore. I'm okay. Okay enough." His throat bobbed, and he glanced over at the machine where Josh was busy working. "I'm not an invalid these days, and I'm a grown man. I can manage my own life again, and I need certain people to back off. Diego is one of them."

He took Audrey's hand between his massive ones. His fingertip skated along the lines of her palm, tickling across the grooves in her skin like he was trying to read her fortune again. "You're important to me, Audrey. Really important. I wanted to spend more time with you, but your schedule's set. You need this job right now. You're doing big things at school, and I want you to succeed so you can graduate in December." He shrugged. "I'm not working and my schedule's flexible. I decided to change it because I can. It made the most sense."

"Diego said you'd be missing some PT and therapy appointments, though, and he has a point. Those are important too, Theo."

His fingers stopped gliding across her skin. Instead, he rubbed his palms across her fingers to warm them. Audrey hadn't even realized her hands were cold until she felt how hot Theo's were in comparison. But it had gradually been getting chillier outside, and she hadn't been working the machine before he came in.

"I'll be fine. I'm healed enough to skip a few weeks, and I can do a lot of the PT exercises at home. Dr. Harper is supportive of all this, and she understands and is excited. I can always call her if I need to. Diego's the one who's overreacting. My mom already has being suffocating and overbearing on lock." The eye crinkles were back again. "I don't need two of them."

Audrey chewed on the inside of her cheek. This was the most self-assured she'd ever seen him. Maybe all this was a good thing. Maybe he felt like he was more in control of his life today than he'd felt previously. She interlaced their fingers and squeezed his hand.

"Okay. I just wanted to make sure."

"Thank you for telling me. I'd have been disappointed and probably a little embarrassed on Monday if you weren't surprised."

She barked a laugh. "And I'm not all that good of an actress. It was partially self-preservation."

"Honestly, you have no idea how much I appreciate that." The way his gaze shifted, she had the sneaking suspicion that he wore a wicked grin under that mask. "And on top of it, now I get to go yell at Diego properly. That'll be fun. For me, not for him."

"I have a really hard time imagining you yelling." Audrey raised an eyebrow. He was so gentle, the idea was incompatible with everything she knew about him.

But it was Theo's turn to hum in amusement. "I have my moments. And I'm going to milk this for all it's worth. Trust me, he's done plenty of things to deserve getting ripped a new one. He's overdue."

They spent the rest of her break chatting before she had to head back behind the counter. Theo was already busy taking out his iPad to stay and work when Audrey remembered what she was originally going to talk to him about today. She turned and rested a hand on his shoulder.

"Before I forget again, I was going to ask you something."

He looked up at her curiously "Oh? What is it?"

"Do you have any plans for this weekend?"

Theo snorted. "Sweetheart, I don't have any plans ever these days, aside from coming to see you. And I'm even freer for the next month than I normally am. What did you have in mind?"

"I'm an officer for Earth Matters, the campus sustainability student group and environmental club at NYU, and we're having a costume party to raise awareness about green energy and university initiatives tomorrow night." She looked down at her hands, suddenly a little embarrassed. "I know it's really dorky, and it's really last-minute, but do you maybe want to come with me?"

His gaze softened and the mask shifted over his cheeks. "Of course I do."

Oh. He'd answered so quickly, and that brightened her right up. She'd been afraid he wouldn't want to be around so many people or hang out around a bunch of college students, nerdy as they were.

She beamed. "Great! I was really hoping you would. But you only have a day to come up with a costume. And the rules are that you have to make it out of things you already have available or can acquire for free."

He chuckled. "I'm pretty sure I can think of something."

Audrey smirked.

"And you know what? A lot of people there will be wearing masks."

Eight

HOW DO I look? He's going to be here any minute."

"Hang on, hang on, I'm almost done, don't move. Relax your mouth." Violet opened her own and Audrey imitated her, trying not to look anxiously over her shoulder at the door while her roommate put the finishing touches on her lipstick. She was terrible at doing makeup and hardly ever wore it, but Violet was more than happy to lend her a hand.

"Why do you even have this shade, anyway? It's so weird."

"Quit talking," Violet snapped while she carefully swept the color across her lips. "It was all the rage a few years ago among the edgier YouTube makeup gurus and I had to try it out. I only wore it a few times, and I'm honestly jealous of how good it looks on your face," she grumbled with a pout. "Never looked half as good on mine."

"It does?"

"*Hush.*" She flipped the tube over and swept a few coats of a clear sealant over Audrey's lips. "There. Once that dries, it ought to hold in place even if you two have an extended makeout session in an alleyway somewhere. But don't touch it, and give it a minute to dry."

"How am I going to get this off if it's blast-proof like that?"

"You—wait, what? What kind of making out are you doing?"

Audrey's cheeks burned. "He's sweet. *I* get kind of intense," she mumbled.

Violet snorted. "Jesus. Okay then. And, well, I guess it *is* your third date." She bounced her eyebrows significantly and thrust Audrey's usual emotional support tube of ChapStick into her hands.

"Right. Th-third—third date."

Her stomach dropped at the reminder.

"Lip balm will get it off. Lots of it. Swipe it on, then immediately wipe it off. The oils in it should do the trick." Audrey tucked it in her clutch right as her roommate passed her a hand mirror. "Just look at my gorgeous handiwork. I'm a fucking *artist*."

"*Whoa*." Audrey didn't recognize the person reflected back at her. Her eyes were dark and smoky, colored with various shades of black and gray and bright, glittering holographic silver eyeshadow. More silver was dusted along her cheeks as highlighter, and the silvery-gray lipstick Violet had just so expertly applied was still drying, but the glossy topper shone gently in the golden fairy lights of their apartment. Her hair was loosely curled and tumbled to her shoulders, and Audrey marveled at how well Violet had gotten it to cooperate. She lowered the mirror and beamed at her as she grabbed her coat. "Thank you. I could have never done this myself."

"You did such good work on the dress, so we had to stick the landing." Violet patted her shoulder just as their buzzer went off, and she gasped and lunged for the button to let Theo in before Audrey could.

"Vi, I'll just meet him on the stairs, you don't have to—"

Violet spun on her heel, her finger raised accusingly and her scowl dark. "*No.* I'm officially meeting Theo. That's my reward for this masterpiece I've just created." She gestured at Audrey's face. "Don't tell me otherwise."

Audrey sighed. "Fine. But at least let me answer the door. He wouldn't tell me what his costume was, and he's mine. I get to see first."

"I'll kill you if you squeeze out without letting me say hi." She glanced down and suddenly ripped Audrey's clutch out of her grasp.

"*Hey!* That's—"

"Where your keys and phone are, yes." Violet grinned wickedly at her. "You get it back when I've met the Sasquatch."

Audrey groaned, but she didn't have time to protest further before there was a knock at the door. She yanked it open eagerly.

Theo stood in front of her, tall and straight, his arms crossed over his chest. He looked like he was about to do something else when he fully registered Audrey in front of him—and audibly gasped.

Both of his eyes were visible tonight, and they widened, the left more than the right, as he took her in before him.

He was not wearing a mask.

"Oh wow," he breathed. "Audrey, you—"

"Theo, what *are* you? Like, a—a *Blues Brothers* mummy?"

He was wearing a suit and a tie with expensive-looking shiny black shoes. A matching fedora topped his head, and he clutched a pair of dark glasses in one gloved hand.

But it was the bandages that threw her off. His entire head, all of his face and neck and hair, had been wrapped in thick, overlapping layers of gauze, covering everything but a sliver for his eyes and a slit where his mouth should be.

Clever.

Not a mask, but certainly not *not* a mask.

"A—a *what*?!" Theo looked down at what he was wearing, and what tiny bit of his brows she could discern furrowed. "Are you joking?" He put on his glasses and gestured indignantly at his chest. "I'm the Invisible Man! From the classic Universal sci-fi horror film directed by James Whale in 1933? Starring Claude Rains and based on the novel by H. G. Wells?" He crossed his arms over his chest and hunched his shoulders pointedly. "You know." He uncrossed his arms and held out a hand as if he were trying to offer her literally anything to grasp on to to get the reference. "You know, right? The iconic film?"

Audrey shook her head and tried not to bite her freshly lacquered lip. "I've never seen it." She grinned sheepishly at him.

The meltdown was imminent.

"Oh my god," he muttered, ripping the glasses off and rubbing at his eyes with one of his gloved hands. "We need to have another movie day, and soon."

She was just about to agree when Violet shoved her roughly out of the way and took her place in the doorway, thrusting her hand out to Theo.

"HI I'M VIOLET TAN I'M SO EXCITED TO MEET YOU."

"AH!" Theo startled and jumped backward from the door, scrambling to tilt his hat further over his face to conceal his right eye. But Violet's grin only grew wider, and she waited patiently while Theo gathered himself enough to take a cautious step forward again, one hand over his heaving chest. His left eye was wide in terror, but he managed to tentatively lift his trembling right hand to slide it over Violet's anyway.

"Uh . . . h-hi, Violet. I'm Theo." He winced as he shook her hand gently, his absolutely swallowing hers. "I'm sorry, I didn't know anyone else was here, and I—"

"No, no, don't worry about it! I was heading out myself, but I've heard so much about you, so I wanted to meet you—and find out what you thought of my handiwork." She winked cheekily at him. "Good makeup on Audrey, right? She looks gorgeous, huh?"

"Yes. Yes, she really does." His eyes shifted back onto Audrey's face. "She always does, though," he muttered softly. Then his eyes landed on Violet's costume, and the gauze shifted up as he raised a brow. "Oh shit—really cool costume." He motioned at Violet's sleek bodysuit. "Are you *The Radioactive Birds of Wall Street*, by any chance?"

Violet's mouth dropped open and she shoved at Theo's shoulder in excitement. "*Holy fuck*, I can't believe you got that!" She gestured down at the outfit she wore, hot glued with carefully placed but as of yet unsnapped glow sticks. "No one knows that Lightm4st3r piece. It's super obscure."

Theo chuckled. "Well, I do sort of run in those circles. I liked that one a lot, but it didn't get much press back in 2019. Kind of a disappointing flop, really."

"I didn't think it was disappointing at all! It might be my favorite." Violet cracked one of the glow sticks hastily attached to her long-sleeved shirt. After a slight shake, it began to glow a bright neon green. "It's just that there were hardly any pictures of it. They only revealed it for about five minutes once at that charity auction before it was snapped up by a private collector. It's a miracle a grainy photo of it even leaked onto Twitter."

Lightm4st3r was Violet's favorite artist. She was really into contemporary art and aesthetics and was one of his 1.2 million followers on Instagram. While he was certainly an enigma, he was also one of the most popular New York accounts on the app, and every time he dropped a photo, it managed to make it all the way into Page Six—and often beyond.

He was a reclusive, faceless street artist who posted cryptic images of whatever piece he was working on, often after he'd placed it somewhere guerrilla-style. He'd started with graffiti, scrawled quickly in the night as highly stylized text on the sides of buildings set to be demoed. More often they were sculptures these days, like the one Violet had decided to embody tonight.

But lately, it had been nothing.

He was something of a ghost anyway, but he hadn't posted anything on social media in well over a year, though Audrey didn't really follow him herself. She only knew this because of how often Violet had prattled on about him, and because he made headlines whenever the glitterati fell all over themselves to bid exorbitant amounts on his art. The only way to acquire a verified piece was through charity auctions, with all of the proceeds going to exactly where the artist directed them, which were always reputable organizations that desperately needed those funds to survive.

At least he seemed to have a conscience.

Audrey did like that.

"Okay, you two can wax poetic over the art scene some other time, but we need to get going." Audrey stepped out of their apartment, swiping her clutch back from her roommate with a glare before sliding her hand into the crook of Theo's elbow. "We need to get there early so I can help set up."

"All right, you kids have fun!" Violet waggled her fingers at them before shutting the door with a smirk. The lock clicked shut and Audrey guided Theo toward the stairs, but he nearly tripped on the first step down.

He was too busy staring at her costume.

"What are *you* supposed to be?" he finally asked, his brow furrowed once more. "Are you a . . . disco ball?"

She shook her head, the corners of her mouth twitching as she tried to hide another smile.

"No, I guess your dress isn't shiny enough for that," he mused. "I feel like I should know this. Are you—grayscale? Monochrome? You look like a palette of some kind."

"No, but you're not far off."

Theo shook his head. "Well, you're beautiful, is what you are. But I don't think I get the costume."

Her dress was made of hundreds of paint chips cut into individual strips and safety pinned all over it in neat, overlapping rows.

Violet had tried to convince her to wear heels to complete the look, but there was no way she'd make the trek across the city to campus in them. She was like a baby giraffe in anything higher than two inches as it was, subways and sidewalks and street grates aside, so she'd opted for a pair of thick gray tights and her (very practical) well-worn Docs instead.

Audrey grinned at him as they made their way downstairs. "I'm *Fifty Shades of Grey.*" In truth, there were far more than fifty shades, but the point got across. She'd found enough paint chips to turn the gray dress she wore underneath into something reminiscent of a flapper costume but made out of paper. Every strip hung and swished under her coat as she moved, not unlike beaded fringe but a lot lighter.

"Aha!" Theo slapped his forehead. "God, I should have gotten that. I'm a sham of an artist."

"To be fair, it's a book-slash-movie that started out as *Twilight* fanfic."

"I should have at least guessed the film version." Theo straightened his hat again with his free hand to reveal both eyes, and Audrey found them evenly crinkled. "*Very* clever, Miss Adams. Where'd you find so many different gray paint chips? They'd never let me walk out of a store with that many for free."

That was the one question she was hoping he wouldn't ask. Her cheeks burned again beneath the silver highlighter. "Uh . . . I, um . . ." She shut the door to her building behind her and pursed her lips. Theo stopped in his tracks, looking down at her with a wary expression. He'd noticed her hesitation. "I . . . sometimes go dumpster diving on the Upper East Side." The burn deepened and intensified. "I found a whole box of them a few weeks ago. I guess someone redid their apartment and their designer finally trashed their paint options, maybe once the project was finished."

"Dumpster diving?" She didn't need to see his entire face to know how deeply concerned he suddenly was under all that gauze. "Isn't that dangerous?" His frown intensified.

Oh no.

"So . . . do you need food? Are you hungry? Because if that's the case, I'll feed you, I'll buy you groceries, I really don't mind. You know that, right? Your tips can't go *that* far, I know they don't. I don't know how you're getting by as it is with inflation and the costs of living here, and if you're not getting enough to eat, I—I don't like that, Audrey, I don't like that *at all*, that isn't—" He was clearly getting more and more upset the more he thought about it, and he scratched anxiously at the back of his head through the gauze. "Or is there something else that's wrong? Are you doing that because—"

She cut him off before he worried himself further. "It's a sustainability thing." She patted his arm reassuringly and kept walking toward the subway. "I'm okay, Theo. I'm not starving."

The look he gave her was incredulous. "You'd tell me if you were, right? If you were struggling?"

She wouldn't, actually.

"Sure."

Her answer had been too quick. Maybe a little too bright.

"I don't believe you." His eyes narrowed. "You were right yesterday—you *are* a terrible liar."

She sighed and reached up to rub her face, but stopped herself at the last second before she ruined her makeup. "All right, fine. No, I wouldn't have told you, but I'm okay. I'm getting by about as well as any of my friends are."

Theo's mouth shifted beneath the gauze, and without warning, he tugged her beneath the awning of a closed shop before putting his hands on her shoulders and running them along her arms. His right hand stopped at her neck, and he looked at it for a second before yanking the glove off and replacing it. His fingers were scorching against her skin, and she shivered at the contact, her gasp curling white in front of her silvered lips.

His eyes searched her own in the weak light filtering beneath the awning. "Audrey," Theo finally murmured, his thumb gently caressing the side of her neck. "I'm serious. I don't want you hurting, especially not when it's something I can fix. You're too precious for that—too good."

"But it's not your—"

He drew in a deep, shuddering breath, and Audrey quieted.

"I can bear my pain, but I can't bear yours," he finally murmured. When he looked away, she finally understood.

He knew what it was to suffer. The thought of her feeling any version of what he must have felt at one point had scared him. It was written in his eyes.

Audrey lifted a hand and tilted his head to make him look at her again.

Someday, she'd have him shed the shrouds he wore.

Someday, she'd have him free of the hurt he harbored.

"I'm okay. I've been taking care of myself for a really long time. I'm used to being on my own. You don't have to worry that much about me."

"Yes, I do. Because someone should. And I want to."

The force of that statement ripped through her. Violet worried about her, and Josh did sometimes too. Gladys did when Audrey lived with her once upon a time. But it wasn't the same.

"I want it to be me who cares for you, Audrey." His eyes were pleading. "So promise me," he whispered. "Please."

He was begging her to let him in.

"All right, Theo. I promise."

She nudged away some of the gauze concealing his mouth, revealing those plush pink lips again. When she ran her thumb across one of them, they parted with a sharp inhale.

"I miss these," she whispered. She tried to let her hand fall away, but Theo's shot up to catch it. He turned it over and pulled her palm to his lips, his eyes never leaving hers—until they briefly dipped to her mouth.

She'd forgotten how dark they could be.

How heated.

How intense.

His lips lingered on her skin for as long as his eyes lingered on hers, and Audrey's breath stilled.

Her heart was pounding so fast, she could hear it in her ears, a constant, low thrum quickening with every shallow breath shuddering across her lungs. Theo suddenly seemed so tall, so wide. Sometimes she forgot when they were at the café, sitting across from each other at the table with their coffee. She forgot how long his legs really were. She forgot how, despite the tremor in his hand, his forearms were corded with thick, hard muscle, how broad and strong his back was. She forgot how he radiated heat until he'd fully wrapped her in his arms. She forgot how he smelled warm and woodsy, like fresh cedarwood and pine, juniper and bergamot, and she forgot how bright and alive and vibrant he tasted whenever he kissed her.

But she couldn't forget now.

Audrey's mouth went dry.

She swallowed.

Theo's eyes dipped down to her throat, and then next to her trembling hands. When did they start shaking? She hadn't noticed.

He wrapped his own around the one he held and pressed it to his chest, leaning forward and closing his eyes as he touched his forehead to hers.

He didn't need to say anything.

His heart was racing just as fast.

Theo drew in several deep breaths before finally opening his eyes. "I'll let you unravel me later," he whispered. And then, a pained laugh. "God knows I already have, sweetheart."

He drew back with a shake of his head. But the next look he gave her shot molten heat straight through her core.

"I hope you know how hard it is not to ruin that pretty makeup of yours before we even get to the party."

His voice had dropped so low, it was almost a growl.

A promise, in and of itself.

AUDREY WASN'T ENTIRELY sure how they made it out of that alcove and onto the train, but they managed it in the end.

She told Theo all about the secret dumpster diving activist group she was a part of while they rode to campus, and how they documented corporate waste around town on anonymous social media accounts.

"It's a little bit of a financial thing, because we do keep a lot of what we find if we can use or resell it, but we also give a lot away, especially when it comes to food. We try to feed as many unhoused people as we can, and corporations and grocery stores toss out perfectly good food every day—the café included."

"Is it illegal? Doing the dumpster diving?" he asked. The look he gave her was pointed, but not at all accusing. He'd leaned forward and was studying her intensely.

Audrey wavered. "Uh . . . well, it's questionable at best. It's not illegal unless you're trespassing. And . . . sometimes we are. I hope you don't judge me for that."

"Ha!" He barked a laugh. "Me? Judge you for that? Not at all. I've done my fair share of questionable things. I was only curious."

That floored her. "*What?!*"

"And I think it's *extremely* sexy of you, by the way. The

whole civil disobedience thing." His eyes glittered with mischief. "Very hot."

She was still stuck on the first part of what he'd said. "What on earth could *you* have done wrong?"

Theo Sullivan? Painfully shy and anxious, deeply romantic artist, a lawbreaker?

It was unfathomable.

Theo laughed again at her expression. No embarrassed huff, no bashful chuckle—a thorough guffaw, eyes closed and head thrown back. The crinkles around them were the deepest she'd ever seen, and a wave of warmth washed over her as she looked at him.

What she would have given to see him unwrapped and fully unbound in that moment.

"I was a right little anarchist shithead back in high school. A budding graffiti artist, which meant I was guilty of a decent amount of vandalism. Maybe a touch of light breaking and entering, and a not-insignificant amount of trespassing. I mean, I was obviously a solo actor, I didn't have that many friends and I didn't run in a gang or anything. But I had a tag and a distinctive style. I was a known entity around the city."

"You hooligan." Audrey shook her head, her grin so wide, her cheeks hurt.

The bandages stretched over a grin of his own. "Oh yes. I almost got caught by the cops once, but I managed to get away at the last second. It was a close call." He leaned over and whispered into her ear. "I was really skinny, and I slipped through a gap in a chain link fence. Pigs couldn't get me after that." She snorted and covered her mouth, and his eyes gleamed with pride. "And at least these long legs were good for something—I was pretty fast, and I absolutely smoked 'em. I didn't manage to get away from my mom, though."

The look he gave her conveyed everything she needed to know about how well *that* had gone over. "She caught me red-handed—

literally. Covered in red spray paint, sneaking back into the house in the wee hours of the morning." He winced. "But that was my only real outlet. I was a really quiet, really angry, *really* broody teenager."

"You're still really quiet, and still really broody."

"And still really angry sometimes, too." Some of the smile faded from his eyes. "I was mad at my mom for being who she was, and for leaving my dad when I was so young. It was rough." Theo shrugged. "But it helped form me as an artist, I suppose." He held up his hands. He'd put his glove back on before they'd gotten on the train. The left one was steady, but that persistent tremor still coursed through the right. He sighed and let them fall back into his lap. "I keep telling myself I'll find my way back one day—to the artist I was before, if not the man."

Audrey plucked his hat away from his head and set it in her lap before sliding her hands around his neck to guide his head down to her shoulder. He let her, and as soon as he made contact, he drew in a deep breath, and his whole body relaxed. "You will," she murmured, stroking the side of his face through the gauze. "I know you will."

No one gave Theo a second glance, perhaps because at least half the city seemed to be celebrating Halloween that weekend. As soon as they stepped out of the subway station at their stop, they were mobbed by undergrads walking around in costumed packs on their way to parties. Music blasted through the streets, and Audrey went cross-eyed trying to count all the sorority Barbies she saw on the sidewalks in high hot-pink heels. The moon was obscured by dark, rolling clouds, but that wasn't unusual—it was always hard to see the light of the night sky when New York was so good at providing its own landscape of stars.

"I like the cut of that suit on you," Audrey said, rubbing her arm along Theo's sleeve while she guided him toward the space her student org had reserved for the party. "You look so handsome in it, and it's a nice change of pace from the usual jeans and hoodie."

"Handsome like Humphrey Bogart?" He quirked an eyebrow at her. "Like Rick Blaine?"

"Even more so. Well, at least I'm sure you are under all that gauze, anyway."

He chuckled, and his eyes—both of them—lit up at her praise. It was fun seeing the change in him as they passed under the campus streetlights. "Oh, well, I already had this suit, as per the rules. And, uh . . ." He trailed off, and the crinkles faded. "I already had the gauze too. Scads of it. And while I'm sure I could repurpose at least some of this, I hope I never need it again."

"I think it's okay if we throw this out for good once we're done here tonight. I'll sign off on that as secretary of Earth Matters." She squeezed his arm. "Plus, it's biodegradable."

When they got to the correct building, Theo held the door open for her and they wandered to the student organization's reserved multipurpose room, where they got straight to work, setting up the party with the other officers.

Audrey claimed food duty, and she and Theo began arranging all the freshly delivered pizzas and prepackaged snacks and drinks. This was one of the few big events they held every year. Most students knew about Earth Matters, and a fair amount of them could be counted on to show up for the free food while they pregamed for the other Halloween parties off-campus. But that was fine. They usually picked up a few new members after this event, often some of the more civic-minded freshmen who wandered their way over out of curiosity and a lack of anything better to do.

It was natural working with Theo like this, and it became almost a dance as they moved around each other in tandem, reaching for more snacks or organizing stacks of compostable paper plates. At every opportunity, Theo shifted closer and closer to her while they worked, brushing his hand against hers, touching their shoulders together here, reaching around her there. Whenever he did, goose bumps prickled across her skin, and Audrey was struck again by his warmth above all else. It radiated out from him, flooded through her, tingled across her arms, right and good and welcome. And as it turned out, they were a good team. Everything was set up in record time, and soon enough, the doors opened and undergrads flooded into the ballroom.

The spread of costumes this year was impressive. There was a contest with a prize for whoever had the best sustainable execution, and the attendees didn't disappoint. There were groups of people dressed as painted cardboard Tetris blocks, an astronaut with a jet-pack made from soda bottles, a snail crafted out of Amazon paper and packaging. One person had shown up as a cereal killer, a costume Theo was particularly enamored with. Miniature cereal boxes from the dining hall were glued to a plain white shirt painted with dripping red blood, all of them stabbed in the center with plastic knives. Audrey's favorite was a movie theater floor: clumps of popcorn and candy wrappers and trash stuck all over a black shirt.

But those were the true nerds or hippies who had enough dedication to follow through on the concept. Most of the rest of the students wandering in were more casual participants, but they seemed to have fun with the games and music nonetheless. A few of the other officers tried to get a dance party going, and Audrey grabbed Theo and attempted to drag him over there with her. But he dug his heels in, and when his eyes grew wide and he shook his head frantically, her heart dropped just a little.

All right, so maybe public dancing was pushing it. He was *very* shy, after all, even if she'd gotten her hopes up about the prospect of dancing with him.

It was okay. She could handle that sort of disappointment.

"AUDS!"

Before she could get too in her head about it, someone shouted at her and she turned to find Kayleigh, the club's president, waving her over from a dark corner. They'd all been so busy setting up earlier that she hadn't gotten to check with her when they came in. She tugged Theo in that direction, and he limped after her.

Kayleigh was a quirky dance and government double major, a total crunchy vegan hippie with swinger parents who owned a hemp farm in upstate Vermont. Tonight, she was dressed head to toe in various shades of brown and covered in leaves. They were real, all of them orange and gold and red, attached to wires and woven over her shoulders and along her arms and in her swirling golden hair.

She moved like chaos incarnate, and the leaves shivered in the breeze she seemed to generate.

"Hey, lady!" she called over the music as they approached. "Wow, look at you, wearing makeup for once." The tiny blonde shot double finger guns at her. "Let me guess: Studio 54 newspaper, and—" She pointed them next at Theo. "Jazz mummy?"

He made a pained, high-pitched noise in his throat, and Audrey strangled a laugh. "*Fifty Shades of Grey* and the Invisible Man."

"Ah, very cheeky. I like it. But your tall drink of water doesn't look so invisible to me." Kayleigh raised an eyebrow at him and put her hands on her hips.

Audrey was almost glad Theo had put his sunglasses back on. She didn't need to see his eyes to know what sort of look he was giving Kayleigh right now. "It's an old film reference. I'm sure you'd see right through him if you unwrapped the gauze."

"That sounds like a good time. Who's under there, anyway? Who'd you bring?"

"Oh! Uh, this is, um—he's my—" She hesitated for a second. They hadn't discussed this, and—

"I'm her boyfriend." He held out his hand. "Theo."

Audrey's heart leapt into her throat.

She didn't know how badly she'd wanted him to be until he said it.

And she'd had no idea he'd say it at all, and with such confidence too.

She swallowed thickly. A wild thrill had just coursed through her entire body.

It was like she'd been struck by lightning.

"Boyfriend, huh?" Kayleigh shook his hand before turning and punching Audrey in the shoulder, breaking her out of her shock. "You've been holding out on me, Audible! I didn't know you had a boyfriend!"

Theo slid an arm around her waist and tucked her comfortably into his side.

It was like she'd been made to fit him perfectly.

"It's . . . new." She was certain her face was on fire. Kayleigh opened her mouth to ask what was undoubtedly another question, but Audrey pointed at the leaves surrounding the club president's head. "So are you . . . Mother Nature?"

Kayleigh's face lit up, and she tossed her arms above her head and twirled dramatically. "I'm the Spirit of Autumn," she said, landing in fourth position and following it with a deep bow. "But you were close. The vibes were right." She grabbed Audrey and shoved her toward the food table in the corner with a wicked glint in her eye. "How about you and your *boyfriend Theo* help clean up? We have to be out of here in twenty before custodial comes in."

They glanced at each other when Kayleigh left them to go talk to some of the other officers, and Theo removed his sunglasses. "I'm . . . really sorry about that," he muttered. What little of his face she could see beneath the bandages was beet red, and he rubbed the back of his neck anxiously. "About the boyfriend thing. I know we haven't discussed it, but you looked so flustered, and I didn't want you to feel—"

"I want you to be my boyfriend." She could hardly stop the

words from tumbling breathlessly out of her lips, and the second they did, he froze. "I'd love to be your girlfriend."

"You would?" he breathed, his eyes widening in disbelief when Audrey nodded.

She glanced down at her elbow. He'd pocketed his gloves a while ago, and his bare fingertips were busy gently stroking her there, as if he couldn't bear to not be touching her somewhere while they talked. No matter how calm he'd been earlier, he was nervous now. She could see it in his eyes, that flash of fear and doubt he so often wore around her.

"You don't think it's too early for me to ask? I can wait if you need me to, I pro—"

He quieted when she reached up to put both hands on the sides of his face. She slipped her fingers beneath some of the folds of the gauze, flipping them up and pushing them gently aside to reveal his mouth. Theo's breath shuddered when her fingertips grazed against his lips, and his chest rose and fell heavily beneath her palms when she dropped her hands there.

Audrey shook her head, a weak, trembling smile breaking through the self-doubt she was desperately trying to hold in check.

The last time she'd hoped someone might want the title, he'd thrown her away like trash. And not for the first time either. In many ways, she *was* trash. She was nothing, and no one terribly important.

But . . .

Theo didn't seem to think so.

He never made her feel like anything less than a treasure.

"Do you have any idea how much I like you?" It was his turn to shake his head, eyes still wide. She patted his chest knowingly and nodded again. He was still so incapable of seeing himself the way she saw him. "It's . . . it's a lot, Theo. Far more than I've ever liked anyone before. I like you so much, it aches."

Theo screwed his eyes shut and surged forward to take her lips in his, lifting a hand and cradling her neck while he kissed her well and thoroughly in the dark corner of the ballroom. The music from the party thudded in the background, drowning out every sound save for their beating hearts. Theo's thundered in his chest beneath her palms, as frantic and needful as her own pulse throbbing beneath his thumb caressing her skin. The deeper he kissed her, the more she burned, the more she *needed*.

She'd never known anyone like him before.

She never wanted to know anyone else.

He pulled away, gasping quietly as he looked at her before burying his face in her shoulder. He smiled against her neck.

"Okay," he finally whispered. He slid his fingers up and buried them in her hair. "No more doubts. I promise."

"Good." Audrey wished she could do the same, but he was still covered in that goddamn gauze.

She was thoroughly tired of the costumes now.

It was time to take off their masks.

AFTER THE PARTY, they left campus and headed back toward Brooklyn, stopping for pizza on the way and eating it while they walked, dripping grease onto the sidewalks and gleefully licking sauce from their fingertips. They hadn't really gotten to eat any of the food they'd been in charge of setting up, and Audrey was starving. The clouds overhead continued to roll and thicken, and gusts of wind picked up tendrils of her hair and plucked at them wildly. But all it did was add to her exhilaration.

Something about being out with Theo now made her feel so terribly, vibrantly *alive*. The way he looked at her—stealing glances here and there when he thought she wasn't paying attention, the light of the street lamps and signs and millions of cascading windows across the buildings of the sweeping cityscape glinting in his eyes—sent shivers down her spine, and she never wanted to look away. The idea of drowning herself in his amber gaze was intoxicating, and every time his fingers sought out hers, sparks skipped across her skin, searing gooseflesh in their wake.

By the time they caught the train and mounted the stairs back up to their neighborhood, the weather had shifted. The clouds were thicker and darker, and thunder rumbled. Theo paused at the top of the stairs and looked up at the sky.

It smelled like rain in the air.

"There weren't any storms in the forecast," he muttered. But as soon as the words left his mouth, he blinked and startled, reaching up slowly to wipe at his eyes. Audrey felt it next: a big, fat raindrop landed on her forehead, icy and bracing. Another came on its heels, and another, and another, until the skies opened up above them.

And poured.

The other people on the sidewalks all scattered and ran, holding up umbrellas or bags or jackets to shelter them from the downpour. Before Audrey could even blink, something dropped firmly onto her head. It was Theo's hat, the brim of it keeping some of the rain out of her face.

She glanced up at him. The gauze he wore was already sopping wet, stuck to and around his features like papier-mâché. Drops of water fell from his long lashes and disappeared into the sodden cotton.

"Come on!" he cried. "My place is closer!"

He grabbed her hand.

And they ran.

Nine

THEY TORE THROUGH the streets, picking up speed while the rain thundered down on them even harder than before.

Despite Theo's best efforts—he'd also thrown his jacket around her shoulders—Audrey was soaked to the bone and shivering, the strips of paint chips wet and curling, hanging limp from their safety pins and weighing her dress down considerably. The cold air burned her lungs as she panted and tried her best to keep up with Theo's long legs while he led them to shelter. But when they turned a corner, his foot caught in an uneven piece of sidewalk, and his fingers ripped away from her grasp as he fell heavily to the ground with a cry.

"Theo!" she shouted. Lightning flashed and thunder rumbled right after it, drowning out her voice. She bent down and helped him stumble to his feet. "Are you okay?"

His face was twisted in pain, but he nodded through a grimace. "I'm fine." He took her hand in his again. "We're almost there."

They kept going at a trot, Theo's limp far more pronounced than it was earlier, until they nearly reached the end of the block. He carefully mounted the stairs of the second to last brownstone at the top of a hill, gripping the iron handrail tightly while pulling a set of keys from his pocket. There was a safety door, and he punched a code into a keypad to unlock it before twisting a fancy key in the front door lock. When it swung open, lights automatically turned on in the entryway and he pulled Audrey inside.

As soon as the doors shut after her, electronic locks clicked into place with a beep. The sounds of the raging storm outside were immediately muffled, and Audrey's teeth chattered while she looked around.

She'd been expecting an apartment building with a foyer and multiple levels, much like where she lived. Much like how most New Yorkers she knew lived.

But this wasn't an apartment building.

This was a house.

And it was *huge*.

Theo hung his keys on a hook near the door before turning to her. "Here, let me take those," he murmured, peeling the coats away from her shoulders before plucking his hat off her head. She let him, her mouth still hanging open in shock, and not even the steady sound of the water dripping from their sodden hems as he hung them on a wall-mounted rack could tear her away from the stark realization that Theo didn't live like she did.

She thought back to all the change he'd shoved so casually into her tip jar over the weeks and months he'd been coming into the café, and suddenly everything made so much more sense. His silver watch flashed in the entryway lights, and her eyes darted down to it. It was usually the fanciest thing he ever wore.

Now she found herself wondering how much something so small could cost.

"I'll get you a towel. You need to get warmed up, it's too cold outside to stay wet and I don't want you to get sick. Come on in and make yourself at home."

"But I'll get water all over your floors."

Theo blinked at her, water still dripping down his own face from the gauze. "They're tile. It'll be fine. I wish I could've saved the original floors on this level, but they were too damaged." He took her hand and pulled her further inside. "Come on."

Oh. She'd thought they were hand-scraped wooden planks.

Even the floors were deceptively fancy.

The foyer opened up into an open living room and chef's kitchen with high ceilings. Floor-to-ceiling windows framed views of the Brooklyn Bridge over the East River, and industrial-style pipe bookshelves were embedded into exposed redbrick walls, all laden with a massive collection of books, movies, and vinyl records. What had to be an eighty-inch TV was mounted with speakers on the wall across from a large, comfortable-looking sectional, and a small home gym was tucked into a corner, outfitted with a recumbent bike, a Peloton slat treadmill, and a fully stocked, top-of-the-line weight rack with matching bench.

Everything looked relatively new, freshly renovated, and impeccably designed in a modern, industrial style. Original exposed beams and brick were juxtaposed with gleaming white quartz countertops and modern, matte-black fixtures, large, top-of-the-line dark stainless-steel appliances, and brand-new ceramic flooring. It was warm but chic, artistic but intentional—and not a speck of dust to be found on any surface.

It was very Theo.

He flicked lights on as they went, and a large neon sign hummed into life on a wall near the kitchen. The words SULLIVAN HOT RODS glowed in classic yellow text around a turquoise vintage car bounded in a red-orange circle, all crafted with neon light. But before she could get a better look at it, Theo tugged her up two flights of stairs, around a corner, and into a bathroom on the third floor.

"Here," he said softly, grabbing a fluffy white towel out of a cabinet and wrapping it around her shoulders. "Actually, do you just want to take a hot shower? Let me get you some dry clothes, I'll be right back."

Audrey pulled the towel closer around her neck. Everything in Theo's house was neat and pristine, aside from the trail of wet footprints they'd just dripped all over his floors. It felt like she'd violated his space by tracking them into his gleaming white bathroom. But he was right: she was freezing, and she bent down to unlace her boots and rip off the tights clinging to her legs. She let them drop with a wet splatter into the sink and braced herself for the tile floors to be achingly cold against her bare feet. But when her soles touched them, they were warm and radiating heat.

She was still busy staring down at the floor in surprise when Theo emerged from the darkness beyond the bathroom, a stack of clothes held in his hands and away from his body so he wouldn't get them wet.

He put them on the counter and grinned from beneath the layers of sopping wet gauze. "Sorry these won't exactly fit, but I grabbed things with drawstrings. You might have to roll up the waist on the pants a couple of times, though."

A few stray drops of water fell from his eyelashes onto the floor, and Audrey stepped over to him. "Do you need help out of that?" she asked, grazing a curious hand against his cheek. "You promised I could unravel you later, and I've been waiting all night."

Theo chuckled and bent down. "I was just going to peel it off myself, but all right. There should be a safety pin up there somewhere holding it all together."

He had to practically fold himself in half for her to be able to reach, but when she finally saw the pin glinting in the lights of the bathroom, Audrey began unspooling the lengths of the soaked cotton. Bit by bit, his hair came into view, then his face. As the gauze fell away, Theo gradually straightened and watched her quietly.

When his scarred right cheek was revealed, she laughed.

It was smeared now, but the red, angry length of the scar on his face had been filled in with black paint and crossed with periodic slashes. Theo grinned crookedly at her, his soaked waves curling around his neck and cheeks.

"I was originally going to try for Frankenstein's monster—you know, the Boris Karloff version? But the paint on the papier-mâché headpiece I made didn't dry in time for me to actually wear it." He pointed up at his head. "I'm glad that didn't work out now. It might have been even messier with the rain." He ripped the last of the gauze away from his neck and tossed it into the sink next to her tights with a loud *thwap*.

"Were you going to actually show your face publicly tonight?"

His crooked grin softened as he gazed at her. "I might've, yeah. It's been a pretty long time since I have." Theo lifted a hand toward his scar, his fingers twitching slightly, as though he didn't quite want to touch it. "Well, I thought about it, anyway," he said with a sigh. "I probably would've chickened out in the end, but it was kind of nice to see it covered. Made it feel less real. I could imagine that it was just like Halloween last year and that nothing had ever happened to me at all. That it was always just . . . paint."

The rest of his grin faded, and he rolled his lips together while he looked at Audrey. "Hey. You're shivering." Theo ran his hands along her arms and wiped some of the dripping water away from her face with the corner of the towel. "Get warmed up and I'll make us something hot to drink. Do you want tea or hot chocolate?" He dug in the cabinet and placed two more towels onto a metal rack near the massive glass-doored shower before turning a dial on the wall. Audrey peered around him and noticed there was more than one showerhead in there.

She'd never seen a shower that fancy before.

It made her feel weird.

"I-I'm going to get makeup all over your towels."

"I don't care. It's fine." He gave her an odd look before bending to search for something in another cabinet. "Don't worry about it, they're just towels. That's what they're for."

A bubble of anxiety rose into Audrey's throat. Everything in his bathroom was so nice and clean and sparkling white, and here she was, barreling into it all, mascara dripping down her face with her garbage dress falling apart. And Theo just stood there, equally dripping in his expensive, ruined suit because she'd asked him to go out with her tonight.

"What about you? You're s-soaked too. You'll need to sh-shower to warm up, right?"

Theo froze. She couldn't see his face, but the tips of his ears poking through his dark hair turned bright red.

"*Shower?!*" His voice cracked. "I'll, um—d-don't worry about me, sweetheart." He huffed a laugh and straightened to face her, rubbing a hand awkwardly along the back of his neck. "I'll—I've got another, um—an-another bathroom. Two others, actually. One's even down in my studio." His eyes widened and he began to sputter. "Oh shit. *THE STUDIO.* Please don't go down there. Don't go down into the basement at all." He held up his hands, almost defensively. "It's an absolute mess and I don't want you getting hurt or anything. Glass everywhere, and uh . . . well, I have some pretty dangerous equipment, and I—I'll just . . . meet you back in the living room when you're done." He motioned toward the vanity and the shower. "Help yourself. Use whatever—whatever you want." The rest of his face turned red, and he backed slowly out of the bathroom. "T-tea or hot chocolate?" he asked again.

Audrey tilted her head curiously at him. Now he was acting stranger than usual all of a sudden. "Hot chocolate?"

"Great. I will . . . make that. For you." Theo turned and limped away, and Audrey poked her head through the doorway to watch him dart back downstairs before slowly shutting the bathroom door behind her.

Theo's shower was the most heavenly thing she'd ever experienced, like something straight out of a luxury spa, and she took her time warming up under the scalding hot water. Hers at home always took a good five minutes at least to warm up, and the water pressure was never quite strong enough to actually rinse everything out of her hair. Theo's was practically a high-pressure massage in comparison, and Audrey moaned as the jets from multiple shower heads pounded against her back and scalp, easing all the tension out of her shoulders. She closed her eyes and leaned into it before using some of Theo's bath products, all of which were in thick glass bottles labeled in a foreign language.

Not that she'd ever thought he was the kind of guy who just used hand soap as shampoo or something, but this did seem to explain how his hair was so good—at least in part, anyway. Hers felt like silk by the time she turned off the shower and reached for a towel, which was thick and fluffy and warm, heated by the rack Theo had placed it on for her.

A built-in towel warmer? Heated ceramic tile? Multiple floors? No discernible roommates?!

What was this?

How rich *was* Theo, exactly?

Audrey paused at the thought, teetering on the verge of panic. She was beginning to feel completely out of her depth when she reached for the pile of clothes Theo had brought her to choose from. And then she smiled.

Just beneath the faded, worn Columbia Lacrosse T-shirt and massive pair of matching navy sweatpants was a familiar black hoodie, soft and fleecy and perfectly broken in. She held it to her nose and inhaled deeply, letting Theo's warm, woodsy scent wash over her. It did make her feel better.

He'd already shown her who he was. He'd visited her apartment, knew where she worked, saw where she studied. Theo didn't seem to care in the slightest that she didn't have much to her name.

Why should she care that he *did*?

By the time she padded back downstairs, clad in Theo's massive clothes with his hoodie hanging down almost to her knees like a dress and his sweatpants rolled at least four times at the waist, he was standing in the kitchen, stirring chocolate milk on the stove with a slight furrow to his brow. His dark hair was freshly re-wetted and curling around his jaw, and gray sweatpants printed with "Columbia" along the leg were slung low on his waist. A black long-sleeved T-shirt stretched precariously tight across his broad chest, revealing far more defined muscle than he'd let her see before, and Billie Holiday crooned from a record spinning in a retro player in the living area. Rain still pelted the floor-to-ceiling windows, smattering hard against the glass while thunder rumbled in the distance, lightning occasionally flashing across the cityscape.

It didn't look like the storm was letting up anytime soon.

Audrey shuffled into the kitchen in Theo's thick socks and put her arms around his waist, burying her face in his side.

"Warmed up now?" he asked, his voice rumbling deep as he slid an arm around her and pulled her closer. She nodded and felt him chuckle. "Better?" She nodded again. She did feel a lot better. "Good." He pressed a kiss to the top of her head before taking the pot off the stove and pouring it into two waiting mugs with his left hand. He topped them off with some whipped cream and picked one up, but stilled and stared at the remaining mug with his right hand outstretched.

It hovered there, trembling, and he screwed up his face in concentration when he tried to grasp the ceramic cup between his fingertips, clearly trying to will his hand to stop shaking. "Come on," he whispered to himself, his voice so low she almost didn't hear him. "*Come on.*"

But his fingers couldn't hold the mug steady, and when he tried to lift it away from the counter, the hot chocolate nearly spilled over the sides from his tremor. He set it down quickly and tried again with the handle. But when the same thing happened a second time, he put both mugs down and glanced at her, despair clouding his expression.

His shoulders slumped, and Theo stepped back sharply from the counter, covering his eyes with both hands. His chest heaved.

It looked like he was trying not to cry.

"Hey." Audrey stepped over and pulled his hands down. As soon as he caught her eye, he closed his and faced away from her.

"I can't even hold a fucking *mug* right now without spilling everywhere and making a mess. I'm a disaster."

"Theo. Look at me." She slid her hands up along the sides of his neck to cradle his cheeks. They were smooth, like he'd just shaved, and he wasn't wearing the silicone scar tape. He'd scrubbed the paint away from his scar, and it was redder than it had been before.

Everything about him right now was stripped bare and rendered raw.

He shook his head.

"I hate myself. I hate that I'm like this—that I'm so broken."

"Don't say that, Theo. I like you the way you are."

She held his hand, but he didn't seem to notice or hear her.

He was still lost within himself.

"How am I ever going to do my art again? Or take care of you? Or . . . o-or—"

"Well, the answer's obvious."

His eyes shot open, and he frowned at her. "It is?"

She smiled softly and picked up both mugs in her own hands. "I'll be the one to hold things steady until you can." She offered one to Theo and waited.

He stared at the outstretched mug. After what seemed like an eternity, he lifted his left hand and plucked it away from her. "Thank you, sweetheart," he whispered. He sniffed and wiped at his right eye. "How are you real?" he asked, searching her face. "Where did you come from?"

"Tampa."

She'd deadpanned her answer, and after a second, he barked a surprised laugh before grabbing her free hand with his.

"Of course. *Tampa*."

He limped with her over to the couch, and once he sat, Audrey curled up next to him and tucked herself under his arm. When Theo punched a button on a remote, a fire blazed to life in the grate beneath the TV, and they listened to the music mixed with the sounds of the rain pattering against the windows while quietly sipping their hot chocolate together. Between the warmth of the drink in her stomach and the heat Theo radiated around her, Audrey began to melt into his chest.

"You've been quieter than usual since we left campus and came here," he murmured softly, combing through her drying waves. "Is something the matter? Is it me? Did I do something?"

He was right in that she'd gone a bit quiet, but he certainly wasn't the reason.

Not exactly.

She shook her head and kept staring at her mug. Theo placed two fingers under her chin and gently tilted her head to make her look at him. "Audrey?" His eyes were warm and soft in the light of the fire, and his brows knit together in concern while he studied her face. "What's wrong?"

She looked away from him and back at the neon sign on the wall.

"That's really cool. Is it from your dad's shop?"

"Yes, it was." Theo chewed on his bottom lip, but he didn't press her.

"How old is it? Is it vintage?" It had the look of an antique neon sign, very much a piece of classic Americana, and she wondered how long the auto shop had been in his family.

"No, actually. It's only about ten years old, maybe?" He pointed at the car. "That one was my dad's favorite—a 1965 Ford Thunderbird. He loved it so much that he wanted it immortalized on his shop's sign."

"Does he have a new sign there now if you have this one?"

Theo shook his head slowly. Something came over his eyes—something deeply sad. "No. The shop is sold now. This was the only thing I wanted to keep from it."

"What happened? Did he retire?"

"No."

He grew very quiet.

A creeping feeling prickled along the back of her neck. She was close to landing on something raw, but she hadn't been able to stop herself from asking the question in time.

"My dad died. About six months ago." His eyes darted over to the console set beneath the sign and Audrey's followed. Now that she was looking at it properly, a black-and-white photo of a very handsome man sat framed beneath the neon sign, lit up by the yellow, turquoise, and red-orange glow. He had the same crooked, roguish smile as his son, the same distinctive nose, and the same crinkles around his eyes as he smiled at the camera. He looked young, about Theo's age now, and he held a grinning toddler on his hip, whose large ears poked through a familiar mop of dark hair.

Her heart dropped.

"Oh. Oh, Theo, I'm so sorry. I didn't mean to—"

"No, it's all right. I just miss him a lot, is all. I always thought I'd have more time with him."

It was Audrey's turn to grow quiet. She could practically feel the grief still lingering heavy and deep in Theo's chest, and he didn't say anything else. Instead, he only tightened his arm around her shoulders and drained his remaining hot chocolate before closing his eyes and resting his head on top of hers.

They sat in the weighted quiet, simply listening to the rain and the music together until Theo finally broke their silence. He leaned forward and set his mug down on the coffee table before running his hand through her still-damp hair. "It's getting kind of late, and I checked the weather earlier. It doesn't look like the storm's going to let up until tomorrow." He paused and breathed in and out a few times, clearly trying to steel himself for something. "Would you . . ." He drew in another deep breath. "Would you stay here tonight with me? Please?"

Audrey's own breath suddenly caught in her throat.

When she didn't say anything, panic flashed across Theo's face. "I mean, I can take you home if you're not comfortable, I don't mind. It's just that—well, it's cold outside, and the rain's really coming down. I'll call us a cab and go with you to make sure you get there safely, but I'd feel better if you . . . stayed. With me."

She swallowed and wrapped her fingers around her mug to contemplate the remaining lukewarm chocolate, searching for how to answer him. This wasn't how she'd been expecting tonight to go.

"Oh shit," Theo breathed, covering his face with his massive palm again. "I've made a mistake, haven't I? I've fucked something up. I've made you uncomfortable. I'm so sorry."

"No, Theo. No." Audrey shook her head quickly and shifted to face him fully. "No, you didn't."

"I know I did. What was it?"

"Nothing. It really wasn't anything."

"I pushed you on the boyfriend thing, didn't I?"

"No, I wanted you to. I—"

"Then I shouldn't have asked you to stay. Was that it?" He looked at her, frantic and worried. "Or, uh . . . it's my place, isn't it? It's too big? I didn't tell you about it. I didn't warn you, and it's—" He ran a trembling hand through his thick hair. "*Fuck*, look, I know it's a lot, but—I-I mean, I wasn't going to bring you here so soon, I just didn't want you to get cold and sick and it was so much farther to your place, and there weren't any cabs around, and—"

"Your house is amazing!" She put a hand on his shoulder. "It's beautiful and warm, and I really like it! If anything, I'm embarrassed by how small and shitty *my* place is in comparison! I practically live in a dumpster!"

Considering how much of her furniture she'd actually found in or next to one of those, it was fairly true.

"No, don't say that! That's not the reaction I wanted you to have!" He sat up all the way and splayed his hands out, pleading. "I really liked your apartment! It was cozy and comfortable and it looked like you, you shouldn't be at all embarrassed by it. It wasn't shitty!"

It was. It was small and shabby and shitty, just like she was. But he was so earnest, it only made her more flustered, and her cheeks burned. This was so embarrassing.

"What? What is it?!" Theo cried. He was fully distraught now.

"It's—um. Well, it's—"

"If it's not my place, and it's not me, then what is it?"

"I haven't done this before!" Audrey screwed her eyes shut and gripped her mug so hard she thought she might crack the thick porcelain.

Theo shut his wide mouth quickly.

It felt like an eternity before either of them spoke again.

"You haven't done . . . what before, exactly?"

She took a deep breath and opened her eyes.

Theo was staring at her blankly, still obviously at a loss. "Sit on a couch in front of the fire? Is that it?" He chewed on his bottom lip. "Well, I guess you probably don't have fireplaces in Tampa," he muttered. "I wouldn't know, though. I've never been to Florida."

"No, Theo." Audrey shook her head. "I've never worn a boyfriend's clothes while sitting on his couch, alone with him in his home." Her face burned even hotter than before. "I've never . . . *stayed over.* With a man. Anywhere. I—" It was really hard to admit this out loud. "I've reached the extent of my experience, and I was afraid you'd start to figure that out soon. I don't know what happens next if I . . . stay here. With you."

"Oh?" His eyes widened and he finally seemed to understand. That only made her even more embarrassed. "*Oh.* Uh . . . Audrey, did you think I was angling for sex or something?" He tilted his head at her and raised both of his eyebrows. "Because for the record, I wasn't."

It was her turn to frown. "But this is our third date."

"No, it's not—we've had way more than that. Right?" He ran a confused hand through his hair. "How are we counting? *Are* we counting? I mean, I've been coming to see you a lot at the coffee shop, so I was thinking those were dates too, and—"

"They were, but this is the third time we've hung out outside of it." Her frown deepened. "There's *expectations.*"

"Wait, what?" He frowned right back. "Why? Did you think *I* had 'expectations'?"

"No, but that's just—that's just the rule, right? Sex on the third date. That's what everyone says."

It was definitely what Violet said.

"It is?" He snorted. "Well, that's stupid. And who's 'everyone,' anyway? Who made those rules?"

He had her there. "I honestly have no idea."

"And that's why you've mostly been so stiff and quiet since we got here?" She nodded. "Has this happened with someone before?" She nodded again and his gaze darkened. "Who?"

Audrey couldn't look him in the eyes anymore—not for this. Her face was so hot, she was sure she would combust, and she stared down at the mug in her hands, running a finger nervously along the rim. "The last guy I went out with, almost two years ago. His name was Patrick. We went out a few times, and afterwards, when we were in his car, he—well, the subject of sex came up, and I told him I hadn't had it yet. I didn't feel ready, and I asked him to . . . slow down." Hot shame rose up into her hairline. "I really liked him. I thought he liked me back, I thought everything was fine, I thought he was okay with what I'd said, but instead, he . . . he just dumped me then and there. Didn't say another word. He took me home, waited for me to get out of the car, and never texted again."

She'd never felt so worthless as she did in that moment.

Even now, she felt just as sick as she did then.

Theo stared silently at her, his mouth slightly open. He barely blinked for what felt like entirely too long, until Billie started to sing another song in the background. He glanced over his shoulder at the record player before seeming to make up his mind about something.

When he stood up from the couch and offered her a hand, it was Audrey's turn to blink up at him in confusion.

"Come here," he said, motioning her forward before taking her mug from her grasp and placing it next to his on the coffee table.

"What—"

"Just come here."

She slid her hand into his, and he gently tugged her to his feet and into his arms. He took her left hand in his right and placed her other hand on his shoulder before wrapping his arm around her waist.

And then he began to sway.

Stiffly, at first. Halting, and certainly unsure. She wondered if his hip bothered him while he moved. It felt like it might.

But regardless of all that, it was definitely something resembling dancing.

"Are you *dancing* with me, Theodore Sullivan? Really?" He'd so staunchly refused to do this with her earlier, and *now* he'd decided to dance? After what she'd just told him? She scoffed. "Isn't this kind of . . . cheesy?"

"Hush, you," he whispered. "And yeah, *it is*. Very. I'm well aware, and don't think I'm not catastrophizing and beating myself up for this choice in my own head right now." His eyes glinted as he looked down at her. They were whiskey and mahogany tonight in the firelight. "But I thought we needed to do something dumb for a second. And if there's one thing I know I look dumb doing, it's dancing." He leaned forward and pressed his cheek to her forehead. "It's why I didn't want to do it in front of everyone at the party. I don't know if you've noticed, but I'm a little self-conscious."

She suppressed a laugh. "I have noticed that, yes."

"And my middle name is Henry, by the way. If you want to know the whole thing."

"Theodore Henry. Got it." She closed her eyes. "Mine's Marie."

"Audrey Marie?" She nodded. "Very pretty. Just like you."

He grew quiet again and swayed with her in time to the music in front of the fire, simply staring at her while they moved together. He was right: it did defuse the awkwardness between them, and when he exaggerated a piss-poor attempt at a twirl and drew her back into his arms, she couldn't help but laugh.

But there was something else. Something about the song he'd chosen tugged at the recesses of her memory.

"This sounds familiar."

He hummed in agreement, the sound of it rumbling from his chest through hers. "Does it now?"

"Where is this from? Where have I heard this?"

"Listen to the lyrics," he whispered. And then he murmured along with them, his breath tickling across her ear. "*No matter what the future brings, as time goes by. Moonlight and love songs, never out of date—*"

Audrey pulled back to look up at him. "*Casablanca?!*" she gasped. "This is the song from *Casablanca*!"

He grinned crookedly at her and nodded, obviously deeply pleased with himself. "Great cover, isn't it?"

"Billie Holiday's version is gorgeous."

"Yes, it is. She's a legend." He smoothed some of the hair away from her face and looked her in the eyes. "Were you really all that worried about me? About this?"

"I got nervous."

"That's not what I asked."

Audrey sighed and rested her head against his chest. He was so solid, so warm. "No. I wasn't worried about *you*. I was ashamed. I got self-conscious and freaked out."

"You shouldn't have. Do you really think *I* would be one to pressure you to sleep with me?" She shook her head and buried her face in his shirt. "How long did it take for me to even show you my face?"

"Too long."

"Too long," he agreed, nodding along with her. "I only asked you to stay because I didn't want to worry about you. And because I love spending time with you—and I thought it would be nice to wake up with you tomorrow." He drew her closer and rubbed his hand soothingly along her back. "I want more. More time, more of you."

"You want more? Greedy," she teased, finally looking back up at him.

"Very." When Theo smirked at her, a single dimple emerged from the depths of his cheek. "When it comes to you, yes, I'm *exceedingly* greedy. Always. And once I thought about you leaving me tonight, I missed you so much that it hurt—even though you were right here with me still."

The song changed to something a little jazzier, and they stopped swaying. The rain still barreled down outside, though the lightning and the thunder had calmed somewhat. Theo's quiet gaze was soft but intense as he watched her, his fingers plucking idly at the hood of his jacket she wore.

"I'm going to be very honest, though, Audrey: I *would* like to sleep with you. I've already dreamed of it more times than I can count." His eyes warmed, and he rolled his lips together as his fingers migrated upward and tugged gently at the hair on the base of her neck. "I mean it when I say you're the most gorgeous thing I've ever seen." His voice dropped lower. "And I won't deny it: I really like seeing you wearing my clothes. It's sexy."

"Oh?" Audrey raised an eyebrow. "This baggy, shapeless look does it for you?" When she pulled her arms away and shook the sleeves of the hoodie down from where she'd pushed them, her hands disappeared completely, swallowed whole into the fabric. It was the most comfortable thing she'd ever worn, but easily five sizes too large.

Theo nodded enthusiastically, and his mouth split again into that familiar roguish, crooked grin. "Oh yes. You have no idea what it does to me, to see you looking so small in my old college practice gear and favorite hoodie like that." He rested his hands on her hips and his face grew serious again. "But I'm perfectly content to wait as long as you need me to. Even if it's forever. Even if it's never." He cupped a gentle hand along her cheek. "When it comes to you, I'm interested in so much more than just sex," he whispered in her ear. "It might even be my lowest priority right now, especially since I'm not entirely sure I'm all the way up for it tonight, given my hip—as *deeply* as it pains me to admit that it hurts today." He drew back from her with a grimace and a sigh. "But if you stay over tonight, I'll even take the couch if you want. You can have my bed, just as long as I can see your face first thing in the morning when we wake up."

She didn't need to think about it anymore.

She lifted a hand and covered his with it. "No," she said with a firm shake of her head.

"No?" His face fell. "Oh." His disappointment was palpable. "All right. That's—that's fine. I understand. I'll call a cab, and—"

He reached for his phone in his sweatpants pocket, but she grabbed his wrist to stop him. "No, Theo. I meant that you're not sleeping on the couch. I'm staying over with my boyfriend and you're not getting kicked out of your bed." She gave him a wry look. "I haven't seen it yet, but I'd guess it's plenty big for the both of us—and probably a lot larger than the twin bunks I have at home. Am I right?"

He stared down at her, his eyes dark and his breathing quick. "You might be."

The last song on the album finished, and though the vinyl continued to spin and crackle on the record player, the house was suddenly plunged into stillness, save for the snapping flames in the fireplace and the rain still pelting the windows. Audrey stood on her tiptoes and slid her arms around Theo's neck.

He was so sweet.

So unlike anyone she'd ever met before.

She'd never known she could ever have something like this.

She'd never known she could have someone like *him*.

"Of all the coffee shops in all the towns in all the world, you walked into mine," she whispered. His lips parted in surprise as he looked at her. The shadows of the fire danced along the curves of his face, alternating between concealing his scar in darkness and revealing it again in the soft, golden light. "You wonder where *I* came from, Theodore Henry Sullivan?" She huffed and shook her head. "I wonder every day what I did to deserve meeting *you*."

When she pressed her lips to his, he didn't hesitate. He only closed his eyes and lowered his hands, placing them on the backs of her thighs to lift her up to the perfect height while he kissed her. Audrey wrapped her legs around his waist and buried a hand in his hair, holding on tight while Theo began to move around the living room. Without missing a beat, he bent down and clicked the remote buttons to turn off the fire and the record player before gathering the empty mugs by their handles in one hand. A quick trip to the kitchen to deposit them into the sink and a few flicks of light switches later, all that was left was the large neon sign from his father's shop glowing in the darkness and reflecting in the glass of the windows overlooking the East River.

He left it on to light the way and hobbled carefully up the stairs, his lips locked firmly with her own.

Ten

AUDREY GENUINELY THOUGHT Theo would simply carry her straight to the bedroom.

But no.

Instead, he plopped her down on the counter back in his huge bathroom with one more kiss before stooping to dig around in the cabinets beneath the sink.

"Theo, what are you—"

He straightened and held out a toothbrush wrapped in plastic from a dentist's office.

"Oral hygiene's really important."

Of course it was.

She took it from him with a shake of her head. "You nerd."

That earned her another crooked grin. "So I've been told—many, many times." He also held up a roll of thick clear tape with blue backing and pointed bitterly at his scar. "And I have to put this shit back on if I ever want this thing to fade all the way. Which I very much do. I fucking hate it."

"Yes, I've gathered."

Given what they'd just discussed, brushing their teeth, doing skincare together, and taking turns in the bathroom felt so oddly domestic, Audrey couldn't decide whether it put her more at ease or only made her feel all the more electric inside her own skin. When

Theo opened the bathroom door again and she tried to hop off the counter to find his bedroom, he grabbed her and set her back up there before reaching for a pair of medical scissors.

"Are you just going to fling me around like this all the time now? Carry me everywhere?"

He leaned down—she still wasn't quite eye to eye with him—and planted a quick kiss on her forehead. "Yep." He dropped the roll of scar tape in her hand. "You're really light. It's fun. Now hold that for a second." And then he glanced at her out of the corner of his eye before crossing his arms and gripping the hem of his shirt.

With a sigh, he steeled himself and yanked it over his head.

She'd been wondering what the extent of his scar was, how far down it ran beneath his shirt. She'd had plenty of time to ponder that, given how broken he'd seemed for a while now.

But she hadn't expected it to be this bad.

The scar ran deep, carved down his neck and through his chest like a river cutting through a canyon. It crossed his collarbone and tore into his right pec, jagged and vibrating, slicing even further down into his ribs and all the way across his arm, deep into the meat of his biceps, and again across his forearm. It was as if someone had tried to cleave him in two with a piece of torn scrap metal, so ragged and violent was the damage across his body.

It also wasn't the only scar he had.

Additional scars, smaller and lighter and altogether shallower, crisscrossed his chest and his shoulders and arms, especially the right. But two more stood out on the left side of his body, both circular and puckered and deep red: one on his left shoulder and the other on the lower left side of his abdomen.

Theo watched her face while she took it all in, silent and anxious, his extraordinary dark hazel eyes wide with apprehension in the bright lights of his bathroom. Audrey pulled him closer, directing him to stand between her legs while she trailed her fingers along the length of his wound. It had healed well, as far as she could tell, though it didn't make the way it tore across the broad, pale expanse of his chest any less devastating.

But the rest of him was beautiful. Just like his face and neck, his chest was dotted with a smattering of dark moles and freckles, each one of them unique and precious. Somehow, with his shirt off, he was even wider than she'd thought him before, and as she ran her hand gently along the scar, his hard, thick muscles twitched beneath her touch. Even if he hadn't played since college, he was still in fantastic shape, still built like she imagined a lacrosse player might be—all dense, solid strength and explosive power, if the way he held her like she weighed nothing was any indication. A little trail of soft, dark hair disappeared beneath the waistband of his sweatpants, and she jerked her gaze back up, face aflame at the sight of it.

"It's bad, right?" Theo's throat bobbed, and he rolled his lips nervously as he swallowed.

"Frankly, I'm surprised you're alive," Audrey muttered, lifting her fingers again in wonder to the deepest parts of the scar on his face and his chest.

"Me too," he murmured. "It's a miracle I lived. I have titanium screws and a plate in my cheek holding my face together. The bone there was shattered, and my hip was even worse. I was in a coma for a few days. I should've died."

"I'm really glad you didn't."

He opened his mouth, shut it, and then swallowed thickly again with a nod. "Me too," he finally ventured.

She turned her attention back to the tape. "All right," she said, rubbing her hands together matter-of-factly. "So do we just stick this on?"

She helped him cover the length of the scar in sections, cutting and placing the clear strips carefully onto his skin. She'd had no idea his wound was that extensive, and she could only imagine how hard it had been for him to show her.

It meant a lot that he had.

When they were through, she tried to hop off the counter again, but he blocked her with his left arm once more before she could.

"I can walk, you know!" she squeaked.

He shook his head and tossed his shirt over his shoulder with his other hand. "Not tonight, you don't." He pulled her into his chest and picked her up. "You have to be right here, against my heart, the whole time. That's the price you pay for choosing to stay."

"So it's like a bridge-troll-toll thing?"

"I was thinking more of a monkey's-paw situation. Unintended consequences versus actual tax."

Audrey threw her arms around his neck and surrendered while he carried her into his room, dipping only to switch on the lamp by the side of his bed before setting her gently down on it. Turned out the entire third floor was the master suite.

And she was right.

His bed was predictably huge.

Wonder of wonders, Theo was, of course, the type of man who had an actual bed frame—thick, sturdy wood in a modern style, low profile and stained a cool walnut. It was a king size, draped in a plush white duvet covered in a multitude of luxurious pillows accented with simple charcoal throws piled at the head, all neatly arranged without a wrinkle in sight. More industrial pipe shelving was mounted to the historic brick walls of the house next to a matching dresser across from the bed, dotted with a smattering of books and photos and fabric storage boxes. A few tasteful paintings hung on the walls in a combination of abstract and modern art styles, all of them in vibrant shades of red. There was no TV in sight, and the windows were uncovered and overlooked the river, just like the ones in the living room.

"Do you wake up at dawn with the sunlight streaming in?" she asked, drawing her legs beneath her on top of the thick covers.

Theo chuckled and shook his head. "No. Just watch." He scooped up a remote from the nightstand closest to the door and punched a button. Machinery whirred and dark blackout shades descended from a thin slot she hadn't noticed in the ceiling.

"My god," she gasped. She turned to face him. "Seriously: How much money do you have? I know it's rude to ask, but this is insane." Then she narrowed her eyes accusingly at him. "Or did you just rent some fancy Airbnb for a night to impress me? Is this all some elaborate ruse? You planned this, didn't you?"

He laughed harder and pulled the covers back, fluffing the pillows and tossing her a few as he went. "No, sweetheart, I promise. Not an elaborate con. But I will tell you a secret if you'll tell me another of yours."

"You want more than my deepest, darkest, I'm-still-a-virgin confession? Violet's the only other person who knows."

"I showed you my scars. My family, doctors, and Diego are the only other people who've seen those."

All right, that was a fair point.

"Speaking of Violet," Theo said, opening a drawer and digging around in it before passing her an extra phone charger. "Do you need to text her?"

"Oh shit, yes, thank you. She'd be one to worry. And she's going to be way too excited about this outcome."

"That makes two of us."

"Yeah, well, Vi will be leaping straight to conclusions all over the place." She pulled her phone out from her pocket and shot off a quick text before turning it off entirely to avoid the inevitable explosive aftermath and plugging the charger into the built-in USB port on the nightstand next to her side.

She looked back up as he was getting ready to slide into bed.

"Wait, Theo—do you honestly expect me to believe you sleep in sweatpants?" She pointed at them. "No one actually sleeps in these things, right? And you're like a walking furnace."

He paused, hand gripping the covers frozen in midair, and gave her a pointed look. "Are *you* going to? Sleep in that getup, I mean. Because—"

He blanched when Audrey reached up and fully unzipped his hoodie before ripping off his ginormous pants and tossing them both onto the edge of the bed, leaving her just in her panties and his circus tent of a gloriously soft T-shirt. The cool air prickled against her bare legs.

"Happy now?" She jutted her chin out defiantly. "You know what? I've already confessed, and I trust you. I'm not going to dance around things anymore." She threw herself under the covers—which, of course, were so soft and silky they probably cost a fortune and had some ridiculously high thread count—and waited, watching him intently to see what his next move was.

Theo rolled his jaw pensively and considered her for a moment. Red crept up the sides of his neck and to the tips of his ears, but he hooked both thumbs under the waistband of his sweatpants and tugged them down sharply, stepping out of them and lifting them up for display before dropping them defiantly to the ground.

Oh.

Audrey's mouth went dry.

Theo was . . .

He was practically naked, and his black boxer briefs did nothing to minimize the massive bulge between his thick, muscular legs. She didn't know much about these sorts of things, but she did know he was big in more ways than one. Her heart raced while she thought about what that thin fabric was concealing, and what Theo had demanded of her right before dropping her onto the bed. But she must have been staring, because he cleared his throat and ran a hand through his thick hair, sending it swirling around his jawline like liquid silk.

"Happy now?" he asked with a shrug, a single dark eyebrow raised.

"Uh . . ." She swallowed and simply chose to nod. "Yes?" Did her voice sound a bit too high? Maybe it sounded too high.

Theo snorted. "All right then." He flicked his hand at her while he pulled back the covers again. "Scoot over. I can't sleep on my right side anymore, I wake up hurting if I do."

Audrey made room on the bed and he finally slid under the sheets, turning out the light as he did. They were plunged into complete darkness, and she gasped and squeezed her eyes shut, curling in on herself when it suddenly swept over her like a death shroud.

That happened faster than she thought it would. She'd be fine, it'd be fine, she just had to—

Theo's warm arms wrapped around her and pulled her close to his chest. "Come here," he whispered. "Cuddling is half the fun of a sleepover. At least, *I* think so, anyway."

But it was too late. The fear had already overwhelmed her. "Theo?" Her voice sounded thin and shaky in the dark, even to her own ears. "You wanted another secret?"

"Yeah, I did. What is it?"

Her eyes hadn't adjusted to the deep blackness of the room, and she couldn't even make out his outline. She turned over and tried to trace it in front of her by running a trembling hand along where she thought his face might be, desperately shoving the panic down.

It wasn't working.

"I'm still afraid of the dark."

"*Oh shit!* I'm sorry." He pulled away from her and the light popped back on. She blinked rapidly and tried to still her racing heart. Theo was facing her again in an instant, his eyes wide and his expression worried. He tucked her under his chin, making soft shushing noises while she trembled. "I'm so sorry, Audrey. I didn't know."

"Yeah, well, I didn't tell you," she finally managed to whisper between deep, calming breaths. "I just didn't think you'd turn the light out that quickly. Didn't even have time to prepare myself to fake composure." A laugh bubbled up in her chest and mixed with a sob. "Boy, you're getting to learn all the most embarrassing things about me all at once, aren't you? First that I'm a huge failure in relationships, and now that I'm a baby who can't even handle the lights being out. God, are you sure you're still interested? I'm actually kind of a mess."

Theo smirked at her with only the slightest wicked gleam in his eyes. "Honestly? I'm glad it's not just me for once." He pressed a kiss to the top of her head. "And besides, do you think I'm not one giant, lumbering ball of anxiety? Have you met me?"

"That's true."

"You weren't supposed to agree so quickly."

She burrowed into his chest while she laughed, and his own chuckle rumbled while he gently stroked her hair. "So what do you do at home?" he asked. "Tell me how I can make you comfortable here."

Audrey glanced up at him from beneath the curtain of her hair. Not a single ounce of judgment was reflected in his gaze while he watched her and waited.

"I have dimmable fairy lights strung through my bed frame. Battery operated, and we put blackout privacy curtains around each of our spaces so the light doesn't leak out and bother Violet." She paused and felt her cheeks burn for what seemed like the thousandth time tonight. "And I also have Petey."

"Petey?" Theo tilted his head curiously.

"Oh no, this is so embarrassing." Audrey hid her face in her hands. "He's my stuffed puffin," she mumbled. "They're my favorite animal. Have you ever seen one?"

"Yeah, on Animal Planet and in pictures, probably. Maybe not in person."

"Well, I love them. They're quirky, happy-looking birds, with striped beaks and vibrant mouths. I like how scrappy they are, and their beaks have my favorite colors—shades of yellow and red and orange, all bright like sunshine."

She peeked at him through the spaces between her fingers. "When I was around four or five, my foster parents at the time took me and their other kids to the zoo. I'd only just been taken from my mom, and I was having a lot of trouble adjusting to . . . well, everything, really. I don't remember much from that time other than crying a lot and having constant nightmares—of all kinds of terrifying things, twisting and lurking and growling in the dark of my room when I was alone. I'd wake up screaming, and trying to go back to sleep was useless. I still don't usually sleep that well, or that deeply."

She sighed. "I don't remember much else, though, including my mom. I can't see her face in my mind's eye anymore. I know I saw it, I know I knew her, but it was so long ago, I wouldn't even recognize her if you were to show me a picture. I only know a handful of details about her situation from having read my file.

"But the one big thing I do remember is when my first foster parents took us to that zoo. They had some Atlantic puffins there in an enclosure with a pool behind glass. I loved them, how cute they were, hopping around on the rocks—and how elegant and sleek they looked when they swam in the water, like they were made for that. Even though they could technically fly in the air, they didn't need to because they could in the water. They were free there.

"When we got to the gift shop, I begged for a stuffed puffin to take home with me, and my foster dad bought me one. I was only in that house for a few months before I had to go to another, but Petey went with me everywhere, to every new foster home, every new school, all of it. And he's still there. Maybe the only constant I've ever had."

"What happened to your mom? Do you know?"

Audrey bit her lip. "She died, maybe around when I was six or seven. Opioid overdose. She was a drug addict, and someone called CPS on her to come take me away when I was about four. According to my file, I was starving—too skinny, the neighbor said. My mom was so strung out, she wasn't feeding me properly."

It hurt telling him this. It was one of her wounds that was always the most raw, always perpetually tender, at least a little, even when she didn't necessarily feel it there. She didn't poke it as often these days, but whenever she did, it ripped right open again, hurting just as deeply and bleeding just as much as it had the first time.

Theo didn't say anything.

He only listened.

"She didn't fight them when they took me. That's always hurt the most, that she didn't try to keep me, that she didn't ever try to get clean so she could get me back. She just . . . let me go, signed me over to the state like I was nothing. Like I was no one to her." Audrey closed her eyes and shook her head. "I've been to therapy. I know that's what drug addicts do: nothing matters as much to them as their next fix. I could never compare, no matter how much I might have loved her. But I still think some part of her must have cared about me—or at least I really want to think so."

"Why do you think that?"

"Because while she might not have fought for me, while she might not have wanted to take care of me—or couldn't—my mom still cried really hard when they took me away," she whispered. "At least, that's what I was told. I talked to the social worker who was there when I tried to find her after I turned eighteen, and that's what she said."

"What about your dad?"

"No idea who he is. There's no record of him, no name on my birth certificate. Maybe he didn't want me either."

Audrey had never said that out loud before.

A knife twisted in her heart.

Theo stayed quiet. He only gazed at her, his eyes deeply sad, until he sat up sharply and ran a single hand over his face with a sniff. He pushed himself off the bed and limped over to his shelves, opening one of the fabric storage boxes and digging around in it for a moment before replacing the top. He limped back over to the bed with something held behind his back and grabbed the remote for the shades, holding down a button briefly before releasing it. The blackout shades lifted and revealed some of the lights of Manhattan in the distance, twinkling like stars in the night sky, and only partially obscured by the lingering storm clouds.

He slid back into bed and revealed what it was he'd retrieved: a woolly stuffed teddy bear, well loved, but still in good shape. One of his eyes was mismatched, lost long ago but lovingly repaired with a black button sewn expertly into place.

"This is Roo—short for Roosevelt." He smiled sadly. "My dad gave him to me when I was little to help keep the monsters in the dark away." He laid down and held it out to her. "I'll keep them away from you now, but you can borrow him if you want."

Roo and Theo suddenly blurred in front of her, and Audrey sniffed as she took the bear and held him to her heart. She couldn't stop the tears anymore, and her chest was wracked with horrible, gut-wrenching sobs as Theo turned out the light again and gathered her in his arms. He kissed her gently through her tears, holding her tightly to his chest and stroking her hair with trembling hands while she cried in his beautiful bedroom.

"I want you, Audrey," he whispered softly. "I want to keep you. I'd never let you go. I promise."

Eventually, she quieted, soothed by Theo's warmth and the gentle lights of the city she'd decided to call home. But even though she'd lived there for six years, it had never quite felt like it all the way; she'd always been a foreigner in New York, a transplant. It was just the latest in a long string of temporary places she gave the moniker to briefly before it was ripped away from her again by the ever-changing currents of life.

But here in Theo's arms, maybe her definition of home had begun to change. Just the slightest shift, bit by bit, now that she'd revealed herself, and he had too.

Maybe home had never been a place, like she always thought it was.

Maybe it was a person.

The strength of her feelings about that truth could have scared her. Should have, perhaps.

Instead, the heat Theo radiated from holding her so closely, so quietly while she cried only warmed her all the more.

It lit something inside of her.

A tiny flame of hope for something more.

Something new.

And something just as beautiful as the man resting quietly beside her.

Eleven

WARM.

Audrey was so warm, and so comfortable.

The source of the heat shifted around her, and that movement was enough to help her swim out of her heavy early morning drowsiness. She opened her eyes to a strange room, and then she remembered:

This was *Theo's* room.

She'd stayed over last night.

It wasn't a dream.

In the gray light streaming through the gap he'd left in his blackout shades, she glanced over her shoulder and found him still asleep. His face was slack, his mouth slightly open while he breathed softly, his hair perfectly tousled around his head like a halo of shadow. A single stray strand fell across his forehead, a streak of darkness cutting across speckled moonlit snow, and she marveled again at how much of his face she could see now. At how much of himself he'd bared to her.

Audrey wriggled closer to his warmth, and when her head shifted on the pillow they'd somehow ended up sharing, Theo responded in his sleep by tightening his arms and automatically pulling her against his chest.

And that's when she noticed it.

Not only was his arm actually beneath her shirt, and *had* been, his hand easily sliding from her ribs to cover one of her breasts entirely with one wide palm, but—

He was also hard.

When he'd pulled her closer, she got an exceedingly stiff idea of what exactly his briefs were barely concealing.

She gasped in surprise, and Theo startled at her sharp inhale, slowly blinking awake, his face twitching as his pupils adjusted to the light streaming through the windows. But as soon as he seemed to realize she was still there, his mouth cracked into a lopsided grin.

"Good morning, sweetheart." He smiled so wide, both dimples revealed themselves carved deep into his cheeks. His scar tape shifted on his face to make way for them, and he leaned over her shoulder and pressed his lips softly to hers. "I thought I dreamed you stayed."

"Nope. I'm still here."

He hummed. "Good."

His eyelids drooped again. He was still half asleep and hadn't seemed to notice where his hand was. Instead, he swept it gently over the curves of her breast, trailing his fingertips along her skin. His other hand was busy burying itself in her hair, absently combing through her tangled locks still silky-soft from his fancy shampoo.

Half asleep, but wholly preoccupied.

Audrey waited, half turned in his arms as she studied his face, wondering when he'd realize what he was doing and where exactly he was touching her. She bit her lip at the thought of the inevitable, impending meltdown and simply chose to snuggle closer anyway.

He'd figure it out any minute.

"How long can you stay?" he slurred, his eyes still shut. But he pressed another kiss to her head, soft and gentle and sweet.

Well. This was unexpected.

Sleepy Theo was *adorable*.

Was he not actually a morning person? He was always at the coffee shop so early. Much earlier than he strictly needed to be, since he didn't work an office job on someone else's timetable.

Either way, she could get used to this.

"I have some homework and reading I need to do, but it shouldn't take me too long. I could stay until this afternoon if you want me to."

"Don't ever want you to leave," he mumbled through a yawn as his hand kept up its caress. "Give you a key if you want one."

"You would?"

"Give you anything you want."

She suppressed a snort. "That's a dangerous promise. What if I asked you for a pony?"

"M'kay." Theo nuzzled into her neck and inhaled deeply.

"Just 'm'kay'?" She was tempted to turn over if only so she could run a hand through his hair. God, she'd never get over how *good* it was. But she was too busy enjoying this unguarded moment. "Where would I keep it?"

"Stables." His mouth fell open and his breathing slowed again. Seemed he was struggling to fully wake up. "Can rent a stall. And tack."

"That's some rich people shit if I ever heard it. You sound like you've done horseback riding before."

"Mm-hmm. Polo." He nodded. "Don't tell anyone. Might ruin my artist street cred."

"I Googled you. Thoroughly. You don't have artist street cred."

One eye struggled to open but failed. "I kinda do, actually."

"What, like Lightm4st3r or something?" Audrey snorted. "Surely not."

Theo's eyes flew open at the name.

"*L-Lightm4st3r?!* What about Li–"

He froze.

His fingers had stilled right as his thumb grazed across her nipple, which rapidly pebbled beneath his touch.

He'd finally realized where his hand was.

Theo gasped and yanked it out from beneath her shirt as if her skin had burned him.

And then his eyes went wide when he felt what was pressing into her back.

"OH MY GOD I'M SO SORRY!" he cried, throwing himself away from her and scrambling backward. His hand slipped off the edge of the bed and he lost his balance, legs flailing and tangling in the sheets, and he fell to the floor with a dense *thump*.

The bed shook with the weight of his fall.

"*Theo!*" Audrey cried, scrambling across the mattress after him. She dropped off the side of the bed and crouched, trying to find where his face might have been, but he'd already cocooned into the sheet. "Theo, are you all right?"

When he groaned, "*How long was I fondling you?!*" in response, she was able to locate his head. She tried to rip the sheet away, but he tugged it back over his face. All she could see was one tip of a flaming-red ear.

"You were fine, I didn't mind!" she shouted, tugging again at the sheet.

"I've ruined everything!"

He gripped it even tighter, his chest fluttering rapidly beneath it as he panicked. So she did the only thing she could think of.

She flung her leg over his waist and straddled him before laying down on top of him, resting her whole weight on his chest.

Theo drew in a deep shuddering gasp and stilled. Audrey waited, burrowing her face into the curve of his neck and running a hand along the left side of his ribs and chest where she knew he had fewer scars. "Calm down," she whispered. He still didn't move, and she was able to slip a hand around the sheet to lay it against his ear. His skin was *burning.*

"Audrey," he croaked, his voice strained. "I'm sorry. After what you told me last night, I wasn't trying to make this sexual, I swear. I was trying to be good. I didn't ask if I could do that, and I'm so sorry, I—"

"It's fine." She nuzzled harder into his neck. "I liked it. My *boyfriend* gave me a sleepy little breast exam and I wasn't going to stop him. Consider this me giving you my express consent going forward."

"Oh." Theo finally lowered the sheet from his face. It was beet red and thoroughly abashed. "Well, uh, I didn't want to make any assumptions, and—"

Audrey leaned forward and kissed him slowly and deeply, drawing his bottom lip between her teeth.

She couldn't help herself.

Too cute.

He was too cute.

Theo moaned, the noise he made rumbling deep in the back of his throat and sending molten heat straight to her core before he made a slightly strangled sound. "That's not—you're not helping things," he gasped when she pulled away for air. He screwed his eyes shut and motioned toward his hips.

"Oh. Sorry." It was her turn to blush. "Are you uncomfortable?" He nodded shortly, and she rolled off to the side, lamenting the loss of the warmth beneath her. The heated floor wasn't freezing by any means, but it wasn't Theo, either.

He turned and looked at her, his eyes wide. Even the right one seemed like it was open more than it usually was, though it was his pupils that were blown abnormally large. The swirling whiskey and amber-green tones in his irises were oddly thin, as if he were trying to drink in every little bit of her light through his gaze.

"I'm trying really hard not to do everything I've ever imagined wanting to do to you right now," he murmured, his voice lower than usual. "And you're making it extremely difficult for me, looking like that. Laying on me like that. *Kissing* me like that." He shook his head before snaking an arm under her neck and drawing her close, planting a kiss on her temple. "Here I was, fantasizing and plotting grand things inside my head for your first time someday—if you want it to be with me—and now I'm ready to toss everything straight out the window and take you on the floor right here and right now. Please don't let me."

She huffed a laugh before resting a hand on his cheek. "I do want it to be you, Theo," Audrey whispered, leaning in close. "And you won't have to wait long, either. I promise."

He tucked a strand of hair behind her ear. "You're going to be the death of me, Miss Adams," he muttered before burying his face against her skin. "But first, do you want me to make breakfast?" He'd said it in the spot where her shoulder met her neck, his plush lips brushing gently against her throat, and when his wandering fingers grazed across a sensitive spot on her thigh, Audrey yelped a laugh and tried to squirm away.

"No! Not there!" she squeaked.

But Theo realized what he'd found, and his attention snapped directly to it. He grabbed her and held her closer, tickling her harder while she laughed and thrashed, his expression lighting up with delight at having discovered yet another one of her secrets.

THEY TOOK TURNS freshening up in the bathroom, and when Theo emerged again, back in his long-sleeved black shirt and gray college sweatpants from last night, it was to find Audrey looking at all the things on his shelves in his living room. He had quite a collection of media, but one thing bothered her.

"Where's all your art?" She turned and watched him in the kitchen while he gathered ingredients. Pancakes, eggs, and bacon were on the menu, all of which he'd refused her help with, and he straightened and gave her an odd look as he placed a flat top griddle across his expansive set of gas burners.

"My art? You've seen some of it. It's around." He gestured absently upstairs.

"The red paintings?" He nodded, and Audrey turned back to the shelves, carefully tugging one of the vintage vinyl albums out to examine it—an old Fleetwood Mac one from the seventies. He had virtually no knickknacks, nothing he might have really needed to dust, and none of it was glass. "Those are really cool, but didn't you say glass was your medium? I thought you'd have some of it on display or something. I'd like to see it."

He looked up at her sharply. "I did say that, yes. But if you want to get very technical about it, you could say I'm actually a mixed-media artist. I *primarily* work with glass, but I incorporate . . . other stuff too. And I have a more traditional design business on the side."

"Then where is all of it?" She pushed the record back into its place until it was flush with the others again.

Theo rolled his lips together and began cracking eggs into a bowl, his right hand trembling while his left held the bowl steady. He frowned and held it up to the light for inspection, but deemed it safe from stray pieces of shell before continuing. "I don't keep a lot of it here. It'd get too cluttered, and uh . . . no, I just don't keep most of my stuff here." He shook his head. "Some of it is down in the studio, though."

"Will you show me today?"

He shook his head even more emphatically this time. "*No.* That's not a space for guests. It's awful, and I'd want to make sure everything was . . . everything was safe before you went down there.

I haven't worked in a while, and I've left it a horrible mess from the, uh . . . the last time I tried."

His neck went red again, and he concentrated on whisking the batter together while Audrey continued to poke around on his shelves. He'd put music on again, something slow and contemporary and shoegazey this morning, streamed from his phone to the retro record console, which was apparently modern and doubled as a Bluetooth speaker. There were a bunch of books and records, most of which were vintage, and a truly impressive array of Blu-ray and 4K movies on his shelves.

"Where did you get all these vinyls?"

"They were my dad's collection. He used to make me listen to them while we worked in the shop together, and whenever he put one on, we played a game where I had to guess the year of the album. He called it part of my 'essential musical education.'" Theo shook his head as he added more flour to the batter and stirred it in. "He was insistent about it. Wanted his son to have taste, he said."

She hummed. "Well, sounds like he succeeded."

"I suppose so. At least, I *hope* so."

Audrey turned her attention back to his collection, but on a second glance, one thing stood out. Nestled at the very bottom corner on the shelf all on its own was a jet-black motorcycle helmet, sleek and cool and expensive-looking, like most of the other things in Theo's brownstone. She bent down and picked it up, turning it over in her hands. It was exceedingly heavy, but it didn't look out of the ordinary.

"Do you have a motorcycle?" she asked, and the sounds of whisking from the kitchen abruptly stopped. "Because if you do, that's really hot. Can we ride it sometime? Or do you—"

"No!"

She wasn't sure how he was able to move so fast with such a pronounced limp, but Theo was behind her all of a sudden, his face as white as a sheet. "Uh, I—I do, yeah, but I don't ride it anymore." He held his hands out and waited for her to pass the helmet to him. "I'll just take that, and . . . put it in its place. Which is definitely not on that shelf." When she didn't immediately hand it over, he plucked it gently away from her with both hands and hurried down the hall behind the staircase, waddling into a dark room she hadn't gone in yet before emerging a minute later, breathing heavily and running a hand through his hair. It flopped luxuriously around his ears, and Audrey pursed her lips with a growing frown.

He went back to making pancakes in the kitchen, and she stalked over to him, watching him closely. "I think you owe me a secret. You didn't confess one last night. And I did."

Theo had been spooning batter onto the heated griddle, the bacon and scrambled eggs ready and waiting nearby. "Roo doesn't count?" He gave her a sheepish grin and some of the color returned to his cheeks.

"No. Roo doesn't count."

"All right." He blew out a deep breath and tapped the spatula anxiously on the counter. "So, well . . . I have a trust fund. In case you didn't gather that." The color in his cheeks deepened.

"You're a nepo baby?"

"Oh god, please don't put it like that." Theo covered his face with one massive hand. "My mom's family is loaded and the trust is from my nana—I was her only grandchild—but I've never really liked using their money. My dad came from nothing, so I've generally tried to make my own way, even though I recognize how much privilege I grew up with." He flipped the pancakes and laid out the strips of bacon to start crisping up. "But that's not how I bought this house, though. That's just what I came from, and what I'm sitting on." He grimaced. "And how I started my artistic practice. Getting into this sort of thing is, admittedly, *very* expensive. The startup costs for equipment can be staggering."

"Then how did you get this place? It's incredible."

He sighed deeply again and winced. "Again: don't tell any other artists. I'll be labeled as a sellout, but . . . I sold some art for a truly insane amount of money in my early twenties. Like, a criminal amount."

"Isn't that the dream, though?" Audrey frowned at him. "To not starve, to hit it big?"

The red in his face deepened even further.

"Yes, it is, in some ways. Not in others. But you know how I hate attention. That's not new." He gripped the spatula tightly in his hands, wrenching it so hard she wondered if he might bend it. "I didn't want it to be about me, the artist, I wanted it to be about the *art*. And if people knew who I was, it would be too much about me. So I sold stuff under another name, and then I invested the money. The proceeds are what I used to buy and renovate this place. It was a foreclosure, and I got lucky. Right timing, right-sized pile of cash, just the right amount of disrepair. I finished renovating it almost from the studs out a few years ago."

His eyes were pleading. "Please just tell people I'm a designer if they ask, and don't mention I have a place like this. I know you don't like lying—and are admittedly bad at it"—Audrey glared at him—"but can you just say it's a decent apartment and not what it is? And besides, I *am* a designer. That's not a lie." He grabbed a plate and started piling it high with golden pancakes, shoving it in the oven to keep them warm before dropping more batter onto the griddle.

"You want me to lie about your success and diminish it?" That was the most unbelievable part.

She wanted to brag about her boyfriend, and he'd just told her not to.

"Yeah, actually. That'd be great." She stared at him and Theo rolled his jaw again with a sigh. "Look, Audrey. I'm dead serious. I don't bring just anyone here. Pretty much it's my mom, my uncle, and Diego who know about this place. And now you. I like my privacy."

"Are you that famous?"

"In some circles," he muttered, turning back to the griddle and grabbing tongs to flip the bacon. "Speaking of, you, uh . . . brought up Lightm4st3r earlier. Do you think he's cool or something?" He shot her an apprehensive look over his shoulder. "Do you like his work?"

"To be honest, I don't know all that much about him. It's Violet who's obsessed with him, and she used to show me his stuff on Instagram, but he hasn't posted in a while, has he?" Audrey began poking curiously around in the kitchen, looking for plates and cutlery. If he wasn't going to let her help him cook, she could at least help him set up. "Do you know who he is? That's the big question, right? Page Six is always trying to suss out his identity."

Theo stared at her. "Uh . . . no. No, I don't think anyone actually knows who he is. But we sometimes run in the same crowd. Some of the other artists I know talk about him a lot."

"That's really cool." She found the plates and set some out next to the stove. "Does anyone know how to get in touch with him?" One of the things that drove Violet nuts was how his DMs were closed, but with that big of a following, it wasn't surprising.

Theo bit his lip and shrugged. "Nope. Not a clue."

He grew quiet, but Audrey's mind had already wandered to something Theo had said earlier. "You had a girlfriend at one point, right? Diego mentioned her."

"Oh god." He covered his face with a hand. "Oh *god*. Did he talk about her?"

"Yeah, a little. Did she live here with you when you were together?"

"*No*," he snapped quickly, glancing away from the wry look she gave him with a groan. "No, I broke up with her about five years ago. She never even knew I was trying to buy a place. No other woman has been here since then. I stayed very single after that. It was better that way."

"What happened?" It was almost more shocking that Theo had even had a girlfriend before, given his general demeanor.

"Oh, don't look at me like that!"

The thought must have shown on her face.

"But, *Theo.*" She leveled a serious stare at him. "Were you the way you were with me with—"

"Yes." He held up his hands in surrender. "She was the one who asked me out first." She didn't think his face could burn any hotter than it had earlier in the bedroom, but it did now. "I don't have a good track record of confidence with women, especially at the early stages. The long story short is that we were together for two years. I was planning on proposing and then Diego found out she was cheating on me." He raised his eyebrows and tilted his head at her. "Sometimes it's really handy having an investigative journalist as your best friend, I won't lie. He's both annoying and nosy as hell, but that occasionally works out in my favor."

"He's protective?"

"He's a pain in the ass." Theo flipped the pancakes bitterly and moved the bacon to a stack of paper towels. "But he saved me a whole lot more heartache and suffering than if I'd have gone through with an engagement, and I'm thankful for that."

"What was she like?" Maybe Audrey shouldn't be prying about Theo's ex like this, but now that they'd come this far, she wanted to know.

He paused, the tongs suspended in midair. They trembled in his hand, and his face grew dark. But it softened again when he met her eyes.

"She wasn't like you at all," he finally muttered, clicking the tongs bitterly as he fussed with the bacon. "She was a mistake, was what she was. She's a curator now at a large gallery. The art world's incestuous, and I never should have gotten involved with her in the first place. In the end, breaking up was an enormous relief."

Audrey didn't press him further.

Theo poured eggs onto the bacon grease and cooked them quickly before turning off the griddle and opening up a miniature sliding door built into his cabinets. It was an appliance garage, and when Audrey saw what was inside, she gasped.

"OH MY GOD, THEO. You have one of these and you come into the café every day? *Why?!*"

It was a jet-black Diletta Bello espresso machine and a matching grinder, a premium at-home version of what she had at the coffeehouse.

It had to cost somewhere in the vicinity of two thousand dollars.

He held up a hand and smirked, a single dimple appearing in his cheek. "Okay, look: call this one a failed pandemic investment. When everyone was in quarantine, I was going to learn how to make café drinks at home, but the machine was kind of hard to use and I only ended up making a few shots of bad espresso with it. But by that point, it was too expensive to get rid of. Sunk cost fallacy." Then he chuckled. "Until I sat down and really learned how to use it—and added a single coffee drink to my repertoire."

"Can I play with it? Please?'

"No."

She put her hands on her hips indignantly. "You didn't let me touch anything with breakfast, you have to at least let me play with—"

Theo turned and grabbed Audrey once again, lifting her at the waist and setting her gently down on the counter across from him with a shake of his head. "Not yet. Don't ruin my surprise. I've been practicing, just in case I ever got this opportunity." He leaned in and kissed her before turning to the fridge to take out a jug of milk. "Hush. Just wait."

And then she watched him work.

He went through the motions she knew so well, she could do them in her sleep, and his brow furrowed in deep concentration while he watched the espresso drip, pulling it at a precisely timed moment before steaming the milk. Theo seemed to hold his breath while he assembled everything, and though he sighed and grimaced when his hand shook and ruined the design he tried so very hard to patiently sketch in the foam, he still held the black ceramic mug out to her proudly in both hands with a soft smile.

It was a flat white.

Not only that, but when Audrey took a sip, she closed her eyes and hummed in pleasure.

He'd pulled a perfect ristretto.

He'd learned how to make her favorite coffee, just for her. No one ever made her coffee. No one besides Josh.

And now Theo.

She opened her eyes and licked the foam from her lips.

"Well?" His expression was anxious. "How did I do?"

"Perfect. It's perfect." She set the mug down carefully on the counter and dragged him all the way over to her, opening her legs wide so he could nestle himself between them and get closer. Theo rested his hands on her hips.

"This is everything I've ever wanted in a Sunday and never had," he whispered. "I think I could do this with you every weekend and never get sick of it."

"Me too, Theo," Audrey whispered back, running her hands up along his neck and burying her fingers in the hair at the base. "Me too."

When he bent to kiss her, her heart skipped a beat. It stuttered in her chest, a deliciously painful flutter of feeling chased by a deep, mournful ache. She didn't want to name whatever this was—not yet. It was far too fragile, far too new to stand on its own. But every glance, every kiss, every moment between them only strengthened it, made it sturdier, built the foundation of it to last.

But for now, she couldn't even breathe it. It was too soft, too delicate, too precious and fleeting. They were both scared of it, *for* it, she could tell. She could tell by the way Theo's breath trembled when he pulled away, how a hint of fear still lurked around the edges of his eyes. But with any luck, and with time, they'd move past the doubt.

The second time Theo's lips met hers, their breakfast forgotten, she tasted coffee on his tongue.

THE REST OF that Sunday was just as perfect as it had started.

Theo was an incredible cook, and he let Audrey play with his fancy espresso machine while he plated up their breakfast. She made him a latte today rather than his usual, just so she could draw him hearts in the foam—which he loved and fawned over far more than she felt was necessary.

But she let herself bask in the warmth of his praise anyway.

After breakfast, they cozied up on the couch again, avoiding going outside in the intense gray fog blanketing Brooklyn after last night's storm, and Theo asked what her favorite movie was.

Audrey bit her lip.

"It's . . . really cliché."

"No such thing."

"Oh, it definitely is." She sighed. "But it's *Anastasia*."

He blinked at her, a curious furrow between his eyes. "The Don Bluth animated movie?"

Audrey nodded and hid her face in the long sleeves of Theo's black hoodie. "Have you seen it?" she mumbled. His chest rumbled as he hummed, and she looked back up to see him shake his head. But he'd already pulled out his phone and was scrolling with interest. Whatever he read gradually softened the frown he wore.

"Oh. I see." Theo tugged her all the way into his arms and onto his chest while he settled down across the long length of his couch. It was big enough for him to actually be able to lay completely flat. "An orphan girl turns out to be a princess?" he murmured, combing his fingers gently through her hair.

"Never happened in real life, by the way. They never found her alive, and they're fairly certain she died with her family, all of them shot and dumped in a communal grave. But I like to think that maybe this was the better version. That maybe it *could* happen."

"Maybe it could." Theo lifted the remote, pressed a few buttons, and fired up the movie.

Leaving was the hardest part. Audrey had hung up her dress in Theo's bathroom last night to dry, but it and her tights were ruined. And besides that, she didn't want to go. She didn't want to leave him.

But Theo insisted she get home and finish her homework. He even swore he wouldn't text her tonight so she could focus—and he gave her a very stern look when she protested and threatened to message him herself anyway. In the end, he won, and he walked her back to her place, dress slung over his arm, mask settled back over his face, and umbrella clutched tightly in one hand.

He didn't stick around to submit to Violet's intense questioning—Audrey still hadn't wanted to turn her phone back on, and when she did, she had 127 unread messages, most of them from her roommate—but he did stay long enough to lower his mask at the top of the stairs, his gaze heavy while he studied her face.

"I need you to know something, Audrey."

"What is it?"

"You make me want to create again. I haven't made anything in a long time. I haven't been in the right place to do that, not like I've needed to be." He glanced nervously over at the door as if he were terrified Violet might open it at any moment before meeting her eyes again. "But I want to show you what you make me feel like when you're around. How it feels deep in my soul to know you now." Theo closed his eyes and pressed his forehead to hers. "I'm going to try."

She didn't know what to say. But she put everything it made her feel into the kiss she gave him before he left her apartment.

Every day that week, he came to the café and they had coffee together (or, at least, Audrey had coffee while he watched and they talked), and he waited for her to finish her shifts before walking her either to the subway or home. On Thursday night, he came over and brought dinner with him again: roasted chicken with Yukon gold mashed potatoes and sautéed green beans, freshly baked sourdough rolls with fancy salted butter, and a chocolate mocha cake for dessert. And once again, he refused to tell her where he'd gotten it.

She missed him that weekend. Her midterms were next week, and she had exams and papers due, so Theo wouldn't hear of him distracting her. It was a firm no when she asked him to hang out after she'd responded truthfully to his question about how much more work she had to do.

Audrey got it done. She wrote her paper and turned it in on time. She even managed to study properly for her exams.

But it was certainly a miserable affair being away from Theo.

Every moment she spent away from him only made her ache all the more.

When she saw him on Monday, her heart nearly burst from excitement, and she only regretted that they were meeting up at her workplace and not somewhere more private. But the good news was that after Thursday, she'd be freer to see him again. They were already planning on spending the entire long weekend together at his house to celebrate once she'd taken her exams.

Which was perfectly fine, because she'd needed time to make a very necessary visit to the university's health services clinic.

Audrey was on her way back home that evening, a fresh prescription for birth control burning a hole in her pocket. She'd never been on it before—there hadn't ever been a need. She'd never gotten far enough for it. But now she couldn't stop thinking about what it might mean to start taking it. And what Theo might say when she told him.

She'd just stepped out of her local Duane Reade with her new meds when her phone buzzed in her coat pocket. Her disappointment was palpable when it wasn't a message from Theo but one from Violet, freaking out about something.

VIOLET✿ | OMG CHECK INSTAGRAM. NOW.

AUDREY | Why?

VIOLET✿ | LIGHTM4ST3R IS BACK!

Audrey frowned as she opened the post Violet sent her. There it was, a new photo at the top of his feed, the first in well over a year. It appeared to be shot in his studio, with only some of the redbrick walls visible in the background amid a bunch of odd machinery. The image featured his messy worktable covered in large sheets of paper with dark black strokes printed onto them, surrounded by pieces of glass tubing. His bare hands were at the center as he compared a freshly twisted piece of glass to the lines on the paper, which was unusual in and of itself. He normally wore jet-black gloves in any photos with his hands, covering every inch of skin. This was the first time he'd ever revealed them publicly.

Huh.

This post was so different from his usual work. It was clearly an in-progress shot of his process, which he never showed prior to releasing a piece. It was only after he revealed his latest sculptures that he posted any of the behind-the-scenes stuff.

The strategy was smart because Lightm4st3r wasn't any normal sculptor.

He was a neon artist.

The reason he was so well-known was because he didn't do it in the classic sense. He didn't post or auction signs like you saw everywhere on the street.

His work was abstract, sculptural, futuristic.

It was exceptional.

It was one of a kind.

The caption of the post was simple, as they often were. Lightm4st3r never wrote any real descriptions of whatever he'd made (unless it was the name of a finished piece), but he usually spoke in song lyrics or quotes from poems or literature relevant to whatever idea he was trying to execute. It always sent the internet into a frenzy of speculation.

This one was especially short.

the wound is the place where the light enters you

It was a Rumi quote. Audrey read it over and over again, wondering what on earth it could mean. But then she froze in her tracks.

His hands—

They were *very* familiar.

Her heartbeat thundered in her ears and her breathing quickened. She threw herself back against the wall of the nearest building and frantically zoomed in on the photo, ripping one of her gloves off with her teeth so she could pinch at her screen more precisely, and *there*: there were all the odd constellations of tiny, raised starburst scars she knew so well, scattered across the backs of those hands.

She knew them so well because she saw them every day now.

Every day, those hands cupped her cheeks when Theo kissed her goodbye. Every day, those hands swallowed up her own while their fingers interlaced on the way to the subway. Every day, the right one shook while it tried desperately to hold onto a coffee mug without spilling it everywhere, just once, just for a moment.

Those hands had sketched her.

They'd cooked for her.

Made her coffee.

Tangled in her hair while they danced.

Gently swept tears away from her cheeks.

Held her while she broke.

Audrey's phone slipped from her fingers. It clattered to the ground, cracking the protective case around its edges.

Theo had tried to tell her, but she hadn't believed him. Not even in the slightest.

Theo Sullivan was Lightm4st3r, the famous, reclusive, avant-garde neon artist.

And now she knew it.

Twelve

AUDREY PRESSED THEO'S buzzer and knocked on the door again. She'd texted she was coming over as soon as she'd seen that Instagram post, and though she didn't say why, Theo's reply was enough to confirm that he probably knew.

Because all he'd said was:

Okay.

But the longer he took, the more she began to worry, and Audrey was just about to buzz again when Theo finally yanked open the inner door. He unlocked the security door and quickly ushered her inside.

Either he'd been working or working out, because his hair and black T-shirt were both drenched in sweat. But his face was paler than it usually was as he helped her out of her coat.

Audrey didn't say anything. She simply showed him Lightm4st3r's post and grabbed one of his hands to hold up next to her phone for comparison. They were identical.

Theo paled even further, but he nodded. "I know. I posted that for you." His voice shook. He obviously wasn't going to deny it. "I didn't know how else to tell you, and I wondered if you might—"

"Recognize your hands? Yeah. I did."

"You—you did. Okay. Wow." He ran one nervously through his hair, sweeping it out of his eyes for once. Audrey was suddenly struck by the nonchalance of it, the practiced motion, and she realized that while Theo was thinking about Lightm4st3r, he must have been acting the way he did before his accident. She'd never seen him *un*cover his face so easily.

He usually tried harder to hide it.

"I'm on a call right now, but uh . . . just come with me, and I'll finish up so we can talk. All right?" He held out his hand, his expression pleading, and Audrey slid hers into it slowly.

Theo guided her to the room tucked beneath the stairs and pushed open a door to reveal a well-lit office. It was the place where he'd hidden his motorcycle helmet after she'd found it on the shelf, and it was nestled carefully into a corner next to a huge motorized sit-stand desk outfitted with three monitors, a massive high-end drawing tablet, a very expensive Herman Miller desk chair, and a high-definition webcam. A stern-looking woman with short blond hair was pursing scarlet-painted lips up on one of the monitors, and she shook her head when they entered.

"Who is this?" She had a light British accent and a voice just as stern as her expression. "Theo, we're having a private call. You know? The whole attorney-client privilege thing? Things that are privileged should probably stay . . ." She waved a sardonic hand. "Privileged? *Private?!*" From what Audrey could see of the office behind her, it was furnished in mahogany shelves lined with leather-bound books.

It looked fancy.

Theo gave Audrey an encouraging squeeze on her arm before stooping and whispering in her ear, "I'll just be a second. Do you mind hanging here?" She shook her head and he limped back over to the desk, slumping tiredly in the chair.

"Imogen, that's my girlfriend, Audrey. She's fine."

"'*Fine*'?!" The lawyer groaned in resignation before rubbing at her temples. "Theo, I swear—"

"We're not discussing anything I wouldn't tell her anyway."

"They're *your* billable hours, so it's no skin off my nose if you want to involve other ears in our conversations. Do what you like with your money."

"I always do," he responded before picking up a pen and scribbling something in his little battered leather notebook. "Anyway, as I was saying, you can tell her assistant no. I've told her no before, and my answer remains the same."

"You know she's not going to take that lightly."

"It doesn't matter how she takes it, only that she does. I think it's ridiculous she's even asking, especially now." His gaze darkened. "And especially because she had her *assistant* do it."

"That's because you're not answering her phone calls."

"And I'm going to continue not answering them. No means no."

"All right then." The scratching of a fountain pen came through the computer's speakers as the attorney made some sort of note. "I'll tell her that. Again."

Audrey busied herself with looking at all the things hanging on the walls in his office while they went back and forth on whatever someone was asking Theo to do. There were a few framed sketches and paintings all done in various styles and colors mixed in with photographs of people she didn't know but who mostly looked vaguely like Theo's relatives. One was a photo of him and Diego, both younger and skinnier, clad in familiar Columbia Lacrosse T-shirts. Theo's wide grin stretched from massive ear to massive ear, which jutted out adorably from the sides of his head. She glanced over her shoulder at the current version of those ears, poking up through his dark waves in the light streaming from the monitor.

He'd grown into them.

She looked at the photo again. Ears aside, the most remarkable thing about it was that this was the first time she'd ever seen a recognizable picture of adult Theo without his scar. It was almost uncanny—she couldn't imagine him without it.

Frankly, he wasn't any less handsome now.

It oddly suited him.

Besides the photos and the artwork, there was a collection of clippings and articles. The walls were covered with write-ups from *The New York Times*, printouts of posts from the BBC, screenshots from a segment on *Good Morning America*, photos from Page Six, even a framed exposé carefully cut out of a *Time* magazine—all of them featuring the art of and speculation around the mysterious Lightm4st3r.

All of this, Theo's secret alter ego, had been tucked away in a small room under his stairs, right next to where they'd cuddled on the couch.

And the deeply introverted artist himself sat right across from her, clad in sweaty workout clothes while arguing with his lawyer.

When her eyes landed next on a wall of diplomas, they widened. Theodore H. R. Sullivan had not only a BFA in visual arts from Columbia University but also a BS in chemistry, both dating from the same year and both designated summa cum laude. A dual degree, with highest honors. Next to those two frames was a larger one, an MFA in studio art from NYU, and, perhaps most shockingly, a valid and recent license as a master electrician. Theo hadn't ever mentioned trade school, but he'd apparently gone there as well.

Were there any degrees he *didn't* have?

"Yeah, thanks, Imogen. We'll talk again soon."

"Take care, Theo. Be careful with the socials. My phone's ringing off the hook, so please warn me next time you're going to post something."

"I will." The Zoom call ended and Theo spun back around in his chair, pressing heavily up from it and stumbling to his feet. He limped over to Audrey and stood next to her, closing his eyes and rubbing the back of his neck. "Sorry about that. Imogen Phillips is my creative attorney. She's kind of like my agent, but better. Manages all the complicated handoffs of art pieces, negotiates charity contracts, brokers press deals, basically does all kinds of things on my behalf."

"You have a lawyer just for your art."

"Yeah?" He opened one eye and winced.

"For Lightm4st3r?"

His wince deepened. "I wanted to tell you. I thought about it. I was about to try when I was making pancakes last weekend and you asked for a secret, but you'd reacted so strongly to me, uh . . ." The tips of his ears reddened. "You were very incredulous about the kind of street cred I might have as an artist, so I panicked and punted to the trust fund instead."

That was a fair point. If he'd told her last week, she might have thought it was a joke.

In retrospect, it felt far less kind of her than she'd have liked it to.

"And, um . . ." Theo trailed off again with a sigh. "In all honesty, it's a pretty big fucking secret. I didn't want to burden you with that, especially this soon out of the gate. Figured I'd put something out into the ether, and at the very least, I could point to it later when we talked about it. But I didn't want to rope you into keeping it with me this early. And I, uh . . ." He attempted to smile, but it twisted into a grimace instead. "I didn't actually think you'd recognize my hands that fast. Not that I'm surprised, you're really smart, but um . . ."

He trailed off when Audrey didn't say anything. She didn't quite know what to say. Instead, she picked nervously at her thumbs and turned her attention back to Theo's wall of diplomas, worrying at her bottom lip with her teeth.

He'd been a trained electrician this entire time when she couldn't even build a working circuit to reliably test her battery design. He had a terminal graduate degree and could teach college if he wanted to. He was a world-renowned artist. He'd been written about in *Time* magazine. He could do so many things. He could date someone so much better, so much prettier, someone who didn't rummage around in garbage in her spare time, who hadn't failed classes so bad she lost her scholarship her freshman year, who didn't work in a café for minimum wage plus tips, who owned nicer outfits than the nineteen-dollar cocktail dress she'd once found in a Forever 21 clearance section. He came from *so* much money, had grown up riding horses, going to private schools, probably summering in Europe, and she didn't even have a passport. He owned a brownstone with a river view in Brooklyn and a two-thousand-dollar espresso machine. He could—

Theo's phone buzzed with a call, and he took it out, glanced at the screen, and turned it off before pocketing it again, bitterness flashing briefly across his features. He stepped up behind her and slid his arms around her waist, burying his face in the crook of her neck and pulling her close to him. He smelled muskier than usual, felt even hotter against her skin than he normally did, and when he inhaled deeply at the base of her throat, shivers coursed down her spine, and she gasped.

"You smell so good," he finally whispered, brushing his nose along the length of her neck. "I've missed you since this morning. I missed having you here." When his arms tightened around her, Audrey closed her eyes and tried to slow her racing heart.

None of this mattered. None of what she'd been thinking mattered.

Theo was still the same person he'd always been.

He just had an artistic persona, was all. So did a lot of people.

Even if that was true, though, it didn't quite make her feel better.

She'd been too preoccupied with her thoughts to respond to him, and she could physically feel the moment he started to panic behind her. "Audrey? Are you mad at me?" His voice trembled when he asked. "What are you thinking? Please say something. *Anything*. Literally anything, I beg of you."

The hurt in his voice helped her find her own. "I'm not mad, Theo. I was just surprised. Really surprised."

As soon as she said those words, he exhaled sharply in relief and burrowed deeper into her neck, his shoulders slumping while he rested his weight on her back. She dug her fingers into his dark hair, and he leaned into her touch, swaying gently on his feet. Theo rocked her back and forth, soothing them both, and Audrey finally found the space to calm her mind and catch her breath.

"It's not every day you find out your new boyfriend's a world-renowned, critically acclaimed artist, you know?" she finally murmured. "When I met you, you were just some sweet, handsome guy wearing a hoodie and a mask who never drank my coffee while it was still hot."

Theo froze on his feet and unburied his face to look at her. "Wait. You thought I was handsome? How would you have been able to judge that? I made damn sure you couldn't see my face."

Audrey twisted over her shoulder to find him absolutely bewildered, his dark eyes wide and confused.

There he was.

Same as always.

She snorted. "Girls just know, Theo. I could tell from the way you carried yourself, the way you talked to me, and even just the corner of your face you showed me." She gestured pointedly to her left eye. "But how was I supposed to know that anxious wreck I had a massive crush on at the coffee shop was actually the notorious *Lightm4st3r*?"

He groaned. "Oh god, I hate that I went with that name. I came up with it when I was a thirteen-year-old edgelord, and I've never been able to get rid of it."

Audrey burst out laughing, and Theo's grin widened as he pulled her closer, pressing a kiss just beneath her ear. "A laugh—thank god," he muttered. His nose tickled in that spot, and she laughed even harder. "From the way you were looking at me when I opened the door, I thought you were about to break up with me after barely a week. That would have been a spectacular record, even for me."

"No." She shook her head. "Sorry, Theo. I might have been freaking out a little, but you're still stuck with me."

"Again: *thank god.*" Theo suddenly pulled away from her and lifted a wry eyebrow, his eyes studying every inch of her as he looked her up and down. "Do you have anything in your pockets?"

"What?" She frowned and turned around to face him. "No? My phone's in my bag. This skirt doesn't have pockets. Why?"

"Mm-hmm. I see." He eyed the strap of her messenger bag across her chest and lifted it over her head, dropping it heavily to the floor beneath his diplomas.

"Theo, what are you—"

Audrey's question turned into a squeak when he bent and picked her up, tossing her easily over one shoulder and locking the tops of her thighs tightly to his chest with his arm.

"*Oh my god*, put me down!" It was entirely unfair how strong he was.

"No."

He shook his head and began to move, leaving the office and making his way over to a door set into the opposite wall. When he opened it, he took a few steps down a twisting staircase, and the upper floor of his house gradually faded away behind them.

"You're going to hurt yourself! Put me down, I can walk!"

"No, trust me, this is better."

"Why? Where are we going?"

"My studio. I don't know if I got all the glass shards picked up when I was cleaning over the weekend, and I'd rather not risk your feet."

"I'm wearing my Docs, I'll be fine."

"Don't want it sticking in them."

"They're steel-toed and they have thick rubber soles. They're literally work boots. I was in the lab today."

"*I said what I said.*" He paused, contemplated something, and then lifted his free hand, jerked her laces free, and tugged her boots off before tossing them nonchalantly over his shoulder onto the landing. They bounced and skidded across his ceramic flooring, disappearing far out of reach upstairs.

"Hey! What the fuck, Theo, those were my shoes!"

He ignored her, gripping the banister tightly and moving carefully downstairs. But the light from upstairs eventually faded enough for Audrey to feel the beginnings of fear rise in her chest. His studio was dark, and it was getting darker still the more stairs they descended.

There must not have been any windows down there.

It was pitch-black.

"Th-Theo—!"

Her heart raced, so fast and so loud, she was convinced it echoed off the walls.

"I know, sweetheart. Hold on. Two more steps. Just a second."

Theo turned and faced the wall when they made it to the basement floor, and Audrey drew in deep, gasping breaths, trying desperately not to panic when her face met the interminable blackness of the room. But right as she was about to close her eyes in terror, Theo flipped a few large switches on the wall—

And the studio exploded into color and light.

Signs of all kinds lined two of the three brick walls of the converted garage studio, the electrified shades of neon gas buzzing in delicate glass tubes. Everything from simple script phrases in various fonts, to classic diner signs, to full, stylized images crafted with light were mounted into the brick, their myriad colors swirling and bleeding into one another on the dark concrete floors and bouncing off the metal garage door. Some of them moved and flashed, some of them were static, and some were brighter than others. But the largest sign was placed in the middle: SULLIVAN LIGHTWORKS, formed in bright, blocky, clean, and modern sans-serif yellow font. But that wasn't all.

There were also the sculptures.

Some hung from the ceiling, neon plays on classic lighting fixtures rendered sharp and cartoonish with their perfectly curved lines in mocking facsimiles of antique chandeliers. Others stood in bases on the floor, upright and three-dimensional, arcing and curving in sweeping, interweaving abstract lines, alternating between chaos and grace, at once delicate and ephemeral, frantic and furious, futuristic and loud.

They screamed, but could shatter.

They were bright, but could break.

These were Lightm4st3r originals, and ones no one had ever seen out in the wild before.

Theo turned again and set her down on the surface of a work table that had been swept clean. There were several tables down there in the studio set between all kinds of untold machinery, tanks of gas and boxes of wires, scraps of metal and endless barrels of straight, glass tubing.

Chaos and beauty surrounded them.

Every color, all shades of blue and yellow, reds and greens, swirling purples and bright pinks, oranges, whites, all of them, every single color she could possibly imagine glowed in the studio space, casting their light on every available surface, dappling them with translucent gradients.

It was staggering.

Theo stepped between her legs and ran his hands along the length of her tights. His calluses caught slightly against the fabric, but all it did was prickle gooseflesh across her skin. Audrey suppressed a shiver at the sensation.

His face was bathed in all the light from his creations, as if it had been refracted through a prism and the colors laid perfectly across his features, mixing and mottling over them, becoming a chaotic palette all on its own. The paint of the cosmos.

"This is it," he finally said, leaning forward and watching her face greedily while she drank in his art, his hands still rubbing gently up and down her legs. The shifting light of his sculptures reflected back at her in his eyes, which dipped briefly down to her lips before meeting her gaze again. "This is my studio. All my work—at least, all that I have here right now."

"It's *beautiful*," Audrey breathed, her voice trembling in awe. "It's incredible." In fact, it was overwhelming. She wasn't sure what to look at first, save for the single blank wall to her right: the only wall Lightm4st3r ever showed in any of his photos.

It must have been left bare to hide the secret of his art.

Even amid the multicolored lights surrounding them, she could see his eyes heat at her assessment. One hand slid up her skirt—his left—and his fingers plucked curiously at the waistband of her tights. "You think so?" The other hand slid to her neck, his tremor vibrating against her flesh.

"Yes. I've never seen anything like it." She swallowed thickly. Theo's palms were hot against her skin, and the heat was rapidly spreading downward across her body, never mind where his fingers lingered on her waist.

"You like it?"

"God, yes. Yes, it's magnificent." She met his gaze. "You're amazing."

The left corner of his mouth crept slowly upward, his lips

spreading wide to allow one single dimple out to play. "I'm making you something, you know. That's what that photo was: it was for you."

His fingers beneath her skirt found the skin of her torso, and she shuddered and gasped at the fire of them. When she opened her mouth, he lunged forward and took her lips in his, more forward, more forceful, more heated than he'd ever been before.

It left her breathless.

"Do you know why I work in neon?" he whispered, pulling away from her slightly so he could look her in the eyes again. Cool air rushed across her neck when he removed his palm, but his left thumb began to make languid circles just above the waistband of her tights, and Audrey shifted and rubbed her legs together, unable to sit still. The sudden urge to move was incessant, unyielding. Theo had never looked at her quite the way he did now, and it made her feel odd. She was hot, burning as if she had a fever, and it was getting hard to breathe, like something heavy had been laid over her chest.

But she still managed to shake her head.

Theo didn't blink. He didn't break eye contact. But his fingers twitched again, and he slid both hands beneath the waistband of her tights. He began to slowly tug them down the length of her legs, carefully alternating sides so they wouldn't tear.

"When I was in high school, I worked in my dad's auto shop on weekends. I didn't have quite the same passion for cars that he did, but there were two things I really loved: welding and wiring."

He yanked the tights free of her feet and tossed them casually onto the surface of the worktable. Audrey barely had time to register the change in temperature below her waist before his hands slid up her legs again, smoothing across her skin and right back up to her hips before coming down, rubbing over and over, cyclical and hypnotic. His eyes were molten, and his skin scorched across hers.

Heat built up in her core.

She shifted again.

"He did regular mechanic work too, but he mostly specialized in restoring vintage hot rods. I'm not going to lie: it was pretty cool to be a teenager and work on classic muscle cars with him, especially when he let me drive his on occasion. He taught me everything he knew, and that's actually how I got the scars on my hands: spark welding burns. You really should wear gloves when you're handling massively dangerous currents of electricity and heat. Don't be dumb like teenage me."

"I-I'll keep that in mind."

"Good."

Theo's fingers had wandered upward again, and when they hooked next beneath the elastic of her underwear, Audrey's heart nearly beat straight out of her chest.

Her breath hitched.

Time seemed to stop.

Theo paused and waited, watching her closely, a question written across his face. He quirked one curious eyebrow at her, and it was all she needed to understand what he was asking. But she couldn't muster up the air for words, so she gave him a tiny, nervous nod instead. No one had ever asked her for this before. But now she needed to know. She needed to know what he might do, and what it might feel like.

His lips cracked into a wicked grin.

The fabric started to slip slowly over her hips, peeling gently down her legs.

Theo took his time.

It was agonizing.

"I didn't really know what I was going to do in college. My mom wanted me to be a lawyer, like her and my uncle and my grandfather, but I have no interest in that bullshit. Never have. I'm too much like my dad. I loved art too much, loved working with my hands too much. I tried law for a year after undergrad, but it wasn't for me. I was miserable, so I left and went for my MFA instead." He flashed her another roguish grin, the twin of the one his father wore in the photo upstairs, though this time, it was paired with a bitter huff. "Turns out I'm the black sheep of the family—I think my dad was the only one who ever understood me. I don't know why I'm still surprised by that."

Her panties snagged briefly on her ankle before Theo tugged them free, and Audrey's cheeks heated when she caught a glimpse of them glistening in the bright blue light of the nearest sculpture. They were soaked through. Theo's pupils dilated further at the sight and his breathing quickened, but he tucked her panties reverently into his pocket before turning his attention back to her.

"Even though I was on an athletic scholarship when I first went to college, my mom still threatened to withhold some finances from me if I didn't do what she asked. So as a compromise for declaring a visual arts major, I promised her I'd do something more 'pragmatic.' Her words, not mine." He rolled his eyes, but it was just a flash. He didn't seem to want to take them away from her for long.

He placed his hands on her hips and pulled her to the edge of the table, nestling himself more firmly between her thighs. His left hand wandered up her skirt and between her legs again while his right slid up her back, bracing her as solidly as he could for what she assumed he was about to do. Audrey's heart thrummed in her ears, mixing with the buzzing of the neon lights surrounding them.

"I wasn't sure what that more 'pragmatic' major would be until I decided to take chemistry for my science credit. And we learned about the noble gases."

Theo's calloused fingertips trailed along the soft skin of her inner thighs. They paused, and his eyes searched her face for one more moment before he slid his fingers up further—and along her slit. She was slick already, unbearably wet, and he closed his eyes and breathed out slowly, gathering himself while he began to stroke her gently.

"I'd already worked with some of them in my dad's shop, actually." His voice was ragged, but he continued anyway, his fingers gentle and slow and soft, circling and caressing and soothing, as if she were the most delicate thing he'd ever handled—as if he were terrified of breaking her. "Hold on to me, sweetheart," he whispered as an aside, bending forward slightly so Audrey could wrap her arms around his neck. She obeyed, twining them around his head and burying her fingers in his hair. He grunted and surged forward when she accidentally tugged a bit too hard on his roots with a trembling hand, but he pressed a quick kiss to the side of her neck before speaking again, his hand gradually increasing in speed.

Audrey gave in with a groan.

She couldn't help it.

Her hips rocked against his palm of their own accord.

"Argon is a shielding gas in welding, so I knew some of their properties. When the gases are inert, you can't perceive them. They're colorless, odorless, tasteless, formless, transient, and, frankly, *extremely* rare. They're completely invisible to the naked eye, their true natures kept hidden from both science and man for centuries, and they have to be manufactured or created in labs for us to use." He paused, and Audrey wanted to die when he did. The lack of friction was unbearable now. "Do you know where we find these gases out in nature?"

She shook her head.

"We find them in the stars."

Theo slipped one finger inside her, and Audrey arched into him with a gasp at the sensation of it. His hands were so big, so wide, his fingers so thick and strong that only one of them was nearly enough to fill her entirely. When he curled it, beckoning, she curled over his shoulder, hardly able to breathe at the rising heat and pressure threatening to overwhelm her at every one of his strong, slow strokes.

"If you take those gases and apply a little energy, a little friction, a little . . . *stimulation* in the form of electricity—" Theo pulled his finger out only to replace it with two, sliding them both in slowly, so slowly, and stretching her carefully, gloriously as he pressed them deeper and deeper inside of her.

God, she'd never felt so full before.

His thumb continued his earlier work, circling gently across her clit while he stroked his fingers along that elusive ridge inside. "If you provide that, they burst into light, explode into color, swirl and form into stars. It's chemistry, yes, but it's also physics, it's metaphysics, it's philosophy. It's everything that drives us and drives the cosmos, the basis of life and light and everything we build upon it.

"When I realized that, I knew what I wanted to do. I saw it then, sitting in that chemistry lab, images of exploding light and sculpture in my mind, electricity buzzing into life, the fabric of the universe stitched in beautiful, vibrant colors. I already sketched incessantly, I already painted, worked with clay, was taking life drawing classes with live models, but everything paled in comparison to the idea I had of this medium."

His brows knit together, but not because he seemed unhappy—he seemed to be seeing something else, something that wasn't quite there in front of him. "Neon is both new and not new, a distinctive piece of America's iconic, early twentieth-century past, over a hundred years old now—but at the same time, the gases you use in it weren't discovered until recently, not compared to other forms of art, other media, other tools and structures and components. It's both traditional and futuristic, classic and avant-garde, of the now and not. But it's grown stale over the years, and it needed its boundaries pushed. I decided to be the one to push them."

"Th-Theo. Theo, I'm—"

He'd increased the speed of his strokes inside her as he talked, pumping his fingers in and out, curling and uncurling, stretching and widening and filling her full, so full, and Audrey couldn't stop herself. She clung to him while she rode his hand, suffering, shaking, *agonizing* through the buildup of an intense wave of pleasure on the verge of cresting. She couldn't speak, she could hardly breathe, she could only bury her face in Theo's shoulder while she moaned, while she burned, while she let herself be consumed by the fire he generated both inside and out.

"Look at me, Audrey."

She'd never heard him be so commanding, so sharp, but it was more than that: there was an urgency in his deep voice she couldn't ignore. It took everything she had to pull away from his neck and face him, panting and hot and so achingly close to breaking.

"I work with neon because it's the material that drives the stars, that fuels the cosmos, that lights up the universe with galaxies. Whenever I ignite a piece for the first time, it's like a new sun bursts into being. There is no greater creative feeling than that," he gasped. What heat she could discern in his face through the shifting, colored lights seemed just as scorching as her own. "It's like I become God." Theo rocked back and forth with her in time with her hips, dipping down to press his forehead to hers and his lips to her own. His right hand slid up and gripped the back of her neck, shaking but strong while his fingers tangled in the sweat-soaked hair at the nape.

"Audrey, I need you to look at me. I need to see it—I need to see when I light *you* up for the first time, brighter and more beautiful than any star. More gorgeous and glorious than any piece of art I myself can ever hope to create."

It was the intensity in his eyes when he said it that sent her over the edge.

It shattered her completely.

Audrey seized and cried out as the wave crested and pleasure crashed through her body, wiping out any sense of self she might have tried to cling to. Instead, the only thing she could grasp on to was Theo, and she dove into him while stars exploded behind her eyes, while heat pulsed across her skin, while her body melted into the fire he somehow always seemed to create, before disappearing into the ether. She went blind, sightless, weightless, soundless and voiceless, save for the ragged screams of pleasure echoing somewhere in the distance beyond the black, beyond the veil.

At some point, she found herself back in her body, the weight of the world back on her chest. Or it would have been—if Theo hadn't been holding her so closely. He was clutching her to him, his hands making soothing circles on her back and stroking her hair, his lips alternating between murmuring gentle praise and peppering tiny, delicate kisses along the underside of her jaw while she gasped for breath and tried to remember how lungs were supposed to work.

"Oh my god," she finally managed.

"Thank you, sweetheart," Theo breathed against her neck. "That was incredible. You're perfect."

"Are you joking?" Audrey was mystified. She'd never come so hard in her life, not even on the rare occasions she had the time and space to touch herself while Violet was out of the apartment, and Theo had done all the work. She could feel how hard he was. His length was pressing against her through his gym shorts, and if it felt like anything he'd just done to her, she knew it had to be agonizing.

And besides: she *wanted* to touch him.

"Theo," she said, stretching out a hand. "Can I—"

"*No.*" He shook his head sharply and pulled away just enough to brush her hair out of her face. "No. Don't touch me."

"Why not?" She frowned at him. "I want to."

Theo sighed and rubbed his eyes. "Two reasons: first of all, if you touch me now, I'm going to come so fast, I'll embarrass myself. I'd rather not." He glanced at her out of the corner of his eye. "And two, I want to wait. I *need* to wait. Because . . ." He drew in a deep breath. "Because above all else, I am a horrible, greedy, *selfish* man.

And once I start, I won't just want a taste: I'll want all of you. A full banquet of your body."

"What was this, then?"

"A preview. Just the scent of a meal to tide me over." He smirked at her, the lights of his artwork glittering in his eyes. "And the only thing it did was make me hungrier. But you have midterms this week, work in the morning, and I can't keep you all to myself right now. So I won't push it any further. Not today. But I needed this all the same, and . . . I wanted to watch it happen here. So thank you."

"Uh . . ." Audrey blinked, dumbfounded. She was the only one who'd gotten the orgasm, but he seemed perfectly pleased by it. "You're welcome?"

He snorted in amusement and flung her tights over his shoulder, stooping again to gather her up in his arms before shutting off his creations and mounting the stairs. The constant, low-grade buzz of the neon lights cut out sharply when Theo's studio was plunged back into darkness, the light of his stars suddenly extinguished.

"Hey, Theo?" she asked as he carried her back up into the soft glow of the lamps on the first floor.

"Yeah?"

"Can I have my panties back?"

He hummed pensively, tilting his head from side to side in deep consideration. "Mmm . . . no. No, I don't think so."

"Oh, come on!" Audrey tried to lunge toward his pocket to grab them, but Theo was too strong. He hoisted her out of reach and threw her back over his shoulder like he'd done earlier, and she had to resort to twisting and pouting at him. "I still have to get home! That walk's going to feel *brisk*."

"You're not going anywhere yet. Didn't you hear me?" She yelped when he slapped her ass playfully. "I'm *starving*. We're ordering Chinese."

Thirteen

THEO♥ | Mountains or beach?

Audrey stared at Theo's message. There was no context, and they hadn't been discussing either beaches or mountains. He'd just sent it out of the blue.

She zipped up his hoodie and started to type. He never gave her panties back, so she'd stolen his favorite hoodie in retaliation. He didn't seem too sad about it when she walked out of the house wearing it, and she loved the way it wrapped her in warmth and smelled like him, all woodsy pine and bergamot and spice.

AUDREY | Are you thinking of going somewhere? I like both

AUDREY | I've never been to the mountains, but the beach is great

AUDREY | Some of them in Florida are really pretty

THEO♥ | No, no, it's the This or That game.

THEO♥ | Don't think, just choose.

THEO♥ | First impulse.

Huh. This was new.

AUDREY | Ok

AUDREY | Mountains, because I'd like to go someday

AUDREY | What do you even do there?

AUDREY | And which would you pick?

THEO♥ | We can talk about that this weekend.

THEO♥ | Chocolate or vanilla?

AUDREY | Hey, wait! You didn't answer!

AUDREY | What would you choose?

THEO♥ | Not the point of this game, and the asker doesn't have to answer.

THEO♥ | Chocolate or vanilla?

AUDREY | Both, and stop making up rules

THEO♥ | You can't pick both, and I'm not making up the rules.

THEO♥ | Chocolate or vanilla?

She wrinkled her nose at the screen. He was *definitely* making up these rules.

AUDREY | Chocolate

THEO♥ | Noted.

She only saw Theo at the coffee shop for the rest of the week. As he'd promised her on Monday, he kept well away from her both physically and digitally during her study hours while she prepped for her Thursday midterm, aside from checking in during the day and visiting over her breaks at work like he did every day. But he still continued this new game at random moments, and just when she was least expecting it, another of his questions would light up her phone.

THEO🖤 | Cake or pie?

AUDREY | GOD THEO, YOU'RE MAKING ME CHOOSE?! 😩

AUDREY | NO

THEO🖤 | Cake or pie?

AUDREY | . . . pie

AUDREY | Fuck you.

THEO🖤 | Patience, sweetheart. We're working you up to that.

She gasped and fully inhaled the cheese puff she'd just popped in her mouth.

"Auds? What's—" Violet was in the kitchen making a snack, and she paled when she turned. "AUDREY!"

Luckily, Audrey managed to cough it up, red-faced and teary-eyed, before Violet actually had to perform the Heimlich maneuver on her. But they—and half of their couch—ended up covered in bright orange cheese powder from the debacle.

Theo, meanwhile, didn't miss a beat.

THEO🖤 | Pumpkin pie or apple?

It took her a few minutes of wheezing to recover long enough to type her answer.

She didn't tell him what he'd just done to her.

Only once that week did Theo break his rule and send her some questions later than dinnertime. He must have been thinking about her before bed.

THEO♥ | Coke or Pepsi?

AUDREY | Coke

THEO♥ | Fancy hotel in the city or Airbnb remote getaway?

AUDREY | Ohhhhh I want both!

AUDREY | I never get to travel

THEO♥ | Pick.

AUDREY | Airbnb, you ass

THEO♥ | Showers or baths?

AUDREY | Baths

Three dots, but they were quick.

THEO♥ | Wait, really?

AUDREY | Yeah

AUDREY | We didn't have bathtubs in a lot of my foster homes, and we don't have one in my apartment now

AUDREY | Soaking in a tub is the height of luxury

THEO♥ | Good to know.

THEO♥ | Back massage or foot rub?

AUDREY | Yes

AUDREY | And don't you dare ask again, I want all the massages, so fuck off

THEO♥ | Alright, fine.

THEO♥ | I'll allow it.

Only one more question came through that night.

THEO♥ | Cozy night in or date night out?

AUDREY | Cozy night in, every time

The hesitancy did reappear for a bit with that one.

THEO♥ | . . . thank god.

Every once in a while, she got him to answer a question of her own.

THEO♥ | I don't understand vanilla being equated with "plain."

THEO♥ | There's nothing plain about vanilla.

THEO♥ | It's the world's most expensive spice after saffron and the flavor complexities depend on the provenance, just like coffee beans or cacao.

AUDREY | Uh-huh

AUDREY | Sure, Theo

AUDREY | Exactly what a boring vanilla person would say

THEO🖤 | BORING??

AUDREY | Yeah

AUDREY | Chocolate people are more fun 😌🍫

THEO🖤 | Audrey, have you ever had REAL vanilla ice cream before?

THEO🖤 | Not made with that artificial vanillin shit, I'm talking the real thing straight from the goddamn orchid.

AUDREY | I don't know that I have, honestly

AUDREY | Still counts as plain, though

AUDREY | It's basic

THEO🖤 | IT IS NOT BASIC

THEO🖤 | THEY CURE THE FUCKING PODS FOR MONTHS, WHICH COME FROM A FLOWER

THEO🖤 | AND THAT FLOWER ONLY BLOOMS FOR 24 HOURS BEFORE IT HAS TO BE HAND-POLLINATED WITH A WOODEN NEEDLE

THEO🖤 | THE ENTIRE PROCESS SCREAMS COMPLEX

THEO🖤 | BASIC???

THEO🖤 | ARE YOU KIDDING ME?

Audrey laughed so hard, she could barely breathe.

Wednesday night rolled around. She and Violet were lounging

around, and she was listening to her roommate rant about her workday while just beginning to wonder what can of soup she should heat up for dinner.

"Can you believe that, Auds? That Hackett would actually say something like that during a *client presentation*?" There was a *thunk* that reverberated through the apartment's walls from Violet's top bunk. "What a dickwad, throwing me under the bus like that, questioning my sales projections!"

Another *thunk*.

She must have slapped the wall again.

"Yeah, yeah," Audrey hummed in response. "I definitely know what that means."

"It means he embarrassed me in front of a potential client! *And my manager!*" A pillow flew out from between the curtains and skidded across their floor. "I hate that stupid, tall ginger with his stupid *freckles* and his stupid *accent* and—"

A text pinged through on Audrey's phone from Theo.

THEO♥ | I ordered you food.

THEO♥ | Should be there in a minute.

THEO♥ | Hope you like it, and good luck studying.

THEO♥ | Don't stay up too late. ♥

A heart emoji? That was a first. She barely had time to stare at the message before her buzzer rang.

He'd sent her Indian food.

Good lord, it was exactly what she needed.

Violet poked her head out between her curtains when Audrey opened the bag. Their apartment was immediately flooded with the heavenly aroma of spices and garlic.

"Whoa, whoa, whoa, wait a second, hold up—" Her roommate slid down and bounded over to peer into the bounty. "Holy shit, did Theo get you Atithi?!"

"Looks like it." Audrey tore into a piece of garlic naan and sobbed. It melted in her mouth. "Violet. *Violet*. How did he know?!" she wailed as she took another bite.

"Oh my god, how much did he order?! Give me one of those!" Violet snatched a samosa straight out of Audrey's hand, but she didn't mind. There was a whole carton of them, plus chicken tikka masala, saag paneer, butternut squash soup, lamb kebabs, basmati rice, daal, mango lassi, and two servings each of kheer, gulab jamun, and rasmalai. Looked like he'd deliberately sent enough for Violet too.

It was so good, Audrey cried real tears into her lassi.

AUDREY | THEODORE HENRY SULLIVAN

AUDREY | Keep giving me food like this and I'll be in grave danger of falling in love with you forever

AUDREY | Are you going to make me marry you just so we can share your Postmates account?

THEO♥ | Great, so the plan is working?

AUDREY | You might get more than you bargained for, though

AUDREY | Violet just informed me that she and I are a package deal and she's moving in with us

THEO♥ | Great, so the plan is working.

The dots appeared again, disappeared, and then nothing.

Audrey waited.

It took another solid minute for his last text to come through.

THEO♥ | Now go enjoy your food and study for your test.

THEO♥ | Goodnight, sweetheart. 😘

Huh.

That last text had taken him an awfully long time to type.

THEO DIDN'T JUST walk her to the subway after work the day of her exams. When Audrey stopped at the top of the stairs where they usually kissed goodbye, he shot her a mischievous look and tightened his fingers between her own. "Come on—what are you waiting for?" he said with a slight tug. "Don't want to be late, do you?"

"Are you coming with me?"

"Yeah."

"Seriously?"

He nodded, the mask shifting up on his face from the grin he surely wore beneath it. "You're mine for the whole long weekend after your exam today. *Mine.* Did you think I was going to let any second of it go to waste?"

They'd made these plans after he'd shown her his studio since she'd taken the rare shift off on Friday knowing she'd probably be wiped after her tests, and even though she'd been lamenting the loss of tomorrow's income, she hadn't known Theo would be making up for it quite this much.

He went with her all the way to the lecture hall, and when she turned to look at him with wide eyes and a sick feeling in her stomach before going in, he lowered his mask and gave her a reassuring nod.

"I'll work out here while I wait for you," he whispered, bending in close to her ear and running his hands along her arms. "Just breathe and take your time, okay? You've got this. Imagine passing with flying colors and walking the stage in a few weeks."

Audrey nodded nervously, and he cupped her face with his hands, curling his fingers beneath her ears and running his thumbs softly along her cheeks. When he stooped to kiss her, his scent washed over her, fresh and clean and warm, and she melted into him. But not for long. He pulled away and wrapped her in his arms, tugging her tightly against his chest for an enormous hug.

"Okay, get in there. No more stalling," he muttered when she didn't try at all to escape. And then to drive the point home, he lowered a hand, ran it down her back—

And very firmly grabbed her ass.

She gasped and jumped back in surprise, and he grinned at her while he lifted his mask back over his face, his expression positively wicked. He'd never done *anything* like that in public before.

"*Theo!*" She tried to hiss his name, but it was awfully hard to do through the laughter bubbling up. "These are my classmates! They're watching!" A few were, it was true. And they seemed awfully interested in whatever was happening.

"I've been dying to do that for weeks. Now go ace your test." He shooed her inside the room with another playful smack on her ass before turning and making his way toward a nearby vacant table and chair.

Audrey gathered herself and took her usual seat, cheeks still burning fiercely. But the warmth in her face and her chest did help steady her nerves while she got out her pencil and settled in.

"LET ME SEE these wires here . . . you might just need to adjust them a bit, hang on. The contact points aren't quite right, and that might be your issue. Hand me those wire strippers?"

After her exam, Theo crouched to examine her battery and circuit in the lab with interest. Once Audrey had gotten started, it was a whole lot easier to ease into a problem-solving mindset, especially knowing Theo was waiting for her outside, and it was more fun than she initially thought it would be to have him there in her capstone lab. But since it was a Friday, they were the only two there.

It was perfect timing.

And the perfect place for him to feel comfortable without his mask out in public.

"I can't believe you told me, 'I know a thing or two about circuits,' and this entire time you've been a fucking *master electrician*," she grumbled, begrudgingly passing him the tool while he plucked curiously at her wiring. "Way to bury the lede."

He shrugged and unwound some of her handiwork. But he was right: on a second glance, she hadn't put that together quite as thoroughly as she'd needed to.

"Yeah, well, it seemed like a useful license to get. I started earning my hours when I was in high school, and then I ended up choosing an art form that uses electricity for the crux of . . . well, *everything*, so I'm glad I decided to follow through."

His brow furrowed slightly while he concentrated, and Audrey had to admit: she loved watching him work, even if she hadn't seen him do his real specialty yet.

Someday, maybe he'd let her watch him in his own studio.

"Sure, but *master*, though?"

"I don't do anything by halves. And I mean *anything*." He raised an eyebrow at her before he finished snipping the wires and rewound them, making sure the copper was thoroughly in contact with the rest of it. "Honestly, this is great work, you just need some minor tweaks." When he went back to his investigation, his phone buzzed with a text, the vibration louder than normal against the wood of the worktable. But he only glanced at the screen and dismissed the message immediately.

"What does your family think of all this? Your art, I mean?"

He froze.

"My family?"

"Yeah. You never really talk about them." She rested her chin on her hand. "If I had a family, I'd never shut up about them."

"I don't talk to my family," he muttered, plucking at more wires and testing their connections. "I was close with my dad. And now my dad is gone." His phone buzzed again, but this time, he threw it bitterly inside his satchel without looking at it.

All right.

She wouldn't press him.

At least, not about that.

"What are you doing for the holidays, then?" She frowned. "Surely you don't spend them alone?"

"Diego's mom invited me this year, which was nice of her. But I was just going to try to work on my piece for the charity gala. I don't mind being alone. It's better that way, honestly." He grabbed a soldering iron and placed it in her hands. "Touch that part up."

Audrey peered at where he'd pointed. He was right: it wasn't properly joined all the way. "Thank you."

But his distraction didn't hide how deftly he'd avoided her question.

Theo studied her carefully as she worked. "What about you? Are you going home to Florida?"

"No. I usually spend the holidays with Violet and her family in Jersey. I can't afford to fly back to Tampa, and I'm not sure I'd call it home anymore anyway." She finished fixing the connection and set the iron aside.

"But what about Gladys? You always speak so highly of her."

She sighed. "I'd *love* to see her. She was the closest thing I ever had to a home and I try to keep up with her as much as I can, but she usually has her hands full with other foster kids. She doesn't have time for me, and can't afford to help me out. You don't get all that much from the state as a foster parent."

"When was the last time you saw her?"

"Before I moved here and started college. Almost five and a half years ago now." She pointed down at her experimental battery prototype. "So what do you think of the design, Mr. Master Electrician? I need a professional opinion before my capstone presentation."

"It looks great. My expertise is more in the practical implementation, not the theoretical, and I don't really work on sustainability—not expressly, anyway. But it looks good to me." Theo leaned his hands on the table surface and rocked back and forth on his heels. "Is your presentation a public thing?" Audrey nodded. "Can I come?"

Her heart raced at his question. He wanted to be there? For her? But she chose a casual shrug rather than show how excited that made her. "It's open to the whole university, so I suppose the public can technically attend."

"So I'm just 'the public' then, huh?" He shifted and loomed over her, his voice dropping low enough to almost qualify as a growl while he pointedly eyed her mouth and rolled his jaw pensively. She had an excellent view of his soft, plush lips from where she stood.

"Yep. Just the public. Just some guy." She bit her own lip and closed the gap between them, sliding a hand up his sweater and trying not to grin as the muscles of his torso twitched beneath her touch. He was somehow the perfect combination of both soft and sculpted, and he shuddered as he bent over her, burying his face in her shoulder.

He'd done this to her in his studio. They were in hers now.

Fair was only fair.

"I'm not special at all?" he breathed, pressing his lips to her neck and settling his hips against her own.

The bulge in his jeans was intriguing.

"Nope." She changed direction and slid back down, her fingers toying with the elastic waistband of his briefs. When she paused, his breathing quickened. "Positively plebeian."

She pushed her hand beneath.

And his breath caught in a sharp inhale.

"You're playing with fire, Miss Adams," he rasped. He'd wrapped her in his arms and his fingers tightened at her back as her own curled in his dark hair.

"Can I touch you?" she whispered back. Her fingertips grazed against something hard and silken, but before she could explore further, he grabbed her wrist and held her still.

"Naughty girl," he rumbled as he finally pulled back and looked her in the eye. His pupils were blown black and wide. "This isn't the right place. I told you: I don't do anything by halves. And I have *plans*." He tossed her hand away and grabbed the back of her neck, yanking her lips to his. When his tongue swept insistently into her mouth, tasting her expertly like he was searching for something, the temperature in the lab was suddenly sweltering. It was entirely too warm to continue working in those conditions.

"We're getting out of here," he growled against her skin. "And you're coming home with me."

WALKING INTO THEO'S house just before sunset felt so different the third time.

It was the first time Audrey had planned to be there, the first time she'd ever done such a thing with any sort of intention, and even though she was so comfortable with Theo now, her body still vibrated with electricity when he shut the door and locked it before helping her out of her coat.

Part of it was the anticipation. He'd kept mum about what he was planning, and she knew he was planning *something*. He was nothing if not deliberate.

Part of it was the length of time. Their longest date so far had stretched overnight, sure, but *three days*? Three days and three nights with one person? What if they got bored with each other? What if it didn't go well? What if they got into a fight? At least they weren't going on a trip and she could go home if that were the case. But even imagining the possibility felt awful, and Audrey tried to shove the thought away from her mind.

The last part of it was the expectation—not his, but hers. She'd started taking her new birth control after going down into Theo's studio.

She wanted more of that. More of *him*.

But she was also scared.

Violet said sex could be a lot of things. It could be good, bad, mediocre, incredible, short, long, painful, soft, intimate, impersonal. It could be any of those things, sometimes all at once, and not knowing for sure what sex with *Theo* might be made Audrey want to crawl out of her own skin with anxiety.

That same restless feeling had coursed through her veins while they made a quick trip to her apartment to grab her things after somehow making it out of the lab with their clothes still on. It didn't let up as Theo helped her pack her bag—and especially not when he peered curiously into her drawers and pulled out her summer bikini.

"What do I need this for?" she'd asked when he'd handed it over.

"You'll see."

"What are we even doing, anyway? How do I pack for this

weekend?" A bikini didn't make any sense at all for how cold it was outside.

"We're going to do whatever you want." His phone vibrated in his pocket, but he took one look at the screen and sharply silenced the call before shoving it back into his jeans, irritation flashing briefly across his face as he turned his attention back to investigating her bed. "Personally, I don't think you need any clothes at all, but trust me: a bathing suit could be fun."

Her cheeks burned at his tone. "Should I bring a dress? Are we leaving the house?"

"We don't have to if you don't want to." He dipped beneath the top bunk and clicked her fairy lights on and off a few times.

"What are you looking for in there?" She put a hand on his shoulder. "Get out of my—" But before she could pull him away, Theo straightened, his smile crooked and victorious. He held a stuffed puffin in his hands. The old, ragged toy looked so small wrapped in his fingers.

"I wanted to make sure you didn't forget Petey. And I needed to officially meet him. He *is* your oldest friend, after all." He held him up and looked at him directly in his beady eyes. "Hullo, Petey." He pinched a wing with two fingers and shook it gently.

"OH MY GOD, THEO, GIVE ME THAT!"

Mortified. She was mortified. She snatched it away from him, her face somehow burning even hotter than before. But before she could shove the puffin in her bag, Theo grabbed her and picked her up, lifting her completely off the ground with only his left arm and pressing her against his side. His biceps bulged against her back and his grip was like iron.

God, he was strong.

"Do you have any idea how excited I am to spend a few days with you? Three whole days?" he murmured in her ear. "And Petey too.

Don't be embarrassed. He can keep Roo company." He pressed a kiss to her cheek.

"You're such a dork." She shoved halfheartedly at his shoulder while she kicked and struggled to be let down, but it was a useless endeavor and she knew it.

"Yeah, and you *like* it. You've told me, over and over again. And I was listening." He nuzzled into her cheek. "It's been long enough for me to finally believe you, and I've seen it—and felt it—for myself. Can't take it back now."

The way he said it—

The way he held her—

It only made everything worse.

And by the time they got to his house with Petey tucked safely in her duffel, her stomach churned with both apprehension and burning hot excitement.

Theo clearly had some experience. He'd known what he was doing down there on that table.

What if *she* was the one who was bad at it?

What if she didn't measure up to who he'd been with before?

But Audrey didn't have time to linger on the thought, because as soon as she'd unwound the scarf from her neck and draped it over one of the hooks in the entryway, two large hands gripped her hips and lifted her, twisting and pinning her against the opposite wall.

"*Mine,*" Theo growled. "Finally."

He held her high enough for her to look him in the eye, and the golden rays of the setting sun spilled along one side of his face. They streamed through his windows overlooking the East River from across his house, highlighting the concentric amber and mahogany rings of one of his extraordinary multitonal irises and plunging the other side into shadow. He ran his hands down her legs and wrapped them around his waist, settling comfortably between them before gently combing his fingers through her hair and tucking it behind her ears.

"You're so beautiful, and all mine."

He was less gentle when he dove forward and pressed his mouth to hers.

The electricity in her skin shifted to lightning along her lips, and Audrey closed her eyes and gasped at the force of it, of him, of how ravenously he devoured her, sucking and nipping at her mouth like a man starved and driven mad by hunger. She buried her fingers in his hair and held on for dear life, giving herself over to Theo's intensity. He was so warm, his hands so unbearably hot, and flames licked across her skin everywhere they touched, curling deep within her belly and pooling there, molten and churning and urgent.

Finally.

Theo slid his left hand beneath her sweater, his fingers deft and questing, and they nudged aside her bra, slipping beneath to cup her breast. His palm was wide enough to cover it completely, and he made a noise low in his throat when her nipple pebbled under his thumb as he massaged it across her skin, the sound primal, guttural.

"My girl is so pretty," he finally managed between desperate, breathless kisses, punctuating the sentiment with tiny nips of his teeth along her jaw. "So perfect." She shuddered and clung to him harder, hardly able to stay upright on her own. Her legs weren't working anymore, and she'd have melted to the floor by now if he hadn't pinned her back against the wall. "So soft. And you smell—" Theo leaned forward and inhaled deeply at the base of her neck, closing his eyes and relishing whatever he found there. "You smell so fucking *good*, Audrey. So sweet." A kiss, whisper soft against her skin, was followed by another, decidedly less soft. "I could devour you whole, ravish you, thoroughly *debauch* you right here, right now if you'd let m—"

The kitchen lights flicked on, and all the heat drained away from Audrey in one fell swoop.

It happened so suddenly, she felt sick. She stopped breathing.

Because they weren't alone.

All the color immediately evaporated from Theo's face. His whole body began to shake when he was flushed with adrenaline, and he set her down quickly as he spun furiously on his heel and lunged for the kitchen, wild-eyed and intent on finding whatever intruder had dared enter his house and interrupt them.

"Theodore."

The intruder spoke.

He froze in his tracks when they both saw her at the same time, the tiny, well-dressed woman making her way around the counter.

Her dark hair was streaked liberally with gray and twisted into a complicated knot at the back of her head. She wore an expensive-looking, expertly tailored navy pantsuit, and she was so small that her high heels did little to boost her to an average height. It didn't matter, though, because she carried herself like a queen: her back was ramrod straight and she wore an expression as hard and cold as iron. But that expression didn't carry all the way up to her eyes. They were wide and lined with a deep, heart-wrenching sadness.

Audrey had seen those eyes before. She saw them every time she looked into Theo's.

He was staring straight into them now.

"Mom?"

Fourteen

"GET OUT OF *my house.*"

Theo's eyes darkened as he stared down at his mother, all shock leaching away from his body and leaving nothing but rage behind.

"I'm so sorry," his mom said calmly, holding her hands up as if she were trying to soothe a wild animal. "I had no idea you were seeing someone."

"That's because we're not currently *speaking*," he spat through gritted teeth.

"I know." His mom's eyes searched his face and she rolled her lips together the same way her son always did before her gaze landed on Audrey, who'd frozen in the entry where Theo had put her down. She peered around him at Audrey and gave her a weak smile. "Hi, dear. My name's Eleanor. It's nice to meet—"

"*Don't you talk to her*," he snapped. His fists clenched at his sides, and his right hand trembled even more than usual.

His voice trembled just as much.

Eleanor closed her eyes and drew in a deep breath before steeling herself and stepping forward, craning her neck as she looked up at him. When her gaze landed on his scar, her expression softened fully into sadness.

"You look good. *Really* good. So much better than . . ." She swallowed and her hands shook as she picked at the edges of her thumbs. "I know you don't want to talk to me, and I know you want me here even less. I'm not going to stay long. I only came and waited to tell you two things." She held up two fingers. "Just two things, and then I'll be on my way."

"Give me my keys back." Theo held out his left hand. "*Now.*"

Audrey never imagined he could be this angry. Every part of him vibrated with fury, and his color was starting to come back with swaths of bright scarlet sweeping up from his neck and spreading gradually into his cheeks.

His mother lifted a hand, almost as if she wanted to cup his face or sweep his hair away from his brow. But she stopped herself at the last second and let her arm fall.

When she didn't give him the keys he'd demanded, the scarlet crept all the way up to the tips of Theo's ears.

He took a single step forward.

"I told you I didn't want to see you once I was cleared to handle stairs again," he hissed. "I never thought you'd come here unannounced like this. This is bad even for *you*." He thrust his hand out more forcefully this time. "Give them back. And you'd better not have made copies."

"I didn't," Eleanor whispered. She plunged her hand into her pocket. "You weren't answering my calls, you weren't answering my texts, you never responded to the letters I sent—even your lawyer said she wouldn't give you any more messages from me because you'd asked her not to." Her lip quivered as she looked at him, and she bit it to hide it. "And I was afraid if I stayed outside, you'd just turn around and leave once you saw me."

"You're right: I would have. That's what 'no contact' is, *Mom*."

Theo waited.

Eleanor's breath shook as she finally pulled a keychain out of her pocket, the jingling of the metal oddly jarring in the thick tension between them. But then she hesitated.

"I came here to apologize to you."

When she didn't drop the keys into his outstretched hand, Theo grimaced and rubbed his eyes, turning on one heel as he began to pace, limping and strained. He couldn't seem to stay still, and he covered his face completely with both hands while he moved.

His mother looked like she still wanted to touch him. She took one step forward, her hand lifted.

"Teddy—"

"*DON'T CALL ME THAT!*" he roared, spinning to face her again. "*You* of all people don't get to call me that anymore!" His expression twisted in disgust. "That version of your son is dead and buried, his body cold and rotting in the ground with Dad. Your Teddy *died* that day."

He looked like he hated himself as soon as the words escaped his lips. But now that they were freed, it seemed as if he couldn't stop them.

Once the dam had cracked, a flood poured forth.

Theo pointed bitterly up at the scar on his face. "*This* is all that's left of him now," he rasped. "I'm a monster. *A simulacrum*. I'm scraps of broken flesh and sinew and bone barely stitched together into a mass of scars and pain and anguish, a fucking *shadow* of the man and the artist I used to be. And you didn't even have the decency to let me try to heal all the way before you came over here to reopen this *goddamn wound*." He tugged at his split cheek, desperate and resentful, and winced at the feeling of it. "Do you even have any idea how much I hurt? All the time, every fucking day?!"

Eleanor sobbed once, but before she could fully break, Theo stormed back over to her, face red and finger pointed accusingly. He was so tall, he loomed threateningly over her, and he almost had to crouch to press his face close to hers.

With every sentence he uttered, with every breath he took, his voice rose.

"This whole time, this *whole fucking time*, you haven't been respecting my wishes. You still kept trying to get in touch with me, kept trying to talk to me, kept sending your assistant to talk to Imogen, and now you've had the audacity to come here? To my own home?"

"I'm sorry, Theo, I—"

But he cut her off with a scoff and shook his head as he turned away from his mother, the disgust written across his face only deepening. "No. No, you couldn't leave well enough alone, even when I said no more than once because I just wanted some goddamn peace in my life for one *fucking* moment, all right?" He splayed his hands out in front of him. "I just wanted to be left alone, without expectations, without having to deal with all of our family's *shit* and you couldn't even do that! And now, *today of all fucking days*, you dare to interrupt *my* weekend with *my* girlfriend because *you* want to talk." He threw up his hands and ran them through his hair. "IT'S ALWAYS BEEN ABOUT YOU."

A tear streamed down his mother's cheek.

"IT HAS *NEVER* BEEN ABOUT ME!" Theo's face reddened as he yelled.

She made no move to wipe it away.

He kept pacing, his limp growing more and more pronounced as he became even more agitated.

"Do you even get it, Mom? No. No, you've never gotten it, not really." He took another step forward. Eleanor held her ground, but she looked so sick, Audrey thought the woman might throw up. Frankly, she felt nauseous herself.

This was something she wasn't meant to see.

But Theo continued. His control had long since snapped, his eyes clouded and unfocused as he spiraled.

"It's always been about you and your career, it was never about me or mine, or even Dad's! He was *never* good enough for you!"

"Theo, that's not at all what happened," Eleanor finally managed to interject, her voice an odd, trembling timbre cutting through her son's. "That's not at all true."

But he wasn't done yet.

"You certainly didn't love him enough to even *try* to stay," he spat. "He died loving you, *still* loving you even after all those years, after you threw him away like garbage, and I never even saw you shed a tear when he was gone."

"Do you really think I didn't love your father? That I don't *still* love him?" Another tear slid down Eleanor's horrified face when she bit out the words. "Is that what you really think?"

"That's what I think and that's what I remember, yes. You didn't bat an eye at his memorial."

Eleanor swallowed and drew in a deep, shuddering breath. A sob wracked her chest, and tears flowed freely from her eyes now. "Theo." She held her hands out in front of her, pleading. "I never stopped loving your father. If you think I'm not also grieving, you couldn't be more wrong." She lifted a perfectly manicured hand and wiped away her tears, but it did little good. They wouldn't seem to stop coming now. "And I'm sorry for giving you the impression I didn't care. I loved Henry. I loved him *so* much, we just weren't good partners. Our divorce had nothing to do with a lack of love. And it had nothing to do with you."

Theo had frozen in his tracks, tears streaming silently down his own cheeks. He didn't seem to notice them.

His mother took a cautious step toward him. "And it's not your fault, what happened that day. It's mine."

He shook his head and took a step back from her. All the blood had drained from his face again, and it was his turn to look sick. "No. No, that's—"

Eleanor put a hand over her heart and sobbed. "It's mine. It's *my* fault. Everything is. I should have stopped Lloyd. I'm the one who called Henry to come get you. If I hadn't, things would be different."

Theo opened his mouth, but his mother held up a hand to silence him. "I had just lost the love of my life—and I almost lost my son along with him. I didn't have enough tears left to cry for Henry. I already spent them all on you when you were in a coma, thinking you were going to die too and blaming myself for everything that happened. I *never* should have asked those things of you that night. And afterwards, I didn't have the capacity left to feel *anything*, much less make space for the grief we've both been processing over the last few months."

She sniffed and wiped at her face again. "I've made mistakes, Theo. I've made *so* many, and God only knows how many I've made with you, most of all. I want to make it right. I want to know what I can do to make it right."

Theo's chest heaved, and he looked at his mother with such pain, such anguish, his face just as twisted and conflicted as his emotions were. He looked like he wanted to yell, to scream, to cry, to break down right there on the floor of his house, all at once.

Eleanor took a step forward and lifted his massive, trembling right fist in both of hers. He didn't fight her when she touched him this time. She gently pried open his fingers and slid the set of his keys into his hand.

"I understand if you hate me, Theo. I do. I hate *myself*." She inhaled deeply, gathering herself for whatever she was about to say next. "I just wanted to ask you to come home for our family Christmas party. Please." Eleanor lifted her eyes to meet her son's. "You're all I have. And I'd give anything for you to forgive me."

Theo stayed silent.

But his eyes grew wide with horror.

"You want me to come to a party?" he finally whispered. "Looking like *this*?"

Eleanor shook her head sharply, her own eyes widening as she seemed to realize her mistake. "You . . . y-you could wear a mask. You could wear a mask, Theo. It's fine, you don't have to—"

"Then you want me to cover it up?" He'd somehow gone even paler than before, the edges of his lips completely leached of color, his pallor almost green. "You want me to cover it up because of the way I look. That's what it is, isn't it?" he whispered frantically. "I'm an embarrassment. I'm still the family embarrassment, after all these years—after all this time."

"*No.* No, that's not what I—"

"It's all a lie. The lie of a perfect family. That's why you want me there, and that's why you want me to cover my face."

Eleanor's own face fell as she watched her son spiral. Her shoulders slumped. Theo looked wild, like he might throw up, like there could be no reasoning with him now. He was beyond hearing.

"I can't believe you just asked me to do this. There'll be questions. Everyone will stare at me, they'll bring up the video, they're going to look at me with pity, like I'm diseased, like I'm damaged goods. I always have been because of Dad, because of what I do, only now I actually *look* like it, and I—I—"

His mom closed her eyes and shook her head as she curled his fingers back over the keys she'd just given him.

He finally froze at the feeling of her hands on his.

"Theodore," she finally said, her voice calm and even. "If you come, I would want you to do what you think is most comfortable." She gripped his hand tightly in both of hers. "You're my son. My genius, handsome, *incredible* son, scar or no scar. And I love you, no matter what." When she lifted his injured hand to her mouth and pressed a kiss to it, another tear dropped from her lashes onto his skin. "I'm sorry. And I love you."

Eleanor let him go, and, with a final swipe of her hands across her cheeks, she dried her tears and turned away from Theo. He stood there, frozen in one spot, swaying on his feet as if it was all he could do to hold himself upright while his mother grabbed her purse from the counter and strode toward the front door, the sound of her stilettos clacking staccato against the ceramic woodgrain tile.

When Eleanor crossed in front of Audrey, she paused and put a hand on her shoulder.

"You're welcome to come too, sweetie. Anyone Theo cares enough about to have in his home is welcome." Her eyes darted over toward her son. He hadn't turned to watch her leave. He stood stock-still with his back to his mother, staring blankly out the window overlooking the view of the East River.

Eleanor turned her attention back to Audrey. "I really would love for you both to come spend Christmas at our family home in Albany. I understand if you have other plans, but I—" Tears lined Eleanor's eyes again, and she tried desperately to blink them away. "The holiday season was already going to be so hard for us this year without his father. It was always going to be bad without Henry. I don't want to make things worse, but I would like to ask that you please consider it."

With one last squeeze on Audrey's shoulder, Eleanor made her way to the front door.

And left them alone.

WHEN THE DOOR clicked shut and automatically locked with a beep, silence descended around them both like the blade of a guillotine.

The last rays of the sun broke through the city skyline in the distance, refracting off of millions of windows and glittering across the water, casting everything around them in a soft, golden glow.

Theo hadn't moved from where he stood in the middle of the floor, trapped between his kitchen and his living room.

He was staring at his father's neon shop sign.

"Theo?" Audrey whispered, finally taking a step toward him. A tear dropped from one of her eyelashes and she lifted a hand to find her whole face was wet.

When did she start crying?

She didn't know.

At the sound of her voice, Theo straightened and slowly turned to face her.

Horror.

Horror was written in his eyes.

He heaved and dropped the keys his mother had left him as he clamped a hand to his mouth. They hit the floor with a clatter and skidded across the tile.

Theo followed.

His legs finally gave out, and he fell heavily to his knees. He only just managed to stop himself from completely collapsing by bracing his left hand against the hard floors.

"THEO!" Audrey rushed over to him and threw herself onto her own knees, brushing his hair away from his face. Tears still streamed from his eyes as he trembled, and he took deep, gasping breaths while he lowered his head and tried not to vomit.

"Please don't leave me," he finally choked out. "*Please don't.*"

"Oh god, no. No. I'm not going anywhere," she murmured, wrapping her arms around his head and pulling him into her chest. "There's no way I'm leaving you." He clung to her while he shivered and buried his face in her sweater, still gulping for air, as though what had just happened suffocated him.

She held him on the floor until he calmed enough to pull away.

The sky outside was gray and darkening by the second, and Theo still looked like he was about to be sick.

"I-I just need a—a minute. Give me a minute," he mumbled, pushing himself to his feet. Audrey rose with him, helping him steady himself until he was able to stumble over to the staircase. "Let me clean myself up. I'll—I'll b-be . . . I'll be right back."

He gripped the banister so hard, his knuckles turned white as he mounted the stairs, his eyes glassy and unfocused.

What she'd just seen with his mother had been so raw, so anguished, it had left her feeling empty inside.

She could only imagine what he was feeling right now. She made her way to the couch and curled up in the corner, drawing her knees to her chest and trying not to cry.

When thirty minutes ticked by and Theo still hadn't come back down, she got even more nervous.

Audrey slung her bag over her shoulder and made her way upstairs. He was in no shape to be left alone for too long, and she was starting to feel a little afraid of what he might do. Fear prickled at the back of her neck at the eerie, empty silence of his house in the aftermath of the argument, and when there was no sign of him on the second floor, she wandered up to the master suite on the third.

As soon as she mounted the landing, she heard the hiss of the shower coming from his bathroom. Light spilled beneath the door, and she pursed her lips while she entered the bedroom.

All right. One mystery partially solved. Some of the unease in her stomach ebbed, but it didn't completely disappear. Perhaps she could settle in while she waited—he certainly hadn't wanted her to leave, and she'd promised him she wouldn't.

But as soon as she saw his bedroom, she stopped in her tracks.

Theo had made some changes.

It wasn't just that Roo sat waiting for her on her nightstand, looking almost comically out of place against the sleek, modern, monochrome design aesthetic of grown-up Theo. It was also that two small black cylindrical machines sat plugged in on both nightstands, standing guard on either side of the bed. Across from them on one of the bookshelves was a new black essential oil diffuser, pumping a steady stream of lavender-scented mist into the air, and on another shelf glowed a beautiful salt lamp. Soft, soothing light in striped tones of amber and orange, pink and gold filtered out from the bulb inside, spilling across the floor and gently illuminating the room in the dark of freshly fallen evening. It was on a dimmer switch, cranked up to maximum brightness.

When she turned on a bedside lamp and clicked the button on one of the new black machines, a steady, droning white noise poured forth—and she clamped a hand to her mouth, suddenly fighting back tears.

She'd told Theo she was afraid of the dark.

She'd told him she had trouble sleeping.

And he'd gone and given her light and sound and scent to help.

He'd tried so hard to make her feel comfortable here, in his room, his house, his home.

He'd made those changes, rearranged his life for *her.*

She let the bag fall to the ground and hurried over to the bathroom door, knocking softly once. "Theo?" she called.

No answer.

She knocked again, more urgently this time.

"Theo?"

When he still didn't answer, panic took over. He'd never not responded to her before.

Audrey opened the door.

Steam poured out in swirling waves, and his outline was silhouetted behind the frosted glass of his massive, luxurious shower. He was seated in some sort of chair, his face buried in his hands, right leg extended stiffly out in front of him.

He was upright but hunched over.

He wasn't moving.

"*Theo!*"

He didn't respond. Audrey eyed the pile of his clothes on the floor and kicked off her boots.

"I'm coming in."

She tore her clothes off before yanking the shower door open. When the steam rushed out at the sudden break in the seal, she could finally see him clearly.

And her stomach dropped.

She'd seen him before, of course, and plenty of times. She had the curves of his face memorized so well by now, she could envision them behind her eyes when she closed them at night, could trace them with her fingers if she suddenly went blind, could draw every multicolored mahogany and amber and light, spring green swirl in his irises from memory.

But she'd never seen Theo fully naked before. And somehow, witnessing all that expanse of his bare form, all that length of *him*, he looked even larger than he usually did. His skin was raw and red, and water streamed down the sides of his face, flowing along his body and across the constellation of moles she loved so much speckling the sides of his torso, intermingling with the plethora of scars and tiny freckles contrasting against his normally alabaster-pale skin. She traced them with her gaze, following them down to the last remaining unexplored part of him she hadn't yet seen.

Her eye snagged on his right hip.

The damage there was extensive.

Far worse than she could have ever imagined.

More deep, puckered scars plunged into his flesh, twisting where they'd had to rebuild his shattered hip after his accident—the hip that caused his limp now, the source of the pain he surely never used to suffer when he was an elite college athlete. The deep scars were thick and wide, angry and red, and even more devastating than what was on his face. That one paled in comparison.

But that wasn't what broke her heart.

It was the way he sat hunched in the chair, his face covered with trembling hands, shoulders shaking as he tried to make himself smaller.

This wasn't the Theo she knew. *Her* Theo.

It was the broken man who'd first walked into her café that one summer morning.

Not the one who'd brought her home and held her while she cried in the dark, sweeping her tears away with his thumbs and banishing new ones with gentle kisses brushed against her eyes. Not the one who loved old movies, who made her coffee, who danced with her in his living room, whose crooked smile and curving dimples she adored coaxing out from the depths of his cheeks with a laugh.

No, that man didn't sit in front of her.

Now it was the one she'd met months ago—the one who could barely string enough words together to ask for a plain black coffee out in public. The one who shied away from cameras, who flinched away from glances, who couldn't look her in the eye. The one who hid himself behind layers of clothing and masks and silence.

Everything Audrey had been worried about up until that moment disappeared in an instant. She'd been so nervous about what staying with Theo this weekend meant, what they might do, what all that might be like, that she'd almost forgotten the most important things:

That it was *Theo* she wanted to be with.

That what happened just now had seemed to shatter every bit of confidence he'd built up over the last several weeks and months.

That in any case, despite his newfound or rediscovered self-assurance, he'd probably been worried about the same things she was.

That he was certainly just as anxious.

Just as nervous.

Just as human.

That he was still grieving.

Still in pain.

Still broken, despite trying so hard to put himself back together again.

And suddenly, absolutely nothing mattered anymore.

Nothing but one thing.

"Theo."

Audrey took a step into the shower and closed the door after her. But as soon as she leaned under the stream of water, she drew back, sucking a hiss through her teeth. It was so hot it had nearly scalded her, which explained why Theo's skin was so raw and red, battered by the unrelenting high-pressure jets streaming from both shower heads. She turned the temperature down to a more tolerable level and stepped up to him, dipping her head beneath the water and bending to try to get a look at his face. She took one of his hands in hers and peeled it away.

When he finally looked at her, his eyes were red and swollen, his chest heaving with tired, labored breaths. He pressed his lips together, rolling them while he tried to get them to stop quivering, but he gave up as soon as his gaze met hers. A single tear slipped out of his scarred right eye and drowned in the water from the shower soaking them both.

"My mom's wrong, Audrey. It *is* my fault," he croaked before swallowing thickly and closing his eyes again, his voice ragged and hoarse. His right hand sought hers out, but it was trembling too hard to catch her fingers. "It's my fault my dad died." He clutched at his heart with his left hand. "It's *my* fault."

"Oh, Theo, no. No." She shook her head. "It was an accident—you've told me that much. If that's true, it can't be your fault. An accident's no one's fault."

His face broke.

And when he sobbed again, Audrey couldn't take it anymore.

She needed to hold him.

If the large medical shower chair he was sitting in could take his weight, it could take hers too. She lifted one leg and slid it around his waist, slipping it through the wide gap between the back of the chair and the seat before following it with the other, using the armrests to balance. When she settled carefully into his lap, she wrapped her arms around his neck and tucked his head under her chin, pulling him close and holding him tight.

Nothing separated them now.

He melted into her.

Theo encircled her in his arms and buried his face in the crook of her neck, his shoulders shaking while he cried. His tears mixed with the water coursing down her bare skin, and it was all Audrey could do to hold him steady, gently combing through his hair with her nails and pressing her lips softly to the top of his head.

She wasn't entirely sure what exactly had possessed her to wrap herself around him like she did. But her instincts told her that he needed to have her skin against his, that he needed to know she understood how raw and vulnerable he was—and how sacred his trust in her was now that he'd finally shown her this part of himself. A part he'd tried so hard not to.

Audrey had never been so close with someone before; she'd never allowed herself to be. It was so much easier to keep people at arm's length, to hold others at bay. If you didn't let them in, they couldn't hurt you. If they held a knife, they couldn't cut deep. Even her past experiences had only been shallow slices of the blade, surface wounds that healed quickly or only left the lightest of scars that rapidly faded to white, mere memories of transitory trauma.

She'd been stabbed once before, and it had been a near-fatal wound to her heart.

She'd learned an important lesson that day, and she'd learned it young. Far *too* young.

If you kept that distance, you could keep yourself intact, whole, safe. You could survive. It was the one lesson she'd learned clearly over the years:

If you didn't let anyone in, they couldn't throw you away.

But Theo was different.

As his trembling hands drew her closer to him, one of them wide enough to span the entire width between her shoulder blades, Audrey knew. She knew with absolute certainty that she'd let him keep burying himself into her so deep, he'd burrow straight into her heart. He'd already found his way there long ago, right where she'd once been wounded so gravely.

Her scar ran as deep as the one on his face, only hers was in her soul.

Theo understood that.

She wanted to feel him against her, inside her, all of him, forever and always, and all the hairs on her neck stood on end when he tilted his head up and pressed his lips softly to hers. His eyes were closed, but his mouth had sought hers automatically, that desperate need for connection innate and instinctive. It was as natural, as easy, as a reflex.

It was as though they'd been crafted for each other, made specifically to slot into the places where there were cracks, each one's pieces fitting precisely into the grooves of the breaks.

She could feel it now, knew it now, clearly and fully.

When he breathed in, so did she.

When her heart beat, so did his.

Something changed between them beneath the hot water as she held Theo and kept him safe and sound in her arms, safe and sound in her heart, all of him finally bared to all of her. There were no more walls, no more barriers, no more secrets. Neither of them could hide anymore.

Everything deepened in that moment.

When Theo finally calmed enough to unbury his face from her neck, pulling back and looking her in the eyes, he drew in a deep breath and searched her face, tiny droplets tumbling gently from his long lashes onto her cheeks. He cradled her face in his hands, softly smoothing her soaked hair behind her ears. He didn't say anything—he only looked at her. And the longer he stared into her eyes, the more she felt it:

The moment their souls entwined.

Or perhaps they'd always been that way, and now was only the moment of knowing. She'd been drawn to him the second he walked through the door of the coffeehouse, almost as though he was so large, his gravity couldn't help but pull her into his orbit.

Or perhaps it was simply that their atoms had always been enmeshed, entangled at the quantum level, drawn inexorably closer until they'd crashed together to form something new, something stronger, their electrons dancing near enough and fast enough to create an unbreakable covalent bond.

It had always been magnetic.

She could feel his heart beat through his chest, thundering in time with her own, their electrostatic pulses synced.

He lit her up like one of his sculptures.

Like one of his stars.

And that light was reflected back in his eyes now when he finally found what he'd been searching for in her own.

"I love you."

When he uttered the words, her heart nearly stopped.

It was the surest thing he'd ever said to her.

Theo's right hand cupped her cheek, its tremor nearly perfectly stilled against her skin. "I love you, Audrey," he said again, his voice stronger, deeper, rumbling in his throat with conviction. "I've made a lot of mistakes. I've said terrible things, and I've left other things unsaid, and I regret it. I regret all of it. But I don't ever want to regret anything with you.

"I could die at any second. I almost did once, and for all I know, I could have an aneurysm right now. And if I went to my grave without telling you how I feel, I'd be tormented with regret and despair for eternity in whatever awaits us when we're gone."

He rolled his jaw, pressing his lips together, and his eyes softened as he looked at her. His brows were still furrowed slightly, as if he couldn't help but be concerned about what he was saying right now, but couldn't stop himself regardless.

"The last thing I ever said to my dad was awful—and then I had to watch him die, maybe even *because* of it. I've been blaming myself for it ever since. I can't even begin to convey to you how much pain I've felt—how much I *still* feel, in my body, my heart, my mind. My soul maybe, if there is such a thing." He shook his head. "I was thinking of ending it before we met, just to make the ache go away. Everywhere, every*thing*, every part of me hurt so much, I didn't think I'd ever feel anything but that pain. And part of me thought I deserved it. There's still a darker part of me that thinks that.

"But you? You've been such a light in that darkness for me. You reminded me that life can be good. That it can be sweet. That I *can* still smile." The corners of his lips tilted up at her now, hopeful and soft. "Knowing you now makes me proud that I kept going—that I'm still here, that I'm still trying. You make me want to get better. I'm not even sure I deserve you, but you make me want to *be* better, because you do deserve someone whole. And I want that someone to be me." His fingers curled around her waist and around the back of her neck. "I'm not whole right now, but I want to be."

She was glad he was holding her steady.

She needed him to.

"None of this is how I thought tonight would go, sweetheart, and I'm sorry you had to see it. I'm *so* sorry. It's not what I had planned.

And I wasn't going to tell you all this. Not today." He closed his eyes and sighed, his chin falling to his chest in sudden resignation. "You don't have to say anything back. I know it might be too soon, but you might as well know how I feel. I owe you that much, especially since I already know it. And I don't want to regret not saying it, even if you don't feel the same way. I'd never forgive myself if I didn't. Not now. Not after everything."

Theo drew in a deep breath. And when he let it out, it shook, but this time in relief—as though a massive weight had been lifted from his broad chest.

They sat there together, the only sound the hissing water of the shower drumming down around them, the weight of his words still echoing against the tile.

Then he blinked.

His eyes widened.

Theo looked around at where they were, and he finally seemed to realize the particulars of their predicament. It was almost as though he'd been so out of his mind, so outside of reality, he'd forgotten.

"*Oh shit*," he breathed, panic immediately crashing across his face. "*Oh*." His gaze dropped down to her breasts, and then to the chair they sat in together. "Audrey, you—you're . . . you're so beautiful, and I—*oh god*. Uh, Audrey, I, uh . . ." His breathing quickened again. The panic was hitting in full force now. "Oh fuck. Oh *FUCK ME*. I just confessed that I love you *in my goddamn shower chair*, oh *no*, you have got to be kidding me."

"Theo . . ."

"You're naked. You're naked, and *I'm* naked, and *you're so fucking beautiful*—and I'm in my shower chair—*and I hate this fucking thing* but I was shaking too bad and my legs felt weak and I didn't want to slip and die in here today but I didn't know what else I could do and I had to wash off the words I said so I tried to burn them away with the hot water and how long have I been in here? But now you're here too and I just told you I love you, and—" Somehow, he managed to pale under the warm water of the shower. "And you saw my fight with my mother, OH GOD."

"Theo—"

"YOU SAW AND HEARD THE WHOLE THING AND THEN I TOLD YOU I LOVE YOU." He ripped his hands away from her and covered his face with them again, throwing his head back under the water. "It's too soon, isn't it?!" he groaned through his fingers. "This is my worst nightmare. *I've ruined everything. I—*"

"THEO."

Audrey grabbed his wrists and yanked them away from his face, dropping them so she could dig her nails under his jaw. "Breathe."

As soon as he felt the tiny pinpricks of pain, he snapped his gaze down to meet hers—and slowly drew in a deep breath.

"Whoever said this would be too soon?" Her voice was even when she asked the question.

"What?" He blinked and frowned at her in confusion.

"Who made that rule?"

"What rule?"

"The one dictating when you can tell me that you love me."

"I . . . don't know?"

"Was it a committee decision?" She bit her lip to stop herself from grinning. "Is there a governing body I don't know about? Some sort of love council? An academy, maybe?"

He blinked at her again, flinching as the water ran into his eyes, apparently mystified by her sudden line of questioning. "It just seems that everyone thinks you shouldn't say it . . . early."

"And who is everyone?"

"I-I don't know."

"And who said this is 'early'?"

"I don't know."

"Well, that's stupid." Audrey pulled his face closer to hers as she echoed his own words from weeks ago back to him. "Especially because I love you too, Theo."

It ached when the words left her lips. Not from the heaviness of them.

From relief.

She'd been carrying them around in her heart for so long now, the hole they left behind from her unburdening was a vacuum that sucked all the air out from her lungs. Until it was replaced with a new, blossoming warmth from the molten look in Theo's widening eyes.

Now it was *his* turn to stop breathing.

"You love me too?" he whispered into her hair.

"Yes. Yes, I do."

He held his breath as she grabbed his face with her hands and dragged his mouth to hers, hungry and desperate now that their truths had been revealed. He clutched frantically at her slick skin, slipping and scrabbling while he tried to cling to her, pulling her as close as he could, almost as though he wanted to press her directly into his heart itself.

"Am I—am I dreaming right now?" He sounded like he could hardly breathe. "Is this real?"

"You're not dreaming. It's real." She beamed at him, unable to contain the feeling. "I love you too."

That was it.

That was what did it.

For all that he'd been still and unmoving earlier, Theo made up for it now. He was a man unleashed, pushed to his breaking, undone and unbridled, and Audrey gave herself over to him, his hands, his lips, his teeth, his tongue. She shivered while he nipped at her neck, her jaw, her lips, cried out when he dipped his head and suddenly drew her nipple into his wide mouth.

When he sucked, she moaned and arched into him at the sensation, gasping in surprise and clawing at his back when a bolt of lightning shot straight down to her core.

Her breasts had never been anything remarkable. Small enough to where she didn't always even need a bra, and most men had never given them a second look.

Theo was treating them as if they were something to worship.

He devoted himself to his task, sucking and licking, laving his tongue against her skin and around her nipples, alternating reverently between the two. They'd pebbled as soon as his lips had touched them, the hard, pink nubs incredibly sensitive in his warm mouth. She moaned once more and felt his smile stretch against her skin.

His mouth was so wide, he'd been able to fit nearly her entire breast inside.

The ache in her chest their words had left behind shifted downward between her legs, and Audrey bucked against Theo in his lap, her hips moving of their own accord. He broke away with a grunt, shuddering forward at the sensation.

It was impossible not to feel how hard he was.

"Sweetheart," he gasped, his chest heaving as his gaze met her own, his eyes dark and pupils blown wide. He looked like he was barely hanging on by a thread. "Sweetheart, I can't hold out any longer."

"I want you, Theo," she breathed. "I need you." Her lids were heavy and her face was scorching, and not at all from the water. "Please. I'm ready. Can we please—"

"Okay. Yeah, I'm done here. Hold on tight." He wrapped an arm around her and pushed up heavily from the chair, swaying slightly under her added weight while he got his feet beneath him with her legs still wrapped around his waist. He shut the shower off and the water ground to a sudden halt, leaving them with nothing but the heavy steam curling against their burning skin.

The urgency was palpable.

"I can walk if you—"

"Don't even finish that thought," Theo growled. "I'd rather die than put you down now—and I mean it. I know what dying feels like. Don't ask that of me again."

She didn't.

Fifteen

THE TOWEL THEO grabbed was almost an afterthought as he rushed out of the bathroom and limped straight over to his perfectly made bed, sending pillows flying through the air and sliding across the floors after he ripped the covers back with one long arm. He left a dripping trail of footprints in his hurry to get them there, an urgency she'd never seen before lighting up his face.

"This isn't what I had planned, Miss Adams," he muttered in her ear while he wrapped her in the towel, dropping her onto the bed before lunging for his nightstand and tearing the drawer open with a trembling hand. "You're making me skip *several* steps."

"Oh yeah? What was originally on the agenda for us tonight, Mr. Sullivan?" She clasped the towel around her neck with an impish grin. He was always so particular.

Theo turned to face her, a white condom packet gleaming between his fingers in the lamplight. Water still tumbled down the sides of his face, sending his dark waves curling deliciously around his jawline, and the way he looked at her so intensely, so darkly, sent flames licking down her spine.

He ripped the packet open with his teeth.

"First, I was going to make us dinner. Pesto gnocchi with homemade focaccia, wine, and a salad—fresh heirloom tomatoes with buffalo mozzarella, basil from my garden, and a balsamic drizzle, topped with flaky sea salt." Theo stepped forward to close the gap between them and placed one wide hand on her waist, pulling her into the center of the bed on top of the towel. He crawled after her, settling over her and dipping down to kiss her, peppering her neck with his lips over and over again.

"That sounds incredible." Something about what he just said nagged at her, even as distracting as his mouth was right now. "Wait. You have a garden?" she asked between breaths. "Where?"

Theo nodded with a hum, twining her hair between his fingers. "The roof. Haven't gotten to show you yet. The weather was too shitty."

"And you were going to make me gnocchi? *Potato* pasta? My two favorite things combined?"

He nodded again, smirking in satisfaction. Then his eyes dropped and his smirk slowly faded. "My god," he whispered, his dark eyes staring reverently at her skin. "Look at that. You've got a galaxy speckled across your shoulders. *Gorgeous.*"

That was right. He'd never seen her freckles before—they'd always been covered. When he leaned down and pressed his lips to one of them, closing his eyes and running his nose softly along all the tiny russet spots she'd so long despised, Audrey felt her cheeks burn anew. She'd never really liked them. Kids used to make fun of her for them in school, calling her a dirty little orphan, permanently flecked with mud.

It didn't help that her foster mom at the time didn't wash her clothes very often.

"I would spend a lifetime trying to count, catalog, and kiss all of your stars." When he did exactly that with another, and another, and another, tracing them all with his fingers and tapping pointedly as he pretended to number them, the corners of Audrey's lips tugged upward despite herself.

Trust an artist to appreciate the paint the universe had splattered her with.

But still something itched at the back of her mind. "You've made me pasta before, haven't you?"

Theo waggled his eyebrows at her, his smug look back in full force. "Maybe."

She sighed and shook her head. She should have guessed. "You've never brought me *anything* from a restaurant, have you?"

His smugness only grew, and he dipped down to nip at her lips again, drawing the bottom one between his teeth. "Maybe I really like cooking, since I like working with my hands. Maybe I got into dough-based foods as part of my PT, since kneading works all my hand muscles so thoroughly. And maybe I quite liked it, and got quite good at it."

"You cheeky bastard."

He cooked.

She'd won the lottery.

He snorted. "That's not all I had prepped. I also made dessert—a surprise—and I had something else planned while we waited for things to cook. An activity for us to do together." He trailed his fingers down her neck and tilted her head to the side so he could press his lips just beneath her jaw. When he grazed his teeth across her skin, she shivered.

"Oh yeah?" Her voice shook as she spoke. It was all she could do to stay coherent for whatever game they were playing now. "What activity?"

"I was going to eat you out on top of my quartz counters."

He—what?

Audrey's mouth went dry.

"You were going to be *my* appetizer," he growled. Theo dipped lower, nuzzling along the swell of her breasts while he mouthed at her nipples again. "Tiny thing that you are—a delicious. Little.

Snack." He punctuated each word with a deliberate suck, smacking his lips with apparent relish.

Oh god.

When his calloused hands grazed across her ribs, she jolted and arched beneath his weight at the sensation. He was steadily making his way lower, sweeping his lips across her stomach, teasing her and tickling her softly with his fingers and his mouth as he went.

"I was going to lift you up, rip those fucking jeans off, and spread your pretty little legs wide for me," he breathed, his breath swirling warm atop her stomach, scalding her far more than the water of his shower had. "Taste you with the tip of my tongue"—he licked it across her skin in a demonstration, dragging it lightly along her hip while his fingers dug into her thighs—"listen to you gasp and scream, watch you writhe, make you beg until my mouth made you see stars."

He pressed a kiss to the top of her mound where her hair curled dark before leaning down and slowly parting her legs with his wide palms, watching with rapt attention while he gradually revealed her sex for a closer inspection. "I've been dying to explore you, you see. I'm really quite the intrepid adventurer." He looked back up at her and raised one dark eyebrow, his expression positively wicked. "I'm curious about what sounds you'll make for me this time. And I want to see for myself if you taste every bit as sweet as I suspect you do."

Audrey could hardly breathe as he tugged her legs over his shoulders, tilting her hips up slightly and sliding a pillow underneath. She'd never done this before, no one had ever been down there like this before, her heart was pounding in her ears, her cheeks were hot, she couldn't *breathe*, and then—

And then Theo lowered his face between her legs.

The second his mouth made contact with her clit, Audrey gasped and threw her head back.

Lightning coursed through her entire body.

Electricity danced beneath her skin.

Theo didn't look up. Instead, his lips continued their ministrations as he mouthed at her slit, languidly kissing her everywhere he pleased, taking his time while he tasted her the way he'd promised he would. But when she flailed on the bed, his left hand shot up to grab one of hers, and he gradually lowered it to his damp hair.

"Hold on tight, sweetheart," he murmured against her inner thigh, pressing her fingers to his scalp while he pressed another kiss to her skin. "Pull *hard*. I like it."

She buried her hands into his thick waves and held on, exactly as he said. And when she jolted and yanked as he grazed a particularly sensitive spot with his lips, he moaned before digging his hands forcefully into her ass, pulling her all the way up to his mouth and slipping his tongue inside.

Audrey closed her eyes and gave herself over to the building sensation as Theo devoured her with the enthusiasm of a man starved and rabid, hungry and desperate. The urge to move was overwhelming, and he helped her when he seemed to sense it by rocking her hips across his face with his hands as he worked, his large nose grazing against her clit and driving her mad with every tilt forward and up. It took them a moment, but together they found their rhythm.

The more Audrey moved, the more she burned.

The more she ached.

It was *agony*.

It started in her fingertips and toes, the simmering heat curling in her limbs before shifting to pool in the pit of her stomach, bubbling and burning and widening and spreading, molten and hot, at once both liquid and fire. Theo sucked again, swirling his tongue around that elusive bundle of nerves before dipping it inside her once more and chasing it with a finger. She was unbelievably wet, and as soon as she had something to clench around, her body seized.

She moaned, the sound originating from deep inside.

The ache was unbearable.

It wasn't enough.

She needed more.

"Theo!" she cried with another gasping, ragged breath. "Theo, please. I-I can't—I need—"

"Not yet," he muttered, looking up at her as he gulped hungrily for air, his eyes just as dark and liquid as the heat pooling inside her, threatening to incinerate her from the inside out. "I need you to come at least once, Audrey. Can you be good and do that for me?" She didn't even have the wherewithal to nod before he licked her wetness from his lips and dove between her legs again.

When he slipped a second finger inside while he sucked her once more, stretching her slowly and deliciously, carefully and with delight as he pumped and curled his hand in and out, she began to break.

With one final, hard tug on his hair, her hands fell from his head and she wound her fingers into his pristine white sheets, twisting and crying out for better leverage while her back arched. Her vision began to fizzle at the edges, grayed and spotty, like snow on an old television screen. Her senses contracted, all sound and sight fading down to a single point:

Theo's gaze, his pupils blown black and wide, the brows framing them heavy and dark while he watched her writhe from between her legs.

When she caught sight of his eyes, they crinkled.

He sped up his cadence. Her pleasure crested.

And Audrey shattered.

Theo's face melded into the twisting background of his room, the lights of New York in the distance refracting off the colors, the reds, blacks, whites, grays, golds, all of them blurring and breaking, crashing into one another and exploding behind her eyes like swirling galaxies colliding in an inexorable cosmic dance, all while her hips bucked. She lost all awareness of her motions save for rolling, rippling, repeating waves of pleasure washing over her again and again, her throat burning as she gasped.

She was blind, suffocating, seizing and thrashing, dead and dying and reborn and living, over and over and over again, cycle after cycle, wave after wave.

It was agony.

It was *bliss*.

But just when she thought she was completely spent, something tingled along her skin, rough and comforting. Audrey opened her eyes and looked into Theo's, soft and warm as he drew himself up next to her. He'd been running his hands soothingly over her body, his calluses dragging goose bumps out from their hiding places and into the light.

"Do you still want more?" he asked quietly, his eyes searching her face.

For all his confidence with his hands and his mouth, he seemed a little unsure now.

But she could feel how hard he was, even through her exhaustion. She lifted a hand and caressed his cheek.

"I want *you*. Please."

"I don't want to hurt you."

She glanced down. He was every bit as big as she thought he'd be—even bigger now than he'd been earlier in the shower, perhaps, wide and erect and beautiful, but daunting in the lamplight—and she swallowed nervously. But when she gazed back up into his eyes, there was no question.

She wanted every part of him.

All of him.

Forever and always.

Audrey cradled his face and ran her thumb along his cheekbone. "You won't. I know you won't."

He leaned forward and pressed his forehead to hers, bracing her neck with one hand while the other dropped between his legs. He carefully rolled the condom over his length before slipping his left arm under her neck and propping them both up on their sides, drawing her close and parting her legs with one of his thighs. They were so thick and wide, even just having one tangled between her legs spread her plenty.

"Like this?" she asked in confusion, though she was glad he was the one positioning her. Her body still felt like Jell-O. "I thought you'd be on top?"

"I did some . . . research," Theo murmured, lowering his hand onto her back and tucking her into his chest. "A lot of it, all about how to do this as gently as possible for you. Your first time shouldn't have to hurt, and I'm going to try my best not to let it. From what I found, beginning in this side position seemed the most gentle."

"Of course you researched this, you nerd." She finally had enough air back in her lungs to speak properly and chase it with a laugh, though her voice sounded oddly tattered to her own ears. But she still tried to bite back a smirk all the same. "Is that why you started where you did?"

It was his turn to chew on his bottom lip, but even that couldn't hide his growing wicked grin. "I would have done that regardless. It's my favorite thing—and you taste *incredible*, by the way." He pressed his lips to hers, plush and red and swollen from his devotion. When his tongue slipped into her mouth, she tasted for herself: sweet, with an interesting tang she hadn't been expecting. He pulled away with a crooked smile. "I could feast on you forever. But it turns out that it *does* help to start with an orgasm or two to loosen you up for . . . *me*." His smile faded and his expression grew serious. "You tell me if anything hurts or if you want me to stop, and I will. I'll stop, okay?" There was no room for argument in the look he gave her. "You promise to tell me?"

"Yes. I promise." Audrey nodded. "I trust you."

Theo pulled her even closer, and she wrapped her arms around his neck. His eyes never left her own, even when his trembling hand circled gently at her clit before grazing her entrance.

"I love you." He whispered the words before he kissed her, long and deep, slowing it down and letting their lips meld and fall in sync. Audrey relaxed into his warm embrace, melting into the heat of his skin surrounding her. He ran so hot normally, but now? Now he was an inferno, the heat practically rolling off of him in waves. She was so preoccupied with the feeling of being completely wrapped in Theo's strong arms in a way she never had been before that she almost didn't feel the tip of him notch at her entrance.

When he started to ease himself slowly inside, she gasped.

He'd been careful to stretch her with his fingers for a reason, but even two of them couldn't compare to the girth of the real thing. It didn't hurt, exactly, but it did pinch. She was still too tight to accommodate him fully, and Audrey closed her eyes and clutched at him, digging her nails into his back with a whimper.

He paused, barely an inch inside.

"Relax for me, sweetheart," he murmured, stroking her hair gently. His voice was strained.

"Can you talk to me?" she breathed. "I'm still nervous. It might help."

"Talk about what?" He raised an eyebrow. "What . . . kind of talk?"

"Anything." Audrey drew in a deep breath and tried to relax, unclenching her tense leg muscles. He was barely inside and she didn't want to stop now, not when she was so close to having him completely. "Literally anything. But not dirty talk. I don't think that'll help me right now. I'm not used to it."

"All right. I can try." He seemed unsure. "At least for a minute. No promises on sustained coherence, though." Theo rubbed circles along her back, doing his best to soothe her while he looked her in the eyes. His were liquid amber and melted chocolate in the soft lamplight of his room. After a moment, he finally seemed to settle on something. "Okay. How about another confession?"

"Another one?"

He nodded. "Yep. I nearly had a panic attack when I first met you."

"Well, that was obvious." She twisted her fingers in his damp, curling hair, enjoying its silky feel.

The corner of Theo's mouth twitched. "No. It wasn't for the reasons I initially told you. It might have been the only time I've ever lied to you—not exactly, but I didn't tell you the whole truth."

This was good, talking like this. This was familiar. She relaxed, and he pushed a little deeper into her. He swallowed a grunt and blinked a little too long, but kept talking.

"I told you I was having trouble coming out in public again after my accident, and that was true. That *was* why I was going out to coffee shops. But the way I acted when I saw you?" He shook his head as if to clear it and thrust a little more, closing his eyes with a strained, strangled noise in his throat. "I panicked because . . . because when you smiled at me as I stepped up to the register, I knew you were the most beautiful thing I'd ever seen. And I immediately forgot every word I'd ever known related to coffee. Or otherwise."

He slid even deeper and moaned. Not quite sheathed, but when she breathed in and relaxed, he began to rock his hips, pulling in and out ever so slightly, teasing her, testing her tolerance.

She nodded at him, and he kept going, his voice even more strained than it had been before.

"I'm . . . glad you didn't see my house at that point. It was a mess. *I* was a mess," he ground out between slow, gentle thrusts, dragging his cock along her entrance and pressing in slightly deeper each time, stretching her and gradually filling her more and more. "I hadn't drawn in months, not since I—n-not since before I was in the hospital, but—" He drew in a shaking, gasping breath. "I couldn't get you out of my head, and it got worse every time I went back to the café. I couldn't stop seeing your face behind my eyes. Every time I blinked, every time I tried to sleep, it was *you* I saw. It was your face I dreamed of."

Breathing was difficult. She started to pant. But with every roll of his hips, she matched him, pressing in closer and drawing him in deeper.

"I felt terrible about it. I thought—*ohhh*, you feel so . . . so *good*, Audrey—I was going crazy. I felt like some creep. Sketches of you were littered everywhere in my house, shakily drawn and horribly composed. I tore them out of my sketchbook and threw them everywhere." His biceps seized around her, and it was a wonder he could still talk, his voice was so clipped and strained. "They weren't you, they were awful, but I-I was . . . uh . . . *shit* . . . I was d-drawing again for the first time when I—*ohhh god, Audrey*," Theo groaned, closing his eyes and throwing his head back. "*God.*"

She moaned, loud and long.

"FUCK."

With one last push and more than a slight pinch, he'd seated himself all the way inside her—sheathed to the hilt and buried deep, finally and fully.

Audrey had watched porn before. She'd even Googled plenty about what sex felt like, watched plenty of films, read plenty of romance novels, listened with rapt attention whenever Violet came back to their apartment with stories of her latest conquests and escapades. She'd never been shy to ask questions, not since Violet knew about her inexperience, and her best friend was more than happy to describe the feelings and sensations and recount everything in great detail.

Songs, art, books, movies, porn, Violet—none of them had prepared her for the truth.

Theo looked back at her, his eyes wide and his chest heaving.

Nothing and no one had warned her.

No one had told Audrey it would feel like coming home.

A single tear escaped from her eye and rolled down her cheek. Theo's face immediately fell, but Audrey smiled and held him tighter, digging one hand into his hair and the other into the strong muscles of his broad back. She wrapped a leg around his waist and rolled to the side and onto her back, letting him roll with her and settle his weight fully on top of her.

But her movement only seemed to alarm him further. "Did I hurt you?" he whispered frantically. "I was trying not to, but I can't . . . Audrey, I—"

"I love you, Theo," she whispered back, lifting her other leg and wrapping it around his waist to join the first. "I feel incredible." It was true. She'd never felt so full, so *alive* before. She bucked her hips up and rolled them, encouraging him to match her cadence once more. "And I want you to keep going."

He drew in a deep breath.

Dove down to kiss her like his life depended on it.

And really began to move.

He couldn't seem to form words after that—nothing coherent, anyway. So instead he spoke with his body, filling her so completely that every bit of her burned. Pressure built in places she'd never known existed inside her, and Audrey surrendered to Theo, to the way his heat enveloped her, how his mouth devoured her, the feeling of his fingers digging frantically into her flesh as they melded together as one, two halves of a whole, lost and then found and then stitched together again, like binary stars in a dancing orbit drawn inevitably closer by forces greater than themselves, by the indelible laws of physics and of the universe, spinning and writhing wildly until they combusted, bursting into something different, something new.

The more he moved, the more she needed him to move, the urge for momentum primal and unyielding. His heat became her own, and he held her so tightly that when Audrey closed her eyes, she wasn't sure where her body ended and Theo's began. All she knew, all she could feel, all she could divine was raw sensation, building pressure, and stunning, ecstatic oblivion.

With every thrust, with every beat, her heart whispered, *I love you.*

With every kiss, with every breath, his whispered it back.

They were both beyond themselves. Theo's lips formed words, but Audrey couldn't hear them, couldn't even discern them over the sound of their hearts beating in time.

And then, all of a sudden, she was gone.

The pressure reached a roaring crescendo, urged into being by Theo and his relentless rhythm while he dragged his length along all the most sacred, secret places within her, filling her so completely, the only thing she knew was that she'd forever feel empty without him there now.

She cried out—or at least, she thought she did.

She must have screamed.

Air tore at her throat, cool and harsh as she came.

And with it, her body melted away.

She dissolved into the orgasm he wrung from the furthest recesses of her being, losing all sense of self, all sense of other, all sense of anything aside from overwhelming, otherworldly union and *pleasure*. But it was so different than any she'd ever felt before—so much stronger, so much more meaningful, earth-shattering and core-shaking.

Her vision filled with light, white and bright and bursting around the depths of Theo's soft, soulful eyes.

And then all of a sudden, her hearing came back.

When he roared, the world rushed back around her, exploding once again into sound and color as he cried out her name.

He came just after she did, riding the wave of her orgasm right after her, every muscle in his body tensing and trembling, just as she tensed and trembled around him. Tiny aftershocks danced along her skin, twitching across her fingers and toes, which curled into Theo's soft sheets as she curled her fingers into his back, pressing half-moon nail indents between the constellations of moles lighting up the negative of the night sky etched there.

Theo slumped onto her, heavy and spent, his right hand shaking while he tried—and failed—to prop himself up. Instead, all he managed to do was shift to the side slightly as he pulled out, letting the bulk of his weight fall onto his mattress while leaving their limbs tangled together. He drew her close, nuzzling into her neck and pressing the tiniest, softest kisses into her still-damp hair while she cradled his head in her arms. They lay together in silence, catching their breath for long minutes, and Audrey marveled at the man still wrapped around her.

In the span of one evening, everything had changed—and yet, nothing had.

So *that's* what this was.

This was what it was to love someone.

It was home.

No one had warned her.

But it turned out she hadn't needed the warning.

She'd known it all along.

Sixteen

WHEN THEY BOTH caught their breath, Theo turned over, grabbed his phone, and immediately ordered a pizza.

"Pizza? Really?" Audrey asked when he locked the screen. "You said we were making pasta!"

He huffed a laugh. "Yeah, sure, but I'm too hungry now—this will be faster than making dinner from scratch. We missed the window on that. It takes a while."

"You tease!" she cried, shoving his shoulder. "Did you only promise me homemade gnocchi to seduce me? Was it all a lie?" He wasn't wrong, it was *way* later than she thought, and her stomach had started to growl.

"Did it work?" Theo asked, raising a wry eyebrow. "Because if so . . ."

She smacked him in the face with a pillow.

And then he made her thoroughly regret it.

She was still laughing and kicking from the ensuing pillow fight when he rolled her up like a burrito in the duvet and carried her over his shoulder downstairs.

"What are you doing?!" she squeaked, still squirming, but not hard enough to throw him off balance. "I'm still naked!"

"Oh, I know," Theo purred with relish. "That's the best part."

He smacked her ass fondly through the padding. “It’s a requirement for building naked pillow forts. It’s even in the name.” He deposited her gently on the floor before ripping all the couch cushions off and tossing them on top of her in a pile.

“What about the poor pizza delivery guy?” she asked with a gasp while she tried to claw her way out of her duvet wrapping. It had been entirely too easy for him to trap her there.

“I’ll put pants on for him. I’m not an animal.” He flopped down on the cushions and took her chin between his fingers. Only her face was visible in the fluffy white folds of his comforter. “But you? You’re going to stay just like this for as long as possible.”

He pressed a kiss to her lips, one of a thousand he’d given her already—and still, it wasn’t enough.

It would never be enough.

Not from him.

He could give her a thousand more, a million, and she’d cherish every one of them.

After Theo retrieved his sweatpants and handed her his hoodie, they spent the next hour perfecting their fort, nestling together in its warmth in front of the fire until the doorbell rang and they were finally able to gorge themselves on a hot, greasy picnic.

Now Audrey knew how heavenly postcoital pizza could taste.

When they were fully sated and the grease had been licked—and then washed—away from their fingers, Theo burrowed into the cushions and held his arm out, motioning for her to tuck in against his side. They sat there and watched the fire in silence for a long time, simply basking in the intimate glow of each other.

It was everything she’d ever wanted.

Everything she’d ever dreamed of.

But there was still a pall over the evening they needed to acknowledge.

“I think we should talk about what happened.”

He hummed. "Yeah, I suppose so." He rested his cheek on top of her head with a sigh, warmth spilling over from his skin and straight into her own. Theo was the best space heater she'd ever encountered, and between his heat and the warmth radiating from the crackling fire, Audrey could easily drift off to sleep in the quiet safety of his arms.

But not yet.

"I didn't like seeing you like that. And that wasn't how I ever thought I'd meet your mom."

Theo sighed again, his chest rising and falling deeply at her back. "I don't know if I was ever going to actually introduce you to her." Then he grimaced and shook his head. "No, that's just the anger talking. I would have eventually, but I wanted us to have more time alone together. I wanted to keep you all to myself for a little longer—something just for me. I wanted to keep you safe from everything else complicating my life."

"What are you going to do?" Audrey turned and ran a hand soothingly along his chest, her fingers stalling over the moles marked there. She was careful not to touch his scar. A reminder of it right now seemed like a bad idea.

"I don't know yet. She's a lawyer, and that's what a lot of our original fight was about in the first place, if I'm being honest—and why I got so upset with her for coming here, even though I think she had good intentions. We probably could have avoided the whole thing if I'd just answered one of her calls or texts, but I was dead set on sticking to no contact for as long as I needed. And I needed more space, I think." He shook his head.

Her brows knit together. "What does her job have to do with you?"

"Everything." He groaned. "My family has . . . expectations. We're old money, you see. And there are conditions to having it most of the time—though my nana made sure that wasn't the case for me. I came into my trust when I was old enough, and that was the only condition. She always supported my art way more than my mom and uncle ever did—my nana and my dad both."

"Why did you freak out about Christmas?"

"My mom hosts a big party every year with her firm—she made it sound like it's just family, but it's not. It's friends, colleagues, clients, politicians, New York glitterati—everyone who gossips. And let me tell you: I've been a fascination for these society people for a long time." He slid his gaze over to meet hers. "I'm the black sheep and they all know it, and so many of them have been dying to see my face since the accident. I was always an oddity to begin with, an outlier, a mistake—the scandalous product of a drunken tryst and a Vegas shotgun wedding that resulted in a vicious divorce and high therapy bills. And now I'm even more of a monster."

"Don't call yourself that. You aren't."

"No. You don't understand, sweetheart. I *am*." He sighed and buried his face in his hand. "I've failed my family and myself in every way imaginable." He tapped at his scar. "This is just the cherry on top of a lifetime of misery. An outward sign of my inner defects."

She grabbed his face with both hands and made him look her in the eye. "Don't you dare talk that way about the man I love, Theo," she growled. "Do you think I would love a monster?"

His bottom lip quivered. He blinked, and tears shone in his eyes for a split second before he shook his head.

"And you know what?" she murmured, drawing his lips to hers for a quick kiss. "From what I saw, your mother doesn't seem to think so either. I saw a woman who loves her son very much, but doesn't know what to do about it. Don't you think?"

He drew in a shaky breath and wrenched his eyes shut, nodding with a grimace as twin tears rolled down his cheeks.

"So what will you do?" Audrey took his hand in hers and interlaced their fingers. His lips tilted up into a watery smile at the contact. "Are you going to talk to her or not?"

Theo drew the back of his hand across his eyes before running it through her hair, gently combing through her loose waves with his fingers. His eyes never left hers, the warmth of the fire reflected in them while he thought.

"I don't know," he finally whispered. "What do *you* think I should do?"

"Oh. Uh . . . well." She rubbed tiredly at her temples, suddenly a bit uncomfortable. This was out of her scope of expertise. "I'm not sure. I've never had a mother or a family to have drama with, and definitely not at this level. I don't think I'm remotely equipped to weigh in."

"Oh god," he groaned, burying his face in his other hand. "I didn't even consider how that sounded to *you*. I bet you'd give anything to have a mother who's alive and cares about you in any way, and here I am, refusing to even give mine the time of day, despite all the rest of it. Do I sound like an asshole to you for it?" he muttered. "I feel like an asshole now."

She shook her head. "No, I don't think so. You're the furthest thing from an asshole. I've never met a man who was less of one, and you wouldn't have done or said what you did if you didn't have a good reason. I know these things are complicated. And you're not wrong for feeling trapped." She tightened her fingers in his. "But I also don't have the context, other than what I saw earlier today—which was two very hurt people, hurting each other, and blaming themselves for it. Will you finally tell me what happened?"

He rolled his lips together pensively, chewing on the bottom one while he thought.

"Audrey . . ." He winced and closed his eyes.

"Just tell me. That's what I'm here for. I signed up for this." She turned and sat in his lap to face him fully, caging him with her legs and combing her fingers through his hair while studying his eyes in the firelight. "It's you and me now, Theo."

He met her gaze, his remarkable eyes never leaving hers—except to dart briefly down to her lips. But when he looked back up again, his expression was the most heated she'd ever seen it.

"How did you get so wise?" He pressed his forehead to hers and breathed in deeply. "You're too mature for twenty-four, sweetheart."

Audrey closed her eyes and breathed with him for a moment, running her fingertips gently along the lines of his jaw. "I've always been alone, and I've always had to take care of myself. I guess I had to grow up really fast."

"You can slow down now, you know. Rest here for a while, stay young for longer." He wrapped her in his arms and tucked her under his chin. "You're safe here with me."

"I know I am," she whispered. "You're safe with me too."

His hand smoothed circles against her back, his fingers gently tracing the curves of her spine. It sent shivers across her skin, but she had the sense that the motion was more to soothe himself than her.

He always had an easier time speaking when his hands were occupied.

"Okay," Theo finally said with a sigh. "I'll tell you about the night of the accident."

Seventeen

WELL, *FUCK*.

Here he was again.

Theo slung his bag over his shoulder and slammed the door of the Thunderbird shut before facing the enormous white colonial manor looming in front of him.

Great.

It was time for the quarterly family dinner—only one obligation among many. Another inviolable Redmond tradition, and part of their legacy.

Legacy. There was that damn concept again, clinging to him like an itching second skin he wanted nothing more than to tear away.

Once every few months, and generally for the holidays, he was required to come up to Albany to spend time with his mother and his uncle. And lately, every visit had begun weighing more and more on him, grating and insufferable and stifling. He scratched absently at his neck.

But there was nothing for it: he was here now, so he might as well get it over with. Rip the Band-Aid off. He was about to take a step forward with a resigned slump to his shoulders when there was a rap on the car window behind him.

Theo closed his eyes and sighed.

The goddamn door must not have latched properly. Again.

What a piece of junk.

He turned to find his father leaning across the front seat, tapping at the glass with a single gnarled knuckle, his white hair gleaming in the setting sunlight. Theo reopened the door with an exasperated look. "What, Dad? Sorry, I'll make sure to shut it properly this time." He narrowed his eyes. "Why haven't you fixed that latch yet? It's been like that for years." Either it caught too hard and wouldn't open, or it wouldn't latch at all, and nothing in between.

"The charms of old cars, kid." Henry flashed him a crooked smile and patted the dashboard lovingly. "She's got as many quirks as I do. This old girl and I have been through a lot together, so go easy on her. She'll be yours one day."

"'Quirks' is one way to put it. I might call it 'well past its prime.'"

"*Hey*—watch it, you." Dark blue eyes glared back at him. "We've both still got it."

Theo surveyed the old bucket of bolts warily. His dad loved that damn car, and he was constantly tinkering with it, forever searching for just the right vintage parts to replace, just the proper fix for this or that, but he'd never quite managed to make it all the way perfect. The Thunderbird ran fine for something from the sixties, sure, but he could've just gotten something more fuel-efficient and environmentally friendly—like a hybrid. Would definitely guzzle a whole helluva lot less gas, and might save the old man a pretty penny.

Henry already had little else but debt to his name. The hot-rod shop wasn't doing so well these days; turned out people in the city didn't have a ton of money to blow on restoring vintage cars, especially when they didn't drive, and especially not in Brooklyn anymore.

But it was blasphemy to even suggest trading such a classic piece of Americana for a Prius. He'd learned that a long time ago.

So Theo kept his mouth shut.

His father pointed at him. "And be nice to your mother when you get inside. You haven't seen her for a few months and I know she's excited to have you here. She misses you."

"Mom misses me? What, have the two of you actually been communicating again?" Theo scoffed. "Was I asleep in the car when hell froze over?" Normally, he might have simply taken his motorcycle on the three-hour trip up to Albany for the weekend, but it had been pouring down rain in the city this morning—and his dad was already headed up here to see his best friend, Jack, anyway. It made sense to ride together.

It also let Theo take a nap. He'd been up late last night working on a new Lightm4st3r piece, and riding a motorcycle on three hours of shitty, tumultuous sleep *definitely* wasn't advisable, particularly in the rain, and particularly on the slick, winding back roads he usually favored. If he was actually going to leave the city, why would he want to stare at the freeway and bumper-to-bumper traffic for all that time?

If he had to come out here, at least he should see trees.

Henry shot him another dark look, but Theo only adjusted his bag over his shoulder again and straightened his leather jacket with a sigh. Why did it feel so tight across his back and shoulders? Was it just him, or was the collar suddenly wrong around his neck? It had always fit like a glove before. He didn't think he'd bulked out *that* much lately.

When his father still didn't say anything, Theo shifted uncomfortably on his feet.

"When have I not been nice to Mom? It's Uncle Lloyd I'm worried about."

There was a reason Theo hadn't been coming around as often. Two of them even, both with Yale law degrees and probably sitting on ancient, heirloom armchairs, sipping at something that cost an ungodly amount of money while they waited for Theo to come inside and for the cooks to make the three of them an unnecessarily large and complex five-course meal.

God forbid either his mother or his uncle actually meet him and his dad outside for once.

God forbid they order Chinese food and let their employees go home to their families at a decent hour.

But it was true that one of them gave him far more anxiety than the other.

He'd learned to be wary.

His uncle had a sharp tongue and even sharper opinions.

Henry snorted. "Just ignore him. You know he's got his notions, but they don't matter. And always remember that they're coming from a good place—he cares about you. I promise." He sat back in his seat and gripped the steering wheel. "I'll be right next door, just one obnoxious compound over. See you in the morning, all right?"

"Can't come fast enough. I'd have rather stayed in the city. I have work to do and I'm on a deadline." He set his own deadlines, but that was true enough. He had goals. There was a charity benefit in three weeks he wanted to slip a piece into.

His father grunted and shook his head. "It's one night. Just enjoy the time with your family, okay? I'll see you later, kid. Love you."

"Love you too, Dad."

Theo shut the door, harder and with just enough of a hitch to get the latch to catch this time, and watched as the car rounded the long gravel driveway leading away from his mother's house, its shiny turquoise paint flashing in the fading light of sunset. Once he couldn't see the glow of the taillights anymore, he ran a hand through his hair, turned on his heel, and made his way slowly up the drive to climb the old redbrick stairs to the house.

With every step, something twisted tighter in his chest.

The massive colonial manor was less a house than it was an estate, passed down through the Redmond line from generation to generation. Classic whitewashed columns framed the pristine, red-painted double doors and bordered a sprawling porch decked out with picture-perfect bench swings no one ever used. Theo's hand stilled when he wrapped his fingers around the silver doorknob embossed with an antique *R*, and he drew in a deep breath, steeling himself before he entered.

There was no avoiding it.

He hated this place.

This was just one of several houses his family collectively owned, but it was the oldest. And while he'd mostly grown up splitting his time between his parents' vastly different apartments in Manhattan and Brooklyn, he'd also been forced to spend most of his childhood summers here, all of them lonely and miserable. The historic house was at once gigantic and also too small, filled with old, inherited things that shouldn't be touched or played with by inquisitive, maladroit hands not yet grown and honed with the dexterity he possessed now. Everything was breakable. Everything was irreplaceable. Nothing was his, not even the bedroom designated for his use and outfitted to his mother's tastes.

He was only a temporary occupant, a transitory traveler through the rooms of a house that had seen many more lives than his pass under its roof, and would see many more to come.

It might as well have been a hotel, not a home.

And it had always felt just as impersonal as one.

As soon as he twisted the knob, his skin began to crawl, and Theo gritted his teeth and gripped the strap of his bag tighter, wrenching his fingers around the leather.

Already the walls felt like they were closing in around him.

It was the unfortunate side effect of having grown up—and having grown up to be rather *large*—that every room in this house, built over two hundred years ago, felt like it was trying to suffocate him.

Why were all the ceilings so low? Did the old wooden beams *want* to give him a concussion?

He shook his head, suppressing a shudder, and wandered toward the library.

That's where they'd be waiting.

The whole house was an odd mishmash of traditional and modern, renovated over and over again throughout the years by its occupants, each of them making changes according to their own tastes. When his nana died, the ancestral seat of the Redmond family fell into his mother's possession while her brother took some of the other properties in the Hamptons, and she wasted no time in making her own fair share of updates. She favored a clean, classical style, a mix of bright, blinding whites and more traditional period-appropriate woods and leathers. Everything was crisp, neat, orderly. Everything had its place.

Perhaps it was why Theo felt so very *out* of place.

He'd never belonged there.

Though he did love the library.

Old, polished mahogany shelves held a truly expansive collection of books, both contemporary and antiquarian, many of their leatherbound spines housing copies of the country's most foundational texts, and all of them crammed neatly—but also haphazardly—into floor-to-ceiling shelves. It was a cacophony of colors and textures, eras and binding, genres and languages, and the books overflowed from the shelves into stacks on the floor, spilling out of order and tumbling everywhere, gathering as much dust as any of his mother's maids would allow.

Someday, an archivist would come in and ruin all that beautiful anarchy.

But it hadn't happened yet.

Theo rounded the corner and two familiar voices filtered out into the hallway.

"—still doing that bullshit art of his, is he? How much does he make per piece, anyway?"

"It varies, Lloyd, but he won't tell me exactly. I only find out when I read the news. His friend Diego usually tries to write the articles about him."

"How ethical is that, keeping your best friend in your pocket at a newspaper? The free publicity for a buddy borders on a conflict of interest, so they'd both better watch it. The second someone discovers his identity, he's—*oh*." Lloyd's head snapped over as Theo hovered in the doorway, ducking so he wouldn't hit his head on the old, low frame. "Ted—"

"Teddy! When did you get here? Why didn't you tell me you were on your way?" His mother leapt up from her chair and hurried over to him, immediately smoothing her hands along his father's vintage black leather jacket. The way she pursed her lips told him she wasn't pleased with his choice of attire: black T-shirt, black jeans, Air Jordans. Lloyd was wearing a three-piece suit, like he'd come straight from a lecture, and Eleanor was still wearing one of the designer pantsuits she favored for court days. They preferred that he dress similarly for these dinners.

But he'd never been that buttoned up.

"Hey, Mom." He bent down and pressed a light kiss to her cheek. "I did text when we left *and* when we got here. Did you not get my messages?"

"I—" She blinked in confusion and then ripped her phone out of her pocket before frowning at her screen. "Oh. Oh, I'm sorry, Teddy, I don't know how I missed those." The lapse was momentary, and her frown was quickly smoothed away with a smile. "But I'm so happy to see you. You look really good."

Lloyd stood from his usual antique armchair and extended a hand. "Hey, Teddy!" His steely blue eyes swept over Theo's shaggy dark waves. "Your hair's getting long, kiddo." He slapped his nephew's shoulder fondly. "You working too hard in that studio of yours to remember that haircuts are a thing?"

Theo rolled his lips together.

Not this again.

Every single time he saw his uncle, the first thing out of his mouth was a comment about his appearance.

He opened his own mouth to say something terse in response but was quickly cut off.

"Lloyd—" Eleanor glared at her younger brother. "Lay off. He's not one of your students. He doesn't work at a firm and he can wear his hair however he wants." She stood on her tiptoes and plucked at the curling ends of her son's thick, dark waves with a smile. "I think it looks handsome. It suits you."

But Lloyd was still grumbling. "He *should* have been one of my students. He has the talent and the brains for it. What a waste." He sighed and shook his head before squeezing Theo on the arm again. "Ah well. At least that hair hides those Dumbo ears of yours, eh?"

Theo's face slowly fell.

There it was.

Another reminder.

His ears *were* too big. They *did* stick out from the sides of his head. He *had* grown out his hair to hide them.

He was always too big, too awkward, too out of place. His mouth was too wide, his teeth too crooked, his nose too large, his face too long, his brow too heavy. It was a wonder he didn't have a permanent bump on his head from the number of times he'd knocked it on the doorways in this old-ass house once he'd hit a growth spurt in his teens. Wedging himself into seats on the subway was an ordeal. He usually just opted to stand instead, trying his best to make himself small and unnoticed in a corner somewhere. Trying his best to stay out of the way. To avoid the gaping stares. Avoid the attention.

He took up a lot of space.

He never fit anywhere.

It wasn't like it was something he'd ever asked for, or even wanted.

He didn't need his uncle, of all people, to be constantly pointing it out.

And *yet*.

The feeling in his chest twisted tighter.

He closed his eyes and counted to three.

"*Lloyd,*" Eleanor said with a sigh. "Do you want me to talk about how *short* you are?" That earned her a glare in return, but she only scoffed and shook her head, taking her son's massive hand in hers. "Come, sit with me, Teddy. Tell me what you've been up to lately." She led him to a chair before turning to the nearby bar cart, pouring a glass of scotch, and pressing it into Theo's hand.

He stared blankly down at the amber liquid. His leg bounced, and he clutched the glass so tightly in his fingers, he half wondered if he might shatter it.

This wasn't a casual question about what he'd been up to. Oh no. It was never as casual an inquiry as she made it seem.

He was always put under a microscope when he came to these things, and it was hardly his fault his mother was too preoccupied to check in on him regularly. She called sometimes, sure, but she was a busy woman, and she'd been juggling a few major corporate cases for their firm. They kept her up and at work until late, and he knew she couldn't be bothered to do more than send a cursory text to her son to ask him about his latest piece—which was already begrudging, given his history. He'd given up on calling her himself.

It was why she insisted on these quarterly weekends so firmly.

It was to alleviate her own guilt.

And to keep a close eye on him.

He tapped his fingers against the glass but didn't drink any of it.

He hated scotch. That was Lloyd's preference, not his. He didn't even really drink. "I've been working on a new piece."

"Oh? For Sullivan Lightworks?"

"Well, yeah, actually—one for Jessica. You remember her, right?"

"Didn't you date her in college?"

Theo stared at her open-mouthed. "*No*, Mom. Jessica's a lesbian." And he never even *had* a girlfriend in college, but he didn't feel like pointing that out now. His uncle didn't know and that was the last thing he wanted him to latch on to. Just another thing to tease him about. "She's the one who came home with me for Thanksgiving junior year? Because she'd just come out and it hadn't gone well with her parents at the time?"

Eleanor pursed her lips together thoughtfully, her brow wrinkling while she struggled to place the name and the time. "Junior year? I'm so sorry, honey, that whole fall is a blur." She turned to her brother. "Was that when we were handling the Henderson case?"

He shrugged.

Theo rolled his jaw in annoyance. "Yeah. Well, anyway, she's opening a new bar called the Cherry Stem. I'm under contract for delivery of a neon sign for it, and it's almost complete. I just need to finish the wiring."

"Oh that's wonderful!" His mother looked relieved. "I'm so glad you're doing more work under your LLC."

Theo's eye twitched.

"I'm also working on a new Lightm4st3r piece. It's coming along nicely, I think." It wasn't. It was going horribly. There was a reason he hadn't launched a new abstract piece in—what was it now? Eight months? Ten? More?

Silence.

The siblings exchanged a glance, and an eerie feeling prickled at the back of Theo's neck. He rubbed his hand nervously along it, and it was burning hot to the touch.

Great. It meant his big, stupid ears had gone scarlet as well.

He drew in a deep breath and held it.

One.

Exhaled slowly.

Two.

"Are you still doing work under that persona?" Eleanor finally ventured. Her question was awfully tentative. A little too cautious. "You haven't done a piece or posted about anything in so long, I'd wondered if—"

"No, I haven't given it up. I've just been a little . . . blocked lately, is all. It happens sometimes."

It had never happened to him before.

Theo held his breath at the empty.

Three.

Lloyd swirled the scotch in his own glass. "You know, Teddy, you don't get much out of that . . . *venture.* Is it really worth it?"

The next breath he inhaled was sharp.

Oh boy.

Here we go.

He didn't get to four.

"You could always just go back to law school."

Theo slammed his glass down on the antique coffee table so hard, some of the liquor sloshed over the edge.

"I'm not going back to law school."

"Why not?" Lloyd's eyes narrowed as he studied him.

"Because I don't fucking want to."

"What, is there something wrong with—"

Theo's heartbeat was rushing in his ears.

"LLOYD."

His uncle startled when his sister stepped in front of him, her arms crossed over her chest. He blinked up at her, his brows still knit into a scowl.

"Enough. We're not getting into that now. Drop it." A bell rang in the dining room, and Eleanor glanced over her shoulder toward the hall. "Dinner's ready. Let's eat before anyone gets hangrier."

Theo rose easily out of his chair and shoved the scotch bitterly into his uncle's chest. When Lloyd shot him a dark look, it brought him a not-insignificant amount of pleasure that his uncle had to crane his neck as far as he did to look up at him. He let go of the glass, barely giving Lloyd half a second to catch it before he swept hastily out of the room.

Thinking about that one miserable year at Yale was the last thing he wanted to do tonight.

It was the last thing he *ever* wanted to do.

THEO PICKED AT his dinner.

Something was off.

Things were even tenser than normal, and he couldn't quite put his finger on *why*, though his mother and his uncle were certainly up to something. They kept glancing at each other the entire time while they ate, their looks significant and heavy. The looks were especially apparent whenever Theo said anything about his art, or Diego, or even when he mentioned a film he'd watched recently.

Eventually, he simply stopped talking.

He fiddled with his phone in his pocket instead.

Maybe he should just . . .

Leave.

Uncle Jack only lived a few minutes away, so his dad could pick him up quickly, right? Or Uber was always an option in a pinch, though it might take too long for one to find him out here.

He could also just walk out.

Lloyd asked him a question, and he snapped his attention back to the table.

"What was that?" Theo idly pushed the remainder of his peas around on his plate. He'd been starving when he got there, but his appetite had gradually waned throughout the evening, only to be replaced with an odd, sick feeling in his stomach.

Meanwhile, Lloyd was going harder on the scotch than he normally did. His face was red and ruddy, and he pointed at Theo with his fork.

"What was that last piece you did about? *The Radioactive Birds of Wall Street* or whatever? I never did understand that one. It was weird even by your standards."

Theo stabbed one of the peas with his fork, catching it perfectly between the tines. Maybe the movement had been a little more aggressive than he'd meant it. "It's a commentary on how rampant capitalistic, corporate greed has become, and how damaging it is—that even the birds who walk near the most iconic symbol of our economy are contaminated by it now. Not even the pigeons are safe." That explanation was extremely reductive, but sure. Good enough.

Something even his uncle should be able to grasp.

"Huh. All right then." Lloyd chewed thoughtfully. "Didn't it only go for twenty thousand dollars at auction?"

"*Yes*," Theo hissed through gritted teeth. "And all of it to a charity that supports women fleeing domestic violence situations." The proceeds from that sculpture had kept their shelter open when it was on the brink of closing due to increasing rent prices, and it had also brought awareness to their cause. They were still operating today because of that auction. "Twenty thousand is nothing to sneeze at."

His father had certainly never had that much money in the bank at once.

"Bit low for you, though, don't you think?" Lloyd put his fork down and tented his hands over his plate. "You could have simply opened up your wallet and paid that amount out to that charity yourself. Your other work has sold for much higher, hasn't it? Orders of magnitude higher."

"Lloyd . . ." Eleanor warned.

All these warnings, and nothing to show for it.

She wasn't going to do *shit*.

Theo let his fork clatter onto the delicate, antique china. He definitely wouldn't be able to finish his dinner now. "It was a little low, yes, but that doesn't take away from its value or its meaning. And I *have* given to that shelter. Several times over."

"Well, that's all well and good. But if your work hasn't been selling for as much as it used to, maybe it's time you hang up your Lightm4st3r cape."

Theo froze. "What?"

"*Lloyd.*" Eleanor slapped her palm on the table so hard, the silverware rattled. "What are you doing?"

He glared at his sister indignantly. "Only what you've been too afraid to do all night. We've been tiptoeing around since the boy got here this evening, and I'm tired of it. You really need to get on with it."

Theo felt all the blood drain from his face. "Get on with *what*?"

His uncle downed the rest of his drink and slammed the glass on the table. "Telling you to put a pin in it. You're floundering."

"*What?!*" Theo pushed back from the table and threw his napkin onto his plate. "Are you fucking kidding me right now?" He looked at his mother. "Tell me he's out of his goddamn mind."

She didn't say anything.

But Lloyd did. "It's time for you to get a real job, Theodore. This Lightm4st3r shit? You're wasting your time. You might as well be a five-year-old still playing with his Lite-Brite." He stood and pointed at Theo. "You stand around in that garage of yours fiddling with tubes and wires for hours on end to do what? Only produce a single piece or two a year?"

"I have a design LLC. I do work. That I am *paid* for."

"Yeah, but you also do a lot of stuff for free, like that taco truck sign, wasn't it? You just gave it to them."

Theo pounded his fist on the table. "They were just starting their business and I wanted to help Tío out. I grew up with him! Do you know how much he's fed me over the years? Do you know how much he means to me? Or Diego? I was glad to do it."

"And no one knows about it—they don't even advertise your business for you."

"I don't need them to!" He ran a hand through his hair.

His therapist would tell him to breathe.

She'd tell him to—

"It's piss-poor management on your part. A stupid decision. It's gotten you nowhere."

"I don't need the money! I don't care!" Theo turned toward his mother. "Mom, tell him. Tell him how much money Nana left for . . ." He trailed off at the look on her face. "Mom?"

She hadn't said anything, and her expression didn't make him feel any less sick.

It was resolute.

"Teddy, your uncle's right, even though that's not how I would have phrased it." Eleanor slowly pushed her chair away from the table and stood, leaning her palms on the surface and pressing her weight against the wood. "I wanted you to come here this weekend so we could discuss the work you're doing as Lightm4st3r—and talk about maybe what's next."

"What do you mean, 'what's next'?"

"I mean calling it quits."

The world narrowed down to a single, horrific point.

Eyes, the twins of his own.

"Call it quits? On my art?" Theo breathed. "You want me to stop? Because of the *money*?!"

Of all the things they could have chosen for this to be about, and they'd chosen *that*?

They had so much of it.

Scads of it.

More than any of them could ever realistically spend.

His mother shook her head. "It's not actually about the money, Teddy. It's about everything else."

"Everything else?" His hands began to shake. This was ludicrous, ridiculous, how could they think that—

"I'm concerned about you. You barely leave your house, and you're so alone. You don't have many friends."

"I don't *need* many friends, I have Diego, and—"

"You're kind of a recluse, and you haven't dated anyone since your relationship with Kendra fell through five years ago."

"She cheated on me!" Anger surged hot into his cheeks at the mention of her name. "How *dare* you even bring her up after what she did! I—"

"I'm not talking about the past, Teddy, I'm talking about the present." She rested her head in her hand and rubbed at the space between her eyes. "I think it's time for a change. I wanted to ask you if you would consider going back to law school and finally joining me at the firm."

"*Why?*" He couldn't disguise the disgust in his voice.

"Your uncle and I are going to retire. We'll make the announcement soon."

"What does that have to do with me?"

"We'd like to pass the family business on to you. It's time to grow up."

The silence in the room settled around his shoulders like a death shroud.

"You're joking. Right?"

Theo glanced between the siblings' faces. Surely this was a joke. She wasn't serious, was she? Where was his dad? This was all a prank. He looked around, half expecting his Uncle Jack to pop out from somewhere and for a real party to start.

But neither of their expressions shifted. Neither of them broke and told him they were kidding.

"No, honey," his mother finally said with a sigh.

"Wha—what is this?" he finally stammered. "What kind of twisted intervention is this?"

"No intervention." Eleanor shook her head. "An invitation."

"No." Theo shook his head and took a step backward. "*No.* Why would you ask me to do this?" He splayed his hands out in front of him. This was stupid. They had *so* much money, none of them even really needed to work in the first place. It was completely unnecessary.

It was obnoxious.

Disgusting, when he thought too much about it.

His uncle groaned. "Don't play dumb, Teddy. You're *so* smart."

"Well, sure, but that doesn't mean I should take over the Redmond family law firm."

"You're the next in line to do it. Are you really going to let over a hundred years of our family's legacy fall into someone else's hands?"

"It's not *my* fault you never had children," Theo sneered.

His uncle's face reddened. "You had a perfect GPA while playing lacrosse and double majoring at Columbia. You scored a one-eighty on your LSATs."

"Do you think I give a shit about some *test scores*?"

"You got into Harvard, Yale, Stanford, *and* Chicago, and for what? *For what?!*"

"I have no interest in law."

"You used to! And then you *squandered* all that raw talent by—"

"I don't want any part of your fucking *family business*."

The walls were too close. Why was the ceiling so low? Or the lights so dim? Why was breathing suddenly so hard? Theo gasped and blinked and tried to calm his racing heart, but it only felt like it sped up at the thought. It was all he could hear, the beating of his heart, the frenzy of his lungs, the way the room seemed to spin.

He couldn't breathe.

Panic.

This was panic.

"What a waste. What an incredibly stupid waste." His uncle's voice cut through the noise. "This is why you need to grow the fuck up, boy. Do something worthwhile with your life."

The symphony of panic in Theo's brain suddenly condensed down to one, single note: a loud ringing in his ears.

And he found his voice again.

"What did you just say to me?" he rasped.

"That you need to grow. The fuck. *Up*." Lloyd rolled his eyes before glaring darkly at him. "This is ridiculous. You're spiraling because we're trying to hand you a real purpose on a silver platter. This is the firm your mother and I inherited—the firm your great-grandfather built from nothing and your grandfather turned into a roaring empire."

"You want me to give up my art?"

"You're not twenty anymore, *Teddy*," his uncle growled. "You need to think seriously about your future."

"It's the only thing that makes me feel alive." Theo's voice shook as he spoke. "You might as well ask me to give up *breathing*."

His uncle shook his head and rubbed at the bridge of his nose. The light danced off the silver threaded through the fading burnished gold of his hair, and he suddenly looked haggard.

"We've all got to make sacrifices in life. Your mother has worked *so hard*—and so have I. Do you know what she's done for you? Do you know what she's sacrificed to send you to the best schools? To make sure you got the best of everything, the best tutors, the best trainers, the best therapists, the best—"

"This is more than a *sacrifice*. It's—"

"Do you have any idea how damaging it could be for us, for our family, if anyone finds out what you actually do?" Lloyd roared. "You'll make us a laughingstock! A joke! The Redmonds, reduced to whatever *this* is." He gestured at Theo's leather jacket.

"What's that supposed to mean?!" Theo bellowed back. "What are you getting at? Why do I have to sit here and justify—"

"You're a lazy, entitled fuckup, Theodore. I know how much you hate your family—and how much you hate our legacy. You could have been something. You could have been some*one*. And instead, you've chosen *this*."

The ringing in Theo's ears grew louder.

It was that word.

Legacy.

The Redmond legacy.

He'd grown up knowing all about their family's legacy, and the expectations that came with it. His family was old and storied, and most—if not all—of his ancestors bore the mantle of that legacy with pride. Lawyers, politicians, public servants, the lot of them. They wore their generational wealth like a badge of honor, carrying it with aplomb and wielding it like a weapon they used to cut through red tape.

His mother's family was one of her greatest assets.

But it was Theo's greatest burden.

The weight of it, the expectations the family name and money carried, their history, their past, all of it was *suffocating*. He was drowning in the depths of it, swallowed by an ocean of a name that didn't fit, that was somehow both too small and too large, that wasn't actually his, that squeezed and restricted him until his skin smarted, until his bones cracked, until his lungs screamed and his heart stuttered.

Everything about the Redmond legacy made him want to peel his flesh off, tear it into shreds away from his sinew and his skeleton so he could step out of it and cast it aside, finally unburdened and finally free.

Suffocating.

The past was suffocating.

And the legacy it left had been slowly killing him.

It must've started at birth, whatever deficiency this was. But ever since he first became aware that there was something wrong with him because of who his father was, because his mother had fallen in love with and got knocked up by her charming mechanic with the crooked smile instead of some guy from some other legacy family with too many houses strewn along the Eastern Seaboard, he'd been feeling it, that sensation in his chest.

He wasn't sure when he realized that he was different, that he didn't fit, that the edges of his particular puzzle piece hadn't been made for the cutout he was being wedged into, but it was early. He was young. Maybe it started when he cried himself to sleep at night after the divorce, screaming for a mother who was rarely there, for a father who was exiled, only to be consoled by a nanny instead—and a bunch of different ones at that.

Then he really knew it when he left Yale. He was the first male born into the Redmond line since they'd been in America to actively reject the university and choose another instead, purposefully eschewing the legacy so many of his forebears had paved the way for previously. He had the talent, the grades, the lineage. It was the best law school in the country, one of the best in the world, recruiters had come after him like crazy—and he'd *still* ripped the silver spoon straight out of his mouth and chucked it across the room like it was nothing.

It was a slap in the face to his family.

And his uncle had taken it personally.

But Theo was the son of a mechanic. What was he supposed to do? Keep showing up with grease stains under his nails from summers spent repairing cars in an unair-conditioned shop in Brooklyn and expect to get along with other kids who spent theirs with staff fanning them and feeding them grapes on private yachts in the Maldives?

Please.

This fucking *legacy*.

It was bullshit.

All of it.

Lloyd jabbed his finger into the middle of Theo's chest. "What have you actually done with your life, huh? *Nothing*. Absolutely nothing." He punctuated each word with another jab. "You have all the potential in the world. You have the brains, you have the background, the ability, the tenacity, and most of all the *privilege*, the extreme privilege of everything *your* mother and *my* mother worked so hard to give you, and yet *you have done absolutely nothing with it*."

The ringing sound turned into a rushing noise.

It was getting louder in Theo's ears.

It grew—

—with

—each

—and

—every

—jab.

"You've squandered it all." Lloyd jutted his chin up at Theo and sneered. "You had your path laid out for you at Yale, the path for your whole entire life, and you flunked out in your first year. And here's the thing: I talked to your professors. They said you were absolutely brilliant in class. Your answers were impeccable. You knew the material, you argued the cases, you did *everything*—and yet you somehow managed to fail every single one of your exams."

Spit flew from his mouth and landed cold on Theo's cheek.

"Imagine that: a prodigy, tanking his own future and throwing away his family name, just so he could give himself an out to go fuck around with colored glass instead. What a goddamn *waste*."

Lloyd shoved at Theo's shoulder, and he stumbled backward as he tried to regain his footing. "Do you know how you've hurt my sister? Do you know how you've tarnished our name? You're your mother's greatest failure. You're the shame of the Redmond legacy, the biggest disappointment this family has seen in generations, and if you keep wasting time on your precious *art*, acting just as lazy as your *father*—"

BAM.

Theo didn't even know he'd raised his fist.

But all of a sudden, all he saw was red.

Lightning crackled across his knuckles and through his arm.

And Lloyd fell to the ground in a heap.

"Don't you ever talk about my dad again."

"*THEODORE!*" his mom yelled as his uncle turned over and wiped blood away from his nose with a groan. As soon as he did, more gushed down his face. "What are you doing?!"

Theo stared at his hand and flexed his fingers over his palm. "Something I should have done years ago," he muttered, almost to himself.

"You broke my nose!" Lloyd spat bitterly as he turned to look at his sister. "You see? You see what I was telling you? The boy has always been too volatile!"

"Volatile?" Theo huffed. "I always just thought I was creative." A strange cold sensation ran through his body. All feeling had been replaced with an oddly liberating numbness—and once it spread, he had no desire to stop it.

He could see everything clearly now.

All of it.

He gazed slowly back over at his mother. "You didn't stop him. You didn't interrupt. You really think I'm a failure, don't you? I'm a disappointment. I'm a mistake."

For some reason, voicing that truth didn't hurt as much as he thought it would.

"Because you called me all the way here to ask me to give up the one thing that makes me feel the most *me*, the one thing I love and I'm good at, the thing that makes me feel *alive*, and you were asking me to do it for you. Not for my benefit: for *yours*."

Eleanor's eyes went wide. "No, Teddy, that's not what I was thinking. I want you with me. I was asking you to join me, to take an interest in the family bus—"

"IT HAS ALWAYS BEEN ABOUT YOU!" His mother flinched. "You have *never* had my best interests at heart, never! I have *always* been your single greatest mistake!"

"That's not true!" Eleanor's face turned red. She stepped over and jutted her chin up at her son. "I love you! I gave you the best I could. I put you in the best schools, gave you the best education, sent you to the best therapists, hired the best tutors—"

"You don't fucking get it! That's not love. None of that was for me, it was all for *you*!" Theo sneered down at her. "You did that to assuage your guilt for never being home because you were a partner at your firm, and for divorcing Dad, and then you put me in therapy because you couldn't understand why I was so fucking angry all the time and why I needed art so goddamn much. It wasn't for me, it was for *you*.

"Do you have any idea what you're asking of me? I TRIED TO KILL MYSELF WHEN I WAS AT YALE!" Theo screamed, all sense of propriety gone now. He could control the words as much as he could control his volume. "I hated every fucking second of being at that suffocating school, trying to live up to your precious *legacy*, trying to shove myself into a box that wasn't made for me—trying to make myself smaller so I would actually fit in your shoes for once. Well, guess what, Mother: *I don't fucking fit*. I never have.

"You want me to cut my hair and wear a suit and get a law degree so my image can bolster yours in the society papers, and you want me to parade around and act like you're the pinnacle of virtue, like you're the best mother in the whole wide world, the most generous mother, bequeathing me the *family fucking legacy* when there were stretches of time growing up where I didn't see you at all for weeks on end, I only saw my *nannies* and my *father* because my own mother couldn't be bothered to come home to her husband and her son because her work was far more important."

Horror flashed over her face, but Theo couldn't stop himself.

"Yes, I tried to kill myself at Yale. Didn't they tell you? Diego knows," he spat. "He came to visit me one weekend and found me passed out on my dorm room floor. He called an ambulance when I wasn't responsive and they had to pump my stomach. How's that for your fucking *legacy*?" He pointed accusingly at his mother. "And now you're asking me to do it all over again? To change my career into something more palatable?

"Do you want me to change my name too? Should I ditch Dad's shameful, low-class, blue-collar name *that you gave me* and take on the Redmond one, just so you can finally put it in the papers that Theodore Henry Redmond the Fourth, Esquire, finally took over the family business so his mother could spend more time yachting in the Seychelles?

"I'm just getting started, and instead of supporting me, you ask me to upend my whole life, my whole identity for *you*. To put my art and my ideas and my future on hold for the sake of yours!" He threw his hands up. "But oh no, poor Teddy the mistake, the blemish on your perfect record, the untouchable half-breed is fucking up again. We'd better protect him from himself and intervene as a *family*, because if there's anything the Redmonds think they're good at, it's circling the fucking wagons and protecting their own."

His face twisted in disgust. "Except they *don't*. You didn't protect me when I was a kid, you didn't protect me when I was at Yale, and you're not protecting me now! Here I am, showing up to these stupid fucking family dinners for *years* when all I want to do is be at home!" Theo ran his hands over his face and frantically through his hair.

Something had broken inside him.

The words poured forth, scalding his throat from where they boiled up in his stomach.

"Nothing I do is ever good enough!" He reached down and tugged at Eleanor's perfectly pressed pantsuit, jerking her forward on her feet. "My opinion doesn't matter. It doesn't matter how successful my art is. It doesn't matter that I'm critically acclaimed, it doesn't matter that I make so much money, I haven't touched my trust in *years*, it doesn't matter that I've raised hundreds of thousands of dollars for charity—none of that is ever fucking good enough. I am never right. I can never live up to your impossible expectations, just because of this *one thing*—just because of this *one difference*.

"I'll always be the black mark on your record. I'll always be the black sheep. I can have the perfect grades, the perfect record, the perfect house, but I can never be the perfect son, can I?"

A scorching-hot tear tumbled down his cheek.

"So, *Mother*," he growled, "this is why my answer is no: because you're so selfish and so shortsighted, you can't even see how you're tearing your own son apart."

The pressure in his chest suddenly wrenched even tighter, and light blue eyes blazed up into his own.

Theo had forgotten about Lloyd. Any focus he could muster had been on his mother.

His uncle had finally struggled to his feet and grabbed Theo's shirt, twisting his hands at his chest and yanking him straight back into his body.

"Get out of my sister's face, you piece of shit."

He ripped his uncle's hands away from his shirt and shoved.

"And you get your fucking hands off of me, you asshole!"

Lloyd shoved back.

Everything became a blur.

Theo had the vague sensation of hearing his mom speak hurriedly to someone in the background while he struggled with his uncle, trying desperately to grab hold of the smaller man. But he was surprisingly quick for an aging, tenured law professor, and Lloyd ducked and wove better than he should have been able to with as much as he'd had to drink.

He shoved Theo away from the table, blood still streaming down his chin and onto the tweed of his custom three-piece designer suit, now torn open under the arms, and he threw his own punch at Theo's face. But Theo caught his hand and pushed it away angrily.

"Come on, old man! You think you can take me?" he jeered. "I've got thirty years, thirty inches, and far more than thirty pounds on you!"

"You little bastard, you—"

Theo tackled him, wrapping his arms around Lloyd's waist and pinning him on the ground while the older man struggled. White flashed across his vision, but the landed punch had little effect: he'd sustained far harder hits to the head in lacrosse, and all it did was flood his vision even further with red.

He couldn't see anything but his uncle anymore. Every shitty comment, every snide remark, every dark look that man had ever shot at Theo suddenly rose to the forefront of his mind, and hatred boiled in his veins. Lloyd had always been like this: odd and bitter, egotistical and opinionated, and if there was one thing he didn't understand, it was his nephew.

He was a bully.

And said nephew had had enough.

Every hit to Lloyd's face cracked across Theo's knuckles like lightning and sent a shudder coursing through his arm, but it was too late now. Every punch was a victory, every glorious blow something that had been lying in wait for years, *decades* even, a lifetime of feeling misunderstood, different, outside, unworthy. Blood splattered across the antique carpet in the dining room, every drop a perfect match to the red Theo so favored in his work, and he painted his knuckles and his uncle's face with it like an artist.

Until a hand nearly as large as his own grabbed him by the neck and ripped him sharply away from his canvas.

"*WHAT THE FUCK do you think you're doing?!*" his father roared, pinning Theo's arms behind his back and dragging him away.

Theo blinked. His uncle was lying still on the floor and his mother was staring at him in stunned silence while tears streamed down her cheeks.

But that only infuriated him more.

"You didn't even do anything!" he screamed at her as his father dragged him out of the room. "You didn't take up for me! You didn't protect me from him! You never really did! You weren't there for me! YOU NEVER HAVE BEEN!"

"*That's enough!* That's enough, Teddy!" His father's fingers dug so hard into his skin, he could feel bruises forming. The world blurred as tears flooded his eyes and the colors of the walls melded together while they rushed past him.

Suddenly, they were outside, the cool spring air bracing against Theo's heated skin.

But it did little to calm him.

All he could feel was his body starting to come apart.

"Get in the goddamn car!" Henry threw him into the front seat and shut the door after him, jogging around and sliding quickly into the driver's side, locking the doors before peeling out of the gravel drive in front of the picture-perfect red-and-white manor.

It was all a lie.

Theo bent forward and put his head between his knees in an attempt to not pass out. He couldn't breathe anymore, and the interior of the Thunderbird fizzled at the edges of his vision, despite the huge, gasping breaths he gulped down like water.

He was going to be sick.

He fumbled for the window crank and rolled it down as fast as he could before plunging his head outside and hurling the contents of his stomach into the dark.

They left it behind in an instant.

His mother lived on the outskirts of Albany, and they rocketed down dark back roads at high speed, his father driving like a bat out of hell back south, in the direction of the city. As soon as Theo rolled up the window and let his head fall back against the headrest, Henry glared at him angrily out of the corner of his eye.

"What the *fuck*, Teddy!" he yelled, gripping the steering wheel so hard, his knuckles turned white. "Were you trying to kill your uncle?"

"I don't know," Theo gasped. "Maybe." He hated him. That feeling hadn't dissipated. "He's an asshole."

But then he looked down at his lap. His hands were shaking. Why were they shaking? They wouldn't stop. They wouldn't stop, he couldn't stop them, and when he turned them over, he flinched and recoiled at the sight of dried, rust-red blood caked onto his knuckles. It was still there, crimson and brown, mixing red with the fresh dark bruises sprouting underneath. His stomach churned again, and he gripped the window crank with trembling, scrabbling fingers, finally latching onto it and holding on for dear life in case he vomited again.

It was disgusting.

He was disgusting.

He was a monster.

And his father was *furious*.

"What happened?" Henry bellowed. "You know he's not going to let this lie—he's a lawyer, for god's sake! One of the best in the country, no less, the dean of Cornell's stupid fucking law school, and you just *assaulted him*!" He slammed his foot on the gas and they raced through the countryside as fast as they could, putting as much distance between Theo and what he'd just done as possible.

They sat in silence while the landscape whizzed by.

It was a long time before either of them spoke again.

"Did you know Mom's going to retire?" Theo still felt sick even asking the question.

"Yes. She told me a few weeks ago that she wants to step down."

The sound of the road purred under the tires of the Thunderbird while Theo turned those words over in his mind.

He was the last to know.

No one had told him, and he was the last to know.

"You—you *knew*?"

"Of course I did, kid," Henry grunted. "You think we don't still talk?" He lifted a hand and wiped the sweat away from his brow. "We may not be married anymore, but we're still friends."

"You fought like crazy when I was little. You could hardly stand to look at each other."

"Yeah, well . . . turns out distance and separate bedrooms do actually make the heart grow fonder. Eventually."

Theo quieted again.

"You knew what they were going to tell me this weekend?"

"Yes."

"And do you know what they asked me?"

"To stop being Lightm4st3r and take over the firm, yeah." Henry cleared his throat and coughed into his hand, shaking his head and blinking as if to clear it.

"And you agree with them?!" Theo sat up again, renewed fury simmering in his stomach. If even his dad thought that—

"No, Teddy." He shook his head. "You're a grown man and you can make your own choices. I don't think anyone gets to tell you what to do."

"Why didn't you tell me?"

"Your mother asked me not to. She wanted to be the one to break it to you—she was nervous, but she was hoping you'd be excited for her. It's a big leap she's taking, you know, stepping down from her life's work." Henry sucked in a deep breath of air and coughed again, clearing his throat once more. It must have been from the yelling—he wasn't in as good a shape as he used to be, and his voice was strained. "She's worked hard when she didn't have to. Her father's firm matters a lot to her. It's a huge compliment that she and your uncle want to pass it to you."

Theo stared at him in disbelief. "Don't you know how *bad* that would be?" He spread his hands out in front of him, pleading. "You know about my episode at Yale. Diego called you when I was in the hospital."

"Yeah. I know. I remember. I took you home." He grimaced. "You think I'd ever forget that day? When I almost lost you?"

"Then how could you think this was a good thing?"

Henry shook his head. "I didn't say that I did, but it's also not my business to interfere. All this? It's between you and your mother and your uncle. I'm not a Redmond. I'm not a lawyer. And God knows I'm not perfect—no one is. But one thing I'm always going to do is protect your mother and support her in her dreams and ambitions. I think this was her way of trying to tell you that she loves you and that she wants to spend more time with you—she wants to make up for the past. She doesn't know anything else, and she's doing the best she can.

"As someone who has a complicated past myself, I understand. I'm comfortable with who I am—and I love her for who she is too, even if we didn't work together." His eyes darted over to meet Theo's, and he wiped more beaded sweat away from his brow. "I still love her a whole helluva lot. I always have, and I always will. There was never anyone else for me, and there never will be."

Theo's preference for back roads came from his father, who always took them when going between the city and the Redmond estate. They both hated the freeways and the perpetual traffic, and the views from the hills and forests of the scenic route were far better, even at night.

Henry sped down a winding road cutting into the side of a hill.

They stared ahead in silence.

"You know, Teddy," his father finally said, "I know you've got your own ideals and opinions about things. I know your morals and values—and the spectacular art you make with them—are important to you. But did you know that you can be just as rigid and stubborn as your mother and uncle are?"

"I don't want to hear it," Theo grumbled. "You're one to talk morals, *Dad*. At least I have them. Mostly."

Henry laughed, and it turned into a cough. "Hey, fair enough, kid. I might be a bit more flexible in terms of what I believe than you, though it doesn't make my opinion any less valuable, you know. But let me tell you, after well over thirty years of dealing with Redmond bullshit, don't think you're at all exempt from it. You're not exceptional just for having the Sullivan name instead. You're one of them too. You're half. Don't discount that."

"I don't want it. I don't want any of their goddamn *legacy*. It comes with a price."

"Everything in life does. Nothing's free. I know you grew up pretty pampered with your trust fund and your fancy prep schools, so maybe you don't *really* know that, despite my best efforts to teach you otherwise, but it's true. It's just a fact of life. So you need to let go of some of this bullshit. Just let it go." He lifted his hand and rubbed at his chest. "What did I eat?" he muttered. "Heartburn is strong tonight . . ."

"It's not like being a Sullivan is a picnic either, you know." Theo shook his head and crossed his arms over his chest, leaning his head on the window to stare out at the black wall of interminable hill outside. The cool glass was bracing on his heated face. His stupid ears were probably still bright red. "I don't want any of this. I never asked for this, I never asked to *be* here, and I just want everyone to leave me alone—including *you*, half the time. I don't know why it's so hard to get that." He sighed. "Why would Mom think this would be a good idea? I'd be a nightmare of a lawyer, and you know this better than anyone. I don't understand why you're being so cavalier about it."

Henry didn't say anything, and Theo shook his head. "Fine. I get it if you don't want to talk about it anymore. *I* definitely don't want to. I'm so sick of this shit, talking everything to death with my parents. It's like you both still think I'm some little kid, but I'm a grown man, and I have been for a while. I hate being talked down to, and everyone in this fucking family still seems to think I can't really handle anything on my own. She should have just told me on the phone. She didn't need to call me out here like this. I . . ."

Theo blinked.

There was more distance between him and the hill to his right.

They were also going awfully fast. His dad never cared much for speed limits and definitely loved to show off the power of his hot rods, but even this seemed excessive.

And the car was floating to the left. That was odd.

Was it the steering? Had it gone out of alignment again?

"Hey, Dad? You're drifting into the other lane. You gotta—"

When Theo turned toward his father, he paled. Something was wrong. Henry looked ashen, and his skin was gray. His eyes were wide as he stared straight ahead at the road, and his breathing was shallow, stilted.

"Dad?"

"M-my arm. Teddy, I—" he choked out, and lights from the other side of the road lit up the rest of his face as he clutched frantically at the steering wheel with his right hand. His left fell into his lap, his fingers twitching.

The curve around the hill brightened.

Then there was noise.

"DAD!" Theo lunged for the wheel as Henry jerked the Thunderbird to the right again, but it was too late. The sound of the semi's horn surrounded them, and all Theo saw was white, blinding light.

White.

Then nothing.

A blur.

Sensation.

Flipping—

Turning—

Churning—

Falling—

Crushing.

PRESSURE.

HORRIFIC, NIGHTMARISH PRESSURE.

Shattering.

Groaning.

And then silence.

It wasn't the sound of him screaming that caught up to him first—no, it was the horrible feeling of the car crumpling around him, the thick, sharp steel of the Thunderbird ripping and tearing at the force of the semi hit. The world turned upside down, then over again, over and over and over, twisting and compressing around him. The jagged, torn steel of the car cut through Theo's body like butter, slicing through flesh as easily as a searing-hot knife, ripping him open and shredding his face. His nerve endings exploded into numbness, and the side of the car crushed his hip as it turned over and over again, tumbling down the hill and into the trees like a rock kicked down a mountain from on high.

He blacked out.

But just as quickly, he was back.

They'd stopped.

His heart thundered in his ears.

For a second, it was the only thing he could sense.

It was the only thing he could hear.

He opened one eye—he could only open one. As soon as he tried to blink, white-hot searing pain shot down his face, and he cried out, his limbs jolting at the feeling of it.

The crash had happened so fast, the pain hit before the sound did.

Then sound came rushing back, all of it at once, but as a ringing in Theo's ears, a hissing noise, far off in the distance.

He could feel his life leaching away, warm and red, sticky, painting his vision vermilion.

And next to him, his father.

Henry's chest rose and fell in slow, jerky breaths, trembling and held aloft by the seatbelt. His left hand still clutched at his heart, his face and snow-white hair were covered in blood, and the rest of his visible limbs were limp and wrenched at odd, uncanny angles.

His body was mangled. The dashboard of his beloved Thunderbird had crushed him when it bore the brunt of the impact.

But he was still alive.

Still breathing.

"D-Dad," Theo croaked. "*Dad.*" It was all he could muster.

Henry's chest fluttered, and he turned his head instinctively toward the sound. His right arm was outstretched toward his son, twisted and broken, but he could still move his fingers. The tips of them grazed Theo's left cheek.

Teddy. His father's lips formed the word, soundlessly, over and over again.

Teddy.

But then they slowed.

Ted.

Te—

T—

His chest stopped fluttering.

His arm went lax.

And then he was still.

"Dad?" Theo breathed. "Dad! DAD! *No! NO!*"

When he screamed, the pain rushed over him again, fully this time, slamming into him like a tidal wave, just as violently as the semitruck had slammed into their car. Nothing but pain, deep and torturous, unyielding and unending. He tried to unbuckle himself and slide over, but the second he moved, he nearly passed out again from the effort—and when he looked down, he saw why.

A tree branch, sticking straight out of his lower left abdomen.

As soon as he saw it, the sensation returned. He *felt it*, felt *everything* in his body.

His face twitched, and he *felt* the metal lodged there.

The shattered bones.

The tattered car door, crushed around his right side.

Blood dripping down his trembling hand.

His chest, ripped open.

His *hip*, ground into dust.

The more he saw, the more it burned, bit by bit as his brain became agonizingly *aware*.

He couldn't handle it, the sheer, overwhelming horror of it.

He lost himself to the burning dark, to the depths of hell.

But the last thing he saw, seared forever into his memory, were his father's glassy, lifeless eyes.

Still staring straight into his own.

Eighteen

A TEAR SLID DOWN Audrey's cheek.

"Oh my god, Theo."

She covered her mouth and sobbed.

He was *alive*.

It was a miracle he was, and she'd never been so thankful for anything in her entire life.

She could have lost him before she even knew who he was to lose.

The thought terrified her.

He nodded and swept the tear away with his thumb before wiping his own aside. "I know. I was incredibly lucky." His own lip quivered, and he drew in a deep breath to steel himself for the rest.

"Somehow, the tree branch I was impaled with through the windshield missed anything vital, and I'm just left with the scar from it now. Same with my shoulder—that was from a bit of metal shrapnel and glass that had to be dug out, but I don't have lasting damage there. My face and arm and hip weren't so lucky." He shook his head. "We hit that semi head-on going way faster than we should have been—way faster than the speed limit.

"That part really was an accident. My dad's foot probably froze up on the accelerator when his arm went numb. But the impact was almost squarely angled toward him, once he jerked the wheel back to the right. He took the brunt of it." He cleared his throat and wiped more tears from his eyes. "But it didn't stop the Thunderbird from spinning and tearing through the guardrail before tumbling down the side of the hill into the trees. The steel on my side crumpled and imploded from the impact, crushing my hip and ripping me open from eye to waist.

"It also sliced through some of the nerves in my arm, broke my face, and nearly cost me an eye." He bit his lip and tried to grin crookedly at her, though it was a piss-poor attempt. "It's actually a really good thing I have such a heavy, Neanderthal brow. It saved my eyesight, if not my good looks."

Audrey sniffed and brushed some of the hair away from his face. "I beg to differ. You didn't lose any of those."

Theo huffed, but his face fell again. "I caused a helluva scene. If I hadn't snapped, maybe my dad wouldn't have had a heart attack. He wouldn't have had to come get me, and maybe we could have staved it off. My mom should have called the police. I was beyond reason." He wrung his hands together, rubbing at his knuckles and picking anxiously at his fingernails. "But doing that would have caused the exact kind of scandal they're afraid of. And anyway, my dad was closer. He was big and tall and strong, like me. I'm sure he was the only person she could think of to help.

"I ruined everything, Audrey. I tore my family apart. I assaulted my uncle, insulted my mother, I might as well have killed my father." He sighed, and his shoulders slumped. "I can't even really do the art I was so protective of anymore, the whole reason for the fight in the first place—at least, not like I used to. And I just wanted to do something good." Another tear slid down his cheek. "I wanted to do something good, something beautiful, something that made an impact, and I *was*. I was doing it, and I was doing it really well. Making an actual difference, bringing awareness to issues, raising money for good charities." Theo's face twisted in disgust, and he tugged at his hair with trembling fingers. "And now here I am, a crippled shut-in, and a failure of an artist."

The bitterness in his voice broke her heart, and she grabbed his hand to stop him from hurting himself.

But he didn't quite seem to notice.

His eyes were empty and unfocused.

"My dad is dead. I watched him die, the car he loved so much a smoldering wreck in the aftermath. It was totaled, nothing but scrap. I sold the shop and the rest of his cars to pay off his debts, but I also just couldn't keep it after that. I couldn't keep hardly anything. Anything except . . ." Theo glanced over at the neon sign buzzing near the kitchen, and now Audrey knew why he'd clung to that piece of his father.

He'd probably made it for him.

"And now I've tanked my relationship with my mom as well. My uncle was always a dick, and I only regret beating the shit out of him because of everything else that happened afterward, but I also hate myself for it. I think about it every day, how *good* it felt bashing his face in, and it makes me sick to my stomach. It was ugly. *I* was ugly. An absolute monster. Does it make me a bully—just like him?" Theo finally looked her in the eyes again, desperately searching her face. "I let his words get the better of me. I failed to control myself. I gave myself over to my basest impulses, threw all my values and ideals aside, and took my anger out on him, just like he always did to me. That makes me just as much of a piece of shit as him, doesn't it?"

She shook her head. "I don't think so. It sounds to me like you were pushed to your breaking point—and that you snapped. I've been there before myself."

He startled and blinked at her in surprise. "Have you really?"

Audrey nodded. "It was in high school. There was a girl there, Abby, and she bullied me relentlessly. I was used to it—I got a lot of shit for being a foster kid. Empathy takes some people a while to learn, I suppose." She drew in a deep breath. "Halfway through junior year, she tripped me outside while I was carrying my lunch tray. I was on the subsidized lunch program, and I only got one meal ticket a day. We had food at Gladys's house, but she was fostering a bunch of kids, and there was barely enough to go around. I was hungry. I needed that lunch. And when I fell on top of it in the mud, I looked up at her—and she was grinning down at me, pleased as punch. So I gave her one.

"I lost it. She was a lot bigger than I was, but I jumped her straightaway and beat the shit out of her. Had to be pulled off of her and restrained by a security guard."

Theo's mouth cracked into a weak, but wicked grin. "That's really hot."

She huffed in amusement. "I love that you think that, darling." She tucked some of his hair behind one of his massive ears, gently tracing the curve of its shell with the tips of her fingers. Now that she knew what had happened, she was all the more thankful for every bit of him she could love.

She loved his ears. He listened to her so well with them.

And they were adorable.

To think that he hated them . . .

It made her ache.

"The principal didn't really think so. I was suspended for three weeks and sent to state-mandated counseling. I think the only reason I still managed to get a scholarship after that was because I was salutatorian *and* I was a foster kid—lashing out was kind of expected of me, to a certain degree. But Abby deserved everything she got, and I refuse to back down about that.

"I don't know your uncle, though he does sound like a real dick. He treated you like garbage. But you can't keep blaming yourself for everything that happened." She wrapped her arms around his neck and snuggled in closer to his warmth, nuzzling into his cheek. "Your dad could've had that same heart attack and died in his sleep. You could have swallowed your words, had the evening go off without a hitch, accepted your mother's offer, and *still* gotten in the car with him and had him die the same way the next day. You can't sit here and keep trying to figure out what you could have done differently."

Theo shook his head. "I don't know about that. I've thought through every scenario, every single possibility. If we'd left in the morning, and if I hadn't gotten into that fight, he might not have been stressed enough to have such a massive heart attack. We might have made it home, or he could have had a smaller one that was fixable. If it was lighter outside, I would've noticed him drifting sooner and could have taken the wheel and avoided the crash. Maybe he wouldn't be dead. Maybe it wouldn't be my fault. Maybe . . . maybe I wouldn't be like *this*." He lifted a hand and ran it down the length of the scar on his face, his fingers shaking. He clenched his fist tightly before letting it fall limply into his lap.

"Theo." She looked him in the eyes and cradled his cheek with her hand. "Listen to me. You have to stop blaming yourself. It was an accident. You can't go back and change the past, no matter how much you want to. Dwelling on it like this isn't going to do any good for your future." She slid her palm along the planes of his face, tracing the ridge of his cheek with her thumb. "I'm not sure I'm going to like the way this sounds, but hear me out," she murmured. "Maybe you should let the past die. Bury it in the ground, and—and forge something new."

He grew quiet.

All either of them could hear was the crackling of the flames in the fireplace.

"Let the past die?" he finally whispered, and his eyes went wide. "Oh my god. I—I've been making this *my* legacy, haven't I?" His bottom lip trembled, and he bit it sharply before burying his face in his hands. "Dad was right: I'm just like *them*."

"No, you're not. It's just that I wouldn't think your dad would want you to cling to this guilt, would he?" Audrey ran her hands through his hair before peeling his palms away from his face. "I'm not saying not to honor him, but it sounded like he loved you a lot. I don't think he'd want you hurting this much. Look at me, Theo." When he still wouldn't meet her gaze, she put her hand under his chin and tilted his face up to make him. "He angled the car away to keep the truck from hitting *your* side head-on even while he was having a heart attack, didn't he? He tried to take the hit so that *you* wouldn't. He protected you. You know that's true, don't you?"

Theo closed his eyes sharply, but it wasn't enough to keep the tears from spilling out. They lingered on his eyelashes for a split second, shining golden in the firelight before finally falling, leaving shimmering streaks in their wake. He sniffed and nodded once—then again, more firmly this time.

The hardest words to say waited on her tongue, and her own heart broke when she finally released them.

"He wanted you to *live*. Your father made a choice, and he chose *you*—he chose you over himself, over anything else." Her own cheeks were wet, the tears streaming down them in earnest now. "And you know what? In a lot of ways, that's more than my mother ever did for me. That's what a parent's supposed to do. He loved you so much. You have to know that."

A sob wracked his chest at those words.

Audrey wiped his tears away and buried her hands in his hair again, pulling his head down to the curve of her neck. Theo's arms shook as they wrapped around her—strong, but still tentative, still broken as they always had been.

"You said he knew who he was, and that he accepted himself, and your mother, even with their complicated past," she said, her voice quivering as she pressed her lips to the side of his head. "Why can't you have the same thing? Why don't you think you deserve that kind of peace? Your dad thought you did. Don't you think that's what he would have wanted for you? For you to forgive yourself, and to let your wounds heal, to stitch them up and let the scars finally settle?" She shook her head. "This isn't living. It's a half-life at best. He can't have wanted you to keep cutting yourself open, slicing over your scars with a knife and bleeding them dry, again and again and again. And I don't want that for you either."

Her hands shook as she held him close, the ache in her heart for him growing with every tear he shed. "Your dad loved you, and if there's one thing I believe, it's that love never dies. It persists. It's what we leave behind—it's what your father left behind for you. It's not his death that keeps his memory alive, it's his love. That's his legacy. It lives on through you." She buried her face in his hair. "And now *I* love you, and I don't want this for you. I don't want you to keep hurting yourself, torturing yourself over this. *I* can't bear you living with such pain. Seeing it hurt you? It hurts *me*." Another sob tore through her chest. "Please let it go," she begged. "At least a little. For me, if not for you. I love you too much for you to keep carrying it like this."

Theo's shoulders shook.

His arms tightened around her, and his fingers gripped so hard as he clung to her, she wondered if he might have left bruises petaled along her ribs and back.

But that was fine.

It was nothing compared to the hurt he felt.

She knew it, by the sound he made.

When he finally set it loose—

And let it go.

She felt where it came from when Theo finally set his grief free. It rose from deep inside him, boiling up from some unknown place, somewhere he'd buried it, refused to fully look at it, refused to let it do more than only simmer constantly beneath his skin.

It wasn't small.

It wasn't just a pool of grief.

It was an entire ocean.

And he'd been lost in it, adrift at sea.

He was spent from treading water, trying not to drown.

He needed a safe place to breathe.

To rest.

So she would be his island.

Audrey closed her eyes and let it wash over her too, clinging to him and pressing her heart to his while he wailed, the sound of it unearthly and uncanny. It vibrated through her, sent shivers down her spine, shook her to her core.

But what it didn't shake was her resolve.

She sat with him, cried with him, kept silent, stayed strong and upright against him, held him tight and stroked his hair while he screamed everything he couldn't voice, everything he'd been keeping wound tight inside for six long months, longer maybe, perhaps hadn't *ever* truly dared unleash.

Eventually, Theo calmed.

He grew quiet.

He closed his eyes, his tears finally run dry, finally spent.

And when he buried his right hand in her hair to draw her forehead to his lips for an exhausted kiss, she didn't feel it move at the back of her head.

His hand didn't shake at all.

Instead, it stayed perfectly still.

For the very first time.

Nineteen

SWIMMING OUT OF her slumber was difficult.

Audrey's eyes were so heavy, she couldn't yet open them. But she could hear Theo somewhere nearby, keeping his voice low through the drone of the white noise machines.

"Okay, good. I'm glad you're on board. Yeah, I thought it was a good idea too. I'm not overly thrilled, though, don't get me wrong, but it feels better than the alternative."

Her whole body was so *heavy*.

And so comfortable.

"Yeah, Audrey and I talked a lot about it last night. And that did help—it helped *enormously*. I told her about the accident. All of it. Yeah, even that part. Thanks. Audrey? Oh, we're doing great. Yeah, I'll tell her—thank you, Amelia. I'm glad she was here too."

Theo's sheets felt like silk against her bare skin, slipping luxuriously along her legs as she shifted. His duvet was thick and heavy and made moving difficult, like last night when he'd first wrapped her up in it. But she finally managed to turn over and blink a little, squinting through the soft pinkish-orange light of the salt lamp cutting through the darkness.

He was sitting on the edge of the bed clad in his boxer briefs, his phone pressed tightly up against his ear, watch already on and glinting in the glow of the lamp. But when she moved, he looked over his shoulder and caught her eye, immediately leaning back to grab her hand and curl his fingers into hers.

She was glad.

She needed to touch him too.

She'd missed him while she was asleep.

"Yeah, I think it would've been so much worse if she hadn't been. I don't know what I might have done."

The corners of his wide lips twitched upward in the shadows, and he shifted his own body, rustling against the sheets while he laid back down next to her, holding the phone away from his mouth slightly so he could kiss her without too much trouble. It looked comically minuscule in his massive paw.

The phone dropped back down to his mouth again, and Theo settled his head on her pillow, his thick, dark waves tumbling roguishly across his forehead.

God, he was handsome.

To think he couldn't see himself the way she saw him.

It was almost unfathomable.

"I'm open to it. I don't want to lose anyone else. I've already learned that lesson once, and that was one too many times. I'll propose it when I see her. I don't know if she'll go for it, though she did say she was willing to do anything to make things right. Uh-huh. Yeah, boundaries, I remember. I will."

Audrey brushed a few strands of his hair away so she could see his face better, and that earned her a full, crooked smile.

"I understand. When can I see you again? Can you squeeze me in soon?" A pause. "Okay, I'll take it. Thank you so much. I really, really appreciate it." Theo pulled the back of her hand to his lips. His eyes darted all over her face, searching her features in the dim light of his room. "Okay. You have a good weekend too, and I'll see you on Monday. Bye."

He hung up and tossed the phone onto the edge of the bed before pulling Audrey into his arms. "Good morning, sweetheart," he whispered, pressing a kiss to her forehead. "Did you sleep well? I'm sorry if I woke you."

She shook her head. "No, it's fine. I woke up on my own."

"Are you terribly sore?"

"No." She couldn't help but smile softly at him while she ran her thumb along the rise of his cheekbone. "I'm a little sore, but not bad. Not at all. You were very gentle."

He closed his eyes and sighed deeply in relief, snaking his arms around her beneath the sheets and drawing her into his chest. His scent enveloped her, warm and woodsy, tinged with musk and sweat and sleep, and she wriggled closer, burying herself in it.

She could stay like this forever, wrapped in his arms. How could she feel anything but safe and loved when his lips pressed so softly against her hair, over and over again, or when his hand combed soothingly through her waves, his palm nearly the size of her head? He was gentle, he was a giant, he was hers.

And she was his.

Their puzzle pieces slotted together so perfectly, so comfortably, so precisely.

And somehow, out of all the places and all the people in the world, the universe had seen fit to let them find each other, and fit each other.

Would she ever tire of this feeling?

It seemed impossible.

"What time is it?" Audrey finally asked with a yawn. She was in grave danger of falling dead asleep again if she didn't say anything.

"It's just after ten."

She blinked in surprise and eyed the blackout shades.

"I had to grab Dr. Harper on the phone between appointments, but I didn't want to leave you in case you woke up, so I tried to keep my voice down."

This was the latest—and deepest—she'd slept in *years*. Barista life meant she was usually awake by 6:30 on a good day, and 4:30 for the rest of them.

Well. Yesterday *was* exhausting. Perhaps it was no surprise she'd been out like a light once Theo had carried her upstairs and made her brush her teeth before they went to bed.

Such a nerd.

She loved him for it.

She turned back over and snuggled closer to him, tucking herself under his chin. His heartbeat drummed beneath her ear as he breathed, slow and steady and strong.

He was alive.

He was safe.

She'd have to keep reminding herself of that for a while now.

"What'd she say?"

Theo rubbed his eyes tiredly. "We didn't have a ton of time to talk, but first, she wanted me to tell you how glad she was you were here last night, and how impressed she is with you—and also that she wouldn't mind at all if you came in and talked to her about why exactly you're so very mature for your age." He shot her a wry glance. "It reeks of trauma."

Audrey snorted. "It's cute you think I can afford your therapist."

His dark eyebrows skyrocketed. "*Oh?*" he purred, burying his nose in the crook of her neck. "You know what else is cute, sweetheart?" he murmured, nipping at the sensitive skin with his teeth. When she yelped, he squeezed her tighter and pressed a kiss there. His plush lips widened into a wicked grin, and he huffed in amusement under her jaw. "That you still seem to think you're going to have to 'afford' anything anymore. That's adorable."

He barked a laugh, full and deep, as if the very notion were ridiculous before peppering her neck with more nipping, playful kisses. She laughed and tried to squirm away, but his biceps bulged and tightened around her, keeping her locked firmly in place and at his mercy.

"It's *very* cute you think I'm going to let you want for anything, or that I don't take extreme, excessive *pleasure* in providing for you." He growled that last bit, his voice rumbling deep in his throat—and, as if to drive the point home, he smiled and took her mouth in his.

She closed her eyes and relished the feeling of the kiss, of him, of his warm, dry hands on the sides of her head, brushing her hair behind her ears, of his lips, soft and gentle against her own. She opened her mouth in invitation, in welcome, wanting, *needing* to feel him somewhere inside her where he'd found his place long ago, and when his tongue darted between her lips, he tasted minty and fresh and cool, like he'd just brushed his teeth. But before she could explore him more thoroughly, he drew back, and with him he drew her bottom lip between his teeth, just barely grazing along it, lingering on their connection as if he were loath to ever be parted from her in any way before he spoke again.

"You'll never want for anything, Audrey," he whispered, pressing his forehead to hers. "Not with me. I'll make sure of that."

The certainty in his voice sent shivers down her spine, and she held her breath as his words fully wrapped around her and settled into her bones.

She hadn't really considered what it would be like to be in a relationship before—what it might be like to actually have someone care for her, to partner with her, to have her back, always, fully and truly.

She'd never had true help before from someone she could rely on who was this close, or who wasn't appointed to her by the state. Friends weren't the same. Foster parents weren't the same, not even Gladys.

Not in this way.

The enormity of that realization, of that change, and of how fast it had crept up on her might have frightened her if it were anyone else.

But now, after everything, that would be like being afraid of her own heart.

She didn't know what to say, but Theo didn't seem to mind. Instead, he only ran a thumb across her lips with a slight smile tugging at the corners of his mouth.

"Dr. Harper reaffirmed that my mother did violate a pretty hefty boundary yesterday. But when she asked me how I felt about what I said, I . . ." He trailed off with a sigh. "I told her I felt like garbage. Not because I was right, but because my mom . . . well, she did try to apologize. She never apologizes for anything, and this time she did. She did at least *try* to, anyway, but I didn't listen. And I screamed at her." He closed his eyes and rolled his lips—the same way she'd seen his mother do. Now Audrey knew where the tic came from. "I have very conflicting feelings."

"She came into your house without permission and dredged up a lot of things in the process."

"Well, yes. But . . ." He tilted his head from side to side with a hum. "I mean, I did give her that key. And I went no contact with her and didn't ask for it back. I could have, and I didn't. I even thought about it once and still chose not to. I didn't even change the locks. I didn't block her number, and I could have. I could have done all that, and I didn't. Maybe that means something."

Theo shook his head again, sending his thick waves tumbling around his cheeks. "I don't entirely know how I feel today, but I do know I feel bad about how I reacted—and about some of the things I said yesterday, even if they were true. My actions and reactions are the only parts of all this that I can control or change going forward." He plucked again at Audrey's hair, arranging the strands carefully around her face. "I wish I'd heard her out a little more than I did instead of leaping straight to anger. I hate myself for that. It's almost exactly the same thing I did the night of the accident. Maybe I haven't learned anything."

It was her turn to shake her head. "No. You were surprised. Your reaction was justified. And you need to stop beating yourself up about *this* too. All right?"

"I did promise you I'd stop doing that. I'll try."

"Are you going to stick to what you decided last night?" she murmured. He nodded, humming deep in his chest with a sigh.

After he'd cried so hard she thought he might pass out, they'd talked. They talked until they ran out of words.

When they grew quiet, Theo ran his hands along her body, slowly, softly. The fire reflected back at her in his eyes, those beautiful irises of shifting liquid gold and amber and dark, deep mahogany, their lighter edges sometimes green, sometimes not, both crystalline and clear, but flecked with a few stray dark spots—freckles, just like the ones dotting his face and body. The most perfect imperfections.

His fingers, sure and strong, had pinched the zipper of the hoodie she wore.

And drew it all the way down.

The second time they made love there on the duvet in front of the fire was so different from the first. She was more ready this time—not at all scared, all the more sure.

And so was he.

She knew with every kiss, every stroke, every caress, that he loved her, well and truly. That he wouldn't hide anything from her. And with every embrace, every cry, every shiver, she knew she loved him too. There was no mistaking it, no denying it, no room for doubt or fear. Her love only grew and deepened in that moment together with Theo in front of the fire, the edges of her blurring into the edges of him, melding into one like liquid metal, forging themselves into something new, honing each other into something sharper, something more.

Waking up this morning, she felt different.

And she could see the change in Theo too.

His shoulders were more square, more set.

For the first time since they'd met, he seemed to take up more space rather than less.

"Do you want to take a shower and get ready?" he finally asked. "It's going to take us some time to get to Midtown."

WHEN AUDREY CAME downstairs from doing her meager best with her makeup, Theo was standing at his kitchen counter, scrawling something in looping, only slightly shaken handwriting on the back of a business card with the fountain pen he normally used for sketching. He glanced up when she padded downstairs, and a crooked grin split his mouth wide.

"You look beautiful."

"Are you sure this is okay?" She looked down at her skirt and sweater, the same outfit she'd worn on their first date. It was a last-minute addition to her bag, but she was glad she'd grabbed it now, even if she was the one who was nervous about leaving the house for once.

It was Theo who seemed oddly at ease.

He tucked the card into his wallet and capped the pen, placing it back in his satchel before slinging the whole thing over his shoulder and holding up her coat. He'd already grabbed it and her scarf from the rack near the door, and he helped slide it over her arms when she stepped over to him, adjusting it carefully around her shoulders before turning her to face him.

"You're perfect. It's very appropriate, trust me." While he looped her scarf around her neck, she ran her hands along his black sweater, admiring the luxurious feel of the cashmere beneath her fingertips.

Theo was immaculate in his turtleneck and slacks, his polished black leather derby dress shoes gleaming in the late morning light streaming through the windows. The sweater hid the part of the scar slashing down his neck, but what was more noticeable was the tiny glimpse of the classic Burberry pattern peeking out from the inside collar of his open black wool coat. Audrey raised her eyebrows.

He never dressed like this, but he looked *spectacular.*

He looked rich.

Expensive.

Everything fit him like a glove.

"Don't look at me like that," he muttered, tucking the ends of her scarf into her coat. "I know what you're thinking. But you know damn well I'd much rather be staying here in a comfortable pair of sweatpants and watching movies with you on the couch. Just because I own it doesn't mean it's my usual fare."

"Could've fooled me. You're dressed like the poster boy of some high-end fashion campaign. And you look damn *good*. Better than I do." Her clothes were secondhand from the thrift store, not some couture brand. She frowned at her worn plaid skirt.

"Nonsense." He snorted and took her chin in his hand, tilting her head back up to make her look him in the eyes. "Impossible. You're far prettier than me. Have you *seen* me?" He lifted his eyebrows and gave her a wry smirk. "You look gorgeous—as beautiful and luminous as a ray of sunshine on a cloudy day. And I look like I've been put through a wood chipper." He laced their fingers together and tugged her toward the door. "This isn't even a contest."

She smiled, but couldn't keep it. "Are you absolutely sure you want to go?" She tightened her hand in his. "You can still say no."

He nodded before pausing and plunging his free hand into a little white box on the shelf near the coat rack. "I'm all right. I'm actually glad this happened—I have some things I need to say today, now that I've had time to think about it."

"Good. As long as you're okay with it. And I'll be right there with you." She stood on her tiptoes and pressed a kiss to his cheek. It was clean and cool and smooth, and he smelled fresh, like his soap and aftershave mixed with his cologne, all cedarwood and juniper and bergamot.

The scent made her mind flash right back to the shower they'd taken together this morning.

It was completely different than the one from last night. Theo had stood behind her under his dual high-pressure shower heads and washed her hair with gentle fingers. She'd closed her eyes and leaned back into his chest, melting in his arms while he gave her the best scalp and neck massage she'd ever had, tilting her this way and that, scrubbing and then conditioning until he was satisfied with his handiwork.

And then it was his turn.

He was too tall for her to do the same for him, so they'd both turned and eyed the shower chair he'd left there last night. Theo pulled it closer and sat heavily, watching Audrey intently. His gaze roved over her body, and he rolled his lips when his eyes traced the path of a water droplet trailing between her breasts.

"See something that interests you, Theodore Henry Sullivan?" Audrey asked, stepping back over and sliding into his lap, much like she had the night before. But this time, it was different.

So very different.

He held his head out of the stream of water for her, and his eyes darkened when she plunged her hands into his thick hair, pulling and tugging gently as she scrubbed his fancy soap into his luscious, shadowy waves.

"I see a lot of things that *greatly* interest me, sweetheart," he muttered, his eyes trailing up her body and finally landing on her lips. "But I was just reflecting on something."

"What?"

"The fact that up until now, you seeing me sitting broken in this thing was maybe my worst nightmare. I thought it was deeply embarrassing, the fact that I needed it at all. Same with my cane—I hate that I need it on bad days sometimes, like when we walked at the park. I left it behind that day because I was ashamed. I didn't want you to see me with it."

"That's silly, Theo. I'd rather you be able to walk properly or shower comfortably than—"

"I know."

He rested his hands on her legs and began to glide them gently upward, sliding them across her slick skin until they finally came to a stop at her waist. His thumbs began to swirl gentle circles there.

"Now I've never been more glad that I was too wide and too heavy for the standard chair. They had to give me one for bariatric patients." He quirked an eyebrow. "Easily holds up to seven hundred pounds, and can truly take a beating, I'm sure. Want to put it to the test?"

Audrey laughed and tilted his head back under the shower stream, using her fingers to comb through and help rinse all the shampoo from his hair. "Not your worst nightmare anymore, then?"

He closed his eyes, and a satisfied, roguish smile cracked his mouth wide open, digging both dimples deeply into his cheeks.

"No, Miss Adams. In fact, I'm pretty sure this counts as a very literal *wet dream*." His hand shifted and dropped between her legs, his fingers stroking and teasing at her clit and her folds, and it was Audrey's turn to gasp and close her eyes. A heat altogether very different than that of the shower began to build in her core, and she rocked her hips against Theo's hand, wrapping her arms around his neck as she rode him. His erection pressed into her stomach, thick and hard, and he grunted when she rubbed against it. Audrey opened her eyes and found his searching her own, water droplets tumbling from his long, dark lashes.

The way he looked at her never failed to send shivers down her spine.

It was as if she was the only thing that mattered.

"Audrey," he whispered. "We don't have to if you're too—"

His words were swallowed by a moan when she wrapped her hand around his length and pumped once before shifting in his lap, lifting her hips, and guiding him to her entrance. She used his shoulders as leverage and slowly slid onto him, exhaling and relaxing as he stretched her, filling her so fully and completely once again. He was still almost too much for her to take, but the ache of him was just as delicious as it had been yesterday, and she savored it, folding forward and burying her face in his neck.

His chest rose in a sudden gasp beneath her, and a chuckle rumbled after. "*God,*" Theo muttered, his voice cracking and strained as he buried his hands in her hair, his arms holding her steady at her back. "Never in my wildest, wettest teenage dreams did I ever imagine I could have someone as beautiful and precious as you."

When Audrey rocked her hips against his, he matched her cadence with his own, dragging his warm, plush lips everywhere he could reach while he held her tightly against his heart.

Neither of them managed to say anything else coherent for the rest of that shower.

But the chair held up *splendidly.*

Audrey smiled again now, and when she met Theo's gaze, she knew he was thinking about the same thing. A single dimple was shadowed into his cheek, his crooked grin as soft as she'd ever seen it. She smoothed a hand over the front of his coat and tugged it straighter across his chest.

"And I'm going to tell you again, Theo: you look really, *really* handsome."

"Thank you, sweetheart." He pulled out a black KN95 mask from the box and stilled for a moment, turning it over in his hands and staring at his fingers entwined with the elastic.

"What is it?"

He shook his head. "Nothing." With one graceful, practiced motion, he slid one strap over his ear and pulled the mask across his face, securing the other side so easily, he could probably do it in his sleep before they left home and headed uptown.

IT WAS A long, quiet subway ride to Manhattan.

Audrey sat next to Theo, still clutching her half-eaten bagel and resting her head on his shoulder as he sketched the people around them in his little black leather notebook. But it wasn't the drawings she was most interested in.

It was his hands.

He hadn't seemed to notice how much the shaking in his right hand had diminished. It wasn't entirely gone, not by any means; she still noted an odd tremor here, a strange twitch there. But the difference from yesterday was remarkable.

It was unmistakable.

After everything, Theo was so much steadier than he'd been before.

When he wrapped his left arm around her waist, she closed her eyes and let the gentle swaying of the train lull her into another light sleep.

He woke her with a kiss on the forehead when they got to their stop, and he led her up into the harried streets of Manhattan, winding through the crowds until they arrived at a massive skyscraper. The doors were busy, constantly opening and closing to accommodate the hustle and bustle of all the professional-looking, buttoned-up office workers dodging in and out.

"HEY!"

Theo's hand had just closed around the handle when they both turned toward the shout. Diego was sprinting toward them from down the street, his woolen coat and scarf flying in the wind. He skidded to a stop and bent, resting his hands on his knees while he panted.

"What—the fuck—are you doing?" he breathed, glaring up at Theo between gasps for air.

Theo raised an eyebrow. "What does it look like I'm doing? I'm going inside to talk to my mother, like I texted you I was. What are *you* doing here?"

Diego straightened and grabbed his wrist. "Are you crazy?" He twisted slightly. "It's Friday. Your uncle's in there too."

"Yeah. I figured as much. Seemed logical, given that he's a partner." Theo twisted out of his friend's grasp.

"What are you going to do if you see him?" When he didn't answer Diego's question, the reporter looked over at Audrey and grimaced, smoothing a hand over his stubbled chin and shaking his head. "*Mother of God.* Audrey, did this asshole finally tell you what happened yet or not?" He jerked his thumb back at Theo. "Surely he's not walking you in there blind?"

"I know what I'm getting into." She put her hand on Theo's arm. "He'll be fine."

"If you say so . . ." Diego shook his head and ushered them toward the door, yanking it forward and holding it open. "Let's get on with it, then. I made up enough bullshit about a family emergency to get out of a meeting with my editor, so you're dead wrong if you think I'm not coming with you as backup."

Theo's eyes crinkled above his mask as he patted Diego on the shoulder. "Thanks, brother."

"Yeah, yeah." He waved them inside. "You owe me one."

The entrance was impressive, with spit-shined marble flooring and chic, light-wood paneled walls sweeping up to tall ceilings dotted with mid-century modern globular light fixtures. The woman staffing the front desk paid them no mind, and Theo led her to a hallway lined on both sides with elevators. When the stainless-steel doors of one opened, he pulled her in and punched the button for the forty-seventh floor.

The higher they went, the more his hand shook.

"Hey," she whispered, tightening her fingers between his. "It'll be okay."

Theo closed his eyes and bent to press his forehead against hers.

"Thank you for coming with me," he whispered.

"Me too, Ted?"

When he slowly turned to scowl at Diego, he shook his head and sighed.

"Yeah. You too, D. You're a good friend."

"That's all I needed to hear."

The elevator dinged and the doors swept open to reveal a sweeping walnut-fronted desk, its top formed out of blue-tinged curving glass with sans-serif stainless steel letters spelling out REDMOND, REDMOND & ASSOCIATES. As soon as the woman seated there spotted them, her eyes went wide.

"*Teddy?!*" she gasped, clamping both hands over her mouth as she stood. "Oh—oh my god, Teddy." Tears lined her eyes. "Is that you?"

"Hi, Maureen." He stepped up to her with a wave. "It's Theo these days. Is my mom busy?"

Maureen stared at him, speechless. She was a middle-aged woman with gray threaded through mousy brown hair and fine wrinkles just beginning to line her kind, round face. "I—I, uh—sh-she—" She glanced down at the phone, and when she reached for it, Theo put his hand over hers and gently set the handset back down onto the receiver.

"I'd rather surprise her. Don't ping her, please."

Maureen swallowed and nodded sharply, still trying—and failing—to blink tears away. "She canceled all her meetings today. She's just been in her office with Nancy all morning. Looked upset when she came in, hasn't come out, and hasn't talked to anyone else."

"Is my uncle around?"

"Yes." Maureen eyed the hall to her left warily. "He's here today."

"Is he in there with her too?"

"No. No, she's—"

"Good." Theo leaned an elbow casually on the counter and drew in a deep breath, both of his eyes hardening as he nodded at Diego. He hadn't arranged his hair over his right eye like he used to, and his scar was barely visible through the thick, dark waves tumbling down his forehead and along his cheeks. "Don't let him anywhere near me."

"Yessir." Diego cracked his knuckles before leaning back on the desk with crossed arms, staring darkly down the hallway to the right.

Maureen stood and reached over the desk to rest a hand on Theo's arm. "Ted—*Theo.* You look . . . you look *so* much better than the last time I saw you."

The mask partially raised over his cheeks.

But his eyes were sad.

"I'm sure I do, though I'm sorry, I don't remember you visiting me, Maureen."

"Oh." Her face fell. "Right. Of course. You wouldn't." She patted his arm and sat heavily in her rolling chair, resting her head in her hand. "You know where your mom's office is. Go on in."

"Thank you." Theo's eyes crinkled at her, and he held out his hand to Audrey. Together, they walked down the hallway opposite from where Diego stood guard, passing walls lined with offices. Some doors were open, revealing people tapping away at computers in shared spaces. Some were private, and a few very lawyerly looking professionals in suits or skirts did double takes. One even stood up sharply and stared open-mouthed as they passed.

Theo ignored them all and headed straight for the office at the very end of the hall. A single, imposing door was cracked, and he rested a hand on the handle, holding it steady as they peered cautiously inside.

From what little Audrey could see, the corner office was huge and flooded with light, the early afternoon sunshine pouring inside through floor-to-ceiling windows. Eleanor leaned against the front of a massive, solid oak desk, somehow looking even tinier than she had yesterday, despite both the height of her heels and her flawless wardrobe. Her gray hair was perfectly coiffed with not a strand out of place. Her makeup was impeccable, her nails pristine. Not a wrinkle in sight on her dark gray pantsuit, and yet . . .

And yet she looked sick.

She was pale, and her cheeks were tinged with green. She was talking to a much taller woman about her age who was just as chic, but much edgier, her silver hair styled in a severe, asymmetrical bob.

Their voices filtered through the crack in the door.

"I don't know what to do, Nance."

"You can't do anything else. He's said no. You need to respect that."

"He's my only son."

"He's grieving." Nancy took Eleanor's hands. "His whole life changed. I'm sure he just needs time."

"What if I've lost him forever?" Eleanor held a trembling hand to her mouth, closing her eyes as if she were trying to stave off tears.

"I deserve to lose him. I understand completely why he hates me so much. I'm a terrible mother. I—"

When Theo pushed the door open and stepped inside, both women's heads snapped over to him.

Eleanor's eyes grew wide.

She looked like she might crumple into a heap on the floor.

The taller woman, Nancy, glanced between Eleanor and her son and blanched, her light brown eyes wide with worry. She put a hand on Eleanor's shoulder and gently squeezed.

"Text if you need me. I'll leave you to it." She hurried out of the room while Theo ushered Audrey inside, keeping her head down as she shut the door quietly behind her.

With Nancy gone, the tension in the room thickened.

Theo stood still and silent as he studied his mother, the very mirror of their encounter yesterday. Only this time, his face didn't flush red. It was inscrutable beneath the mask.

After a long moment, it was Eleanor who finally broke the silence.

"Theo," she finally whispered, as if she still couldn't quite believe that he stood before her now. She stepped forward and fumbled for a nearby armchair before sinking heavily into the plush, leather cushion. As soon as she did, she buried her face in her hands and began to sob.

"I'm so sorry, Theo," she finally gasped, tears streaming down her face. "I'm so sorry. I'm *so* sorry."

He met Audrey's gaze, and when she nodded at him, he reached up and tugged the mask away from his mouth before shoving it into his coat pocket and stepping over to his mother. He dragged over another chair and sat next to her, hands clasped and elbows resting on his knees while he waited patiently for her to catch her breath.

When she finally calmed down enough to look at him, he rolled his lips together and began to speak.

"You sent me into a tailspin yesterday. It was ugly. I wasn't ready to see you yet. I wasn't ready to talk to you yet, and you still pushed it. I've only ever been more upset once in my life." He glanced over his shoulder at Audrey and smiled softly. "But I'm okay now." When Eleanor opened her mouth to speak, hope lighting up her face, Theo held up a hand to stop her. "That doesn't mean that *we* are okay, though."

He reached into his coat pocket and pulled out his wallet, freeing the little card Audrey saw him writing on earlier from one of the slots. "I decided to come today because Dad would have wanted me to. I'm here because he can't be. He loved you. He was proud of you. And I know that what you do here, you see as your service, your purpose. The way you give back to the community and do pro bono work, the way you try to make things better for so many people within the legal system—I get that." He sighed and flicked the card between his fingers absently, anxiously. "In some ways, we're not so different. Because for you, this is your art, isn't it?

"Rejecting your legacy is about as fair as you asking me to give up mine. I know you didn't understand it that way at the time, and if I'd had the wherewithal and the mindset to explain it to you like that then, I would've. But I didn't. And now we're here. Frankly, in that respect, I don't think that part is a bad thing, even though it's caused me a great deal of pain." He huffed sardonically. "*A great deal.*"

Theo stared Eleanor straight in the eyes, unyielding and unblinking and intense. "You weren't there for me when I was growing up. I know you get that intellectually now, even if you didn't then. But that doesn't mean I'm going to do the same thing to you that you did to me. As I see it, there's only one way to break patterns, and it's by doing things differently—by not repeating them. So here's me, actively choosing not to repeat a cycle of abandonment." He nodded. "I'm here. I'm going to do better and *be* better than you were for me by modeling what I want from *you*. And that's support. And acceptance."

He leaned forward and finally handed her the card. "That doesn't mean this is a carte blanche to start over." He tapped the thick, creamy cardstock. "It's literally not a blank card." He shook his head. "Thank you for the invitation, but Audrey and I won't be coming home for Thanksgiving this year. Or Christmas. Or any other holiday. Maybe not even next year, or possibly *never*, I don't know yet. That depends on what you do from here on out. And you and I still aren't on speaking terms—let me be exceedingly clear." His full lips pressed into one thin, tense line, so hard they almost disappeared completely. "Today is a onetime deal. A goodwill gift. An exception. And unless things change, I will not be doing it again.

"Even if things *do* change, I want my privacy respected, and I want it respected religiously. It's a hard line. In either case, I will not be going back to law school. I will not be taking over the firm. If you want to talk to me, if you want to start making things better, you have to start here." He pointed at the card. "Joint therapy sessions with Dr. Harper, and independent ones on your own. I'll make time for the joint ones if you will." His face softened and he inhaled sharply. "I don't want to lose anyone else. There aren't—we don't have a lot of us to lose, and I don't want to have any more regrets. But we also can't keep going on as we have been. You agree, right, Mom? And—a-and you said you'd do anything to make it right. Did you mean it?"

He couldn't hide the hope in his eyes.

They were begging—*pleading* for his mother to see it.

Despite everything, Theo Sullivan still had hope after all.

Eleanor drew in a deep breath, still struggling to stem the tide of tears streaming down her cheeks, and nodded. "Yes. I did say that. And I meant it. I *mean* it." She wiped some of the tears away from her face. "You were right: I wasn't around. I never prioritized you enough. I didn't protect you. And above all else, I didn't understand you—and I didn't try to. I'm so sorry you felt so alone. I want to fix it. I want to fix it now before it's too late, if I have even half a chance." Her hands shook as she tried to suppress another sob. "I'll make the time. I'll do whatever it takes. I swear it."

A weak, tentative smile tugged at the corners of Theo's mouth. "Okay. Good. I'll see if you follow through—and I hope you do." He motioned again toward the card. "Turn that over."

When Eleanor did, her eyes grew wide, and she glanced at Audrey. But it was only a split second before her gaze was back on Theo's face. When she nodded, he turned in the chair and motioned over to Audrey, who walked up next to him. He stood and wrapped his arm around her waist so he could tuck her firmly into his side.

"Mom, this is my girlfriend, Audrey Adams." He beamed down at her, true light dancing in his dark eyes. "She's an electrical engineering student at NYU about to graduate in a few weeks, and she's working on sustainability, so I hope I see you prosecuting more companies who break environmental law in the future." His smile widened. "Audrey's incredibly smart, incredibly kind, really funny, makes a mean ristretto, and I thought I knew what love was until I met her. Turns out I was wrong." The crinkles around his eyes deepened. "But I know now."

Audrey smiled back up at him, and pride warmed her chest as her gaze met his. But it was only for a moment. She took a step forward and held out her hand to Eleanor, who stood as well. She was so short, she only came up to just under Audrey's nose.

"It's really nice to meet you, Ms. Redmond."

Eleanor wrapped Audrey's hand in both of hers, holding it tight. "Oh, my dear. It's so wonderful to meet you too. But please—just call me Eleanor." Her mouth bloomed into a wide, relieved smile as she looked between them. She pulled her phone out of her pocket and tapped the screen. "Would you like to stay for a bit and have coffee? I'll ask Maureen to bring us some."

Audrey looked up at Theo.

He smiled.

And nodded.

She turned back to Eleanor. "We'd love to stay."

"Thank you." Her face relaxed, and she typed out a quick message before pocketing the phone again. Theo let Audrey take his chair so she could chat with his mother while he grabbed a third from the seating area and pulled it nearer to the coffee table, close enough for him to hold her hand. Once he was settled, Eleanor turned back to Audrey and clasped her hands in her lap.

"Now: how long have you two been tog—"

"DON'T YOU DARE GO IN THERE, YOU PRETENTIOUS PRICK."

"GET YOUR HANDS OFF OF ME!"

"FUCK YOU, MOTHERFUCKER!"

There was another shout and a sudden commotion out in the hallway, the sound of a short scuffle followed by a dull *thud*. The floors and walls of the office shook, rattling Eleanor's framed diplomas against the drywall, but before any of them could react, the door burst open.

A short man with graying, burnished gold hair and light blue eyes stood in the doorway, his suit rumpled and askew, swaying as he struggled to shove away a spitting-mad and swearing Diego.

They both froze as soon as their eyes landed on Theo.

Theo sucked in a breath and gripped Audrey's hand so hard, she half wondered if he might break it. There was no mistaking his expression as he stared at the man. It could only mean one thing.

This was his uncle Lloyd.

Audrey knew immediately. While he shared few traits with his older sister aside from some resemblance in bone structure and stature, the man's nose was slightly crooked, with a telltale bump at the bridge—and several new, thin pink scars slashed across his skin, still healing a few months after being broken open and stitched back together.

All the blood drained from Lloyd's face, and his mouth dropped open.

But before he had half a chance to say a single word, Eleanor had already launched herself out of her chair, lunging toward her brother with her teeth bared. He startled as she pressed one perfectly manicured finger deep into his chest.

"*Get the fuck out of here, Lloyd,*" she growled, a deadly look in her eyes. "I don't want you near my son. You take one wrong look at him, and I'll castrate you myself. And I'll do a lot worse to your balls than what he did to your face. You understand?"

When Lloyd's gaze darted back over to his nephew, Audrey rose from her chair and stood in front of Theo, meeting his uncle's look with a dark one of her own.

It didn't matter what Eleanor threatened.

If that man so much as *breathed* in the direction of hers, he'd have hell to pay.

"Sorry," Lloyd muttered, looking down at the floor. "My mistake. I thought you weren't busy."

"You thought wrong."

Without another word, he slunk away from the door. Diego grabbed him and shoved him roughly back into the hallway before Eleanor slammed the door after him so hard, it rattled in the doorframe.

She turned back to them and rolled her lips together.

"As I was saying—how long have you two been dating?" She made her way back to her chair and perched on the edge, crossing her legs primly, one right over the other. "I want to hear all about it. Please tell me as much as you're willing to."

"It hasn't been long—we met this summer." Audrey smiled at Theo as she sat back down. Warmth and relief simmered molten in his amber eyes, soft and sweet and grateful. “But I’m deeply in love with your son. I’ve never met anyone like him before.” She squeezed his hand. “He’s extraordinary.”

Eleanor’s expression softened. “That he is.”

Maureen brought in a pot of fresh coffee, setting the tray and mugs down between them and wiping her eyes with her sleeve as she hurried back to her desk.

They spent the rest of the morning talking.

It was sweeter than Audrey ever thought it might be.

Twenty

ONCE LLOYD WAS properly subdued and exiled back to his corner, Diego hurried back to his office, citing his editor's impatience—as well as his own deep satisfaction. If there were any consequences, he assured them it was all worth it, if only because he finally got to shove Theo's asshole uncle around. Truly a lifelong dream of his, apparently.

Maybe Audrey understood why Theo loved Diego like a brother now.

Maybe she kind of did too.

After they spent about an hour talking with Eleanor, they left.

And they ran.

It was Theo who took off first, fast but limping slightly while he tugged Audrey along behind him. They flew down the street, dodging trash cans and skirting along sidewalks, and it was all she could do to keep up with him.

They rounded a corner and Theo pulled her to the side of a building, leaning up against the nearest brick wall and ripping his mask off. His breath curled white in the cold air, and just as Audrey stumbled after him, the early winter chill burning her lungs when she freely gulped it down, he grabbed her and spun her around.

And laughed.

It wasn't that anything was funny, exactly, only that his relief—

his utter *relief* at having just done what he did—was palpable. His laughs turned into gasping groans, and he buried a hand in her hair, clutching her to his chest while he rocked her back and forth. "Thank you, sweetheart," he whispered. "Thank you for being there with me."

"Always," she whispered back. "I'll always be there for you."

Finally, he calmed and he put her back down with a crooked smile. "Wanna go home?"

Audrey matched his smile with one of her own. "God, yes."

They still had almost three more full days to spend together.

She couldn't wait anymore.

The first thing Theo did when they got back to his house was put his phone on Do Not Disturb. And once they changed clothes, he got started in the kitchen, and they made—and did—all the things he'd promised her yesterday.

Watching him expertly work dough with his hands was a new fascination for Audrey. The practiced dexterity in his fingers, the way his brow furrowed in determined concentration, the expertise he'd gained with persistence, all of it was beautiful.

But while the focaccia baked in the oven, Theo had his own feast.

He didn't have to ask. He didn't have to say one word. He simply turned around after setting the timer and she knew what was coming purely based on the dark, heated look in his eyes. His enormous hands gripped her waist and lifted her up onto his countertop as if she weighed nothing at all before tugging off her joggers and sliding her underwear down. The cool quartz at her back gave her goose bumps when he laid her down and ran his hand reverently along her body, and her mouth suddenly went bone-dry as soon as he spread her legs and lowered his face between them.

He made her come three times on his tongue before the timer went off.

He also showed her how to make gnocchi, and together they shaped the little pasta dumplings, munching happily on fresh, hot focaccia dipped in herb-infused oil before Theo took her up to the third-floor master suite. He opened a door she'd assumed was a closet, but it turned out to be stairs leading up to the rooftop, where he had a garden full of herbs and fresh basil.

And a hot tub.

Her mouth fell open at the sight of the city skyline in the distance, visible from where the covered tub sat waiting. She turned to look at him, and he waggled his eyebrows at her. "I told you to bring your bathing suit, didn't I? Now you know why. Though we could always just go buck nak—"

"You've been holding out on me this whole time!" she cried, punching him lightly in the shoulder. He staggered backward in mock pain and surprise, clutching his arm dramatically.

"Ow!"

She shoved him again.

"Why didn't you show me this any of the other times I was here?!"

"The weather was shitty! And I was saving it for this weekend!" When she lifted a hand for the third time, he caught it easily and grinned wickedly at her. "It was my present to myself for being able to handle stairs again. Figured I needed something that felt nice after all the PT I've had to do. I may not have a tub in the master bath, but I do have *this*." He lowered his voice and whispered in her ear. "After we eat, we'll get in. I promise."

It was Audrey's first time making homemade pasta, and dinner was everything she could have wanted: fresh basil and tomatoes and mozzarella, pesto and cheese, soft pillowy gnocchi, perfectly crisped focaccia, flaky sea salt and balsamic glaze, just as he'd promised. It more than made up for the wait. But Theo had also promised her one more thing, and he turned around and pulled an unmarked tub of something out of the freezer before grabbing two spoons from the drawer.

"Close your eyes," he murmured.

She did as she was told.

"Open your mouth."

Ice cream, cold and velvety smooth slid onto her tongue. It was thick and luscious, luxurious in its mouthfeel, and tiny bursts of flavor, floral and caramel, fruity and sweet, alternated with odd ripples of spice and sunshine and richness across her tastebuds, shooting through her mouth and making it ache slightly at the sensation.

"Now *that*, sweetheart, is real vanilla ice cream."

She opened her eyes to find Theo watching her eagerly. He was practically bouncing on his heels with anticipation.

"What do you think? None of that artificial aftertaste, huh? Not like the industrial shit."

Audrey pressed her lips together and drew in a deep, contemplative breath. "I don't know. I think I need another bite. Just to clarify my thoughts." She opened her mouth and when he obliged, she tasted it again, savoring it deeply even while she bit her cheek to stop a grin from giving her away.

"It's wonderful, Theo," she said, still trying her best not to smile. His face lit up in victory. "But I still think it needs some chocolate syrup."

The victory was short-lived.

"Chocolate syrup."

His face had fallen, his expression stony and incredulous now.

"Yeah. Hershey's would be great."

Theo's expression darkened further, and he closed his eyes and drew in a long breath, as though in deep, unrelenting pain. He stabbed his spoon into the ice cream container and crossed his arms over his chest.

"Hershey's."

"Mm-hmm." Audrey beamed at him. "Would make it just that much—"

"The crap that has thirty ingredients in it."

"Precisely." She nodded. "Goes perfect with vanilla. Covers it all up nicely."

"You only need *five* ingredients to make chocolate syrup."

"But I like the—"

"The garbage kind?"

She nodded again, more enthusiastically this time, her grin definitely getting the better of her now.

Theo stared at her. After a moment, he rolled his jaw and shook his head. "You're a horrible person. You don't deserve my homemade ice cream. I'm going to need you to give it back."

"You—what?"

Without warning, he lunged forward and grabbed her head with both hands, pressing his mouth to hers and forcing his tongue inside, swiping it around and licking with wild abandon.

Audrey let out a muffled shriek and tried to struggle away. "Ew, no, Theo!" she screeched when she finally pushed him off of her, but he only chased her mouth with his again. "*Theo!* Stop, that's gross!"

"I don't care! *Give it back!*"

"NO!"

"That took me two days to make! You don't deserve it! GIVE IT BACK TO ME!"

She tried to run, but he caught her easily and swept her up into his arms, squeezing her tight and tickling her on all her most intense spots while she squeaked and struggled.

"I'm sorry, it's delicious, I didn't mean it!" she cried through bouts of laughter. "I lied, it's the best thing I ever tasted!"

"You're awful!" He picked her up, still kicking, and pressed his nose against her neck, burying his face in the crook of her shoulder while he feverishly peppered her skin with kisses, punctuating his sentiments with tiny, aggressive nips of his teeth, biting just hard enough to leave marks behind. "But I'm going to *make* you appreciate it!"

In the end, he won.

He also finally showed her how he worked.

Turned out that bending neon glass took an enormous amount of skill and dexterity, and Theo was absolutely incredible with his hands, even with his lingering tremor.

And he was equally incredible with his mouth.

When he first described the process, he'd left out the fact that he had to blow into the glass tube at the same time as bending it over an open flame, puffing air through a rubber straw–like contraption into the glass to keep it hollow while he bent the exact angles corresponding with the pattern he'd made. The work required deep concentration, extreme precision, and a fair amount of speed. And if he ever made a critical error, he'd have to scrap the entire glass piece and start over.

"I make more mistakes now than I did before the accident," Theo explained. She was perched on one of his worktables, watching him with fascination. The process was slow but mesmerizing. "My hand shakes or spasms at odd moments, and it fucks up the curves I'm working on half the time. So it takes me a lot longer to complete things now. I don't know how that's going to play into my art—or my business—and I'll be lucky to get any piece finished at this rate."

He sighed and shook his head. "The first time I tried a few months ago, I wasn't ready yet, and I could barely grip the tube at all. I couldn't do *anything*. It was a nightmare. I got so frustrated, I smashed the Lightm4st3r sculpture I'd been working on before my dad died. And then I just . . . left it there for months, all the glass shards strewn about the floor. It's why I didn't want you coming down here when you stayed over that first time. I wasn't kidding about it being a mess." He eyed his work in progress. It sat covered in a sheet in the corner, shrouded in mystery. "I'm still not sure I can pull off this piece in time for the charity auction. It's . . . not good right now."

Audrey frowned. He was doing so much better, but it must have been bad for him to destroy the sculpture completely. "Is there anything I can do to help? Can I hold something steady for you, or . . . ?"

Theo tilted his head at her. "That's a good question. Wanna try it out? See what it's like?"

She grinned and launched herself off of the table and straight into his arms. He smiled softly as he tucked her into his chest and handed her a scrap piece of glass while he reset everything.

"Okay. I'm going to work the air tube, and you're going to try to bend a curve into the glass, just like the one on that pattern over there." He covered her hands with his, demonstrating how she would heat the glass over the flame, working it carefully back and forth. "You want to bend it when it's pliable enough not to snap or shatter, but not when it's so hot that it just melts in your hands. You want to stress it enough to bend, but not break. That's where it transforms."

"How am I going to know where that point is?"

He placed the air tube in the side of his mouth and smirked crookedly at her, one parenthetical dimple appearing in his cheek. "You've gotta *feel* it. That's where the artistry comes in." He huffed in amusement. "Well, one of the places, anyway. Artistry and *skill*." He fired up the gas again and relit it before trailing his fingers gently along her hands. "All right, sweetheart. Let's see what you've got."

It was so much harder than he made it look.

Even though Theo's hands guided her, even though she pulled the glass from the fire when he tapped her arm, even though she did her best to twist and bend the tube against the pattern laid out on the nearby table, her curve was still horribly misshapen. After the sixth attempt, Theo took a look at her handiwork, raised an eyebrow, and tried—and failed—to suppress a grin.

"Ahhh," he finally hummed. "Very kinky."

"Hey! I tried!" She punched him in the shoulder for the dig, which only made his grin widen. The glass did, in fact, have several kinks in it. But she had a greater appreciation for the smooth beauty he wrought from nothing now, and she wiped the sweat away from her brow while glaring up at him in mock indignation.

"I know," he purred. "And I liked it."

The way he said that sent shivers down her spine, and she tried to escape back to her perch, cheeks blazing—but Theo didn't let her. He grabbed her and held her close, sweeping kisses across her neck and beneath her jaw, his eyes closed and mouth still stretched wide with pleasure. She knew he wasn't lying. She could feel how much he liked it pressing up against her back.

Fine.

She melted.

And let him bend her to his will this time.

He was very good at it, after all.

~

THREE DAYS SHE spent, playing with Theo and loving him like this, letting him love her like he did.

Three days they spent, with their phones quiet and dark, their notifications silenced, their focus only on each other.

It was the best weekend she'd ever had.

~

WHEN THE WEEKEND was over, Theo walked her back to her tiny studio apartment where Violet was waiting anxiously to hear about how everything had gone.

But her roommate didn't even know the half of it. There was no way Audrey could tell her who else Theo actually was.

Lightm4st3r was a big deal.

He didn't want the attention.

They'd talked about it, though, and Theo wasn't actually opposed to letting Violet in on the secret provided she could keep it—perhaps if she signed an NDA—but it was Audrey who wasn't convinced. Her best friend probably needed time to get to know him separately from the artist identity she idolized, and Theo promised to make friends with Violet. He was shy and nervous, but he'd try.

They reached the top of the stairs in Audrey's building, and Theo slowed his ascent, stopping just short of the landing. Audrey turned and glanced down at him over her shoulder. He didn't move, and she couldn't quite interpret the look he had in his eyes.

"What is it?" she asked, stepping back down to stand with him. "What's wrong?"

Theo shook his head. "Nothing. I—"

"Tell me."

He ran a hand through his hair before ripping his mask away from his face while he mounted the last few steps with her to reach the landing. "Audrey, I, uh . . ." He drew in a deep breath. "I was just thinking about going back to my house."

"Oh?" She raised an eyebrow. "Is that a problem?"

"Yes." Theo rested his hands on her hips. "I can already tell, especially now that we're here. It's a big problem."

"Why? Your house is incredible. I love it. It's the nicest place I've ever been."

"That's just it: it's a nice place when *you're* there. But you won't be there when I go back." He shifted on his feet, rolled his jaw, pressed his lips together, all the things he always did when he was anxious or reticent. His fingers twitched and tightened at her waist. "I have to go back there alone, without you. And I know it won't feel like home anymore if you're not there. Not now. It'll be way too empty. Way too quiet."

Her face fell when Theo was the one to voice the same thought that had been plaguing her the entire walk back to her place.

She hadn't wanted to leave his.

It was an odd feeling to realize that she'd started thinking of his house as her home.

Before she could say anything, Theo plunged his hand into his pocket and pulled out a familiar key. He set it in her palm and curled her fingers back over it gently.

"I wanted to ask you to move in." The tips of his ears reddened as he blurted it out. "You don't ever have to leave my house again."

She stared down at the key in her hand.

"I know this is a big step." He took her hands in his. "But I've thought a lot about it, and I need to be honest about what I want. And that's *you*." He leaned forward and pressed his forehead to hers. "You feel like home to me."

"I know," she whispered, pocketing the key before burying her hand in the loose waves at the back of his neck. "You feel like home to me too."

"Will you think about it?" His lips brushed against hers, their softness and warmth tantalizing. "Please?" And when his thumb pressed firmly into her cheek, tilting her head to the side, his fingers tightening and curling against her neck just so, so urgent, so wanting, so—

Oh.

"Theo," she breathed as she leaned into his touch, her mouth already instinctively chasing his. "You're cheating."

He pressed his lips to the corner of her mouth. "Cheating how?" Her nose was next, and then the other corner.

"You know how."

Somehow, her chest was pressed all the way up against his.

When did that happen?

His right hand slipped beneath her sweater, vibrating against her skin as he nudged his fingers under the band of her bra and caressed the curve of her breast. "I'm not doing anything." He was just as breathless as her, and she gasped as his thumb grazed across her nipple.

He swallowed it with a kiss.

"We could have this every day." His voice rumbled deep in his chest, and all it did was make her want him a thousand times more. "We could have this all the time."

Audrey drew his face into the crook of her neck, holding him tight and tucking him close.

But in the end, she sighed.

"I'll think about it." She could practically feel all the hope flee his body at her words, and she squeezed him tighter. "It's not that I don't want to—it's just that it's sudden. And I'd feel bad."

He pulled away from her and frowned. "Bad? Why?"

She smiled sadly at him. "I come with a lot of baggage, Theo." She swept some of the hair away from his face and tucked it behind his ears. "A lot of baggage, and a lot of loans."

"So?" His frown deepened. "You can save money by living with me and pay them off. It's not like you'll have to pay me rent."

"I don't want to be financially dependent on you, especially not this early."

"Well, then you could just let me pay your loans for you. Then you wouldn't be financially dependent on anyone."

She stared at him. "Theo, they—they're six figures. I have well over a hundred thousand dollars of debt."

Going out of state for school was expensive.

Flunking her first semester of college because she couldn't cope with the change and losing her scholarship was expensive.

Living in New York was expensive, even if all of this had been her dream.

But he didn't even blink.

"Okay."

Okay?!

"No, you shouldn't have to pay that for me. It's not your burden, it's not due to your mistakes, it's not—"

"It's not that much."

Her mouth dropped open.

"No. No, it *is*, it's *so* much, and then I'd be indebted to *you* instead." She shook her head. "What if we broke up? What if—"

"I'd still feel good about doing it even if we weren't together."

"No, I couldn't do that, that's far too generous, I—"

"You saved my life, Audrey." It was his turn to smooth her hair away from her face. "You made me feel alive again, so if anything, I owe *you*." He leaned forward and kissed her forehead again. "You wouldn't be indebted to me because this is just one part of working to build a life together—I have the means to do it, and I want to. And besides, you give me so much in return every single day. You'd never need to pay me back. You already have."

Her heart was beating so fast, she was certain it would pound straight through her chest.

"But I understand if that's a lot to take in right now."

Something nearby thumped. There was a muffled swear, and when Theo eyed her door warily, she remembered where they were.

Violet was probably listening on the other side.

"Just think about it, sweetheart." His mouth cracked into a crooked, unsure smile. "Okay?"

"Okay." She took his hand in hers and squeezed. "Come visit for a while?"

A shadow shifted from beneath the front door and disappeared.

He nodded and picked nervously at the fingernails on his free hand. They'd talked about this before coming back, and it was a big step he was about to take. But Audrey had faith that her best friend wouldn't let her down, even without prior warning. It had to be authentic.

When she opened the door and ushered an unmasked Theo inside, Violet turned from where she sat innocently on the couch and her mouth dropped open in shock, her eyes immediately landing on the right side of his exposed face. But it was only for a split second, and she chucked the book she was pretending to read (upside-down) onto the coffee table before bounding over to them eagerly, an irrepressible grin growing rapidly across her face.

"Oh my god, HI THEO!" Violet grabbed his hand and yanked him further inside. She barely came up to his chest, but her grip was so strong that his eyes widened and he stumbled forward with a grunt, nearly tripping over his own enormous feet. But he recovered his balance enough to straighten and rub the back of his neck. Every bit of his face was burning red-hot now, and it did make the scar stand out even more than usual.

"Audrey didn't tell me you were coming inside this time! Are you gonna hang out?"

"Uh . . . yeah." He glanced nervously at Audrey while she hung her coat on its hook by the door. "Yeah, I figured I'd stick around and chat for a bit, if that's okay by you."

"Okay by me?! I've been *dying* to talk to you! So come on then! Come sit down! *And give me that damn bag—*" Violet wrestled it over his shoulder, and Theo looked vaguely terrified as she dropped it onto the ground and kicked it ruthlessly toward Audrey's bed. It skidded across the worn wooden floors and bumped to a stop against their bunks, and he flinched at the force of the impact.

Honestly, his reaction wasn't off base.

Violet could be . . . *intense.*

She dragged him to their tiny loveseat and shoved him onto the cushions before rushing into the kitchen. "Hey, do you want something to drink? We've got Coke Zero, water, key lime LaCroix . . . oh and maybe—"

Audrey slid onto the spot next to him and laced their fingers together while Violet continued to rattle off their options. "You see?" she whispered in his ear. "She couldn't give less of a shit about your scar. I told you."

"My face feels naked," he whispered back. "I hate it. Can I put the mask back on?"

"No."

"Oh god," he breathed. "Please?"

"You told me to tell you no when you inevitably asked." Audrey caressed his right cheek. "You look fine. You're doing fine."

"She's staring at my scar, I know she is."

"She's literally not, her back is turned right now."

"She looked when I first walked in."

"That's because she's never actually seen your whole face before. It's not because of the scar, I promise. She doesn't care, she's just excited." She squeezed his hand. "Give it some time. It's just practice." She leaned over and planted a quick kiss against his cheek. "You got used to being unmasked around *me*, didn't you?"

"Barely," he grumbled.

"Theo, what did you think of the new Mila Herrera gallery show?" Violet called over her shoulder. "Have you seen it yet?"

"Oh, uh . . . y-yeah," he stammered. "Mila's a friend of mine, so—"

"OH MY GOD, are you serious?" Violet shrieked, bounding back over clutching an assortment of cans she dumped unceremoniously onto the coffee table. "That's amazing! Are you into performance art? I heard Lucius Scott is going to be doing something new soon. Do you know him too?"

Theo blinked at her. "Uh . . . actually, yeah, I do?"

"*Holy shit.* You're so cool." Violet leaned forward with deep interest. "I really want to see your stuff, you know. You're almost impossible to Google. I only found, like, one article about you from a while back, and the pictures of your paintings in it weren't high quality. Surely you have a portfolio or something?"

Theo rolled his lips together. And then he raised an eyebrow.

That was an idea if ever she'd seen him have one.

His eyes glittered with deep mischief.

"What was it you do again, Violet?"

It was her turn to recoil and blink in surprise. "I studied fashion design and work at a department store's corporate offices. Why?"

"Oh. *Perfect.*" From the way his head tilted, he must have been struggling to hide a smirk. "You know what? I need a favor. Do you think you could help me with something?"

She hummed with wary interest. "Maybe. What is it?"

"Well, I was thinking . . ." Theo trailed off and chewed on his bottom lip. "Tell you what: give me your phone. I'll text it to you."

"OHO!" Violet ripped it out of her pocket and shoved it at him with glee. "Secret favors? Intrigue? You know I'm already in. *Give me your number.*"

"Sure thing."

"It's gonna cost you, though."

"I expected nothing less."

"Oh no," Audrey groaned, burying her face in her hand as Theo typed his number into Violet's contacts. "Maybe this was a mistake. I never should have introduced you two."

"Can't take it back now."

The smugness dripped from her roommate's voice.

"But anyway, as I was saying—should I grab us snacks? Are you hungry? And OH, THEO, what did you think of—"

His fingers twitched and tightened in Audrey's after he passed the phone back to Violet, and he leaned down and buried his face in her shoulder when her roommate darted back over to the kitchen, an endless stream of art-world gossip tumbling from her lips while she gathered chips from the cupboard.

But no matter how many times Audrey saw him reach for his pocket, he still didn't replace his mask for the entire hour he stayed.

Twenty-One

THE SOUND OF the crowd in the auditorium rumbled backstage.

It vibrated through Audrey's feet, her chest, her fingertips, the low-grade hum of thousands of people talking punctuated by cheers rising periodically higher for someone as they crossed the stage.

Air horns.

Shrill whistles.

Whooping screams and enthusiastic catcalls.

The cries of big families, large friend groups, every proud supporter here and celebrating as the graduates crossed the stage and left school behind for good, off to pursue new lives and careers on fresh horizons.

It had been a few weeks since Theo's reconciliation with his mom. They were actively going to therapy, but he'd scheduled those extra sessions in the mornings while Audrey worked, so she saw him a little less at the café than usual—a huge departure from their routine earlier in the fall. But that was all right.

Because these days, she spent all her free time with him.

Every day, he picked her up from the café after work if he wasn't already there waiting for her shift to end. Every evening, he cooked or bought her dinner. And every night, they slept together, alternating between making love in his luxurious king-sized bed or chastely cramming themselves into her tiny bottom bunk. Violet let them break the one roommate rule they had in place on the condition that Theo bought or made her dinner when he was there, which he was only too happy to do, and she'd nearly died laughing the first time she watched him squeeze his wide frame into Audrey's twin bed.

Both of them were unwilling to sleep separately now that they knew how good it was together.

But they couldn't keep this up forever. It was time for things to change. *Really* change.

And now Audrey was graduating.

She'd given notice at the café that morning.

She folded the corner of the note with her name scrawled on it back and forth, over and over, wearing a deep, frowning wrinkle into the thick cardstock.

One chapter closed, and another just beginning.

It was so strange to even contemplate leaving the place that had saved her five years ago when she failed her first semester and lost her precious scholarship. She hardly knew what to do if she wasn't pulling espresso shots, and it hardly mattered that she'd had several interviews at reputable engineering firms and startups over the last few weeks—none of it seemed real.

Not even when she gave her capstone presentation in front of a bunch of industry people invited by her professor to critique her work while Theo grinned beneath his mask in the audience, his eyes crinkled the entire time he looked at her.

Not even when the representative from her dream company approached her afterward and asked to see her résumé.

Not even when she'd finally received a call with an offer to be a junior engineer at a green energy startup firm.

Not even when Josh squealed and grabbed her when she told him, twirling her around on the spot.

"I'm so proud of you, Audgepodge!" he cried. "Maybe I'm next, huh?"

"Next big Broadway star Josh Lemaire?" She waggled her eyebrows at him. "I think your big break is right around the corner."

He beamed at her, wide and gleaming.

"Certainly doesn't hurt that ya boy was cast in *Les Mis*!" He bounced her again. "Grantaire! Can you believe it!"

"Yes!" She buried her face in his neck and laughed. "I can! And so can Diego, I take it?" Theo's best friend had been coming around to the coffee shop a lot more lately, leaning over the counter while he flirted with the cute barista with the flawless mahogany skin and the brilliant smile. These days, he was lingering over his coffee to write while glancing back up at the register. Frequently.

A lot like how Theo had.

"Oh, well . . . I—I don't know." Josh's cheeks reddened.

That was a first.

She'd never been able to embarrass him about a crush before. Must've meant he really liked him.

It was nice to turn the tables a little for once.

"Erin Thalia Acosta, bachelor of arts in English, summa cum laude."

The graduate a few places in front of her stepped onto the stage to raucous cheers and Audrey folded the corner of her card over one more time, barely stopping herself from ripping it off entirely. All these people with huge, loving families, gaggles of friends, and certainty about their futures, and here she was with none of that.

She peered anxiously out into the crowd from the wings of the stage, but the faces were drowned in shadows from this angle.

Theo was out there somewhere with Violet and Diego, that much she knew. Josh said he'd try to come if he could swap shifts. Some of her professors were gathered on the stage in their full academic regalia, their silly hats and tassels and garish robes with striped hoods hanging down their backs like some strange relics of bygone institutions, broken out of dusty storage just for the occasion. But that was it. Audrey only had, what? Three or four people to her name?

More cheers for the next graduate erupted.

She looked down at her card again before handing it to a waiting staff member.

It didn't matter that her section wouldn't be as loud as the others.

The people she *did* have were the absolute best.

Quality over quantity anyway.

Life was happening. Things were changing, and changing *so* fast. She felt like she was standing at the edge of a cliff overlooking the ocean, deciding if she should jump and wondering how cold the water below would be.

The idea of having a job *not* as a barista was exciting—and terrifying.

Audrey stepped up to the side of the stage. The girl in front of her crossed next, beaming at the sounds of an air horn blaring through a gaggle of wild screams from her friends and family, smiling even wider as she shook the dean's hand and grasped her diploma, pausing for a quick photo before continuing.

"Go ahead, honey," the staff member said, nudging her forward. "You're up."

"Audrey Marie Adams, bachelor of science in electrical engineering, cum laude."

The crowd was quieter for her than it had been for the others. She stepped out and squinted, blinded by the bright lights while she made her way across the stage toward the waiting, smiling dean of her school.

She slid her hand into his and shook it.

"Congratulations, Audrey." He handed her a leather folder.

They both smiled and the flashbulb of a camera popped, blinding her anew.

Then she heard it.

A shrill whistle pierced through the low hum of the crowd, loud and strong. She turned her head, looking for the source of it, her eyes finally adjusting to the lights.

And there he was.

Theo, with his face bare, both pinkie fingers shoved into the sides of his wide mouth, his whistle bold and robust.

Then there were the cheers. Everyone was there: Violet, her sister, their parents, Josh, Diego, everyone who mattered to her here in New York, *everyone* had come. Even Theo's mother, Eleanor, was there, standing quietly at the end of the row Audrey's motley family had claimed, clapping with a wide smile on her face.

But a voice, one she hadn't heard in person in years, broke through all of it.

"That's my babygirl! My sweet Nuggie!"

Audrey froze. "Gladys?" she whispered. She looked up at the dean and felt a tear tumble down her cheek. "My—my foster mom is here?"

He shrugged, but Audrey couldn't stay to explain.

"Um . . . thank you."

She gripped her diploma and tore off the stage, black robes flying behind her while she ran.

She couldn't believe it, but the image was already seared into her mind, unmistakable and solid and real. It was really Gladys Kane, the foster mother she'd loved so much, and somehow she wasn't in Tampa, she was *here*, standing next to Theo with her pure, snow-white hair contrasting against her dark brown skin, looking so much tinier and more wizened next to him than the last time Audrey had seen her more than five and a half years ago. Even her Coke-bottle glasses had somehow gotten thicker, but she was still just as remarkable, just as kind, smiling just as proudly as she had been when she'd taken Audrey to the airport to fly to college.

Audrey barreled through the line of graduates waiting backstage and ignored the staff members trying frantically to direct her back to her seat, turning instead and sprinting into the auditorium through one of the side doors. It bounced open on its hinges, banging into the wall behind it, and Audrey ran up the sides of the aisles, heading straight toward where her rowdy, ragtag gaggle of friends and family waited, screaming even louder for her as she approached.

But she didn't have far to go. Gladys saw her coming and had already made her way to the end of the row. She stood there, waiting for her with her arms spread wide.

Audrey threw herself into them and melted into a blubbering mess, her shoulders heaving while she sobbed.

"My girl," Gladys murmured, gripping her with a strength that belied her years and rubbing circles soothingly on Audrey's back the way she always had when she was younger. "Look at you! Graduating with honors! I'm so proud of you, baby!"

"What are you doing here?!" Audrey finally managed to hiccup between sobs. "I never thought you'd be able to come to New York."

Gladys pulled away from her with a smile and lifted a wrinkled, weathered hand to wipe the tears away from Audrey's cheeks. "You know, I didn't answer the first few times that man of yours called me. I didn't know a Theo Sullivan and didn't have that number in my phone, so I thought it might be a scam when he offered to fly me up here. You know how they get you by promising you free vacations and the like? At my age, you have to be careful." She chuckled. "But after his third voicemail, I looked him up on Google and finally called him back. And I thought to myself, you know what, Gladys?" She tapped a pensive finger against her cheek. "Maybe you could use a bit of a trip to go see your Nuggie." Her smile widened. "You've never been to New York, and it could be really nice seeing snow this time of year too. Just in time for Christmas. Good change of pace."

The tears hadn't stopped falling, and Audrey dried her face with the sleeve of her robe, sniffing through a laugh.

Theo sidled up behind Gladys, his grin shy and his hands jammed into his pockets as he looked down at Audrey. "Surprise, sweetheart."

His mask was nowhere in sight.

"Theo, your mask! And you—" Audrey covered her mouth and sobbed again, looking between the two of them. She hardly knew what to do. "You did this?" she finally asked him. "How did you find her?"

He jabbed his thumb over his shoulder at their row. "Violet helped me. She went digging in your phone for the contact info when you were in the shower, and she slipped it to me a few weeks ago. It took some convincing, but once I hired a professional nanny for the week to make sure everything at home with the kids would be okay, Gladys agreed to come up."

Her foster mother leaned forward and cupped a hand around Audrey's ear. "It wasn't the nanny that did it," she whispered. "He's a fine-looking man, Audrey. You've nabbed a handsome one. I came across his college lacrosse photo online and decided I needed to judge for myself how attractive New York men might be, if they're all cut from this same cloth." She squeezed Audrey one more time before drawing back with a wink. "Now get your ass back down there!" Gladys shoved playfully at her back. "You still need to toss your cap, or whatever the traditional nonsense is! Get back to your seat so I can take some videos for my friends on Facebook!"

Audrey barked another laugh but didn't obey—not just yet. Instead, she leaned around Gladys and reached out for Theo. He stretched forward and took her hand in his.

"Thank you," she said, her voice still shaking. "I love you."

"I know." He grinned and squeezed her hand. "I love you too. You'll get plenty of time with her. We're all going out to dinner afterwards."

"We're really going out to a restaurant?" He'd staunchly refused to tell her anything about what he had planned for today. Now she knew why.

But they still had never been out to eat at a restaurant together, not with how uncomfortable he was about his scar.

Theo nodded. "I made reservations weeks ago."

"You did?"

"Yeah." His grin was as crooked as she'd ever seen it. "We're getting Italian at Carmine's so Gladys can see Times Square." He brought Audrey's hand up to his mouth and brushed the back of it with his lips, a kiss so gentle and delicate, it was almost fragile.

But she felt every bit of what he wanted her to through it. She could barely contain it herself.

It amazed her how a gesture so small could contain such multitudes.

"I've been practicing not hiding my face in public so I could do this today. For you." He ran a hand through his hair and shrugged. "You were right. People don't really give a shit." He glanced back at the stage and shooed her away like Gladys had. "Now go back! You're missing your own graduation! We'll find you after!"

Audrey did as she was told.

She was a weepy mess while she twisted her tassel from one side of her cap to the other and then tossed it in the air with everyone else in her winter graduating class.

She never thought she would feel so light closing the chapter of this part of her life.

Maybe it was because the next one shone so very bright.

Twenty-Two

SHIT, I'M RUNNING late. He's gonna be here any minute! Vi, do you know where my clutch is?"

"Right here in front of you, dummy."

"Oh fuck." Audrey smacked her forehead and took the bag from Violet, who immediately gasped and started fussing again.

"Your *makeup*! DON'T TOUCH YOUR GODDAMN FACE!"

"I'm sorry!" she wailed while Violet grabbed some powder and setting spray and fixed what she'd just smeared. It apparently hadn't set all the way yet and she'd already forgotten she was wearing it. "I'm not used to this!"

"Which is exactly why Theo asked me to help you!" The way Violet huffed was rather smug, but Audrey supposed that was to be expected.

She had to admit she looked *amazing*.

It was her first black-tie event. Her new dress wasn't going to wear itself, and every time she thought about it, she grew more and more nervous.

He'd managed to finish his sculpture after all—just in time. He was convinced it was terrible, but he'd done it all the same.

And he needed a date to go with him to unveil it to the world.

The question of the gala came up a few weeks ago before graduation, and that's when she discovered there was treachery afoot. It was Violet who'd broached the topic a little too casually: "Hey, Auds, Theo was telling me the other day when you were in the shower about some charity auction gala. What are you planning on wearing?"

He wasn't over at the apartment for dinner yet and Audrey had her nose deep in a book, studying for a final while her roommate puttered around in the kitchen, making herself a plate of predinner snacks. She'd glanced over her shoulder, her face entirely too innocent all of a sudden, and it was her expression that gave Audrey pause.

"My little black cocktail dress," she replied with rapidly narrowing eyes. "It's the nicest one I have. Why?"

Violet hummed, her lips pursed, and swept to the side in disapproval. "You can't wear a cocktail dress."

"Why not?"

"Theo said it was black tie."

"Yeah, and? I'm sure *he'll* be wearing one, and my dress is black. That's like the same thing, right?"

That earned her two brows raised sky-high and a sharp look. "Oh no, Audrey. No, baby, no." Violet slapped her forehead with her palm so hard, she nearly stumbled backward. "Black tie and cocktail are two extremely different things. You need a *gown*."

"A gown? Like a *ball* gown?"

"Yeah, babe, like a ball gown. Like red-carpet stuff."

She'd never felt the blood drain from her face so fast.

"Oh shit," she whispered. "I didn't even think to Google that."

"*Ohhh*," Violet drawled, stretching the word out with sudden wicked intrigue. "Oh no! Looks like we'll need to go shopping! What a travesty!"

"How much do these things usually cost?" The panic was real now, and Audrey set her book aside while she lunged for her laptop. “How much am I going to have to spend for this? I didn’t think–”

“Calm down, Audity, I’ve got you.” Violet’s grin was absolutely predatory now. “We’ll find you something affordable that fits, don’t worry. Step into my office tomorrow after class and I’ll get you sorted.”

Audrey should’ve known the whole thing was a setup. She really should have. The fault of her naïveté was set squarely on her own shoulders when Violet dragged her into Saks Fifth Avenue under the pretense of window shopping, or “looking at examples of gowns for us to emulate,” as she said–as giddy as a schoolgirl for Audrey to try on and pick up the items she and Theo had already reserved ahead of time just for the occasion.

Apparently, Audrey’s (former) best friend had a *great* deal of fun picking out her dress for the gala the week prior. Theo hadn’t wanted Audrey to know how much everything cost, so he’d enlisted Violet to do his dirty work for him in secret, while also keeping her choices a secret from *him*. He wanted to be surprised too.

Their betrayal was uncovered when Audrey was suddenly thrust into a dressing room where the nicest dress she’d ever seen was waiting for her.

It was even worse when the damn thing fit like a glove and no one would tell her the price.

Traitors, the both of them. *All* of them. Salespeople included.

Violet couldn’t stop smirking while they tried on the shoes she’d picked out as well. The red-soled stilettos soared higher than Audrey was typically used to, but luckily she at least knew they’d be driven to the event. No long walks across street grates for her this time. She could manage for one evening.

“Stop looking so pleased,” Audrey grumbled when the shoes fit just as well as the dress.

"Oh no, I don't think so." Violet's grin only grew wider. "I just got to play the best game of Barbie *ever*. You're going to look phenomenal. Theo will lose his shit when he sees you."

"How did that go down, anyway? When he asked you for help?" Audrey tugged the heels off and placed them gingerly back in the box, wrapping them up carefully with the tissue paper. They probably cost more than a month of rent based on how beautiful they were, and on the fact that they were handmade from real Italian leather, according to the text stamped inside. She'd look up the price online later out of spite.

Violet snorted. "Your boyfriend is *awfully* trusting. We met up while you were in class for a long lunch one day. He brandished his black American Express card at the salespeople and then set me loose in here without a budget. It was like something out of *Pretty Woman*, a real Richard Gere kind of move. He's lucky I didn't spend the entire GDP of Luxembourg."

He gave Violet free rein with his credit card? Was he crazy? He was playing with fire. "He was that trusting with you because he's sweet and he thinks you're a good person." Audrey shot her roommate a dark look. "Even though he's wrong and you're actually a horrible, lying *traitor* of a friend for keeping this from me, and for not telling me how much he spent." Judging by the feel and thickness of the fabric of the dress, it had to be obscene. "He didn't need to. I don't want him to waste his money."

Violet ignored those last two remarks and sniffed imperiously. "Well, Theo knows the truth and he's an excellent judge of character. And he obviously doesn't care about the cost and can afford it. It's why he's my favorite."

"So what did *you* get out of the deal, huh?" Audrey wrinkled her nose and thought about tossing some of the tissue paper in Violet's face, but that seemed uncouth. Saks was too fancy a place for shenanigans. "I know he gave or promised you something."

"No?" Violet's voice was far too light and her expression far too innocent.

"Don't lie to me," Audrey grumbled as she retied the laces of her combat boots. "*Spill*, you asshat."

"Fine. He let me pick out some shoes for myself—god, they're *incredible*, the Louboutins I chose are so fucking beautiful, I've been ruined for other heels forever." She pointed and glared at Audrey. "He's the best man I've ever met and if you break up with him, I'll kill you."

It was Audrey's turn to snort. "I never thought you could be bought so easily. All it took was a pair of shoes?"

"Don't be ridiculous. It was a pair of *Louboutins*—don't call them *shoes*—*and* all the times he's bought me dinner. He knows how to treat a lady." Violet buffed her nails idly against her sweater, completely nonplussed by the accusation. "He also promised to show me his studio after the gala."

Audrey snapped her head up and tried to school her expression into submission. "Oh yeah?" She winced at how high her voice had suddenly pitched.

"Yeah, but he said I might have to sign some paperwork first. What the hell does he do that's so secret, government-contracted art or some shit? Now I'm *really* intrigued."

"Uh . . ." The panic was definitely creeping up now, but there was nothing she could do about it. If Theo wanted to tell Violet he was her favorite notorious reclusive artist and neon sculptor, that was his deal. "It's, um. He's just, uh . . . been working on something special lately, and he wants to stay tight-lipped about it."

"Never heard of signing paperwork to view a studio before, but I've never been much *involved* in the art scene, I only follow it. Maybe it's more common than I think it is?"

"I have no idea."

"Just how loaded is he, anyway? What does his apartment look like? No one with chump change just casually flashes around a black Amex like that."

Panic. Full panic and deflection mode now. Audrey glanced around for the salesperson they'd been working with and waved her over. "I think we're done here. Do we have to do anything else to leave, or . . . ?"

The night of the gala, Audrey wriggled into her new dress and shoes, closed her eyes and tried not to wrinkle her nose while Violet applied her makeup, complained loudly and repeatedly as her roommate swore when she attempted to curl Audrey's hair (it was only being mildly cooperative), and crammed a tube of lipstick and her phone in a tiny metallic-gold clutch before there was a knock at the door. As soon as she heard it, Violet threw the makeup brush onto the vanity and made a beeline for the bathroom.

"Hey, where are you going?!" Audrey shrieked, twisting indignantly in the chair at the sudden abandonment.

"I'm out!" Violet shouted through a crack in the door. "Trust me: you'll want privacy." She slammed it shut and the sound of the pipes knocking and the shower roaring to life filled the apartment.

Audrey rolled her eyes and pressed up from the chair, trying her best not to topple over like a baby giraffe on her new designer heels while she answered the door. When she pulled it open, she gasped.

She knew Theo would be wearing a tux. It was a black-tie charity gala.

She hadn't been prepared for him to look *that* incredible in it.

He always looked good, he always smelled clean and warm and woodsy and citrusy, even when he was simply wearing sweatpants. But tonight, he was *resplendent*. He stood tall and straight in his tuxedo, the cut of it perfectly tailored for his broad shoulders and trim waist. It fit him like a glove.

Everything about him oozed wealth, right down to the Piguet watch she'd never seen before and the gold cufflinks glinting from his wrists. His shoes were so shiny and pristine, they flashed in the light when he shifted on his feet, and he must have gotten a haircut. His hair was slightly shorter than it was yesterday and had been expertly styled with some sort of texturizing wax, the dark, shadowy waves tumbling perfectly to frame his bare face.

No mask tonight. He was going to the party as himself, scar and all.

She'd never be tired of such unobstructed views of him.

Without the mask, he looked like a prince, not her shy, introverted artist boyfriend. Everything about him sparkled today, down to his perfectly manicured nails and fingertips, no longer stained black with ink from sketching like they so often were.

"Oh my god," she whispered, breathless. "Theo, you look amazing." He was so handsome, she had to brace a hand against the doorframe to hold herself up. Suddenly, she felt so hot, she didn't really need the coat she was clutching, and she sucked in a sharp breath to try to calm the rapidly growing heat simmering in her core.

But Theo hadn't moved. He hadn't even blinked.

He stood frozen in place, staring at her with his mouth agape—until he shook his head and swallowed.

"I—" He gulped again, and his right hand wandered near the edge of his jacket, stalling just short of plunging inside at the last second. He lifted it instead, fully trembling now, and ran it over his freshly shaven face. "Holy shit, Audrey. *Holy shit,*" he whispered through his fingers, suddenly doubling over and bracing his other hand on his leg to keep upright. His breathing was heavy and labored, and he sounded on the verge of hyperventilating. "*This* is what Violet chose?" he wheezed. "Is she trying to kill me?!"

It seemed she wasn't the only one left breathless.

"Do you like it?"

"*Do I like it?!*" There was an odd, desperate growl tingeing the edge of his voice, and when he tried—and failed—to draw in a deep, calming breath, he glanced up at her. His pupils were blown black and wide, the swirling amber-green of his eyes reduced to a thin ring of color around them. "It's taking everything I have not to tear that dress off of your body *immediately*," he croaked. "You're the hottest thing I've ever seen."

Violet had chosen an off-the-shoulder designer dress. It was made of a thickly knit, scuba-like fabric, constructed in wide strips crisscrossing in layers that tightly hugged the meager curves of Audrey's body, the length barely grazing the tops of her stilettos. Tiny cutouts at her waist and hips showed tasteful glimpses of golden, freckled skin, teasing at what lay beneath—though the long slit running nearly to the top of her left thigh left far less to the imagination.

Violet had gone for maximum sex appeal while still being black-tie appropriate. And while she was plenty covered, Audrey did feel like she was walking temptation, in part because of the color. The dress was dyed a deep scarlet red, and she would be wearing a lip to match.

Audrey wondered if her roommate knew red was Theo's favorite color.

She put a hand on his back. "Breathe," she whispered. "Theo, I—"

He swallowed the rest of her words with a kiss.

The force of it took her aback, and she would have toppled over if he hadn't grabbed her first. But she couldn't deny the way he made her feel. That heat pooling in her stomach only simmered hotter when Theo growled and nipped at her lips, the sound and feel of it hungry and desperate. The sensation of his enormous, calloused hands cupping her jaw and wrapping around the back of her neck made her feel the same, and she pulled him close, all thoughts of makeup and hair and galas escaping straight through the rapidly forming cracks in her brain.

Did they have to go anywhere?

Surely it was unnecessary.

It was just a party.

What if they just went straight to his—

It was Theo who ripped himself away first with a sudden gasp. It seemed like it took everything he had, every last scrap of sanity he could dredge up from the depths of his hindbrain to put any sort of distance between them, and the sudden tightness and visible bulge in his trousers wasn't lost on her. He cleared his throat and tugged absently at his pant leg, obviously trying to calm down before they completely ruined the artistry that had been so carefully performed to make both of them look like this tonight.

"Sorry," he rasped. He might have pulled away, but he hadn't been able to take his hands off of her, and his fingers trailed longingly down the bare skin revealed by the low back of her dress. "Couldn't help it."

"Me neither," she whispered back with a grin.

"Your dress might be a problem for me tonight."

"Is it inappropriate?"

"No, it's perfect," he murmured. "It's just . . . not the sort of thing I was expecting. I love it. I *really* love it."

The warmth in her stomach spread all across her body, and Audrey slid her hand into his. She needed to touch him again. "Shall we?"

Theo eyed her shoes and shut the door behind her. "How about you put on your coat and I'll carry you down? I don't want you doing stairs when you don't have to."

She wrinkled her nose at him while he helped her slide her arms into her coat. "I can get down some stairs, Theo. I'm worried about your leg, and I'm not that clum—*oh!*"

She squeaked when he didn't wait for her to answer and instead scooped her into his arms, gently but firmly cradling her against his chest, almost as though she were his bride.

Her cheeks burned so hot the second she had that thought, they had to have matched her dress.

Instead of protesting further, she only wrapped her arms around his neck and studied him quietly while he carefully carried her down the few flights of stairs to the door, meditating on the curves of his face and the dark moles speckled across them and how strong his arms were for him to lift her so easily like this.

When looking at him felt too intense, she let a hand fall to inspect the bow perfectly tied at his neck, trailing her fingers along its edges and tracing its shape. Was this what he would look like if they got married? Would he wear this same tux, or one like it? And then another thought crept into her mind:

What would it be like having Theo not as her boyfriend, but as her husband?

She shook her head to clear it.

That thought was too big for tonight.

Before she could let herself be completely overwhelmed by it, they stepped outside into the cold and the snow and their driver ran to open the door to a sleek black Lexus. Theo set her gently down inside, making sure all parts of her dress and coat were safely tucked in before circling around to the street side of the car.

That odd feeling Audrey had was still vibrating in her bones, burrowing down and settling deep into her marrow when the doors shut and they sped off to the gala.

THEY WERE QUIET nearly the whole ride to the Plaza Hotel.

Audrey applied her lipstick as Violet had instructed, and when she snapped her compact shut, Theo's fingers slid across the supple leather of the seats and laced together with hers. He kept looking at her, his eyes roving up and down, but always landing back on her face—and though he didn't say anything, especially not with his mother's longtime driver, Wesley, in the front seat humming contentedly along to the radio, he didn't have to. It was written all over him, in the way he leaned toward her, how rosy his cheeks were in the flashes of gold from the streetlights outside, how his smile softened the curves of his plush lips and the sharp planes of his face.

God, did she love him.

"Oh, I almost forgot," Theo finally said, startling a little. He'd been so intently focused on her, but now he finally broke his gaze and leaned forward, reaching around to the front to grab something Wesley passed him before sitting back with a thin, black velvet box clutched in his hands. "I picked this up for you on the way over."

Audrey shook her head in disbelief when he placed it in her lap. "Theo, *no*. Did you—?"

He rubbed a hand on the back of his neck and tried to hide a smile. "Yeah, I might have borrowed some family jewelry from the safe deposit box. With Mom's permission, of course, and with one condition: she wants pictures." He pointed at her lap. "Open it."

She flipped open the box and blanched.

"A-are you crazy?!" she sputtered, gazing back up at him with wide eyes. "I—Theo, I can't—"

"Sure you can. Here, let me help you put it on. Turn around."

"You can't be serious."

He raised an eyebrow at her and gave her a stern look. "Oh, I'm quite serious, Miss Adams."

"This isn't a family heirloom or something, is it?"

He ignored the question. "We're going to a black-tie gala and there's a dress code. This is a Manhattan glitterati event. You're going to be mingling with a lot of very wealthy people, and you should look the part. Just for one night. It'll be fun, I promise."

She frowned at him. "But I'm not—I-I'm just a barista from Florida. I'm not one of them. I don't know—"

"Quit worrying," he said softly. "I'm glad you're not one of them. I wouldn't want you to be. And besides, you're just borrowing. It's like a costume." He took the box from her and twirled a finger in the air in silent command for her to twist in her seat. "Now, I didn't know what color your dress would be, so I had to go with the most neutral thing." When she obeyed, he brushed her hair away from her neck. "It's not *my* fault that just so happened to be a whole bunch of antique diamonds."

Audrey glanced at him over her shoulder while he swept the diamond-encrusted necklace around her neck. It was strung with five rows of diamonds curving along her collarbones into a vee that dipped lower and dripped with a much larger diamond suspended at the lowest point. It was cool and heavy, and Theo looked exceedingly pleased with himself while he fastened its clasp.

Even with it on, she could see how much it sparkled beneath the passing streetlights.

"There," he whispered, pressing a kiss to the nape of her neck before leaning back in his seat and snapping the box shut. "You were already gorgeous—but now you're *ready*." He took her hand again and interlaced their fingers once more.

Only when they got close and found their place in the line of cars waiting to pull up outside the hotel did he squeeze once and finally let go. Lights flashed in the distance as someone got out of a car.

"Are you okay being photographed?" she asked with a worried frown. "Should we go around the back? Or did you bring a mask?"

Theo shook his head slowly. He was as resigned as she'd ever seen him. "No. I'm going as I am. It'll be better to get it all over with at once like this—rip the Band-Aid off." He sighed and looked at her again. "At least this way, so many of them will have pictures of me that it'll be hard to sell my new likeness as an exclusive. But are *you* ready, sweetheart?" He tucked a stray lock of hair behind her ear. "You're showing yourself to them too. Don't be surprised if we end up in the tabloids. The Redmonds are an old, well-known New York family. We even have our own charitable foundation I'm representing here tonight."

"I'm all right so long as I'm with you."

"Okay. Then let's do this."

Wesley stopped the car and someone opened the door from the outside. The paparazzi didn't start yelling in earnest until Theo unfolded his long legs and stood, stooping to help Audrey out next—and then they seemed to realize who he was.

"Theodore! Theodore Sullivan, look this way, look here!" Lights from the cameras bounced everywhere, blinding Audrey and making her see spots. She clung to Theo's arm and he helped her stay steady before shutting the door.

But as soon as Theo lifted his head and showed the right side of his face to the red carpet, all hell broke loose.

Between the inordinate amount of flashbulbs popping off and the photographers' screams, it was practically a feeding frenzy.

"What happened to your face?!"

"Where did you get that scar?"

"Look here, Mr. Sullivan! Look here!"

"Were you in an accident?"

"Was it from when your father died?"

Some of them realized that probably wasn't the right approach and quickly shifted tactics.

"Is your mom planning to retire?"

"To your left! Your left!"

"What do you think of the Supreme Court ruling for the latest case she argued?"

"Over here, Theo! Over here!"

"Who's your lovely lady? Is this Audrey Adams? She's a barista, right?"

Theo had been ignoring them all until that last one, and he whipped around to glare at the photographer, who took a step back at Theo's dark expression.

"She's an engineer," he snarled. "*And* a barista." The man paled and lowered his camera, but another paparazzo chose that precise moment to snap a photo of the two of them right in front of Theo's face. He only blinked and glowered at both men before ushering Audrey inside the hotel, his hand pressed protectively into the small of her back.

It was a relief to be in the warmth and away from the cameras, and once Audrey checked her coat, she and Theo made their way around the charity auction gala, snatching bites of food from the passed plates of hors d'oeuvres and clutching flutes of champagne to their chests in the crowd.

"How do these things work?" Audrey asked, standing on her tiptoes to whisper the question into his ear.

Theo pointed at a table against the wall. "Most of the items up for bidding tonight are listed and shown over there. They'll bring out the real things during the actual auction. The piece we're here to see is already primed in the back, and will be rolled out on a platform and turned on in the dark as a surprise at the end of the scheduled programming." He waggled his eyebrows at her with a crooked smirk. "I heard rumors from Lightm4st3r's creative attorney, Imogen Phillips, that one of his sculptures might be making a last-minute appearance, and everyone in society knows I've been after one for some time now—even though I've been unsuccessful in winning so far."

"Ah, I see," she hummed. "Is that how it is?"

"Yeah." He shrugged with a dramatic sigh. "I've been outbid so many times. I just can't win. Not rich enough, apparently. I'll probably never get one."

Audrey suppressed a snort and Theo wrapped his arm around her waist, tucking her into his side. She didn't miss how his fingers skimmed the edge of her gown, lingering over the tiny patches of exposed bare skin at her torso and hips, spreading warmth everywhere they touched.

"So what do we do until then?"

"We dine, we dance, we avoid schmoozing at all costs. I don't want to have to pretend like I don't hate everyone but you here," he muttered with a grunt. "And the auction's only part of the scheduled programming after the dinner, which'll end relatively early. But most people will stay and keep celebrating until the wee hours of the morning."

The corner of Audrey's mouth twitched.

"What?" he asked, suspicion slowly dawning across his face. "What did I say? What's funny? You look like you want to laugh."

She did. "You just mentioned dancing."

As soon as she pointed it out, his expression fell. "Oh. Oh *no*."

"*You* said it." Audrey reached up and pinched his cheek with an impish grin. "Not me. And you can't take it back now."

He glanced over his shoulder at the dance floor, where a not-insignificant number of people were swaying in time to the live band. "Fuck me," he mumbled, rubbing a hand over his eyes. He lifted the champagne to his lips and downed it with a disgusted grimace.

"Oh, I most certainly will later."

Theo sputtered so hard, he nearly spat the champagne all over her, barely managing to recover in time. She patted his back amiably while he choked and gasped for breath.

"Yep," he wheezed. "Both you and Violet are trying to kill me tonight, I'm sure of it."

Audrey grabbed his hand and set her empty champagne flute on a nearby tray. "Come on, Theo. Dance with me. Please?"

The more he looked into her pleading eyes, the more she could see him break—until finally, with a strained groan, he let her drag him onto the dance floor, reluctant and limping. This time, Audrey was the one who took his hands and placed one at her back. He slid it up to a more chaste height, but before they could start swaying, she reached behind her to slowly lower it again, trying her best not to shiver when his calloused palms grazed the bare skin of her back, only to finally settle just above the swell of her hips.

Theo raised an eyebrow once he clasped his free hand with hers and they began to move. "Ah, so that's how it's going to be?" he muttered. "*Scandalous*, Miss Adams. We're in polite society tonight." His fingers tightened at the small of her back and his smirk grew all the more crooked.

"I thought we agreed I was actually feral. I thought that meant I wasn't fit for polite society anyway." If her eyes glittered, she couldn't be held responsible. "I *do* like to go rummaging around in dumpsters, scavenging through trash to find treasure, after all."

"I know you do. Hardly a typical genteel hobby, and as something of a garbage person myself in some ways, one I find particularly endearing." It was his turn for mischief to light up his gaze. "And again: I never said I was afraid of scandal. Rather think I sort of embody the concept, all things considered."

She closed her eyes and let him guide her slowly around the dance floor, both of them focused on each other's movements while they let their bodies sway in time to the music, their currents synchronized and melded.

Theo wasn't nearly as awkward as he was that time in his house. Despite the limp, he still moved with enough grace and coordination to betray his athletic past, and Audrey began to suspect that he might've greatly exaggerated his lack of skill in this arena. Maybe he was actually quite good. Maybe he'd actually had some lessons growing up. Maybe—

"*Wait*." When she gasped, she opened her eyes and found him watching her closely.

"What? What is it?" He slowed and raised an eyebrow.

"You took me to a ball," she finally whispered accusingly, eyes wide while she looked down at her dress, her shoes, the necklace. "This is your version of a *ball*."

"And?" The other eyebrow followed the first, but there was an amused, expectant tilt to his lips paired with it now.

"The only thing I'm missing is a tiara, isn't it? And it's only because your family doesn't own one."

"*Yet.*" He held up a finger. "We don't own one *yet*. But I could rectify that if you wanted me to, princess." Theo's smile widened in deep satisfaction.

Audrey was still stunned. "This isn't *Pretty Woman* like Violet thought. We didn't *have* to come to this—you just wanted me to . . ." Audrey bit her lip. "You wanted to let me be Anastasia."

Theo tilted his head back and forth as if weighing the accusation. "Well, I do try to come to these at least once a year. I was due." He tugged her closer and held her tightly against his chest, tucking her head beneath his chin and running his hand soothingly along her back while they continued to sway. "But I also thought it might be fun."

He placed his lips next to her ear and chuckled, low and strong. "I had an opportunity and I took it," he whispered. "I watched your face during that part of the movie, you know. You were so focused on the screen that you didn't know it, but I watched you light up, and I'm not sure I'd ever seen you look that dreamy before—at least, not then. Not yet." His hand pressed more firmly into her back. "If you were that thrilled by the mere idea of going to a ball, did you really think I didn't want to know for myself what it might be like if you *lived* it, even just for an evening?"

Audrey stopped swaying. She cradled his right cheek with her hand, sweeping a thumb along the length of his scar with a bemused shake of her head.

"You are a ridiculous man with ridiculous notions, Theodore Sullivan." It was her turn to huff a soft laugh. "I hardly know what to do with you sometimes."

He caught her hand and brought it to his lips, his eyes molten and dark, amber warmth mixing and mottled with cool, forest moss.

"I'm a very *reasonable* man with very *practical* notions, Miss Adams," he growled. Then he looked up at the heavens and sighed deeply before gazing back into her eyes with resignation. "And very little shame about how much I love you. So much so, I'll even sacrifice my hard-won dignity at your altar if you want me to dance in public with you. I know that about myself." Another raised eyebrow, and his grin was wolfish once more as he leaned down and murmured, "And I'm pretty sure you know *exactly* what to do with me."

"I do. And it's move in with you."

He stopped in his tracks. "What?" he breathed. Everyone else around them kept dancing. "Really? You mean it?"

"You're not the only one who had surprises up their sleeve tonight." Her smile widened. "I want to move in—with you. Before I start my new job. New year. New us."

The band finished their song and the rest of the dancers stopped to applaud. But Theo didn't move. He just stared at her, smiling softly, frozen in time and space, his eyes lined with tears and glimmering with wonder in the glittering lights of the ballroom.

Audrey didn't applaud either. She was too lost in the gaze of the man standing before her, and she knew. She knew he was the only one for her, the only one who ever would or *could* be for her, if only because she couldn't fathom ever having eyes for anyone else.

She saw him.

And he saw her too.

He always had, even when she couldn't see herself.

AFTER DINNER, THE auction began.

Though the Redmond family usually sponsored a large table for this particular multi-charity event every year, Theo had opted to purchase a smaller, more intimate one for just the two of them—meaning they had the entire table to themselves for the night. But despite not having to entertain his family's foundation's donors, it didn't stop people from approaching them.

Turned out Theo was fairly well-known in high society, which shouldn't have surprised her. What did, however, was how none of them seemed to know he was an artist. A few asked him about his graphic design business, but most interrupted their dinner to give their condolences regarding his father or ask after his mother or inquire about Audrey. No one mentioned the wreck explicitly, but nearly everyone's eyes immediately fell to his scar and rarely left.

Theo smiled and nodded politely and kept up appearances through gritted teeth, and it only became more genuine when he got to talk about Audrey, and how proud he was that she'd just graduated and accepted a job at a green energy startup. She blushed whenever he heaped praise upon her, and they both sighed in relief every time another person finally decided to leave them alone.

"Is it always like this?" she eventually asked.

Theo shook his head while he focused on cutting his steak. His hand was shaking a little more than it usually did these days, and she had to wonder how much of that was from stress—or nerves. "No," he muttered. "Diego tried to keep things out of the papers and Dad's obituary didn't mention the accident, but word got out anyway. They're coming around to gawk at me."

"I hate that they are." She placed her hand on his arm, and when he looked up at her, his face softened.

"It's fine." He shrugged. "I don't really give a shit anymore. They can stare all they want. Only one person's opinion about my appearance matters to me." He lifted his fork to his mouth and glanced at her out of the corner of his eye. His lips twitched, and she swore she saw the ghost of a crooked smile cross them, if only for a split second.

After dinner and during dessert, the lights dimmed and the auction began. Among other things, there were two dozen art pieces up for grabs that the public knew about, and as soon as the auctioneer launched the sales, Theo leaned his elbows onto his knees and his expression shifted, growing stony and determined.

When everyone else followed suit, it became apparent:

This auction was serious business.

The gala attendees were enthusiastic and brutally competitive, and Theo was no exception. He bid on—and won—an art piece by a relative unknown early on, explaining to her in a low voice that he knew of the artist he'd bought and they'd likely take off in the next few years, so what he'd gotten was actually a steal. Plus, the money went to a good cause and he was also keeping up pretenses.

Who would suspect a bidder in the auction was secretly one of its entrants?

The façade Theo kept up appeared to work like a charm. Most of the people who'd stopped by their table really seemed to believe he didn't work—that he was just a spoiled trust fund kid with a casual interest in art and philanthropy, and that was it. Things couldn't be further from the truth.

After about an hour, the final listed piece sold, but instead of raising the lights, the auctioneer held his hands up. The crowd, some of whom had obviously been angling to leave and had already risen, paused at their tables in surprise. Others, the serious collectors who might have heard the rumors Theo's lawyer had spread, leaned forward in anticipation, their excitement palpable.

Theo merely folded his hands pensively over his mouth. His face was unreadable, but he wasn't fooling her: he fidgeted the way he always did when he was anxious, his leg bouncing up and down, one finger tapping at his lips.

He was afraid this piece would be a failure, the same way his last one had been.

"Now, everyone," the auctioneer said, "you might have thought the bidding was over, but we have one more special, surprise piece up for grabs by a local artist you may have heard of: Lightm4st3r."

Whispers and murmurs swept through the ballroom like wind rushing through trees.

He gestured theatrically behind him, and two men wheeled a platform out from behind a partition at the back of the stage. Theo's sculpture was covered with a tarp, but the only thing it did was conceal the shape of the piece. Whatever he'd made was well over six feet tall and sprawled almost as wide at the base.

"It's a last-minute entry we received this morning, benefiting two very deserving foundations. Fifty percent of the proceeds from the sale will go to A Home For Juliette, an organization dedicated to improving the lives and living conditions of foster children across America. The other fifty percent are for Fostering Freedom, which provides college funding, tutoring, and support to foster students fresh out of the system who go on to pursue their undergraduate degrees."

What?

Audrey whipped her head over to find Theo watching her closely, a tiny satisfied smile concealed beneath a seemingly pensive finger.

I love you, he mouthed.

This was for her.

This whole thing was for her.

If she was as determined to kill him tonight as he kept claiming, then he seemed even more dead set on making her cry.

And this time, he won.

Her lip quivered and she sniffed, one traitorous tear escaping the jail she'd tried to confine it to. Theo leaned over and swept it away with his thumb. "Don't cry, Miss Adams," he whispered. But that only made it worse. She choked back a sob, and Theo pressed a kiss just below her ear before pulling a handkerchief out of his pocket and gently dabbing her cheeks with it. "The fun's only just begun. You don't want to miss what happens next."

"The piece is a neon sculpture, so please be patient while we turn off the lights to show the work to its full effect."

One by one, every bit of light aside from the signs illuminating the emergency exits was switched off, and the entire ballroom was plunged into darkness for a full minute, maybe even two. It was so quiet, you could hear a pin drop—but you would've been able to slice through the excitement with a knife, it was so tangible.

The piece was finally switched on and a collective gasp swept through the crowd.

The initial flash of color was so bright, it was as though a star had exploded before their eyes.

The audience fell silent as they took in what was before them, and Theo's fingers grasped for hers. Audrey grabbed his hand and squeezed it hard, unable to pull her eyes away from the stage—because what he'd made was extraordinary.

Like all of Lightm4st3r's pieces, it was an abstract neon sculpture molded around a metal frame. It was hard to describe what it was—not exactly shapeless or formless, and not at all haphazard, but definitely evocative.

What this one evoked was pain.

Breathtaking, devastating, all-encompassing *pain*.

It was the lines of it. There was something about its edges that tore at Audrey from the inside of her chest when she gazed at them, as if someone had taken a serrated knife with a hacking hand and tried to violently cleave her in two. It curved and twisted like a heart squeezed and lit aflame, its fire leaking and spilling and bleeding out along the floor in reaching, grasping, gasping tendrils, tortured and dying, fading into darkness at the iridescent, black-painted ends crawling away from the scene of an accident, leaching across asphalt like blood mixed with motor oil.

The hands that had shaped the structure were angry, hurt, desperate. The red neon forming the tall sides of it—swept as high up as Theo could get them on the scaffolding he'd constructed—looked like it had been made with a shaky, manic hand as it sliced its own wrist open, to bleed it dry, to splatter its lifeblood along the ground. It was raw. It was chaotic. It was brutal.

It was all those things, yes, but it was also *beautiful.*

It was beautiful in its form and its construction. At first glance, it looked unfinished, haphazard, disjointed, but Audrey knew better. She'd seen how hard it was to bend glass, the precision it required, and she knew every bend, every chaotic kink weaving in and out and between other tubes equally edged, equally hurt, equally pained, frustrated, *violated*, every single one had been purposeful, crafted, and refined, the trembling of Theo's dominant hand harnessed and intentionally channeled into the shape of things, turning and twisting the imperfections of the sculpture into something new.

This was Theo's pain, personified and publicly displayed for the world to see.

But it wasn't just pain. The outer shades of dark, angry, almost bloodlike red light tinged copper faded as the sculpture folded in and twisted inside and around itself, first to a dark pink or two, and then to an orange, an amber, shades of yellow and white, then, finally, to a single vivid light blue tube blazing from the dead center of it—where the core of the flame, its soul, might be nestled. The further Audrey gazed inside, squinting at the brightness of the sculpture, the more she noticed that the tubes had curved, softened, straightened. It was as though the piece had soothed itself, faded from fury to tranquility, from pain to peace, inner or otherwise.

Despite everything, a nascent kernel of hope burned brightly within, ready to emerge from a cocoon of devastation—like a phoenix rising from the ashes, reincarnated and born anew.

The auctioneer's voice echoed across the ballroom, jolting everyone out of their reverie.

"Lightm4st3r has stipulated that this piece is called *arterial rupture and pulmonary crisis after interstitial fractures of right side ribs 1-3 and left side 4-7 with subsequent hemorrhagia.* Or: *bleed out and break your heart until it opens.*"

Murmurs rustled across the ballroom at the title of the sculpture.

"That's one helluva name he came up with," Audrey muttered out of the side of her mouth, still wiping stray tears away with Theo's handkerchief. They'd rolled down her cheeks again when his art was unveiled. "Do you think he could've added more words to it? I don't think there are enough."

He gave her a tiny, nonchalant shrug. "Yeah, well, he never claimed to be good at titles. He's not a wordsmith," he muttered back. "Just look at what he called the piece he did right before this one. Derivative and lazy as fuck."

She snorted, but the auctioneer wasn't done. He cleared his throat when the lights were turned back on and Theo held his breath. "The bidding will start at ten thousand dollars."

It didn't stay there.

As soon as the auction was launched, the ballroom descended into chaos.

People began bidding left and right, scrambling to hold up their paddles, standing at their tables, trying frantically to beat one another to the punch. Theo got in on the action long enough to help drive the price up, but it turned out he hadn't needed to at all: the sculpture quickly hit a hundred thousand dollars—then two—then five, and he bowed out.

Many others did not.

The price soared above five hundred thousand dollars, then

seven fifty, a million, two. Theo's eyes widened and he grew very still in his chair once his sculpture passed that threshold, continuing to climb and climb and climb—until it finally topped out at a whopping *4.21 million dollars*.

Eventually, the gavel came down.

And it was all over.

The auction packed up. The winner, some billionaire art collector, was congratulated. The stage was returned to the band, and attendees went back to their desserts and drinks and socializing. More people joined in on the dance floor than were there before dinner, and still Theo sat there quietly, staring blankly at their white tablecloth, his lips parted and mouth slightly agape.

He didn't eat his dessert, so Audrey polished it off for him when he passed it to her absently (the best crème brûlée she'd ever had, if she was being honest. She liked it more than the chocolate mousse she'd chosen. Maybe Theo was onto something with his vanilla obsession) and finally tapped his shoulder.

"Theo? Are you all right?"

He turned and looked at her, his eyes falling to her empty dishes. He ripped her napkin out of her lap and threw it onto the table before grabbing her clutch and hand in his to pull her out of the seat.

"Where are we—"

She didn't have time to finish the question. He was already moving, and she with him, his long legs increasing in speed from a walk to an uneven, limping trot while he aimed for one of the exits, the side door that led to the rest of the hotel's event spaces. They wound their way across the dance floor before bursting into an empty hallway, where Theo suddenly hoisted her off her feet and half threw her over his shoulder.

"*Theo*," she hissed. "I can walk, for god's sake!" Sure, maybe not as fast as him in her heels, but *still*.

He shushed her, his face growing redder by the second, and

headed straight for a dark glass door across the way. He yanked the handle and breathed a sigh of relief when he found it unlocked. He drew them both inside and shut the door after him.

It was a meeting room, fancy and well-appointed like she always imagined a high-powered CEO's board room might be. The curtains were open and moonlight streamed through the windows, mingling with the lights of the city and dappling the floor in shifting shades of silver and gold. But she didn't have much time to reflect on how nice the room was, or what they were doing there. Because as soon as the sounds of the gala were cut off behind the closed door, Theo set her down—

And promptly caged her against the wall with his arms.

The wall shuddered with the force of his impact, and he panted heavily, his expression wild, his hair mussed from running his hands through it. When he tilted his head, a soft golden shaft of light fell diagonally across his face, highlighting his eyes.

His pupils were wider and blacker, more bottomless, more of an abyss than she'd ever seen them before.

Their darkness had swallowed him whole.

"I've never sold one for that much," he breathed. "It's a new personal record—by a *lot*. It blew everything I've ever done completely out of the water." He shifted and his biceps bulged, the muscles of his arms and back straining against the seams of his beautiful jacket while he rolled his shoulders and pressed his palms harder against the wall. Audrey swallowed when he settled in front of her, rocking on his feet until he was satisfied with the solidity of his stance. "And it's all because of *you*."

Heat rippled off of him in waves. They washed over her now, pinking her cheeks and quickening the cadence of her heart. He was so close, the scent of his cologne, warm and spiced and woodsy, filled her nose. It was heady and intoxicating, and though she'd only had a glass or two of champagne, Theo's intensity, the smell of him, the sight of him looking so untamed, so *wild*, made her head spin.

"I didn't do anything," she whispered breathlessly with a shake of her head. It took everything she had to form the words.

"Yes. You did," he insisted.

"No, I—"

Audrey sucked in a breath when Theo braced a hand on her neck and buried his face in the crook of her shoulder, inhaling deeply once, the sensation and depth of it full of longing. He groaned and dragged his soft, plush lips against her skin, and she shivered while they traced the curves of her neck before dipping to the swells of her breasts. A quick tug with a single finger was all it took for him to free one from its confines before he drew it into his mouth, kissing and suckling at her as though he might die if he didn't.

"You did this," he rasped against her skin, his voice low and desirous while he worked at her with his mouth. "It's your fault."

"Theo—"

He sucked harder, and Audrey arched her back against the wall and writhed, unable to hold still any longer under the feeling of his tongue over her nipple. She put a hand on his shoulder to try to draw him closer, but he only grabbed it, sought out the other, and pinned them above her head with one massive paw, encircling both wrists with just his thumb and forefinger to thoroughly trap her there.

He pulled her neckline down further to free her other breast. "If I hadn't met you, I couldn't have made that." He drew it into his mouth, laving at her nipple and worshipping the hard, sensitive bud with his tongue between breaths. "If I hadn't met you, I don't know where I'd be. Dead, probably."

"Theo, we're—w-we're in public," she breathed, barely managing to hold onto any last threads of decency. They were unraveling quickly enough as it was, especially with how hot she felt caught in Theo's orbit. She was beginning to burn; already her own skin was becoming unbearable, never mind the feeling of the dress and how it clung to her. Maybe Theo *would* rip it off and free her completely. It'd be a relief from the flames licking across her skin. "We should call Wesley. We should—"

He jerked his gaze up to meet hers again, his mouth red and swollen and wicked. "*No.* I can't wait anymore." His eyes, normally so kind, so sweet, so often sad, glittered instead with mischief. "Theo's not here right now," he purred, caressing her neck with his free hand and swiping a careful thumb along the edge of her jaw. "It's *Lightm4st3r's* night. And you know what? He might be reclusive, but he's not quite as upstanding as Theodore Sullivan is. He's done some things in his time." Darkness simmered in his gaze. "And do you know one thing he's not yet guilty of? *Public indecency.* I think we should change that. *Now.*"

"Are you trying to collect broken laws like Pokémon or something?" she gasped. "Theo, we should—"

He dove forward and took her mouth in answer, nipping, biting, sucking at her lips, her tongue, her neck, every bit of her he could reach, frenzied and manic, hurried and desperate and hungry. All thoughts fled from Audrey's mind, chased away by his heat, his fervor, his insistence, and instead, every remaining shred of rationale and decency was replaced with wild, irrepressible *need.*

Audrey needed him, and she didn't care how.

He let go of her hands to free his own and lifted her off the floor, palming her ass through her dress and pinning her back against the wall with his hips lodged between her legs. He was unbearably hard, and when he kissed her again, it was so deep, so passionate, he stole her breath. She hardly knew what to do with herself.

But Theo knew.

His hands didn't stay idle. While one wrapped around the back of her neck, trembling but strong, he ran the other up her dress beneath its slit and along her thigh. His calluses skated across her skin, but when he reached the curves of her ass, he stopped. His brows knit together in confusion, and he shifted his hand again, his fingers searching for the edges of her underwear.

When he didn't find any, his throat bobbed.

"Good god," he whispered, his voice ragged and strained. "You've been bare under this dress the entire time? This whole evening? *And I didn't know?!*"

Audrey's cheeks were on fire, their momentary pause allowing words to filter back into her brain. "I forgot about shapewear," she mumbled, biting her bottom lip. It was a rookie mistake. "And the dress was too tight otherwise, it would have shown the panty lines. Actually, it would have shown through the slits anyway. So I just—"

Theo closed his eyes and threw his head back, his expression one of utter bliss while he mouthed *Thank you* to the heavens. "I should have bought Violet *two* pairs of shoes."

Her back slid down the wall while Theo lowered them both to the ground, pressing soft kisses to every sliver of exposed skin along her hips and torso while he knelt carefully in his tux. He parted her dress at the slit with reverent hands and a rapt look on his face, tugging the tight, stretchy fabric slightly higher onto her hips and lifting her right leg over his shoulder as a brace. Before Audrey could fully comprehend what was happening, Theo's fingers dug deeply into the flesh of her waist and hips to hold her steady—before he plunged his face between her legs.

It was his nose she felt first, nuzzling against her sex, drawing languidly up and down her folds and over her clit. Then his lips, soft and gentle, grazing and mouthing along the inside of her thighs.

When she felt his tongue, she moaned.

It was too loud.

She clamped her hands over her mouth.

"*Theo.* We're g-going to get caught," she whispered through her fingers.

"Then try to stay quiet." His voice was muffled, but she could feel the vibrations of it and the wickedness of his smile against her cunt when he paused, his lips forming the words through his devotions. "*If you can.*"

"But—"

"I'm *busy,*" he growled. "You taste incredible—so sweet, and all mine. Let me be greedy, just for tonight."

That was the last thing he deigned to say.

Theo was already lost to his art, to his adoration, to worshipping at Audrey's altar, and only his shadowy halo of hair was visible through the slit in her dress, his head bobbing slightly as he feasted on her. She dug her fingers into his waves, grabbing and pulling while she fought for purchase, and he grunted in pleasure when she did, merely pressing the blade of his tongue more forcefully against her clit before shifting and plunging it inside of her, licking and tasting what he found with abandon.

Audrey closed her eyes and arched her back against the wall, barely managing to stifle a moan by biting into the side of her hand hard enough to imprint it with the shape of her teeth while she began to ride his face. A shadow passed their doorway, the light streaming in from the hallway darkening for a moment—but instead of sending fear coursing down her spine, it only fanned the flames of her arousal, making it stronger, more intense. She bucked harder, her hips finding their rhythm in time with Theo's tongue, with his mouth, his face wet and hot with her slick, and together they found their cadence, falling into time like the beats of a song.

The darkness of the meeting room blurred into black velvet around her, the edges of the table and the golden light tumbling through the glass door melding together while she lost herself. The only thing she was aware of was Theo, his silken hair in her hands, his fingers pressing deep into her flesh, his nose and lips and tongue alternating over her clit, the burn of the fire within her growing and spreading every time he closed his mouth over it and sucked, as forcefully as if he were trying to drain her dry of all the nectar she contained.

His mouth was music and she danced to it, chasing its tempo, its tenor, its time, until together, they finally reached her crescendo. When she cried out, Theo snaked a hand upward across her body, smoothing his palm over her exposed breasts before plunging his thumb into her mouth to help stifle the sound.

That only made her come harder.

When she closed her lips around it and sucked, he jolted forward between her legs with a groan. Suddenly, the warmth of him was gone, the cold, empty air rushing along her legs, but only for a second. Before she'd even finished coming, before she could sink to the floor limp and spent, Theo's thumb was gone from her mouth, replaced with his tongue and the taste of her, his strong arms now wrapped around her back, lifting her up and pinning her more forcefully against the wall.

"Need you," she rasped when he broke away to breathe, the air searing her throat. "Want you. *Now.*"

She hadn't needed to ask.

His belt had already fallen to the ground.

As soon as the words crossed her lips, he thrust inside her, sheathing himself to the hilt in one smooth stroke. He swallowed her groans, and she wrenched her hands into his back, twisting her fingers into the fabric of his jacket and wrapping her legs around his waist to cling to him for dear life, pulling him closer while he pounded her into the wall.

The force of Theo's thrusts wracked through her while he plunged deeper, faster, harder than he'd ever dared to before. It was almost too much, the way he filled her, the way his length dragged deliciously along the ridges inside her, the way he found her limits—and yet, somehow, she was able to take him, match him, hold him, stroke for stroke. She hardly felt the wall at her back. Instead, it was only Theo's lips while he sucked and nipped at her neck, beneath her ear, along her jaw, hard enough to leave marks and still leave her wanting more.

More.

It was always the need for more.

He wasn't the only one who was greedy.

They were the same.

They always had been.

The pressure built inside again and Audrey surrendered to its currents, gasping and panting as the wave grew and crested into an even larger swell than before, curling and tumbling when she barreled over and crashed into the shore. She went blind with pleasure and buried her face in the side of Theo's neck, digging her nails and teeth into his skin, biting hard while she tried to stifle her cries with her last remaining speck of consciousness. He grunted, growling deep in his throat as he thrust into her again, once, twice, a third time, his entire body stiff and straining while she clenched and fluttered around him, milking his own orgasm from him and pulling him deep into her core where he belonged, where he'd always been, where she wanted him most, always and forever inside her where she could hold him dear and keep him safe.

Theo slumped against the wall over her, barely able to stay upright. Their chests heaved, and as he bent forward and pressed his lips softly to hers once more, stroking her neck tenderly with one straining, trembling hand, sweat tumbled down Audrey's brow, the droplet mingling with and matching Theo's own. They stood there, foreheads pressed together while they panted, their breaths still in sync with each other as they tried to catch hold of reality again now that they'd come back down to earth. Even though Theo held her tightly against him, it was a miracle he was even still standing, and he was leaning heavily against the wall when he finally opened his eyes and his mouth split into the beginnings of a crooked smile.

But before he could say anything, the golden light spilling over the floor near them from the hallway darkened—and this time, the shadow didn't pass.

Theo's smile faded, and they looked at each other in wide-eyed horror. Theo was still inside her, pants unzipped and pulled down just enough to allow him access, and he pressed forward, practically smothering her against the wall in an attempt to shield her from whoever might open that door.

They held their breaths, waiting for the errant jiggle of a door handle or the sound of footsteps thudding across the carpet. Theo shifted and pulled them both slowly along the wall, maneuvering them deeper into a dark corner of the meeting room and away from where the angled light had spilled. Audrey hardly dared look in the direction of the door—her heart was thudding so loudly in her ears, she was certain whoever was on the other side could hear it pounding from there.

But nothing happened. No one entered the room, and after a few seconds that seemed to stretch into eternity, the shadow left, letting the light spill inside once more.

They exhaled and let their shoulders slump in relief.

And then, when they looked at each other—and down at Theo's pants—they both snorted and started to laugh at the same time.

"Oh my god," Audrey finally wheezed, hugging him tightly and burying her fingers in his hair. Between the wax he'd styled it with and the way she'd been grabbing it, it was the messiest she'd ever seen it. He looked thoroughly debauched, like a man shipwrecked and only recently liberated from his wilderness exile. "What did we do?"

With her breasts still freed from the bonds of her gown and the rest of it hiked up around her waist, she was sure she didn't look any better.

"I look that put-together, huh?" The crooked smile was back, doubly dimpled, thoroughly roguish, and not at all remorseful. He smoothed some of the hair away from her face, tucking her once-artful waves more or less back where they should go before tugging up the fabric of her gown to cover her.

"How are we going to get out of here like this? Is my makeup completely trashed?" She blinked at him and tilted her head toward the light, hoping he might be able to see.

"You're the most beautiful thing I've ever seen—just as you are." Theo leaned forward and pressed a kiss to her nose before pulling out and setting her carefully back on the ground. He took out his handkerchief and used it to clean her up, wadding it into a ball and stuffing it hurriedly back into his pocket. Both of her shoes had fallen off somewhere and her legs felt like Jell-O, so she clung to him while she steadied herself and tried to remember how to walk properly again and *not* wobble like a baby deer on a ship at sea. "Though I might have kissed away all your lipstick. Pretty sure that's long gone." He ran a hand along his mouth and shrugged sheepishly.

So much for Violet's bulletproof date-night lip color. "Uh-huh. Sure. And now you want to go back out *there*?" She grimaced as she bent and slipped her shoes back on. Truthfully, she wasn't sure she had it in her to go back to the ballroom where everyone might stare at them, and at Theo's scar—

And his suspiciously wrinkled shirt and jacket.

"Actually, no." He tucked himself back into his pants and tried to straighten his jacket, smoothing his shirt somewhat before patting curiously at his hair. He only managed to tame it slightly when he ran a hand through it. "Want to go beg for some more crème brûlée from the kitchen and then call Wesley to pick us up out back once we get your coat? I'm ready to go home."

"Are you regretting giving your dessert to me now?"

"Yes," he said, bending forward and stealing another kiss. "I paid enough money for that table. I want the cherry on top of my night after all." He raised an eyebrow and leaned down to whisper in her ear. "But you're still the best thing I've ever tasted, sweetheart. Nothing can top *you*." He kissed her, low and slow this time. "And I can't wait for you to come home with me—for good."

When she swatted at him and headbutted him playfully, he only smiled wider and folded her into his arms. Once he tucked her into his side, they glanced out into the hallway and walked out as if nothing at all noteworthy had ever happened to either of them.

No, nothing noteworthy at all.

And somehow, that second caramelized custard—nicked from the kitchen and eaten barefoot against a wall in the service hallway of the Plaza Hotel—tasted even sweeter than the first.

Twenty-Three

A FEW WEEKS LATER

IT WAS A Saturday at exactly 2:15 p.m.

And Violet was a ticking time bomb.

"Sign here," muttered Theo's lawyer, Imogen, pointing at the stack of papers as she towered over Audrey's tiny ex-roommate. Zoom had not done the woman justice: turned out she was something of an Amazon and was nearly as tall as Theo himself.

It made for an interesting picture when she and Violet stood at his kitchen counters.

"And here. And initial here."

Violet shoved her curtain of sleek, dark hair behind her ear and groaned as she shook out her hand. "What is his studio, fucking *Fort Knox*?" Without warning, she attacked the paperwork with such renewed vigor, she nearly knocked the remainder of her latte onto it. Audrey leapt forward to grab the half-full mug while the wide-eyed lawyer stumbled backward, teetering on chic sky-high red-bottomed handmade Italian leather stilettos.

Violet hardly noticed.

"I swear to God, this better be worth it," she grumbled while she scribbled the last signature with a pointed flourish. "I need to know what in the actual *fuck* Theo is doing as art that requires this much secrecy *or I am gonna die*."

"Don't you think that's a bit of an exaggeration?" Imogen's red-painted lips pursed while a single platinum blond eyebrow soared. "It's simply a matter of security, not death."

"Who's dying now?"

The heavy *thump* of a cane followed by another and another echoed off Theo's expensive tile floors as he finally made it up the stairs, not looking too worse for the wear, all things considered. He'd slipped on the ice on his stoop a few days ago and was still suffering for it, though every day was getting better.

Violet threw her head back. "Me! I'm dying, Theo."

"You sure about that?" He eyed her wryly.

But she wasn't to be deterred. "Yes, very sure, because you won't show me your art without a *goddamned* NDA."

"Hey, at least you're here now, right? And besides, we can't have you dying. Ali would be so disappointed."

Fire blazed in Violet's eyes. "Don't you dare bring up that prick Alastair Hackett to me, *Theodore*. I don't care if you happened to play lacrosse together at Columbia, I don't want to hear one more fucking word about that man."

His smile was soft and crooked as he stepped over and jabbed a finger into her ribs, chuckling when she flinched and dodging her retaliatory shove before he made his way to stand next to Audrey. Once he was settled, he turned to his lawyer. "Thanks for coming out here, Im." He extended a hand. "I know it's a bit of a trek for you."

Imogen's hard expression softened as she clasped his hand, her eyes dropping down to his right hip before darting straight back up. "Of course, Theo. You don't need to be out and about—especially not after having fallen like you did."

He waved her off. "I'm all right. I've had worse." He jutted his chin at where Violet had decisively slammed her pen down on the counter. "Are we good here?"

Imogen nodded. "I'm satisfied," she drawled, sweeping the completed NDA paperwork into a fancy zippered leather portfolio. "I believe you're up. And I'd like to come down as well before I head out—it's been some time since I've had the pleasure of seeing your artwork in person."

"Ah. Okay." He laughed nervously and rubbed the back of his neck, which was rapidly turning red. "All right. Um . . . Violet, I guess you can—"

He didn't even get to finish before she made a beeline for his studio door.

"No, wait!" He shot his hand up with an alarmed look. "Wait a second! Hey! Come back here, you can't just—"

"I SIGNED THE FUCKING NDA, I'M GOING IN."

Theo waddled frantically after her, but it was too late. Violet had already wrenched it open and was at least halfway down the stairs by the time he managed to grab the doorframe to hold himself steady.

"Don't touch anything or go any further until I get down there! It actually *is* dangerous!" he called, his voice trembling as he grabbed Audrey's hand and gripped it tightly. He leaned on her heavily while she helped him down the steep staircase leading into his dark studio.

It was still a little strange, remembering that she'd moved in with Theo only a few short weeks ago. That his place was now theirs. That there was no more splitting their time between beds, no more schlepping clothing back and forth from the itty-bitty studio she shared with her best friend. No more having to coordinate schedules or spend time going between his place and hers. No more missing him when they were apart. No more café, even—not since she'd started her new job at the sustainable tech startup Greenwise Technologies.

Now she got to wake up every morning wrapped safely in his arms.

Make him coffee over breakfast.

Sit with him in the kitchen while he cooked dinner.

But not as a visitor anymore, because now this house was her home too. Theo was her home. And she was so happy.

Bliss was the taste of him in her mouth.

The sight of him sound asleep next to her in their bed.

The feeling of his body melding into hers.

The scent of roasted coffee beans.

And the sound of Billie Holiday lilting in the air.

"Yeah, yeah, I read the paperwork, you're not responsible for any bodily harm I may incur," Violet yelled back, her voice echoing slightly.

"Yeah, but still! I don't want anything to happen to you!" Theo's hand tightened on the cane, making the padding groan and squeak as they rounded the corner and found her waiting at the bottom of the staircase, leaning casually against the wall and smirking in the slim sliver of light pouring down from upstairs.

He still hated using his cane, but admitted that he hated it a lot less with Audrey around now.

"Did you honestly think I wasn't going to let you do whatever big reveal you have planned? You think I've waited all this time only to miss out on that shit?" She stood on her tiptoes and punched Theo fondly in the shoulder. "I just wanted to give you a heart attack."

"*Why?!*" he wailed, flashing her a look like she was absolutely out of her goddamn mind. "Do you not think I've been through enough this year? A heart attack? Are you trying to kill me? *Again?!*"

"You're fine, Teddy." Violet's smirk widened. "I'd be willing to bet that the very strongest part of you is your heart."

He froze and grew quiet, still leaning on Audrey. "That's . . . a-awfully generous of you to say," he finally stammered, taking another tentative few steps down to meet her at the bottom. "But for the record, I'm pretty sure it's actually my chest and back. I still have trouble gripping a pen sometimes, but I can bench three-twenty-five."

"Is that good?"

"Yeah, it's a lot. I exercise when I'm anxious."

"I assume that means you work out near constantly, then," Violet replied, rocking back and forth on her heels while she waited for Theo to hobble over and fiddle with the light switches. "But I'm sticking with my answer."

"I hope yours is as strong as you think mine is," Theo muttered as Imogen floated down the stairs after them, her arms crossed over her chest and her face unreadable. Audrey eyed the attorney's shoes, envying her ease with such tall, pointy heels. "Okay. Are you ready?"

"Boy, am I ev—"

He hit the switch.

". . . er."

All the neon lights in his studio exploded into life.

Violet's mouth dropped open.

She went completely silent.

This must have been what Theo felt like when he first showed this to me, Audrey thought, watching her best friend take in the full truth of Theo's secret. His hands were so warm, hers started to sweat in response. But Audrey knew he was nervous about this; he always was about sharing the things most precious to him.

The things that mattered most.

Violet, for her part, had gone awfully quiet. "You—*neon*?!" she finally gasped, gathering herself as she trotted over to stare at the signage on the far wall. The large, yellow letters of SULLIVAN LIGHTWORKS were on proud display and took up the most immediate visual real estate. Violet lifted a hand in wonder as she traced the perfect curves of the massive sign with a single finger.

"You do neon art?" She finally spun on her heel with her mouth fully dropped open. "Oh my god, that's so cool! Okay, for real: Do you know Lightm4st3r? I know I've asked you before, but surely you must, especially if you both work in the same medium. There can't be that many neon artists working in Brooklyn." She wandered around and began peering at some of the other more traditional signs on the wall, standing on her tiptoes to look at the wiring behind them before leaning back and contemplating the colors and the shifting, flashing shapes.

Theo and Audrey exchanged a glance—and then both turned to look at Imogen. The attorney was busy staring in disbelief at Violet, her perfect, platinum eyebrows raised high in surprise.

Audrey met Theo's gaze again. She shrugged.

He sighed, closing his eyes as he rubbed the bridge of his nose.

"Uh . . . well, no, there's not that many of us. It's a niche art."

"So you're saying that's a yes?" Violet called over her shoulder. "Yes to knowing Lightm4st3r?"

"Yeah, Violet. I know him."

She spun on her heel and clapped her hands together, shrieking in excitement. "OH MY GOD IS THAT WHY I HAD TO SIGN THE NDA?!" She trotted back over and ripped his hand away from his face, tugging eagerly at it. "Can you introduce me? I have so many questions I want to ask him, all about his process and his inspiration and—"

"Well, you're looking at him, so fire away, I guess."

Violet quieted. Her face fell.

She blinked.

A little too much.

A little too rapidly.

"What?"

Audrey wasn't sure Violet was breathing.

Theo rolled his lips together and pointed behind Violet. "His commercial art is on the wall you were just looking at. But, uh, that's . . . well, his latest abstract sculpture he's working on is over there. Because it's the latest one *I* am working on." He winced and twisted the handle of his cane in his other hand until the padding groaned again. "Me is he. I am Lightm4st3r."

Violet let go of him like he was suddenly on fire and staggered backward until she knocked into one of his worktables. Her eyes were as wide as saucers.

"You . . . are him. You're him? You're Li-Light . . . m4st3r?" she stammered. "The notorious reclusive Radon Renegade of Brooklyn?"

"Radon is radioactive and I don't use it, that moniker is a misnomer."

"The Argon Apostate?"

"As far as I'm aware, I've never been excommunicated from any church."

"The Neon Ninja?"

"I'm nowhere near that nimble anymore."

"The Helium Hellion?"

"Since when have I ever actually raised hell?" Theo splayed his hands out indignantly. "*Where the fuck did all these nicknames come from?!*"

But Violet only shook her head in disbelief. "You? Sweet, sweet Theodore Sullivan, too shy to ask Audrey out, are the scourge of the *New York Post*?"

Theo rubbed the back of his neck and sighed. Even in this light, Audrey could tell that his ears had flushed pink, if not scorching red.

"Um . . . yeah? That's me."

"No one's ever seen your face."

"Well, obviously not *no one*." He grimaced. "But now you know why we needed an NDA." He shrugged sheepishly and winced, shifting anxiously on his feet. "I mean, I'd really appreciate it if you didn't blow my cover. I don't want the attention." The low buzzing of his sculptures and signs was the only noise filling the space, punctuating the uncomfortable silence stretching between them.

"Holy shit, you're not joking," Violet finally breathed. "I keep waiting for someone to tell me this is a prank, but you—" She suddenly spun around and gasped when she looked at where he'd pointed behind her, paling in the bright, multicolored light of his artwork and clamping her hands over her mouth.

Theo let out the breath he'd been holding.

Audrey took his free hand again and wove their fingers together, leaning her head on his arm and resting there as they all quietly studied his work in progress. It was raw, he'd told her, still only the beginnings of his next work. A sketch, essentially. He'd needed something to do with his hands after getting some of his confidence back post–charity auction, so as soon as he could, he'd set to work fiddling around in his studio. The end result was going to be stunning.

Imogen stepped up behind them and put her hand on Theo's shoulder, resting the other casually on her hip. "It's good," she murmured. "I can see where you're going with it, and if it's the direction I think it is, it's going to be very good, Theo. Well done."

"Don't congratulate me yet," he muttered back. "I have to finish the damn thing first. I've only just started."

"You will." When Audrey uttered the words, he looked down and smiled softly. "You'll finish it. And it'll be brilliant." The light in Theo's eyes was everything she needed. It was brighter than the sun.

But Violet, meanwhile, seemed to be at a loss for words.

This new sculpture wasn't anything like the last one. It wasn't an expression of his pain, or rage, or grief. It wasn't chaotic, or frenetic, or filled with terrible, trembling fury mixed with agonizing beauty.

This one was all curves, the welded scaffolding and initial neon tubing sweeping and smooth and soft.

This one was all lightness, the first strokes of radiance laid down in yellows and whites and bright oranges, all of it full of joy, of sweetness, like Popsicles eaten during the height and heat of a summer's day.

It was like hope.

It was like the sun.

It was how Theo felt now, with Audrey, and she with him.

It was how he saw her, how he lit up whenever she entered the room. How she lit up for him in return.

It was how he loved her, in the soft, golden glow of dawn. And how she loved him back in the dulcet, amber tones cast over the city skyline at dusk.

She knew, because he told her.

He told her every single day.

Violet spun back to look at the three of them. Tears shone in her eyes, and she kept glancing between Theo and this new sculpture. "The whole time?" she finally managed to gasp. "You've been listening to me babble on about how much I love your work the whole goddamn time?!"

Theo's neck turned even redder. Audrey could tell how hot his face had suddenly become even in the bright, multicolored light of his studio, and she knew if she were to reach up and rub one of his ears, she'd find it blazing. "Yeah?" He shrugged helplessly. "It's not like it wasn't flattering." He limped over to where Violet stood. "It's not like I can just blurt that sort of thing out. Page Six would pay a *lot* to uncover my identity, and they're not the only ones."

"That's putting it mildly, don't you think?!" Violet punched him bitterly in the arm.

"Ow!"

Violet drew in a deep breath. And Audrey knew the dearth of words was about to be over.

She braced herself for the onslaught.

"HOLY SHIT, THEO. YOU'RE FUCKING LIGHTM4ST3R?" Violet pointed at his scar and angrily wiped her tears away. "Is this why you don't do graffiti work anymore? Why you disappeared for almost a year? WAIT."

She ran her hands frantically through her hair, making it swirl wildly with static and pushing her bangs up to practically stand on end. "OH MY GOD THE SCULPTURE WAS ABOUT YOUR ACCIDENT. Holy fuck, Theo, the photos were the most incredible thing I have ever seen. Can you get me access to see it in person? Do you know the billionaire who bought it? Surely he'll let you visit. Maybe if we all wear masks, can I see it? Or wait—wait wait wait, what about any of your past sculptures? Or any that you haven't shown?"

Violet finally looked around at the rest of the ones behind his newest, and Audrey could have sworn her legs nearly gave out. They shook and buckled, and Violet had to grab onto the edge of a table to hold herself upright.

"Holy fuck, I'm in Lightm4st3r's studio right now." Violet seemed to be having trouble breathing and looked like she was on the verge of hyperventilating. She patted the top of the worn wooden table as if she couldn't believe it was real. "There's shit in here no one has ever seen, oh my god." She whirled around and faced him again. "Over my dead body would I rat you out." Madness gleamed in her eyes. "But you are never getting rid of me now. I am gonna be down here constantly, creeping on you while you work."

Theo's smile might have stretched into a grimace. "That . . . might make it a little hard to actually do the work, Vi," he said, gently resting his hand on her shoulder. "I don't like attention, remember? Neither identity of mine does."

"Oh. Right, right." She nodded sagely. Her face fell a little.

"But you can take a look at my progress whenever you come over. I'm happy to let you have sneak peeks."

That perked her right up.

"Brilliant. I'll take it!" She bounced on her heels and pointed back to his newest work. "All right, fine: what's she called? I'll need to know. I want all the dirt, and I want it before you release any of it publicly. I signed my life away in blood to keep your secrets, so you'd better fucking make it worth my while now."

Theo chuckled. "Well . . . I don't know for sure yet."

He glanced down at Audrey.

"But I'm thinking the working title for Instagram might be *the sun can't touch you if you burn yourself*."

IT WAS THE best evening Audrey had had with Violet in a long time.

After Imogen left, they spent what must have been hours in the studio, but the time flew by. Theo answered as many questions as he could until he and Violet were both blue in the face before they made their way back upstairs to his office, where he got to share all the articles and newspaper clippings and screenshots with her.

It was fun, watching her best friend be so filled with joy.

It was fun, sharing another secret between them.

Audrey hadn't liked keeping that one.

After dinner, Theo called Violet an Uber, and as soon as she was safely tucked into a five-star luxury ride, he flopped back onto the couch next to Audrey, blowing his dark hair out of his eyes with an exhausted puff of air.

"My god," he whispered. "I knew that would be a lot, but—"

"But you loved it too, didn't you?" Audrey grinned when Theo held out an arm and she snuggled up close, curling into his chest and closing her eyes.

"Yeah. Yeah, I did," he said, softly running his fingers through her hair. They'd turned on his fireplace while they'd waited for their food delivery, and they both quieted and watched the shadows of the flickering flames dance across the exposed brick walls. "I forgot how much I love talking about my art. It really sucks that I can't with most people, even though that's my own fault."

Audrey cupped his right cheek, tilting his face toward her own. She swept her thumb across his scar, and his lips spread up into another slow, soft smile at her touch.

"I know. I'm not exactly the best at keeping track of all the art world stuff. I like it, but Violet lives for it. She's so *intense*."

Theo nodded sagely. "That she is. And at least she seems to like what she does, according to Ali, even if it's not yet the entire dream. He says she's good at it. And that she's *terrifying*. Sounds like she regularly threatens to eat him for lunch."

Audrey raised an eyebrow and tilted her head up to meet Theo's gaze. "Oh? Is *that* what Alastair says?"

He bounced his brows right back at her. "Uh-huh. He can't shut up about her, whether he's ranting about whatever she did to him most recently, or about how wonderful she is. He thinks he sounds begrudging, but I'm fairly certain he's been in love with her for months now. At least that's the subtext." He frowned slightly and tapped a finger to his lips. "Or supertext, maybe? Is that what you call something that's *so fucking obvious* it doesn't even count as subtext anymore?"

She snorted and snuggled even closer into his side. His arm tightened around her. "Well, don't tell that to Violet. She's still convinced she hates him, not that she thinks or talks about him constantly, or even that tall, lanky gingers are exactly her type and have been since at least middle school. I didn't even know Jersey had that big of an Irish population, but apparently they do."

"What? Oh my god, what a revelation." Theo didn't even attempt to properly feign surprise. "Violet might like Alastair? He might be exactly her type? This is news to me. Absolutely earth-shattering information."

She snorted. "Don't you *dare* pretend to be an expert in these things, Theodore Henry Sullivan. You couldn't even tell that I had the biggest, most awkward crush on you when you were coming to the coffee shop and that was *pretty fucking obvious* if you ask me." She tugged his ear. "If you remember, I had to ask you out first."

"*Oh?*" he purred, leaning in even closer to whisper against her lips. "Did you now?" He slid his left hand up her neck and buried his fingers in her hair, stroking hard and pulling it in just the right way to make her shiver. "I'm pretty sure I was pining for you much earlier than you were for me, but perhaps I'm wrong."

Audrey hummed. "I don't know. I liked you from the beginning."

"I could barely breathe from the moment I saw you."

"Well, I had to ask you to kiss me," she pouted. "When the hell were you going to do that?"

"Eventually." He grinned at her with dark delight. "And that's not exactly how I remember it. I remember simply being a gentleman and not wanting to pressure you."

"I remember having to demand that you not go so slowly."

"Ah," he crooned. "I see that we're at an impasse. So why don't you remind me again how I kissed you on our first date? I'm not sure that's burned deep enough into my memory."

"You need a reminder, huh?" Her breath had quickened. Her *body* burned.

It was always like this with him.

She always wanted him.

Always.

Theo nodded and hummed, just barely brushing his mouth against her own. "I mean, I think it might have gone something like this, but I'm not sure. Tell me if I'm wrong, and I'll try again." He curled his fingers beneath her jaw, his calloused fingertips grazing across the sensitive skin as he gently tilted her mouth up to meet his. She flung one leg over his hips to carefully settle into his lap, straddling him on the couch cushions.

Theo was getting harder and harder by the second.

"That's not how it went," Audrey muttered.

"No?" Theo breathed, snaking a hand beneath her sweater and bra to palm one of her breasts. Her nipple hardened to a tight peak beneath his touch, and she sucked in a sharp breath when he lightly pinched her.

"Nope. Not that either," she gasped. "Like you were ever so forward in your life."

"Well, fuck me," he chuckled. "I guess I've just completely forgotten, then."

Liar.

"Why don't you show me, sweetheart? I think I need my memory jogged."

"Mmm. Okay, fine." She cupped his face with both hands. "Close your eyes. And don't open them. No peeking."

Those extraordinarily unique hazel irises of his glittered with mischief before they disappeared behind their lids, his long, dark lashes sweeping half-moons across his high, pale cheekbones. "Yes, ma'am."

They grew silent, and Audrey took her time to study him. It never ceased to amaze her how handsome he was, despite what he might have thought of himself. He was beautiful, even with the scar, perhaps even *because* of it in some ways, and she ran her thumb gently along its length, as quiet and soft as a whisper. This must have been what he was doing that night, she realized—why he took so long to press his lips to her skin.

He'd wanted to look at her the way she looked at him now.

He'd wanted to study all the dips and curves and planes of her face.

He'd wanted to capture them in his memory—just in case she might not have wanted to go out with him again after that night, despite what she said. Despite all of her clear reassurances to the contrary.

For the space of a second, Audrey's heart ached. That would have been a very Theo thought, even as far from the truth as it was then—and even farther now.

As far as she was concerned, he was stuck with her.

She would never give him up.

She loved him far too much.

Audrey leaned forward and drew her nose across his face, tracing it the same way he had with her all those months ago. His mouth dropped open and his breath trembled at the sensation of it, only for it to catch when she pressed her lips first to one brow, and then to the other. Now he knew what it had felt like when he'd done this to her—when he'd dragged his lips across her eyelids and her cheeks, briefly rested them at the tip of her nose, tilting her head this way and that between his hands as he completely ruined her for first kisses.

And made sure she wouldn't ever want another man.

She could practically hear his heart thundering in his chest. And when she finally pressed her lips to his, he broke and surged forward, pulling her closer so he could bury his hands in her hair and utterly wreck her mouth with his own.

He'd already wrecked her for anyone else, after all. Absolutely destroyed all other prospects in claiming her as his.

The truth was, she'd always been his.

She had been from the very beginning.

Theo moaned when she opened her mouth to allow him in, wanting him deeper, closer, just the way she always did, and when he swept his tongue inside so softly, so expertly, Audrey couldn't take it anymore. With her eyes closed, her hands dropped to his lap, and she fumbled at his belt buckle, finally wrenching it away and tossing it victoriously behind her. His zipper was next, and as soon as she had access, she plunged a hand into his underwear, pulling it down slightly to palm at his length while she ran her free hand along the hard stretch of abs hidden beneath his undershirt and sweater. He moaned again, the sound rumbling deep in his throat when her fingers wrapped around him.

"I don't think this is what happened next," he breathed, sliding his hands up her sweater to rip it over her head. The clasps of her bra were next, and he flung it away from the couch as he mouthed at her neck. His hands were occupied with her breasts, caressing and massaging them, pinching and soothing in equal measure before his right hand slid down into her jeans and gave her clit the attention it was begging for. As soon as he touched her between her legs, his skilled fingers deft and circling and teasing, she shuddered and groaned.

"Doesn't mean I didn't want it to." Audrey gasped again when he suddenly sucked at her collarbone. Now that it was cold and she was always covered up, Theo seemed to take extra pleasure in leaving marks behind on her body. No one else had to know except for them. It was another delicious secret they shared. "And besides, how would you know? You said you couldn't remember."

That earned her a derisive snort. "As if I could ever forget, sweetheart." Her zipper was next, and he hooked his thumbs in her belt loops and yanked her jeans down forcefully. They both grunted as she shifted on his lap slightly to rip one leg off fully, and then the other before turning her attention to Theo's own sweater. Warmth washed over her as soon as she pressed herself to his chest. The man was a raging inferno, a walking space heater, and he radiated that heat even more now through his undershirt than he had when there was a thicker barrier between her and his skin.

Audrey positioned herself over him in his lap. As soon as she was settled, he drew one nipple into his mouth, sucking hard and laving at the bud for a moment before letting it go with a gentle *pop*. She grabbed his head and held him to her chest, directing his mouth to the other breast with a soft inhale.

She was already soaking wet.

Her body always responded to him like this now.

Quick and desperate.

"How's your hip?" she murmured, sliding her hand back into his underwear while he dutifully suckled at the other nipple. It was easier straddling him this way than having to ask him to get up or lift his legs to take his pants all the way off, which was sometimes a clunky, hobbling affair.

He came up for air long enough to answer her. "Feels plenty good enough for this today. I—*oh god*." Theo shuddered and buried his face between her breasts when she pressed up and positioned him just so, right before sliding down his length.

And sliding home.

They both paused for a moment when he was fully seated inside her and gazed at each other silently. Audrey knew he was thinking the exact same thing she was: How was it that they managed to fit together so perfectly? So gloriously? How was it that it felt like this each and every time?

It seemed impossible.

It seemed entirely too good to be true.

And yet . . .

"I love you," Theo breathed. He cupped her face with both wide, warm hands. "I love you so much."

Audrey dug her fingers into his dark hair, marveling at how thick and soft it was. She rolled her hips, slowly at first, and then a little more insistently when he dropped his hands to her waist and dug his fingers firmly into her flesh.

"You light me up like nothing else," she whispered in his ear. "Like no one else." She nuzzled into his cheek. "Tell me again how you love me."

Theo took her mouth with his and drew her bottom lip between his teeth. It was already swollen and red from before, and the tiny, sharp bite of pain was exquisite. Sparks skipped along her skin. "'Brother, bear the needle's pain and draw out the poison from within,'" he quoted breathlessly, rocking his hips up slightly to meet hers. Audrey gasped as he plunged deeper inside, hitting that spot she never seemed to be able to reach herself. Heat surged in her core and rose through her body, simmering all the way down to her fingertips.

She moaned, and he chased it with his mouth, pressing another kiss to her lips—longer this time. "'Break free from the prison of your mind and rise up, kill the self, master your fate. If you do, you'll command the heavens.'" Theo's lips skated down her jaw, and he sucked another small bruise beneath her chin, punctuating it with a thrust of his hips. "'The sun can't touch you if you burn yourself.'" She moaned again, deeper this time. She could feel it hovering, the inevitability of her release, and she kept up the punishing rhythm of her own movement as she tried not to combust. The flames threatened to consume her.

But not yet.

Not just yet.

Audrey buried her face in Theo's neck, sucking hard for air as she rode him. "'Its light slips by those who hold fast to the radiance of suffering.'" He only dug a hand in her hair to hold her closer to him, even while he snaked his left hand down between her legs again. "'To the peace found through pain.'" His fingers found the bundle of nerves there, and he began to gently stroke and circle it, matching the cadence of her hips, the pads of his fingers pressing harder as she ground into him. "'The thorn blooms into a rose. The drop becomes an ocean. The—oh god, Audrey. *Audrey!*" he rasped, swallowing down a moan of his own.

He was close too.

But he managed to rally enough to finish the poem.

"'The fragment of a soul unites with the infinite.'"

With one final thrust of his hips, he made her see stars.

Audrey cried out and gave herself over to it, seizing and shivering in his lap as she drew his own orgasm from him. Her nails bit into his back just as firmly as Theo's fingers pulled against her scalp, and together they sat there in their living room, on their couch, riding the waves of their bliss between drinking their pleasure with their mouths.

Then, there was silence.

And softness.

Theo leaned back on the couch, cradling her on his chest as he laid them both down. He was still inside her, but she didn't want him to leave yet. He was warmth. He was love.

He was home.

Finally, he broke the silence.

"You saved me from my prison. From my pain. You are my light." His voice trembled as he spoke, just as much as his right hand once did, lifting to sweep her tousled hair away from her face. "My infinite love." Tears lined his eyes and glinted in the firelight. "My beautiful Audrey." He sniffed, and a quivering smile cracked across his wide mouth.

"I love you too, with all that I am." Audrey closed her eyes as she cupped one cheek and pulled his face closer so she could press her lips to the other. "You shine just as brightly for me, you know." She smiled against his skin. "My brilliant Theo."

That, at least, was no secret.

It was a truth she'd never stop sharing with him.

THEO'S EPILOGUE

IT WAS THE scent of strawberries and honey that woke him this morning—like it did every other.

Theo tightened his arms around Audrey and nestled closer, breathing in deep, awake but unwilling to open his eyes.

Not yet.

When she no longer smelled like coffee, temporarily on her days off back when they first met, and permanently after she'd finally quit her job at the café, he thought she smelled like summer: all sunshine and sweetness and light.

It made sense. That's what she was to him, so of course she'd smell that way.

He buried his nose in her hair now, letting the heady, sleepy warmth of her body curving against his wash over him, soothe him, settle into his bones. He wasn't ready to wake up fully—not yet. He needed more time.

He'd always needed more time.

It was sweeter this way, savoring her like this, like she was one of his dreams. Because for him, she was. She was his most beautiful dream.

And every time he opened his eyes, he was terrified he'd find that she was *only* a dream.

He was terrified to find himself alone again.

THE ACCIDENT WAS exactly two years and five days ago.

Theo knew because he counted: another day he managed to beat back the looming specter of death was another victory in the game of life. Another tally added to his scoreboard.

One more tick mark.

One more point.

One more win.

But it was one year, ten months, and twenty days since he woke up alone in his house for the first time after he'd lost his father—and himself.

Every bit of his body and mind had felt like they were being torn apart and burned away.

And he'd considered throwing the game entirely.

ONE YEAR, TEN MONTHS, AND TWENTY DAYS AGO

PAIN.

Searing, incredible pain shattered across his face when Theo rolled over onto his right side in his sleep. All of a sudden his pillow was made of broken glass, stabbing and tearing into his skin, driving an ice pick straight into his brain.

He screamed.

He flipped onto his back again, fumbling for the pain pills on the table next to his bed. But his hand was shaking too hard, and he couldn't quite grab the bottle. His stitches were only freshly out of the wounds on his arm and they were still raw, still red, still aching, but no longer bleeding. At least, not on the outside. But his grip was still shot, his nerves still damaged, his skin still burning, constant pins and needles and electric static jolting down his shoulder and across his palm to the tips of his fingers.

He leaned too far to the side and nearly passed out from the pressure on his right hip.

Theo froze in his bed, gasping like a fish out of water, and even that movement was painful, given how difficult it was to open his mouth wide with the lingering swelling from his wound. The ragged way he sucked for air through the fire searing across his body and face made his throat burn.

Coming home alone this early was a disaster.

It was stupid.

Fucking *idiotic*.

Why did he demand this?

He coughed, drew in a slow, steadying breath, and finally managed to grab the little amber bottle, holding it still enough to twist the cap open with his left hand before immediately swallowing two pills dry. He rolled back onto his pillow and traced every bit of their journey down his esophagus, watching the shadows dance on his ceiling with his one good eye and trying not to panic when the meds slowed their descent and stuck in his throat.

Why *did* he insist on coming back so soon?

Everything was fuzzy. He couldn't even remember coming home. He did have a few memories: the sound of shattering glass and him screaming at someone—his mother, probably—while he was standing upright, leaning heavily against a wall for support. Then a different kind of screaming, a gut-wrenching wail, doubled over and anguished, as if his soul were being ripped apart. Wetness on his face. His hand tugging at his hair. A deep, aching sense of emptiness and disgust.

Aside from that? Not much. There were only vague impressions of movement, the sensation of rocking, and the feeling of someone helping him up the stairs, a familiar, soothing male voice murmuring while a strong arm held him steady at his back.

He glanced over at the cane propped up next to the bed. It was one of those aluminum ones with four feet and a curved, padded handle, telescoping and set almost at its maximum for his height. He hated it. He fucking *hated it*.

This was what he'd been reduced to:

A cripple.

He blinked, and the memory of bright, approaching lights flashed in his mind, blinding him anew.

His world shattered again along with it.

> ***Dad's dead.***
>
> ***Nothing but glassy eyes surrounded by crumpled steel.***

Oh.

Right.

That was why.

It was because being in that house again had been unbearable.

His breathing stuttered now under the sheer weight of it.

> ***Dad's dead, his corpse buried deep and rotting in the ground, and it's your fault.***

A tear slipped out of his left eye and rolled down the side of his face.

Theo didn't remember much, but he did remember being trapped in his mother's house. The feeling of those old, white walls and low ceilings closing in around him.

> ***It's all your fault.***

The smell of musty, aging wood, painted over in a dozen layers. Too-short doorways he had to duck under. Whispers outside his room, talking about him in hushed tones, thinking he couldn't hear.

His ears hadn't been damaged in the slightest.

He wished they had.

> ***You killed him.***

The sensation of wanting to tear his skin off if only to relieve the incessant guilt crawling beneath it like spiders skittering along his bones, and the horrible, crushing knowledge that even if that were an option, he couldn't. He wasn't capable anymore.

YOUR FAULT.

He held up his right hand.

You're the shame of the Redmond legacy.

The biggest disappointment this family has seen in generations.

It shook so violently, he couldn't even grip a drinking glass for fear of dropping or shattering it. It was only his cup from the hospital with its plastic handle and wide, clear straw and leak-proof top that he could manage now.

You killed your own father.

A fucking sippy cup for a grown man.

He didn't want to touch it.

It sat empty on his bedside table.

You deserve to die too.

It was useless.

He was useless.

What could he do with his life now, like this?

You're a piece of shit.

Fucking garbage.

Lloyd was right all along.

Theo turned onto his left side. His blackout shades were down, but he was sure it was afternoon already. It didn't matter.

Nothing mattered anymore.

He thought about the little amber bottle sitting next to his bed. There were more pills in there. Everything hurt. Maybe he should take another dose—or two. Maybe three, or four.

Or twelve.

But that would mean he'd have to try to open it again.

He closed his eyes.

Maybe if he did, he wouldn't wake up this time.

It'd be a relief, in the end.

~

ONE YEAR, NINE months, and seventeen days ago, Theo left his house by himself for the first time.

He wouldn't have if Amelia hadn't made him.

He sat across from her now, gripping his cane tightly in both hands, twisting it over and over again. Maybe this time, he'd manage to break it. Maybe—

"I'm really glad you made it out here, Theo. It's nice to see your face."

"No, it's not," he spat without thinking. He swallowed bitterly, closed his left eye, and shoved his cane to the side. His right eye was still buried under layers of gauze. Last week had seen another reconstruction surgery to his face, trying to more elegantly piece together his shattered cheekbones beneath the wound slashing across it, marring the vision he had of himself—not that he'd had the courage to actually look in a mirror yet.

He hadn't truly seen himself in months.

And, of course, there was the titanium plate holding those cheekbones together. Screws mixed with sinew, metal and muscle, welded permanently inside his head.

He'd die with that in his face now.

Ironic, really. It was metal that tore him apart and nearly killed him. And now it was the only thing holding him together, both there and in his hip. The reason he'd been injured in the first place was the only reason he could walk. What had ripped open his face had patched it back up.

If there was a god, he sure had a wicked sense of humor.

Fuck him.

Theo didn't find him at all funny.

"It *is* nice to see you in person. I've been really worried about you." Amelia dug her bare feet into the soft carpet between them and leaned forward to gently squeeze his hand, her lavender-dyed hair swirling around her kind face like grape cotton candy. It was one of the reasons he'd picked her as his therapist years ago, her choice of hair color. She liked to keep it bright, or pastel. Never natural. Always cheerful. It was part of her style, her art.

Theo liked that.

He did love color, even if he didn't wear it much himself.

"I can barely see *you*." His left eye watered. When he lifted a hand to wipe the tear away, a button on his sleeve brushed too close to the gauze on the right side of his face. It snagged and pulled, and he cried out and recoiled, then flinched again at the fresh wave of pain rolling swiftly on the heels of the first.

Even minor expressions were excruciating.

His therapist tilted her head at him, her brows knitting into a soft frown. "Are you not taking your pain meds?" He shook his head slowly, and her look of horror grew. "Theo, you just had surgery. You're still recovering. You need—"

"I don't want to take them."

"Why not?"

> ***Because you're a piece of shit who killed his own father.***

Fuck.

He'd been here for a whole five minutes and Amelia was already poking around in dangerous territory.

And unfortunately, she knew him well enough to read when he was lying.

"Because I deserve to feel it." The truth didn't hurt as much to say as he thought it would, but he clutched at his chest all the same. His heart always ached now, ever since his father's had given out. Ever since Theo had been the one to break it.

It was almost unbearable.

"I need to *feel* it."

"Why?"

"Because if I don't, I'll forget. If I . . . maybe if I feel the pain, I'll still feel him too. I don't want to be numb."

Amelia sat quietly for a moment. "Do you really think you'll forget your dad?" she finally asked.

"Yes. No." He shook his head before resting it in his left hand. "Well, not just Dad. *Everything* that happened. There's already so much I can't remember." He'd lost two whole months, some of that to a medically induced coma, the rest to a haze of pain and medication. It was an unsettling feeling, knowing why things were fuzzy and still not being able to grasp them. Who knew what he might have said or done when he was in recovery?

"Right." She narrowed her eyes. "But why else?"

He hesitated. The last thing he wanted was another hospital visit of any kind—but this was the other reason he'd chosen Dr. Amelia Harper over other therapists. Because while she was soft and kind, and an established, respected leader in her field, she was also sharp and incisive while still being understanding. When he needed answers or counsel, she usually had it, whether he liked it or not. A tough-love approach with a gentle delivery. And he trusted her immensely.

"Because I don't have them anymore."

Both eyebrows skyrocketed. "Why?"

"I was afraid of what I'd do with them. Sometimes I thought about taking too many all at once, so I flushed them down the toilet. And then I felt horrible because I should've properly disposed of them, but I didn't want to leave the house to do it. And Diego wouldn't have done it for me. He would have made me take them. Or . . . I don't know." Theo drew in a deep, trembling breath. "Either way, I didn't want him to know."

Amelia pursed her lips and looked down at her notebook. She scribbled something and then tapped her pen on the paper. "When *was* the last time you left the house?"

"Today is the first time I've left by myself for anything but doctor stuff. Diego went with me to my other appointments and took me to my most recent surgery. But I don't remember that. I don't remember going. I still have trouble with my memory sometimes."

He glanced at the door, already dreading going outside again now that he'd thought of it. The walk here was bad enough. People on the street stared at the gauze on his face and gave him a wide berth like he was some kind of monster. Like they knew he'd been disfigured. Like they knew he was trash. And then a kid had pointed at his cane and he and his mother both gawked in wide-eyed horror at Theo before darting quickly in the opposite direction while he limped down the street.

He must have looked horrible, even with his hood up and his face covered as best he could manage. But scaring women and children while he lumbered around? That was a new low.

Well. He *was* basically sewn together like Frankenstein's monster, wasn't he?

The walking dead.

Maybe he should just put himself back in the ground and be done with it.

"What about your art? Have you gone back to your neon projects?"

He blinked. An image flashed in his mind: shaking hands, loud, angry music, his chest full of rage, the rippling heat and whirring sound of flames and feeling of sweat dripping down his brow, soaking into gauze. Nothing was working. Nothing was steady. He saw red through one eye.

And then he saw it on his hands. Everything was shattered, lying broken on the ground in jagged shards, blood dripping from his palms and tainting the crystal scarlet.

"No."

It was all still there in his studio, hidden behind the door, a graveyard of creative corpses.

There was that same irony again: he worked with glass, and now he was shattered himself, broken into a million pieces, left lying on the floor.

He didn't appreciate the symmetry.

"What about sketching? Painting?"

He shook his head. Touching a pen or a paintbrush was out of the question right now. He'd rather die than have to witness how his skills had crumbled and deteriorated.

The one thing he was good at, gone.

Why are you even here?

"What do you do all day, then?"

"I sleep. A lot. I walk—*hobble*—on the treadmill. I try to lift weights, poorly. I stare at the TV." Staring was more accurate a word than watching. Watching implied attention, absorption. But the shows only sounded like static in his brain, white noise whirring in the background of interminable days and restless nights. He couldn't even say *what* he usually put on. Some baking show, maybe. That was his best guess.

"Are you talking to your mom?"

"No. I told her not to contact me when I left for home. She's tried to call, but I haven't answered. Diego lets her know I'm alive so she doesn't freak out enough to actually come over."

"What about your other friends? Have you been seeing any of them?"

"Diego comes over every day."

"Anyone else?"

"I don't want to see anyone else."

"What do you and Diego do?"

Theo shrugged. "Sometimes I order dinner, sometimes he brings it. I miss cooking, but don't trust myself with a knife. He offers me a beer or a cider or a Coke, I have water instead, and we watch movies. He tries to get me to talk, I don't say anything, and after he helps me change my wound dressings, he goes home and then comes back again the next evening."

Her expression softened. "He sounds like a good friend to me."

"I guess." He hung his head. "I don't deserve him either."

"What makes you think that?"

Wasn't it obvious?

"Because I'm broken." Theo threw up his useless hands. "I was defective before, but now I can't do *anything* anymore. I'm a barely ambulatory shell of a man, hardly existing, and even then for *what*? It's my fault my dad's dead, and while he might have loved me, I don't deserve it from anyone else."

"We've been over this, Theo. You are not responsible for your dad's death."

"It doesn't change anything."

"Where's your evidence for that? Or for your earlier statement?" She tapped the pen on the pad, more forcefully than before. He could tell she disagreed with him, though her expression stayed neutral. "Where's your empirical evidence for being undeserving of love? Why do you think others merit love and care, but not you?"

Theo quieted.

"Did your dad think that? Because from what you've told me, I don't think that came from him."

You're the shame of the Redmond legacy.
The biggest disappointment this family has seen in generations.

"I don't want to go there today." He might have snapped at her with that, but he didn't apologize, and she didn't ask him to.

Amelia glanced down at her notebook again before reaching for a nearby file folder. What was she getting? He started to get nervous. He should have kept his mouth shut.

"You're not going to recommend me for inpatient treatment or anything, are you?" The thought of having to go back into the hospital made his heart race and his stomach churn. He wanted to stay home. He wanted to be alone, where it was at least safe. Where no one could see him like this.

Amelia shook her head. "No, Theo. I know you. You wouldn't be here if you didn't actually want to be. You came out of your house today to talk to me, after all, and I know that was hard. It speaks to your resilience. You're still trying, and you're still talking, so you must want to live, despite everything."

It was true. He hadn't managed to completely quash that pesky will to survive.

His left eye twitched a little at the reminder.

She rifled through the folder, plucked a page out from one of the sections, and leaned over to give it to him. It was a pharmaceutical information sheet. "But what I *am* going to do is call in a prescription for antidepressants to your pharmacy. We'll try Lexapro first. I want you to pick it up, start taking it regularly, and then tell me how you're feeling next week. And the week after that. And the week after that. And if we need to adjust things or try a different kind, we will. If you're game for it, that is."

He stared down at the paper.

"All right. I'll think about it."

"And I want you to start going out in public."

Theo jerked his head up at her so fast, he grunted in pain when his stitches pulled at the movement. He covered his eye with his *stupid fucking piece of shit* hand and tried to hold it there. Pressure through the gauze sometimes helped with the pain. "You want me to do *what*? Looking like *this*?!"

"Has your doctor told you that you can't go out?"

"Well, no."

"You're here now."

"Sure, b-but I'm going in for my follow-up appointment next week. I'll know more then," he gasped.

"Then I want you to try afterwards if your surgeon clears you for it." She pointed at him with her pen. "Theo, the last time you were out in public was in early April. That was over three months ago." She eyed the double-walled insulated stainless steel mug he always brought with him. He liked having something in his hands during sessions. Or . . . hand. "You like coffee, don't you?"

"Yeah."

"Then I'm giving you an assignment: I want you to go sit in a coffee shop." She held up her hands, placating but stern when he started to frantically shake his head as much as the pain would allow. "You don't have to stay long: fifteen to thirty minutes, tops. Five minutes, if that's all you can manage. I'll even take *one*. Consider it exposure therapy. I just want you to talk to someone who's not me or Diego. Have you talked to anyone else?"

"Imogen, once or twice."

"In person?"

He shook his head again. "Phone. Or Zoom. With the camera off."

"Who else?"

"Doctors. My PT, but he comes to my house. Same for the massage therapist, and I knew him from before. We don't talk much."

"That's it?"

"Yeah."

"In three months?"

"That I can remember."

"Then go talk to a barista, or someone new. *Anyone*, Theo. Order a coffee, have an actual conversation if you can, and try to stay out for a socially acceptable minimum length of time." She tucked her pen behind her ear. It swept some of her hair away from her face and sent it swirling around her jaw like a lilac cloud. "Try it once. See how you feel. Journal about it. Then we'll debrief."

He held up his hand. It was horrifying how much it shook. "I can't write—not like this. How the hell am I supposed to journal? I'm right-handed."

Broken piece of shit.

Amelia pointed and leveled a stern look at him. "Not without practicing, you can't. That's what you do in PT, right? Relearn how to move, strengthen muscles that have been injured or atrophied?" She tilted her head at him again and raised an eyebrow. He'd figured out a while ago that it was one of her tells—that she used it when she was trying to drive a particularly strong point home. "And that's what we're doing now: practicing. Strengthening your social—and physical—muscles. That's all. A café is low stakes. Go to one you've never been to before. If it goes poorly, they're a dime a dozen, and you never have to go back to the one where it went sour. This is New York. No one will know or care. And at the very least, you will have gotten some coffee out of it."

WHEN THEO LEFT, he went straight home.

He didn't go to the pharmacy. He threw the information sheet in his recycling bin. Instead of doing what Amelia told him to, he hobbled up the stairs with his cane and limped into his bathroom. The LED lights were stark and bright, and, not for the first time recently, he almost regretted renovating this place. Maybe he should have kept the dim, half-broken antique fixtures after all, even if they were ugly and not up to code and would have certainly shorted out and burned the house down.

What a shame.

It might have taken him with it in the fire.

After he ripped his hood and cap away, he swallowed and lifted a hand, tugging at where Diego had tucked the tail of gauze into the layers last night. Theo began to unravel while he started thinking about his new assignment.

Go out in public? Like this? He'd barely been able to manage today as it was. The usual ten-minute walk had taken him thirty both ways, and his heart raced the entire time, caught up in his throat like the last time he'd taken those goddamn pain pills instead of staying put in his chest where it belonged or shutting all the way up and stopping like he still half wanted it to.

He tugged the last of the gauze away, plucked off the clean cotton padding underneath, and steeled himself to look in the mirror. He'd only seen a glimpse of his uncovered face once: at the hospital before his last surgery, while his surgeon marked where he was going to cut, Theo turned his head and caught sight of himself reflected in the side of a stainless steel cart. It was enough to know what sort of state he was in, and the answer wasn't good. He'd been avoiding it ever since. He hadn't even shaved. His hand shook too much anyway, even for an electric razor.

But now that Amelia had brought up going out in public, he needed to know. He needed to see.

Theo lifted his eyes and finally faced himself.

A stranger stared back at him.

That . . . that wasn't him, was it? It couldn't be. His hair was long, brushing his shoulders now when it had previously been at his jawline, last he remembered. He hadn't shaved since Diego helped him with that before his surgery, and his beard was growing in, dark and patchy and haphazard. He lifted a hand, and so did the thing in the mirror. He grazed his fingertips against his swollen right eye, and when he recoiled, so did the reflection. When he closed his good eye and opened it again, it was still there, staring straight back at him.

The reflection he found was torn and broken, red and splotchy, bruised, battered, bloated, distended. His left eye was lined with a dark circle of exhaustion, and his right? Oh god, his *right* . . .

He tried to open his right eye, but it was still mostly swollen shut from the aftermath of his facial surgery. The massive slash down that side from the wreck had split him deep, shattered bone, severed muscle and sinew. Nerves had to be repaired, plates installed, everything cobbled painstakingly back together, and the result? The result was a raging deluge of stitches, what seemed like hundreds of them zippering down his face and neck from above his brow to his jawline, wicked and pointed and black, twisting deep into his skin.

It was a torrent of trauma.

He wasn't even done yet. He had another surgery scheduled for mid-August, a scar revision. Because the trauma was so bad, they already knew he would need it.

The more he looked, the worse it got. That side of his face was lopsided and sagging, mangled and—

And *ugly.*

He was ugly.

No, it was more than that.

MONSTER.

He was a monster. His outside matched the inside now. He was horrible and misshapen, his soul shredded and dissonant, and his body the same: broken and half dead and wholly deserving of it.

That's the face of a man who killed his father.

He loved you.

And you killed him.

Theo's stomach revolted. He heaved.

He launched himself at his toilet.

Several stitches popped and tore straight through his flesh while he vomited so violently, nothing was left inside him but despair.

"JESUS *FUCKING* CHRIST, Theo!" Diego roared when he shoved himself through the door later that night. "What the hell did you do to your face?!"

"I looked at it," he mumbled. "And then I threw up."

Diego grabbed his head with both hands and turned it side to side, holding Theo in the light so he could better see. "You popped your goddamn stitches. You're bleeding—it's oozing. This could get infected. We should probably take you to the ER. This is serious."

"No. I'm not going anywhere tonight."

"What? But—" He quieted at Theo's expression. "Then you need to go in tomorrow and get them to fix it ASAP. Didn't that hurt?"

It did. It was agonizing, a thousand times worse than throwing up in the past had ever been before.

Deserved it.

"It was an accident. It's not like I meant to do it."

Diego pinched the bridge of his nose with his thumb and forefinger, screwing his eyes shut and shaking his head. "*Madre de Díos*," he muttered to himself. But after he drew in a deep, steadying breath, he looked at Theo once more and patted his shoulder. "Come on, buddy. Let's get you patched up."

While Theo showered, Diego shoved their dinner in the oven to keep it warm and then went upstairs armed with fresh gauze and antiseptic and butterfly bandages. Theo sat on his shower chair in the bathroom in silence, wrapped in a towel, his hair dripping water down his shoulders while his best friend helped him carefully shave and then clean his reopened wound with antiseptic.

It was a long time before Diego spoke. He was unusually quiet. Normally, he chattered like a magpie about his day while they performed this new ritual.

"You know something?" he finally said while using clean cotton to dab at Theo's face.

"What?"

"I can't do this forever," Diego muttered, setting the cotton aside and grabbing the butterfly bandages. He opened the packet and placed one carefully over some of the popped stitches.

"I know. This isn't fair to you, but I'm really grateful you've been here for me. Thank you." Theo's voice shook. "But if you don't want to help me with this anymore, I can always hire someone to—"

"I'm not talking about that." Diego placed another across the wound, his eyes firmly locked on Theo's cheek. "Unfortunately, you're like my brother. With four sisters, I always wanted one of those. And because of that sad truth, I'm going to keep coming here every single fucking evening, even to the detriment of my sex life. Which is horribly barren right now, I hope you know." His dark eyes darted over to meet Theo's for a split second before turning back to the task at hand. "Talk about a dry spell."

"My deepest condolences to you and your blue balls." Diego's definition of a dry spell was something like three weeks. For Theo, it was already more than five years.

Now it would likely be even longer, if not permanent.

Who would want to have to deal with all this? Who would ever want to look at his face?

He couldn't even look at *himself*.

"Thanks. We appreciate it. But can you at least do me a favor?" Diego began replacing the padding over the gash. "You know my best friend, right? You remember him? His name's Teddy. Real tall, dark hair, has a big nose and huge ears. Does art. Might have a new scar or two on his face, but I hear chicks dig that sort of thing." He carefully wound the gauze around Theo's head. "If you see him around, can you tell him to come back? It's been a while since I've seen him, and I'm real lonely without him." When Diego tucked the tail of the long, cotton strip back where it belonged, he finally looked Theo in the eyes fully—and his lip quivered. He rubbed his eyes angrily and glanced away. "Will you do that for me? I miss him. A lot."

Theo rolled his lips together. If he hadn't locked his mouth shut tightly, he wasn't sure what might have broken through the dam he'd been so desperately trying to construct in his chest over the last several weeks. But he finally managed a nod.

"Yeah. If I find him, I'll tell him."

It was a lie. Theo was fairly certain Diego's best friend recently died in a horrific car accident.

He was dead and buried in the ground next to his father, Henry.

But it didn't feel like the right time to tell him that.

He didn't have the heart.

Without warning, Diego's hand shot up to Theo's hair and roughly yanked his face toward him so that they were almost nose to nose. Theo stared at him in shock, one eye wide.

"And by the way," Diego growled through his teeth. His grip was like iron and he pointed at Theo accusingly. "Don't you *dare* leave me. You think I can't see you thinking about it? I'm not an idiot." He shook him for emphasis. "If you follow through on anything you're contemplating, just know that I'll find a way to raise you from the dead so I can kill you again myself, so help me God. Do you understand me?" His grip tightened on Theo's scalp. *"Do you understand me, Theodore?"*

Theo's throat bobbed as he swallowed and nodded slowly. "Yeah. Duly noted."

"Great, thanks. Appreciate it." Diego let go of him, and he sniffed and wiped at his eyes before patting Theo hard on the shoulder. "All patched up. Get dressed and let's go downstairs, I've got tacos from Tío in the oven—he sent your favorites. What movie are we watching tonight?"

IT WAS ONE year, nine months, and one week ago that Theo set foot inside a café for the first time. Diego had come over two days prior for July Fourth and nearly passed out from shock when Theo told him that he was actually going to go out in public.

Things couldn't get much worse than they already were.

He might as well try.

They were grilling steaks on Theo's rooftop when he brought it up, and Diego immediately insisted on helping him find just the right coffee venue.

"Bean Me Up, Brewtiful Morning, Jurassic Perk, Roaster Coaster," he muttered, rattling off café names from some listicle. "Oh, hey, how about this one—you're a huge Star Wars nerd, right? This place just opened."

Theo leaned over and squinted at Diego's phone. "You've got to be fucking kidding me. A themed café called Java the Hutt? How does that even make sense?"

"It's a *java hut*—just look at the photos. A riff on a coffeehouse. Get it?"

Theo shook his head. "Absolutely not. Way too kitschy. Look at that décor—I bet their coffee is shit."

The photos were insane. Every bit of wall space was covered in Star Wars memorabilia and mixed with flashing lights probably meant to look like stars or laser cannon bolts. They barely had room for a counter and a few tables. High reviews, though—but mostly from really nerdy usernames commenting on the ambiance and fighting about Star Wars fan theories among one another. No one mentioned the drinks. None of those usernames or profile photos looked remotely like they belonged to a woman.

"It's all about the gimmick and nothing about the craft. And I don't think I'm a fan of that kind of clientele—they probably all hated the cinematic masterpiece that was *The Last Jedi.* Absolutely not."

"Fine. Ruin my fun." Diego scrolled down the list. "Is this one less *pedestrian*? More your usual kind of nerdy? It's a literary reference. You read." He tapped the name a few down from the first and opened up the website. "Surely it's bougie enough for you, you fucking hipster."

"Javawocky?" He reeled back in disgust. "Who the *hell* is coming up with these café names?!"

In the end, Theo settled for a normal-sounding coffeehouse called Uncommon Grounds that was highly reviewed and only a five-minute walk from his house. He still wanted to pass out when he thought about going, but Diego pointed out that he could wear a mask. He had a box of black KN95s on his counter, and Diego grabbed one from it.

"Here, put this on." He shoved it into Theo's hands. "And let's see . . . your hair's grown out a lot, so we can work with that. Hand me that cap, let me work some magic." Theo bent down and Diego helped arrange his hair over his right eye. He pulled up his hoodie and pointed him toward the bathroom. "Now go look at yourself in the mirror."

Theo's eyes flicked over to it. He'd pinned a few towels above it to cover the reflective surface there and in every bathroom after he made the mistake of facing himself a week prior, and the idea of sweeping one aside wasn't particularly enticing.

"It's okay. I believe you."

Diego crossed his arms over his chest and tapped his foot impatiently. "Hear me out, Theo: you look normal. Can't even tell. You look just like you did pre-accident during the pandemic when you stopped getting haircuts while we were all in quarantine, I promise. You can go outside and no one will look at you twice."

Theo hummed nervously, but limped over and swept aside one of the towels all the same. And when he saw himself, he looked . . .

Fine.

He was fine.

He closed his eyes and sighed in relief. His surgeon had given him the okay to not wear the gauze during the day anymore, and most of his stitches from this round were removed, though not all—not the parts where he'd torn them. The swelling in his right eye had gone down enough for him to see a bit out of it now that some repairs had been made—though he didn't love how his eyelid couldn't open as wide as it used to. Some of the tiny muscles and nerves were severed in the accident, and his doctors weren't sure how much he'd heal and how much movement or feeling he'd ultimately regain. But with his hair arranged like this to cover it, the cap and the hoodie concealing the scar on his neck and eyebrow, and the mask, he almost looked like he did before.

He saw himself again, or someone who looked a little like him.

He buried his face in his hand in relief.

"There you go, bud." Diego grasped his shoulder. "See? You can go outside like this and no one will notice. It'll be okay."

THE OPTIMISM WAS short-lived.

Diego had to work, and when Theo arrived alone at the coffeehouse he'd chosen, it was packed—turned out it was a popular spot for remote workers. The music was slightly too loud and it seemed like everyone in there was trying to talk over it. Every table was full and either covered with laptops, being used to hold meetings, or both, and the line to order was practically out the door.

Theo eyed the people around him nervously. The fact that it was this crowded probably meant they had good coffee, and he was already this far. He'd walked all the way over here, so he might as well try to order. He didn't want to turn back now.

But it was taking a long time. Even though there were four baristas manning the espresso machines and two at the registers, the constant whir of the grinders and the gurgle of milk frothing and the hissing of steam wands all began to grate on him while he waited. The more sound there was, the louder it seemed to get.

BANG.

He jumped. Right when one of the baristas pounded some espresso, someone behind him pushed too close and touched him, grazing their arm against his freshly healed right-side ribs, and he nearly leapt out of his skin. His heart was beating so hard he could hear it in his own ears, and the longer he was there, the faster it pounded and the more frantic it got. All of a sudden, he was lightheaded. He swayed on his feet.

BANG.

BANG BANG.

His palms were sweating, and even his left hand was beginning to shake. Someone turned up the music—unless he imagined it—and the person at the register yelled their order over the din.

The world blurred.

The floor shifted under his feet, the floorboards suddenly twisting and buckling like a ship at sea.

Theo started to lose his footing. He clutched his cane for dear life and leaned heavily onto it.

He was nauseous.

Something was wrong. He felt weird. Something was sitting on—or *in*—his lungs and had curved around his ribs, wrapping its hands around his neck and *squeezing*. Why was his chest suddenly so heavy? Oh god, he was having a heart attack, wasn't he?

Was his left arm going numb? It sure was shaking a lot, and he could hardly feel it, his fingers felt and looked so very far away. It had been years since he'd eaten spray cheese, but it was his dad's favorite snack, bright orange spray cheese on saltines, a whole can at a time, he could still hear it and smell it when he thought about it, maybe he somehow inherited it in his arteries and he had high cholesterol by proxy, why was it so loud, had everyone always talked that loud? Someone left a steam wand hissing, and it rang in his ears, drilling the sound down to one vibrating, high-pitched note overtaking everything else, screeching inside his own head like tires squealing on asphalt and—

Theo turned and bolted, barreling through the crowd behind him with his cane in his haste to limp back outside and back home to hide where it was safe.

Where it was quiet.

Where maybe, just maybe, he wouldn't die.

~

"IT WAS ONE café, Theo." Amelia's voice sounded tinny and far away through the phone's tiny speakers. "It was one café and one panic attack."

"I thought I was dying." Even now, his chest was still heavy. Even now, just thinking about it made breathing difficult.

"But you didn't die, which proves my point: that you *can* do it. You managed to stay there for a few minutes before it got too overwhelming, and I'm very, very proud of you for that. That took guts. Pick a quieter place and try again. It'll be all right." He took a shaky breath, and she must have heard him. "Yes, breathing is good. Don't forget to do it next time. Now go get back up on the horse again."

"I thought you were supposed to be gentle with me and my feelings, Amelia."

"You know very well I'm not that type of therapist. You chose me for a reason, and it's because I know you can handle it. We'll talk soon."

It was another five days before he screwed up enough courage to try again, in part because he had therapy the next day and he knew

Amelia would ask him about it—and he didn't want to fail his assignment.

Goddamnit, that was why she'd phrased it that way, wasn't it? She knew he had to win at school. He was competitive and had always been at the top of his class for a reason.

He never liked feeling like a failure. He didn't wear it well.

Last week's debacle was certainly an abysmal one. Couldn't even go into a *coffee shop* anymore?

What the hell would his dad think of him now?

You're not dead yet, kid.

Stop acting like it.

My son's brave, not whatever this is.

Was he brave? Had he ever really been?

Another pang of guilt rippled through him at the thought, a fresh wave of grief right on its heels. But Theo glanced at the Post-it note he'd stuck to the bottom of his mirror last week after his conversation with Amelia and tried to shake off the feeling.

He'd rolled up the towels on his mirror just high enough to reveal his mouth when he crouched so he could at least see while he flossed—oral hygiene was important, after all—and he'd slapped the words there as a morbid reminder, the ink shivering and shaking across the ironically cheery yellow backdrop in this new version of his handwriting:

TRY NOT TO KILL YOURSELF TODAY

The second half of that reminder was one he hadn't actually been able to bring himself to write:

Dad would never forgive you if you did.

He drew in a deep breath and gripped the edge of his bathroom counter while he steeled himself. "Right," he muttered at the faucet. "Try not to kill yourself today, Theo. You can think about it again once you've had some coffee. Just go get some fucking coffee. It's not that hard. You used to do it all the time." He zipped up his hoodie, tugged the hood over his cap, and pulled a mask onto his face before stepping out into the summer sunshine to try again.

Just like he did every day.

One halting step at a time.

When he arrived at the coffeehouse he'd picked out without Diego hovering over his shoulder, he hesitated on the sidewalk, eyeing Déjà Brew cautiously from the outside. It was clean and modern and had a good design. It was smaller than the first one. He liked the logo. The reviews were excellent. And it didn't seem *too* crowded.

Plus, it was only about a fifteen-minute walk from his house.

His hip still ached, and he still limped, but at least he was leaving the cane behind more now. It was doable. His physical therapist would be happy with him for exercising.

Maybe Amelia was right. Maybe things would be easier now that he'd broken the seal.

Maybe that was the hard part.

Theo steeled himself and pushed open the door. Instead of too-loud alt-rock music, soft, soothing lo-fi played over the speakers. There were some tables open, not all of them completely monopolized by remote workers, and everyone who *was* working wore headphones and typed quietly. And there were only two baristas, one working the machine, and the other at the register. He couldn't see their faces through the line to order, but he could tell that much from the matching aprons they wore.

He waited, shifting nervously on his feet. The middle-aged bleach-blond woman in front of him turned and glanced at his mask, scowling slightly up at it, but she didn't say anything. That was fine. As long as her eyes didn't linger on his face for too long, he could live with that.

And then it was his turn.

The blonde stepped away from the register, and when she did, Theo was finally able to focus his attention on the woman working it.

And all the breath was immediately knocked out of his chest.

He might as well have been hit head-on by another semi.

It wasn't the same as before when he couldn't breathe at the other café. There, his chest felt like it had been put in a vise, like something had gripped his heart and squeezed, or like he was back in the Thunderbird tumbling down the mountain, the hard steel of it searing into his flesh and crushing his ribs, crumbling them to dust and shredding his face more and more with every flip.

No, this was nothing like that.

When this woman smiled at him, it was like the clouds parted and revealed the light of the sun for the first time in months. It was as if he'd been sitting in a dark cave all this time and only just now stepped out into the light, blinking and blinded but warm.

She was the most beautiful thing he'd ever seen in his entire life.

She was radiant.

"Hi! Welcome to Déjà Brew. What can I get started for you?"

At the sound of her voice, every word in the English language he'd ever known immediately abandoned him.

Those were words. He knew those were words, but what was she saying? What was she asking? Start *what*?

What did he come here for again?

"Um . . ." He started to sweat. It was exceedingly hot in here, wasn't it? He tugged at the collar of his hoodie before remembering he had a scar there he was desperately trying to hide, and he scrambled for something, *anything* to grasp on to. He looked up. Right. A menu. Coffee. He glanced back down at the woman, who was watching him with a quizzical eyebrow raised.

Oh god, she knew. She had to know what he was thinking just now, and none of it was even remotely appropriate.

Maybe *this* is where he should die. It'd be less embarrassing than whatever was happening now if he did.

"One . . . l-large Americano." Good, yes. Those were coffee words. It was the first thing his eyes landed on when he looked at the menu. That was appropriate for a coffeehouse.

Her eyes were gorgeous.

Bright spring green flecked with gold.

It was a good thing she couldn't see his cheeks. He was sure they were on fire, scorched red and raw from the inside out.

"A large Americano?" She repeated the order and he nodded. "For here or to go?"

"To go."

Better, yes.

Good.

Good words.

Good words?

Fuck me.

Oh shit. He didn't say that out loud, did he?

Tiny russet freckles dotted daintily across her button nose like flecks of paint flicked from a delicate brush with a deft hand.

He couldn't tear his gaze away from them.

"Room for cream?" He shook his head. "Name?"

Fuck. What the hell was he called again?

Idiot. That was his name.

"Theo." Did—did his *voice* just crack? What, was he fifteen again all of a sudden?

Jesus Christ, get it together, you imbecile.

Pull yourself together.

How could he when he was still so broken?

The woman wrote his name and order on a cup and was about to pass it off to her colleague when he had a sudden thought and lifted a hand to stop her before he could stop himself. "Wait!"

She paused.

"Uh . . . c-can I get that extra hot, please?" There was no way he was taking his mask off here, but he'd come this far. Might as well go for the extra credit and sit for a minute at a quiet table. That was definitely the reason he suddenly wanted to stay.

Definitely.

The only reason.

"Of course you can." Her smile was softer this time, and her eyes never lingered on his mask or tried to search out what was hidden behind his hair. She simply looked at him like he was normal. Like she was kind.

He liked the way that felt.

He rubbed the back of his neck while she rang him up at the register. Her hair was a pretty chestnut color, and a single strand had slipped out at the base of her bun and curled into a perfect, loose spiral at the nape of her neck. When she turned her head, the morning summer sun caught in it and glimmered a warm gold.

Oh god.

He pulled a twenty out of his wallet, and, without thinking, dumped all the change she handed him into the jar next to the register.

It was easier than trying to wrestle bills and coins back inside the leather folds with his damaged hand. He didn't want her to see him struggle.

But her beautiful eyes did widen in shock at that.

"*Whoa.* Wow. Thank you, sir! That's—"

The panic rose. She'd noticed. What he just did apparently wasn't typical.

For fuck's sake, Theo.

Be normal for once in your goddamn life.

Oh god, he'd fucked up, hadn't he? He was weird just now, that was weird, that was abnormal, people didn't tip that much, *oh god.*

Before she could thank him further, Theo retreated, claiming a table in the corner as swiftly as he could and only darting up once from his chair to grab his order.

He made it exactly forty minutes before leaving.

Extra credit indeed.

But it was because his hand was busy doodling that tiny curl at the base of her neck over and over and over in his sketchbook. He had to keep stealing glimpses of the gorgeous woman at the register the entire time, just to make sure he got the curves of it right. It had to be perfect. He had to get it right.

He couldn't do much.

But he could sketch that.

AUDREY.

Her name was Audrey.

He went again to the café the next week. And then three times the week after. He went five times the week after that, but two of those were in the afternoon and someone else was working behind the counter, some dumbass named Steve who forgot to make his coffee extra hot and also left room for cream when he said he didn't want that, which was how Theo discovered Audrey only worked the morning shifts.

Every time he saw her, she was more beautiful than the last.

He, meanwhile, remained an inept, bumbling *idiot*.

He stumbled over his words, stuttered, forgot what he wanted to order even though it was the same goddamn thing every time, felt fuzzy in his head and unsteady on his feet. It was like his brain and his tongue had joined forces to lock up and fuck him over and there was absolutely nothing he could do about it except keep trying.

Meanwhile, she beamed at him and remembered his name and his order for him, and while it sent warmth surging through his body, while he wanted to feel special, he was sure he wasn't. She probably had a boyfriend—she was far too pretty not to. She was also good at her job and he was just another customer, even if he tipped well, but he had no idea how to talk to her and didn't want to bother her while she was working. And even if he did, every time he went home and caught even the barest glimpse of his reflection, the warmth he carried back in his stomach with the perfect coffee she made him would suddenly leach away.

She had no idea who and what was really beneath the mask.

It didn't seem to stop her from trying to talk to him, though.

Her smile was radiant, and she was funny and sweet. She was trying to get him to smile back, to laugh with her, he knew that. But every time he came close, his scar pulled across his face and his heart wrenched in his chest, another constant reminder of the life he'd had ripped away.

But he did start drawing again.

His dad would have laughed.

A girl, huh?

A girl got to you, Teddy?

You're a chip off the old block after all.

(There he is.)

(That's my boy.)

Theo wanted to draw her, to keep something of her for himself. There was no way he'd ask for a picture or take one in secret, oh god no. No, no. This was bad enough. He didn't want to be a weirdo—or, well, more of one than he already was. But maybe if he could sketch her from memory . . .

He started practicing again.

He tried to draw more than a single curl of hair, and ink flowed onto the paper to sketch the lines of her face, shaky and misshapen at first.

But over the weeks, it began to change. He got better. It started to look something like his style again. He began drawing other things, and painting too, with watercolors. They were easy to use and it didn't matter if his hand slipped or shook. The vibrant shades of it brightened up his life a little, made it less gray, chased a fraction of the gloom away, beat back the voice in his head that said hateful things to him. At least a little.

And one day, he had an idea. He took the coffee Audrey made him and he laid a brush to paper, filling in the shadows and lowlights of his portrait of her with the art she'd made for *him*. Every time he brought home her coffee he added to it, layering the fresh brew atop the old, deepening the stain, enriching the image, adding depth and dimension, just as he was getting to know her better, even if only by the tiniest of measures.

Whenever he held the portrait to his nose, he closed his eyes and could feel himself there with Audrey, the scent of coffee—of *her*—overwhelming his senses and filling him with warmth.

He loved the café now.

It was another safe place added to his short but slowly growing list.

UNTIL IT WASN'T.

One year, seven months, and twenty-two days ago was a bad day.

That nasty blond woman ripped his mask off and revealed how grotesque he was to the world.

To Audrey.

She saw.

She saw him for what he really was now.

DISFIGURED.

UGLY.

MONSTER.

He didn't leave the house for a month after his mangled face went viral. The comments online about his appearance and the calls from reporters weren't even the worst part of it all. They were bad, but they only confirmed the things he already thought about himself.

The worst part was that he'd lost his little leather sketchbook in the ordeal.

It wasn't his plans for the charity benefit and sketches that he mourned.

It was that he'd lost his portrait of *Audrey*.

The only good thing he'd made since the accident.

The only piece of her he'd been able to keep, just for himself.

The tiny bit of light he'd found had slipped through his trembling fingers.

Diego found him sobbing in the middle of the living room floor that evening, his house torn apart around him, papers strewn everywhere, storage boxes overturned and emptied, clothes ripped out of his dresser and flung about carelessly. All hopes of having mislaid his sketchbook somewhere at home were gone.

It had to have fallen out of his pocket, maybe even at the coffeehouse.

He'd been keeping it close to his chest.

He couldn't go back for it now.

Yes, you can.

Get your ass back there, kid.

Go get her.

"I can't."

"Yes, you can, Teddy." Diego knelt on the ground and grabbed his shoulders. "Just go back and ask if they have it, for god's sake."

"Audrey saw my face, Diego. *My goddamn face*." He'd just had his final scar revision surgery last week, and with it, new stitches, new pain, new pulling and tugging and wrenching and aching, all of it a fresh reminder of what he was. It was still raw, and the salt of his tears burned as they rolled along it.

"So what? You said she was nice! If she really is, I don't think she'd care! No one who cares about you gives a flying fuck about a stupid scar!"

"I'm not going back. I can't go back. I can't face her again. Not like this. Not now." He dove within himself, covering his head with his arms as he collapsed into his lap, sucking for air while he sobbed. It felt like fingers had wrapped around his throat. He couldn't breathe. The thought of going back and facing Audrey now was too much to bear.

Nothing Diego said could change his mind.

It was over.

Well.

That's disappointing.

Of course it was.

That's what he was: a disappointment.

> ***You're the shame of the Redmond legacy.***
> ***The biggest disappointment this family has seen in generations.***

His father's voice in his head faded.

The little sliver of peace he'd stumbled upon was gone.

And something inside him died all over again.

IN THE END, Audrey found *him*.

It took her nearly two months, but she did.

The next day, Theo sat across from her at the café, staring at her in disbelief while she smiled at him, while she touched him by sliding her tiny hand over his and keeping it there. He watched her mouth move, and her lips were telling him that she liked him, that she liked his drawing, that she'd seen it and didn't think he was a stalker or a total creep.

What?

He'd spent those two months fixated on that little Post-it note on his mirror.

TRY NOT TO KILL YOURSELF TODAY

He thought about it. He thought about it every day.

You're not dead yet, Theo.

Stop acting like it.

Get busy living, or get busy dying.

Just fucking pick one already.

Make up your goddamn mind.

I'm tired of this shit.

But the truth was, if he had, then he really never would have been able to see Audrey again.

Part of him clung, white-knuckled and straining, to that tiniest glimmer of hope. He didn't know why.

And now he was here, sitting at a table with her, their two coffees between them. He couldn't believe he'd almost forgotten how stunning she was in person.

His face ached. The stitches were long gone, but he swore he could still feel them most of the time. His plastic surgeon told him his nerves were healing, and that increased pain was actually a good sign. His cheek was full of pins and needles and tiny lightning shocks beneath the silicone scar tape whenever he brushed it by accident or winced too quickly or sometimes from nothing at all. It burned now, odd and electric, but that was nothing compared to the feeling of Audrey's skin atop his, cool and soothing against the back of his scorching hand.

That was a different kind of electric.

He'd spent two months driving himself mad trying to recreate the part of her he thought he'd lost while the artistic flame she'd lit within him struggled to survive. He never wanted her to know how many half-finished drawings of her face he'd angrily crumpled and then recycled at home, how much ink he'd wasted trying to recreate the soft curves of her smile, the waves in her hair, the light in her eyes.

He was right to throw it all away.

Every one of his sad attempts paled in comparison to the real thing.

Maybe he was something of a hack after all—his uncle certainly thought so, and plenty of critics too. But maybe it didn't matter anymore. Not if what was happening now was real.

Of course, the fact that Audrey had found him at his therapist's office was *mortifying*. Lisa winked at him when she handed him the note, and when he read it, he almost threw up before hurtling back upstairs to pound frantically on Amelia's office door. He nearly gave her a heart attack, but he was convinced he was having one himself.

At least he'd been the last client that day. She probably wouldn't have extended their session otherwise.

Now he held his sketchbook again, safe and sound. All his pre-accident plans for his upcoming projects were recovered.

But none of that mattered, because the most important drawing he'd ever made was back in his hands.

And with it, the most unexpected confession.

He went home, stripped off his hoodie and the sweat-soaked shirt beneath it, and laid his bare back down on his kitchen floor to stare blankly at the ceiling in wonder, letting the cold tile soothe his burning, feverish skin. He'd been sweating *profusely* under all those protective layers during that entire encounter. But he could deal with it.

You see?

You got the trademark Sullivan charm after all.

I was beginning to doubt.

Because for some reason, Audrey liked him. She actually liked him. She'd even *touched him.*

Despite his limp. Despite his horrifying, butchered face. Despite his shyness, despite it all—

She asked him out.

She wanted him to come back to the café, to sit with her and talk with her.

He actually had a date.

It was literal years since he'd been on a date. He hadn't been out with anyone at all since he'd broken things off with Kendra, and that was five years ago now.

It was a goddamn miracle.

Maybe God was real after all.

Maybe she'd finally decided to give Theo a break.

~

IT WAS ONE year, five months, and twenty-five days since Theo decided to try to see Audrey every day.

It was one year, five months, and twenty-three days since Diego yanked Theo's favorite hoodie off over his head without even having the propriety to unzip it first and shoved "real clothes" at him and did his hair before Theo ruined it with his black baseball cap and then spent the next thirty minutes yelling at him about it.

Diego made him get ready so early, Theo had time to go all the way to Levain and back to bring Audrey cookies, and also pick up flowers before he met her at the park.

It was one year, five months, and twenty-three days since they went for a walk, and saw *Casablanca*, and ate birria, and she demanded that he kiss her and she was wonderful and amazing and smelled like strawberries and honey and her lips were so, so soft and so was her hair and her skin and her taste, oh god, she'd felt and tasted so *alive* and it had taken every bit of willpower inside of him to stop himself from devouring her right then and there on her stoop and it was the best day of his entire fucking life and he *knew.*

He knew he was a goner.

He knew he'd never met anyone like her and never would again.

He knew no one else was for him.

He knew he was already falling so deeply in love with her, he would do anything for her. Absolutely *anything.*

And that feeling only grew over the following weeks.

There he is.

That's my boy.

It was one year, five months, and seventeen days since he sort-of-voluntarily showed her his face and she called him handsome. Audrey called him *handsome,* and smoothed her thumb along his scar, and kissed away the tears tumbling down his cheeks at her words and at the way she looked at him, and he realized she wasn't lying. She really did think so.

Her touch there felt like lightning.

It shocked him to his core.

Not so bad, huh?

This whole living thing?

Good choice, kid.

I'm proud of you.

It was one year, five months, and two weeks since she stayed with him after getting drenched in the rain, and he made her hot chocolate with trembling hands and they danced poorly in front of the fire and held each other in the dark while confessing some of their deepest secrets. She fell asleep in his arms, and he slept better than he had in months with her warmth curled against him now that he wasn't alone.

It was one year, five months, and two weeks since Audrey told him she would hold his mugs for him until he could again.

Since she said she wanted to be his girlfriend.

Since he woke up with her in his arms, and promptly tumbled

out of bed because of *what the hands attached to those arms had been doing in his sleep*, and that was how he discovered she was the most ticklish on the spots roughly three inches above her knees and halfway down her ribs and where the curve of her left shoulder met her neck.

It was one year, five months, and two weeks since he got to make *her* coffee for once.

It was one year, five months, and thirteen days since Theo went back down to his studio. He grabbed a broom and a dustpan and swept up all the shattered dreams he'd left strewn on the floor, and then he fired up his burners and chose a length of glass tubing.

His hands shook, and they shook horrifically. There was nothing to be done about it now, nothing more than he was already doing with only marginal improvement. But this time, he leaned into it. Instead of fighting it, he let his new state guide the vision—because Audrey seemed to really like his hands just fine the way they were. And if she liked them, maybe he could grow to like them again too, flaws and all.

He started to make things again.

Yes, get back in the shop.

Working with your hands will clear your head.

It always did mine.

It felt *good*.

It was one year and five months since he posted an ungloved photo of those hands Audrey liked so much on Lightm4st3r's Instagram, wondering if she might see, if she might know. And she did. So he took a chance, and let her into his soul, and showed her his studio—and, with those hands, the stars.

But it was one year, four months, and twenty-seven days since he saw his mother again.

Since seeing her shattered him completely, all over again, straight to his severed soul.

Since he felt like he lost his father all over again.
Since he remembered what he was:
GARBAGE.

> ***Your fault.***
> ***Your fault.***
> ***YOUR FAULT.***
>
> ***His voice in your head isn't real.***
> ***It's wishful thinking, a lie, a dream.***
> ***Dad's dead and it's your fault.***
> ***You killed him.***

It was one year, four months, and twenty-seven days since Audrey was there to hold him together when he nearly came apart completely.

Since her words actually managed to penetrate his soul—because she was beautiful and honest and good, and she couldn't lie, and if she said it, it had to be true.

It's not your fault, Theo.

It was an accident.

He tried to save you.

You're alive because he sacrificed himself for you.

Your dad loved you.

It was one year, four months, and twenty-seven days since he confessed that he loved *her*, truly, madly, deeply, with every fiber of his being.

Since she confessed the same.

It was one year, four months, and twenty-seven days since they made love together for the very first time.

Since his world was completely changed because of it.

Since he started to feel whole again.

Since he started to *live* again.

Theo knew because he'd been counting the days.

IT WAS ONE year, four months, and three weeks since Theo met up with his mother for their first joint therapy session. When she arrived and sat with him in the waiting room while Amelia finished up with another patient, she took a little dark green velvet box out of her purse and set it gently on the arm of his chair.

"Here you go. Nana's ring, as requested."

When he opened it up, his heart leapt into his throat.

There it was: his grandmother's ring, a beautiful antique emerald cut in the shape of its name, set in a band of smooth, delicate yellow gold and surrounded by a halo of small baguette-cut diamonds in an art deco style. It looked like a starburst.

It looked like Audrey.

"Thanks, Mom." He snapped the box shut and tucked it into his interior jacket pocket for safekeeping. He was glad she followed through. It was what he'd asked for, written on the back of Amelia's business card he gave her the day he went to her office:

> *I want Nana's ring, the antique emerald one from the 30s.*
>
> *I'm going to ask Audrey to marry me.*
>
> *She's the one.*

"Are you sure, Theo?"

He glanced at his mother out of the corner of his eye. She hadn't said it with judgment—only curiosity.

"Yes."

"You didn't ask me for a ring for Kendra. You bought hers," she pointed out.

Theo heaved a deep sigh. "Well, she never ended up finding out I even got her one, did she? And honestly, that should have been an indication. If it was real, I would have asked you. I was an idiot. I'm glad I could return it."

"You were young." Eleanor reached over and took his hand. He looked down at it, but didn't stop her. She was here, after all. That meant something. "You're *still* young. And so is she."

"I'm not that young." And neither was she. Theo hadn't really *looked* at his mother in a long time. The sight of how small his mother's hand was against his—and how much older it seemed, how much more frail she was now than when he'd last thought about it—made him ache.

Kid, she's not gonna be around forever, you know.

Someday, I'll have to come get her.

You need to take care of her until then.

I still love her a whole helluva lot.

I always have, and I always will.

Someday, she'd leave him for good.

Someday, he'd lose her too.

He turned his hand over and gently squeezed her palm.

The gesture wasn't lost on her. Her face softened, and he saw himself in her eyes. "You're still my kid. You'll always be my baby. No matter what."

"I know." The corner of his mouth twitched under his mask. "I'm not asking Audrey tomorrow, I just want it on hand for when I do. I'll know when the time's right." He reached up and pulled off the mask so she could see all of him and read how serious he was. "And I wanted it now in case you and I have another falling out, or in case you get too busy with litigation or something and stop showing up for these sessions. You don't have a good track record of consistency. Look at how many of my lacrosse games you missed when you told me you'd be there." He tilted his head at her and gave her a pointed look. "I was aware, you know. I looked for you in the stands, every time. And you were at court, or at a briefing, every time. I always asked Dad."

Eleanor winced deeply. She hung her head and sighed. "I know you did. You're right. I deserve that. I'll keep taking my licks." She squeezed his hand back. "But I'm not going to do that anymore, the whole 'misplaced priorities' thing. I'm here now, and I'm going to keep coming. And besides, I want to get to know my future daughter-in-law. If she doesn't have a mother, she will soon enough, because that's a role I want to fill. And I want to do it well."

"I'm going to hold you to that. Audrey is the most important thing in my life." He quirked an eyebrow at her. "Last chance."

"Oh, I know. I know you're not fucking around, Theo." She raised an eyebrow right back, the twin to his own. "You are *my* son, after all. And I love you."

He rolled his lips together. "I love you too, Mom."

It was true.

It was still there.

It had never left. It had only been buried.

The door opened, and it was time.

And though they had an understanding, it didn't mean that any of this was going to be easy.

~

ONCE HE HAD the ring, Theo thought about it every day.

He thought about it when Audrey was curled into his chest, clutching at him and whimpering in her sleep. She had a tendency to cling to him as though she were terrified he might leave her. He never would. It was an impossibility.

He held her as tightly as he could.

He would have opened up his chest again and kept her safe inside his own heart if it were possible.

He thought about it when he made pancakes for her on Sundays, watching the bubbles in the batter rise and pop with the sound of bacon and eggs sizzling next to him while greats like Billie Holiday and Etta James played in the background and Audrey fiddled with his fancy espresso machine, making them entirely too much and too many kinds of coffee in her delight with a new toy.

He thought about it when he watched her study, her nose wrinkled in concentration, some of her chaotic, loose waves making a daring escape from her hair tie and sweeping along the sides of her face.

He thought about it when he tucked those rebel strands of hair behind her perfectly-sized ears.

He thought about it while he heated and curved and bent the glass for his art, sweat dripping down his back and flames reflected in his eyes.

He thought about it while they made love.

Being inside her was unlike anything he could have ever fathomed, and every time they came together, every time she let him take her, every time he tried to meld his body and his soul with hers, he found that the well inside him where his love had sprung was unfathomably deep, and it only went deeper each time. Inasmuch as he could, he thought about it then, although it was less a coherent thought and more an instinctual knowing. A truth.

They were made for each other.

Every day, it only became more evident.

Every day, his desire for her, his love for her, only grew.

He never thought he could love someone so much.

He was never so happy to be wrong.

THEO ALMOST PROPOSED right after he got the ring.

He carried it around with him everywhere, and he thought about it so much, it was practically a reflex to reach for his pocket.

But the first time he automatically sought it out during Audrey's graduation dinner, he stopped himself.

And panicked.

Something inside him, some wild instinct, *panicked* at the perfection of it all: not because it was too much and he wanted to run, but because it was so precious, he was terrified to lose it. Terrified that if he didn't ask her that question, if he didn't ask her to stay with him forever, if he didn't ask her to codify what they had into law, something would happen and he'd miss his chance. He'd miss his chance if he didn't do it *now*.

"That's a trauma response." Amelia sat across from him during their next session, her legs crossed under her on the couch and her chic, flowing pants billowing elegantly over the sides like silk. They were a slightly darker shade of lavender than her hair and her shirt, and he marveled at how well she managed her monochrome color palette. That was actually really difficult to do if you didn't have high color acuity. "The need to rush like that, I mean. It's coming from anxiety."

"What do I do about it?"

"You're intellectual, but also creative and visual. Let's try this approach: you can visualize removing it from yourself and looking at it impartially. That's one way." She set her pad in her lap and mimed plucking something off of her back, holding it in her hands and handling it almost as if she were trying to corral a massive ball of unwound yarn. "This is what mine feels like when I hold it. It lives on my upper back, like I'm wearing a little creature in a backpack. It sits between my shoulder blades and tenses up when triggered. If you were to peel yours away from yourself and take a look at it, what does it look like for you?"

His brows knit together. "I'm not sure it looks like anything. But it feels . . . itchy." He scratched at the scar on his neck. "And it lives in my stomach." The more he thought about it, the more he felt vaguely nauseous.

"That's good. That's a start. Now imagine it. Tell me with your artist words. How would you draw a representation of your anxiety?" She tilted her head and tapped her pen against her notebook. "Actually, you're the rare client who won't shy away when I ask them to really do that. Get out your sketchbook."

His left eye twitched at the thought, but he sighed and dug into his satchel anyway. After uncapping his pen and flipping to a blank page, he readied himself and waited.

"Talk me through it, Theo. Tell me how you felt when that happened. Let's find it in your body and figure out what it looks like. If you identify it, you can be more aware of it."

He scowled at her but complied. He *was* paying for this, after all. This was supposedly some of the best therapy money could buy. Dr. Amelia Harper was world-renowned and she'd written actual textbooks used to train other therapists. Surely she knew what she was doing.

"Fine."

"Let your mind go blank." She took a deep breath and closed her eyes, and he followed suit. They sat there in meditative silence, relaxing in the quiet for a few minutes before Amelia spoke again. "Focus only on the paper, and what you feel in your body when you think about your anxiety."

When Theo opened his eyes, his hand moved the pen smoothly across the page. He let his gaze go slightly unfocused like he often did when he was first visualizing a sketch, straddling the liminal mental boundary between his creative vision and its physical representation.

"Where does it live?"

"It lives in my stomach, like that's its lair," he murmured, sketching a human figure roughly his size and shape. He thought back to the graduation dinner and fished around in his memory for the latent seed of panic he'd felt. "It expands when something brushes against it, draws itself out like a plume of smoke. But it's more than that; it has more form than just smoke. It sticks. It's thick and viscous, like tar. It crawls up my back, twists itself around the sides of my ribs, over my shoulders, wraps around my neck." His hand was fully automatic now, his eyes completely unfocused. He didn't see the pad of paper before him at all, only the image in his mind.

"Does it talk to you?"

"Yes," he breathed. "It whispers things to me."

"Like what?"

"That I'm not good enough. That I've failed. That everyone can *see* that I've failed, or that I'm a hack. That my art is actually shit. That I don't deserve any good things I might have. That my life is a waste and I don't deserve to live it. That I'm trash. That I'm a garbage person."

"Do you think that's true?"

"No. Yes. Sometimes." He frowned as he drew until a thought wormed its way through the static—and he grunted. "Audrey doesn't think so, but she also *really* loves garbage. Says she finds treasure buried there all the time that was just tossed when it shouldn't have been—when it was still perfectly good, or even pristine. Scavenges a lot of it while dumpster diving." The corner of his mouth swept upward and his entire face warmed, softened, relaxed. "It's one of my favorite things about her, actually. Her ability to see through to the true heart of something and find the value in it when others don't."

"That's an interesting observation."

He hummed. He might have wanted to comment on Amelia's amused tone, but what he was doing right now was far too engrossing. He couldn't quite pull his attention away. Instead, he kept sketching.

"What else does your anxiety say?"

"That something bad will happen to me, or that I'll die soon, or even worse: something bad will happen to people I love. Something bad will happen to Audrey. I'd rather die again myself than let anything bad happen to her."

"What was going through your mind with her at the dinner when you had the ring in your pocket?"

The thing was taking clearer shape now. "I wanted to propose that night because I was afraid maybe something would happen and Audrey would leave. But it's not her fault I'd think that. She tells me all the time she would never leave me, she loves me too much, and she can't lie. She's terrible at it, and I learned to pick out liars a long time ago. What she tells me is true. I know this intellectually. But it's still *my* mind that has trouble believing it." His hand kept moving, kept circling, shading, lining, forming, filling.

"What else, Theo? Any other reasons?"

"Yes." His brows knit together more firmly. He could feel the mountain range rise between his eyes, hardening his expression. Darkness began to overtake the pad. "I had the thought that I needed to marry her because that way, I could take care of her if I died. I could give her an inheritance with my trusts, or if not that, then with my investment income. I could keep her safe that way."

"Do you think you're going to die soon?"

"No. Yes. Sometimes." He chewed absently on his bottom lip as he drew. "Sometimes I think about dying, and I'd never forgive myself if I left her, especially now. She has no one, except for me and her foster mom down in Florida and a few friends. They're good, solid friends, and they love her, but not like how *I* love her." He shook his head sharply. "I know her. Maybe not every single detail, not yet, but I *know* her. I know her in my bones, in my soul, and I love her so deeply I feel it there too. I love her with my whole body and heart and soul, and *I* want to take care of her.

"I have more than enough. I have too much. I want to share it, but she won't let me. What if something happens? What if something goes wrong? What if I throw a blood clot and die? If I did that and we weren't married, I can't take care of her if I'm gone. What if she can't pay those loans off and she loses her job and goes hungry again? What if she's alone again?" He tried to shove down a sob, but failed. The despairing thought was overwhelming. A tear escaped his right eye and slid down the length of his scar, dropping onto the sketch and blurring some of its darkness.

"So you love her, and you want to make sure she's taken care of. Those are noble reasons to propose, Theo."

"But—"

"But are they the right ones? Are they coming from the right place?"

His hand spasmed, splattering ink over part of the paper where he hadn't intended for it to go. But it didn't matter. He was done anyway, and he dropped the pen when electricity jolted again through his fingers, jerking him partially out of his reverie. He grabbed it before it could roll onto the expensive Persian rug beneath his feet and scrambled to cap it before he made a bigger mess. And then he actually looked at his drawing.

It was horrifying. A black, twisting specter vaguely in the shape of a gigantic, ephemeral shadow-man burst forth from Theo's stomach. It was wrapped around him and bent over his shoulders, its large, bulbous head tilted forward and down while it crouched over him threateningly. Something about it was almost spiderlike in the movement he'd evoked.

But that wasn't the most disturbing part. The shadow-thing's hands were wrapped around Theo's neck, tenderly caressing his skin like a lover might all while long, distended fingers choked the life out of him.

Whenever he panicked, he couldn't breathe.

"Is it male or female? Does it have a gender?"

"It's male," he muttered. Theo blinked and recoiled in disgust.

He hadn't been expecting to draw anything at all, much less something like that, and so fast. What the fuck was this? He finally glanced back up at Amelia. Her notepad was covered in writing. Had she hypnotized him or something? He turned the sketchbook around and showed her the drawing. She took it and analyzed it silently.

But she didn't seem bothered by what he'd drawn—in fact, she seemed exceedingly pleased. She finished her notes with a satisfied nod and handed him back the sketchbook.

"How do you feel about *not* proposing, given what you just drew?"

As much as he didn't want to look at it again, he made himself. That seed of panic in his stomach grew all over again, and he rubbed a hand across his torso, trying to quell it. "I felt like it was too soon. And I was right." He shook his head. "We've only been together a few months. I mean, I don't want to rush it anyway, I was going to wait no matter what, but . . . I thought I was ready. I actually thought I was *ready*, but if this is what was looming over me? I'm not. I'm definitely not."

He held up the drawing again, brandishing it frantically in front of her. "I-I don't want this to be the foundation of my marriage, Amelia. I don't want this looming over me, over *us*. I don't want to build a life or a family based on fear. I want it—*him*—gone."

A tiny, knowing smile tugged at the therapist's lips. "Well done, Theo. Great work today." She pointed at the drawing with her pen. "There's your demon. Now that we know what he looks like, we can fight him—together. You're not alone. I'll help you."

When he went home that day, he couldn't say he felt great. But he did feel more prepared, somehow.

He wasn't ready, but that was okay. Now he knew why.

He still had a demon to exorcise.

He'd promised Audrey that he'd keep her safe from monsters—including his own.

And he wasn't letting it anywhere near her.

~

THE ART OF timing was everything.

It was something both he and Audrey had in common.

When working with glass, you have to know when it's ready, when it's tempered, when it's the perfect time to pull, to bend and shape, to manipulate and form it into what you envision it to be before it cools and hardens.

Coffee was the exact same.

If you pull an espresso shot too early, it isn't developed yet. The flavor is too weak, too unsteady, not robust enough to serve as the foundation of a drink. Wait too long, pull too late, and it becomes bitter.

The art of timing a proposal was everything.

Of course Theo thought about asking her at the gala. He had the ring tucked in his inside jacket pocket, just in case he changed his mind. And they looked so *good* together, it would have been so easy. He could have proposed, had Wesley drive them to the airport, thrown down his credit card at the ticket counter, and caught a first-class flight straight to Vegas. They had twenty-four-hour chapels there. They were dressed and ready. The pictures would be perfect.

He thought about it.

It was possible.

But he didn't act on it. The moment didn't feel right yet. Their foundation wasn't ready. It was new, and the materials were strong, but their mortar hadn't yet set. Their glass wasn't tempered. Their espresso wasn't developed.

That, and the impulse was still tinged with too much desperation for his liking. A little too much panic, a little too much fear of loss rather than the thrill of the future. He felt his demon wrapping its fingers around his throat again.

And besides, their friends and family would kill them. He knew his mother would. Diego would be even worse about it, and he didn't want to even *think* about what Violet would do. Smother him in his sleep, probably. Then perform a ritual to summon his soul back from Hell so she could kill him again—with Diego's help, most likely.

Better not chance it. Things were going too well.

Theo let the thought pass. He breathed, he relaxed, and he waited.

But this time, letting the desire go didn't twist in his gut the same way it had before. This time, he focused on Audrey, and he thoroughly enjoyed *himself* in the process.

He stopped worrying about it so much.

How could he worry, when life with her tasted so sweet?

Like strawberries and honey.

~

WHEN AUDREY MOVED in with him, Theo's life started all over again.

It felt like he was really being given a second chance.

It was everything he could have wanted.

She started her new job about a week later, and Theo surprised her when she got home by filling the house with fresh flowers. He loved the way she lit up when she saw them, and after that, he made sure to always have some around, in the kitchen or on her bedside table. He even made a few glass vases to keep them in, just for her. Just because.

Just because the flowers reminded him of her.

So soft, and so sweet.

They fell into a new routine. When Audrey didn't have to get up at four in the morning anymore, she started sleeping—really, truly sleeping, first until six, then seven, then eight. She'd always seemed to sleep better with him around anyway, but now he thought it was because she finally felt truly safe and secure under his roof and in his arms. Now she felt protected. Or, at least, he liked to think so.

On her second weekend as a full-time engineer, she was so tired, she accidentally slept until noon.

Theo let her. She looked like an angel freshly tumbled down to earth, hair spread wildly around her face and across their pillow, dark lashes fanning delicately across her cheeks, mouth open and drooling slightly on his shoulder while she snored softly into his neck.

Beautiful.

A king bed, and she mostly insisted on sleeping on top of him, even now.

She was chaotic and precious, even in her dreams.

On those weekends when she did wake up before noon, he'd cook breakfast and she'd brew him coffee. They'd eat standing at the counters or curled up on his couch, never at the dining table, and they'd talk, or read books, or cuddle while they watched trashy reality television and classic movies, or they'd go out later and spend time in the city and with their friends.

They had a tendency to use the dining table for . . . other things.

And then one Sunday, one year, two months, and sixteen days ago, Theo woke up before Audrey did.

That was no surprise—he usually did now.

They'd left the blackout shades up that night while they fell asleep to a clear winter sky, the city's lights glowing brightly beneath a smattering of twinkling stars, and early morning light poured through the windows. Theo turned his head and looked at Audrey, snuggled peacefully into his side. It was extra cold out, and she'd fallen asleep cozied up in his favorite hoodie. *Her* favorite hoodie. He was fairly certain he hadn't gotten to wear it once since he'd let her steal it from him.

His ears burned when he noticed how small she looked in it.

But that wasn't all. A shaft of golden sunlight had fallen across the bed, glowing in her hair and casting her in an angelic halo.

She was so beautiful, she stole his breath away.

He stared down at her, silent. Waiting.

His breath quickened.

Something tugged at his heart, rolled in his chest, stirred deep in his soul.

An urge.

"I have to draw you."

Theo whispered it before he could stop himself. The light was perfect. He had to. It was a compulsion. Once he spoke the desire out loud, he couldn't stop it, and he sat up, looking frantically around the room for where he'd tossed his sketchbook.

Audrey stirred at his movement, snapping him at least partially out of his wild frenzy.

He leaned over and pressed a kiss to her temple, first one, and then the other when she shifted and nuzzled drowsily into his neck. He gathered her up in his arms and pressed one to her lips next, whisper soft and gentle, as tender as he could make it. She pawed at him, making groggy noises deep in her throat while she tangled her fingers in his hair.

"What is it?" she slurred when he finally pulled away, her eyes still closed. "What time is it?"

"Early." His fingers were already unzipping the hoodie, drawing it slowly down her front and trying to make as little noise as possible. "I'm sorry if I woke you, sweetheart. You go back to sleep. Just relax. I'm going to take care of you."

"Hmm?" She opened one eye when he pressed a kiss between

her breasts. Her brows knit together. "What are you doing, Theo?" Her nipples had tightened into hard buds at the sudden assault of cool air around them, and Theo grunted as he shifted his body over her, ignoring the sudden sharp pain in his hip at the movement. It subsided once he settled and drew the duvet over his head, tucking it high enough to cover her as he slid further down, dragging his mouth along the length of her body and leaving languid, lazy kisses between her breasts and along her stomach while he pushed himself to the foot of the bed.

When he didn't answer her and instead hooked his fingers beneath the elastic of her panties and tugged them gently down her legs, she drew in a sharp breath.

"You're supposed to be resting." She was more awake now. "You should—"

"Can't rest. I have to draw you," he muttered, burying himself beneath the covers and pulling her underwear fully off.

She propped herself up on her elbows and lifted the blankets up to peek at him. "Now? You want to do that now?"

"I always want to." He ran his hands eagerly along her legs, wrapping his arms around her thighs and digging his fingers firmly into her soft, velvety flesh. "I think I'm in the mood for breakfast in bed."

She looked so goddamn beautiful, staring down at him in concern.

"But you—"

"Let me take care of you, Audrey," he growled, his pupils blown wide and his attention already lost in the sight of the rosy pink petals between her legs. "You've taken such good care of me. Let me make you come, and then let me draw you. I need this."

He didn't wait for her answer.

But she gave it to him anyway as soon as his lips touched home.

"*Yes,*" she gasped, throwing her head back onto her pillow, closing her eyes and writhing beneath the movements of his mouth. He groaned into her sex, savoring the sweet taste of her and taking his pleasure in her own. He loved the noises she made, loved the way the air seemed to scorch her throat while she panted, loved how he'd learned to wring orgasms from her body like this.

It made him feel powerful.

He gripped her legs tightly and splayed her wide before him as she arched her back and grasped for the headboard. He drank every last drop she deigned to give him, feasting upon her as though he'd been starving.

When she wound her fingers in his hair and pulled as she came, riding his face and screaming his name with his nose buried between her folds and his tongue thrust deep inside of her, he nearly came himself.

But he didn't stop at one. Oh, no. He wanted *more*.

He once told her he was an excessively greedy and selfish man.

He showed her now what he'd meant that day.

He kept going, and Audrey begged him to stop, pleaded with him for more, told him she couldn't take it, screamed "*Yes, Theo, yes*," until her throat was raw and ragged, until he made sure she was boneless, until stars seemed to explode into being against the cosmic background of the universe behind her eyes—

Until he knew there was nothing but the feeling of him worshipping between her legs.

When she slumped to the side, her chest heaving and limbs shaking, he finally released her. Theo slid out of bed and hobbled over to his art satchel. He threw it over to his shoulder and dragged himself around to the other side of the bed, pausing only to lift Audrey up and peel her completely out of his hoodie before tossing it unceremoniously atop the duvet.

She was so limp and breathless, her skin so flushed with heat and sweat, she didn't protest.

He gently laid her back down and sank heavily into the armchair in the corner.

"Don't move," he murmured, pulling his large sketchbook and tin of charcoal out from his satchel. "Stay just like that. Leave your hair right where it is. The light is perfect. *You're* perfect."

Drawing her like this made him feel more like himself than he had in a long time.

Everything else faded away once his focus took over, and for a blissful stretch of time, there was nothing but him, and her, the sun, and his sketch. The room disappeared, and with it, the ache in his hip and the shaking of his hands. The charcoal moved smoothly across the paper, capturing the soft curves of Audrey's mouth, sweeping along her body, tracing the dark strokes of her lashes, spilling over the edges of the pillow with her hair.

After a few minutes, she came back to herself enough to tug at the duvet, seemingly still shy. But when he looked up from his work and locked his gaze with hers, something shifted in her face. He could only assume it was the intensity in his eyes reflected back at him in her own that made her slowly drop her arm, fully baring her breasts to him again. Eventually, she kicked the rest of the duvet away from where it had tangled in her legs, and relaxed while she watched him watch her, studying him and lying on her side with a soft, knowing smile.

One of his own tugged at his lips, crooked and mischievous.

He put every bit of his love for her in that drawing, his hands gentle when he repositioned her, adjusting her to his liking to start another. And then one more, each one better and more relaxed than the last.

He'd never done this with someone he loved before. He'd only ever drawn nude live models in classes, and it was nothing like this.

This was the most intimate, electrifying thing he'd ever done.

And given the way Audrey was looking at him now, unabashedly posing for him, glowing and reveling in the warm, winter sunshine streaming through their windows, he was certain she felt that way too.

He loved her.

Every piece of her.

And he knew she could *see* it.

Only a fool wouldn't be able to see it in his eyes, in his expression, in the way his gaze softened, how his hands took such care with her, how he stilled for a minute, just to gaze at her, for him and for no one else before he began to draw anew.

And given the way Audrey padded over and slid carefully into his lap once he finally set his sketchbook aside, wrapping her arms around his neck and pressing warm, languid kisses to the underside of his stubbled jaw, he knew she understood. He knew she understood why he'd needed to do this.

He didn't know how long he held her in that chair, smudging black charcoal all over her arms and her neck while he traced the lines of her all over again, tapping across her freckled constellations, smoothing along the white slashes of her own scars, the few that he found.

But no matter how long it was, it still wasn't long enough.

It was never enough.

It never would be.

THE DAYS AND weeks passed. They framed the drawings he'd made of her and put them up in their bedroom, the rare example of his own art he was actually willing to display. He let Audrey try her hand at cooking and then immediately revoked the privilege. She adjusted to her new job not at a café while he kept working on his art. His physical therapist, Andy, came back to his house for their appointments and they started working together in earnest again.

His limp began to fade.

"We'll have to retrain your gait," Andy said with a pensive hum. "You walked with a limp longer than you should have, and you don't need to anymore. But you're in the habit of it now, so we'll work on it. It'll suck, but we'll train up your muscles and get you back into proper form."

It did suck.

But after six months of work, Theo walked almost normally again. Almost—but not quite—like he did before the accident. He hardly ever needed a cane anymore, and didn't mind so much when he did.

It happened so slowly, he didn't even notice.

And something else happened so slowly, he didn't notice—until he finally did.

It was eight months and thirteen days since he found himself in an optometrist's office, staring at a mirror while wearing a new pair of glasses, all because he was out for a run one morning and the street signs were a little too blurry for him to read.

He didn't think he could hate having something on his face more than his scar.

But he was wrong.

He may or may not have been scowling deeply at his reflection when Dr. Hamilton came up behind him and patted him on his shoulder. "That's a good pair Willow helped you pick out," the older man said kindly. "They really suit your face." At least he didn't completely hate the design of the rounded, plastic, tortoiseshell frames. At least they were classic. It was the fact that they had to be on his *face* that bothered him.

Why was everything aimed at his fucking face these days?

What did he ever do to deserve that?

Constant insult to injury. Or even *injury* to injury.

"I can't wear these all the time." Theo shook his head and pulled the glasses off. "I can't wear these in my studio. I work with too much fire and heavy machinery, I need to be able to wear goggles and welding shields, I need—"

"It's only until your contacts come in. They're on order, and it'll be good to have a pair of glasses in case you need them as a backup, or for around the house."

He gave the doctor a pleading look. "Can't I have LASIK?" The fact that something *else* was wrong with him bothered him more than anything. What was it now? Glaucoma? A brain tumor? Some other degenerative disease? *Was he going blind?!*

With his luck, he'd lose his sight within the year.

"Son, you're slightly nearsighted. LASIK is a more serious surgery than most people think, especially for something so small. This isn't a big deal. And your eyes may actually improve over time. I don't want to sign off on something if you don't need it."

"I've never needed glasses before."

Dr. Hamilton huffed. "You're, what? Thirty-three? It's just a consequence of getting older. It happens to most people."

"But—"

"Growing older is the goal, you know. You *want* to get glasses, Theo. You *want* to make it long enough to need them. It's a privilege. Every year you make it is a victory. Growing old is an honor, not a right. It's never a guarantee. You know that better than most. Plus, it keeps me employed." He patted him once more and then moved on to his next patient, leaving a quiet Theo behind with his thoughts.

He was still sitting with those thoughts when Audrey came home from work that evening. He was dreading showing her. He hadn't even told her he had the appointment.

But he did appreciate how he could see every one of the stray hairs escaping from her bun as she bustled inside, her face sweaty and red from the summer heat.

"Theo, I'm home! How was your—"

She stopped abruptly after she locked the door and turned to look at him. Her mouth dropped open and she let her work bag fall to the floor, forgotten.

"You . . . got glasses."

"Surprise," Theo deadpanned while he threw up his arms in a halfhearted, mocking celebration. When Audrey didn't say anything, when she only walked toward him slowly, he let his arms fall and his shoulders slump. He couldn't read her expression. That couldn't be good news. "Oh no," he groaned, hiding his face in his hands. It was more awkward than it usually was, given how hard he was trying not to smudge his new lenses. "They look terrible on me, don't they? I knew it. I hate them."

He glanced up at her through his fingers when she stepped in front of him. Her eyes were wide as she continued to stare down at him, and the faintest of blushes was beginning to tinge her cheeks pink.

She swallowed.

Theo frowned and shook his head. "You don't like them either, do you? I'm only going to wear these until I get my contacts. I—"

"You look so fucking hot."

"I—" He stilled. *What?*

"Who the hell helped you pick those out?" Audrey's voice was oddly strained and her breathing had quickened. Something prickled in warning at the back of Theo's neck. He lifted a hand and rubbed at it nervously.

"Uh . . . Willow? Some girl who works at the glasses fitting desk at the optometrist's office? She—"

Before he could finish that thought, Audrey pounced.

She lunged forward and threw herself in his lap, straddling him while grabbing wildly at his hair to drag his mouth to hers. "You look like a sexy professor in those," she growled against his lips in between sharp nips of her teeth. "You've been squinting for a long time. Why the fuck didn't you get glasses earlier?"

"*WHAT?!*" The word might have come out a little strained and confused, but it was because she'd already plunged her hand under the waistband of his jeans and was busy palming his cock while she writhed in his lap.

"Recite poetry to me again, Professor Sullivan." When she sucked on his bottom lip and drew it slowly between her teeth, oh god, holy *shit* he was so incredibly hard, and—

"*Oh*. Oh, Audrey, I . . ." he gasped. "I, uh . . . I h-have an . . . an MFA. It's a terminal degree, I could actually be a college professor if you wanted me to be." Her face turned even redder at that, and when she pumped her hand around him, he moaned. "Poetry? You want poetry? Anything you want, sweetheart, I know some e. e. cummings, a lot of Rumi, I could—"

Before he could finish that thought, she pressed her lips to his neck and sucked on a particularly sensitive spot beneath his jaw, and words completely escaped him.

His brain short-circuited.

By the time Audrey was done with him, the buttons from his shirt were scattered all over the floor. The shirt itself was nowhere to be found. His pants were . . . somewhere, and his new glasses might have been sitting more than slightly askew on his face while Audrey lay beneath him, cradling his head against her bare chest and stroking his hair while practically purring in contentment on their couch.

And Theo thought that maybe, just maybe, he could live with wearing glasses after all.

~

IT WAS SEVEN months and two weeks ago that they had their first real fight.

And of course, it was about money.

Audrey's student loan repayments had kicked in. Theo saw the statements where she'd left them out on the table—and confronted her about it.

It didn't go well.

"I don't understand why you just won't let me pay them off for you!" He held his hands out, pleading after who-even-knew-how-long they'd been arguing. "It's stupid, Audrey! I have plenty of money, fucking *scads* of it, and you're paying a ridiculous amount of interest! That's how these banks get you for life, they're predatory like that. You're not even paying the principal, and you won't be for *years*. It's a waste of your paycheck."

"Stupid?!"

As soon as she repeated the word, all the blood drained from his face.

He'd fucked up.

"I-I didn't mean stupid, Audrey. I'm sorry, I didn't mean it, I meant *stubborn*, I used the wrong word, I—"

Her face was red, and she'd already turned on her heel and ran halfway up the stairs. He followed, a strange, hollow feeling sinking into his stomach. *"Audrey—"*

"I'm not *stupid*, Theo," she shot over her shoulder, tears already streaming down her cheeks. "I may not be as smart as you, but I know the fucking numbers! I'm the one who signed my life away for them."

"You're *so* smart, this has nothing to do with—"

She stopped and turned to face him fully. "It's *my goddamn problem*, and I don't need you to save me! Quit trying to steamroll me just because you're so used to having your way. Everyone's right: you *are* spoiled. You have no fucking idea how privileged you are. You've never had to really work for anything. Everything has always been easy for you!"

She disappeared.

He froze on the stairs and listened to their bedroom door slam.

She didn't come down, and he didn't try to go up. He didn't bother sleeping in any of the extra bedrooms on the second floor either. Instead, he relegated himself to the couch.

That was what he deserved.

He stared at the shadows on the ceiling until long after midnight. It was no use.

He couldn't sleep without her now.

The stairs creaked.

And when he looked over, Audrey stood there, a blanket wrapped around her shoulders.

She must not have been able to sleep either.

Her face was a mess.

It broke his heart.

When he held an arm out, she rushed over to him, throwing herself onto his chest and wrapping her arms around his neck while she sobbed into his shirt.

"I'm a horrible, stubborn bitch," she finally wailed. "I'm sorry, Theo."

"You're only one of those things, sweetheart." When she jerked her head up to glare at him, he couldn't help but flash her a crooked grin while wiping her tears away with his thumb. "*Stubborn*," he whispered. He kissed the tip of her nose when she wrinkled it at him. "And I'm sorry too. I shouldn't have pushed."

She sniffed and wiped at her eyes with her sleeve. "Yes, you should have. You're right. It'll cost less if I let you pay them off now." She held up a finger. "But you have to let me pay *you* back."

His grin only widened. "No, that's not how partnerships work. You won't owe me anything. And besides, you've already paid me back a thousandfold, as far as I'm concerned. I owe *you*. Your college education is nothing in comparison to what you've done for me."

Her frown deepened. "But that's—"

"Then consider it the rest of the scholarship you *should* have had—the one you had at the start, and would have kept if you'd only had the right help. Which you deserved, by the way. Why do others deserve help, and you don't?" He brushed the hair out of her face and tucked it behind her ears. "Think of it as a scholarship from the Redmond Family Foundation."

"That's not a real thing."

"Yes, it is." He raised an eyebrow. "Did you forget that my family has a charitable foundation? I don't joke when it comes to money. And besides, what's yours is mine, and what's mine is yours. Your debt is mine. My wealth is yours. We're partners. That's how it works."

Her face broke, and she buried it again in his shoulder while she cried. He let her sob on top of him for a while before carrying her upstairs to bed.

Theo was never more pleased or relieved to see an account paid down to zero in his entire life.

IT WAS SIX months ago that he didn't even see his scar anymore.

He realized it while he was shaving. He was looking in the mirror, tilting his head this way and that, trying to get rid of every bit of stubble for Audrey. She liked running her hands along his smooth skin in the mornings, drawing her lips along his freshly shaven jawline, closing her eyes and breathing in the scent of his aftershave. He liked the way it made him feel.

And it was then he noticed that . . .

He hadn't noticed it.

It had been weeks since he'd even really paid the scar much mind. Months, even.

It was long healed, completely closed, and had thinned considerably, given all the treatments he'd gotten. Now it was nothing but a fine, white line slashing across his face—and he was already pale enough to where it wasn't particularly distinguishable. Even his eye opened almost as wide as it originally did, the muscles and sinews knit back together, the nerves mostly healed. Only a slight bit of asymmetry in his cheekbones betrayed the titanium plate lurking beneath.

Theo set the razor down on the edge of the sink and stared at his reflection in wonder.

There he was.

He never thought the day would come when he'd see himself again.

But it had.

And it happened so slowly, he didn't even notice.

Because he was too happy to care about something so small and so insignificant as a scar.

IT WAS THREE months and sixteen days since Theo entered another piece into the annual charity auction. And it was three months and sixteen days since he beat his own record and raised over five million dollars for the domestic violence shelter he'd failed a few years ago.

He'd wanted to do better for them, so he tried again.

Their director fainted when she heard the news.

Maybe he shouldn't have kept it a surprise.

He was going to have to change how he did things.

He couldn't have people hurting themselves over a bit of art.

THEO KEPT GOING to therapy.

Weekly, at first. Then once every two weeks. And then, one day, Amelia recommended that he go down to once a month.

They were running out of things to talk about.

And over time, the grip his anxiety—the demon who lived in his stomach—had on him loosened.

Until he didn't feel it hardly at all anymore.

Until he could look at a photo of his father and only feel grief rather than guilt.

Until he stopped worrying so much about dying.

Three months and twelve days ago, he ripped that dark drawing of the specter of his pain out of his sketchbook and burned it.

When he did, he felt lighter than he had in years.

As soon as the edges of the paper curled into ash, he pulled out his phone and booked two first-class international plane tickets in the spring.

It was time.

AUDREY WAS HIS best friend.

She was more than the love of his life.

She was more than his soulmate.

She was his own heart, plucked straight through his rib cage and made flesh. More than his better half, she was his better whole. She was his family, and he was hers.

And he wanted to make an even larger one with her.

It was two months since he started wondering what it might be like if maybe the house wasn't quite so quiet anymore. What it might be like if they added someone else to the mix.

It was two months since he wondered what Audrey thought about starting a family. He knew she wanted kids—they'd talked about it, but only in the abstract, the theoretical. Now he wondered about the practical. Maybe biological. Maybe adopted. It didn't matter.

He could wait.

But he wondered.

And first things first:

He wanted it official.

It was one day since they'd left New York. Audrey came downstairs yesterday morning at 8:30 like she always did on weekdays, standing on her tiptoes to press a kiss to Theo's cheek while he made her lunch before she headed over to the espresso machine.

He loved cooking for her. Lately, he'd been making little Japanese-inspired bento boxes. He especially liked making those because they required knife skills—and his hand hardly shook at all these days. Audrey was the envy of her coworkers for them, especially for the pictures he drew and the notes he wrote on her napkins.

What he put on there was always a surprise.

It wasn't always for other eyes.

Theo liked the idea of being a househusband. It suited him. He'd much rather stay home and work in his studio than work somewhere else with other people, and he liked taking care of his wi—*girlfriend.*

. . . girlfriend.

That word was too small for what they had.

It didn't fit anymore.

Time for a change.

He looked up from the sandwich he was cutting and glanced over his shoulder. "Everyone knows you're leaving early today, right? Wesley and I will be there in the Bentley at three."

The espresso machine whirred, and he watched quietly while Audrey frothed the milk and rotated her wrist, expertly mixing it into the crema of both of their flat whites, floating a quick little concentric pattern in the foam. She swept the last of the milk through the middle of it and flicked her wrist with a flourish at the end, transforming the foam of his into a series of layered hearts before setting it down next to him. He leaned over and kissed the top of her head in thanks.

"How could I forget? I've been *dying* to leave all week." Then, a scowl. "I can't believe you won't tell me where we're going. I had to get a *passport*, but you won't tell me for which continent?! And you won't even let me pack my own suitcase? How long are you going to keep me in the dark?"

He had a blindfold and earplugs already prepared. His lips broke into a crooked, wicked smile. "As long as I can, sweetheart. It's too much fun for me. You know how I love surprises."

Audrey groaned. "Fine." She took the finished bento box he passed her and tucked it safely into her work bag. "Safe for work napkin today, or not safe for work?"

"Decidedly *not* safe." The sound of her snort was such a rush.

She held up an accusing finger. "And you're going to pack me underwear for this trip, right?" She gave him a stern look. "I mean it, Theo. Give me some fucking underwear this time. I don't want a repeat of Christmas."

"Absolutely not. You don't need it. Commando for ten days."

She shoved at his shoulder before grabbing his collar and yanking his head down for a kiss.

It was the second best Christmas he'd ever had. The best was their first, when it was just the two of them exchanging gifts in his family's quiet, snow-covered cabin in the Catskills in front of the fire. But this past Christmas at his mother's house in Albany had felt like coming home in a different way—a new way, and one that actually fit.

There was no big, extended Christmas party filled with aging Manhattan socialites making incessant small talk at him, no Uncle Lloyd, no house servants cooking big, stuffy, formal dinners. Instead, it was just the three of them: Theo, Audrey, and his mother, wearing matching flannel pajamas and eating Chinese food with chopsticks straight out of the cartons while they lounged on the couch in the den and watched *It's a Wonderful Life*.

It was perfect.

His dad would have loved it.

Audrey certainly did.

He spent yesterday packing their bags (including *some* underwear for Audrey) before Wesley picked him up. They went and got her next.

Then they went to the airport.

He kept her in the dark for most of the flight.

But she knew where they were when the pilot announced that they'd landed over the intercom.

And she cried.

THEO FINALLY OPENED his eyes.

Sunlight streamed through the billowing white curtains of their Airbnb apartment in the third arrondissement, spilling across the light-stained chevron-laid wooden floors. The night air was cool, so they'd left one of the windows cracked open while they slept, and the sounds of traffic crept through and mingled with their portable white noise machine. Somehow, the noises of the cars and the people were different here than they were back home in Brooklyn.

It was a big city, but still different.

He watched Audrey sleep and ran whisper-soft fingers through her hair so as not to wake her. She was curled into his chest, her eyes closed and her legs tangled with his, her breath warm against his skin. She'd changed from when they'd first met—her hair was longer, her curves softer, her cheeks more filled out.

Somehow, she was even more beautiful, more radiant, more precious.

Maybe it was because he knew her now.

She stirred in his arms, and he knew she was awake when she

yawned, arching her back while she stretched. After a moment, she finally opened her eyes.

"Good morning," she murmured. Her lips twitched into a soft, sleepy smile, and she nuzzled deeper into his neck. "We're in *Paris*."

"Yes, sweetheart," he hummed, tightening his arms around her with a dreamy sigh. "We're in Paris."

"What are we going to do today?"

Theo tucked her under his chin and buried his nose in her hair, inhaling deeply while he thought back to the texts from their friends that had come through once they landed:

DIEGO | Good luck tomorrow, Tedward! You've got this! She's gonna cry

VIOLET | I swear to God, THEODORE

VIOLET | I swear to GOD

VIOLET | If you forget to record my baby's proposal so I can see it

VIOLET | I WILL RIP OUT YOUR INTESTINES AND HANG YOU WITH THEM MYSELF 😠

ALASTAIR | Bloody hell, Violet, what the fuck?

VIOLET | I MEANT WHAT I SAID 🔪

VIOLET | IT'S NOT *MY* FAULT HE DRAGGED HER TO PARIS INSTEAD OF DOING IT HERE

ALASTAIR | Wouldn't YOU like to be proposed to in Paris???

VIOLET | . . .

VIOLET | . . . are you—?

ALASTAIR | NOT WHAT I WAS SAYING

ALASTAIR | Let's talk about this offline

There was a large stretch of radio silence in the group text before it picked up with a new timestamp.

ALASTAIR | Violet

ALASTAIR | My love

ALASTAIR | Petal

ALASTAIR | My sweet pookie bear

ALASTAIR | Please come back inside

DIEGO | Your sweet pookie bear, Ali? Really? 😏

DIEGO | I'll be your sweet pookie bear. 😘

ALASTAIR | FUCK

ALASTAIR | FUCK

ALASTAIR | SHIT

ALASTAIR | OH FUCK NO

ALASTAIR | DELETE THIS

ALASTAIR | NOT MEANT FOR THE GROUP

Theo nearly had an aneurysm trying not to cackle when he read that. But Ali would be fine.

Violet was quick to anger, but never one to let it linger. And Ali knew how to grovel with the best of them. So much so, Theo half wondered if the man had a foot fetish sometimes.

He didn't want to know.

JOSH | . . . good luck, man. Godspeed. 🫡

JOSH | Theo, Audball loves you. She'll say yes

JOSH | But seriously: record that shit or you'll be in for it when you get back home

JOSH | Violet will be out for your blood and I'll help her hunt you down

Those weren't the only texts he had waiting for him.

His mom's had come through the latest. Looked like she was up burning the midnight oil prepping for a big court case.

But that wasn't important. What *was* important was that she fulfilled every promise she'd made him in therapy, and more.

He teared up when he read her messages.

MOM | Make sure you call me when she says yes.

MOM | What time is your brunch? I think it'll be about 4am here.

MOM | I'll have my phone on, you make sure to wake me up, I don't care about sleep, it'll be a miracle if I get any anyway

MOM | I'm too excited

MOM | I want to FaceTime with Audrey as soon as you slip Nana's ring on her finger.

MOM | And make sure to text Gladys too. She'll want to know.

MOM | I can't wait for you to come home.

MOM | Your father would be so proud of you.
I know I am.

MOM | He would have loved Audrey like his own daughter. I know I do.

MOM | And I love you. ♡

It was true.

Dad would have loved her. He would have loved her so much.

Audrey was the only one who didn't know it yet, but Theo had already made brunch reservations at a café—a real one, in a historic building with classic cast-iron tables outside and bursting with fresh springtime flowers, covered in wisteria and surrounded by blossoming pink cherry trees. In about an hour and a half, they'd sit at their table outside in the sun and order baguettes served with butter and fresh strawberry jam, freshly baked pain au chocolat, orange juice, œufs cocotte with toast and cheese and whatever else. And they'd order café au lait, rich espresso mixed with milk. Just the way Audrey liked her coffee best.

Theo would pull out the emerald engagement ring he'd been carrying around in his pocket for the past five hundred days—

—he'd kneel before her—

And he'd ask for her hand.

He'd kneel with a decent hip, with relatively steady hands, without fear, without anxiety, only a heart filled with hope and love, and he'd ask Audrey to be his forever. To let him be hers for the rest of their lives.

And he would stop counting the days.

Because now he wouldn't have to anymore—he would just live them with her.

He would do anything for Audrey.

He would kill for her. He would die for her.

But these days, what he wanted most was to *live* for her.

The corner of Theo's mouth twitched, and he felt both dimples fold deeply into his cheeks when he smiled—as wide as he ever had.

"Figured we'd head out to a café and start with some breakfast. And coffee."

SCENT HAS A stronger tie to memory and emotion than any of the other senses.

They met in a café at 8:17 on a sunny Tuesday morning.

Whenever Theo thought of Audrey, he could always smell freshly roasted coffee in his nose, just the same as when he first laid eyes on her.

The scent of thick, rich espresso, brewed dark and strong.

And while he could still taste the chocolate from her lips at the park, feel the popcorn between his fingers while they watched *Casablanca* at his favorite theater, see the way the bright orange neon sign he'd made for Tío's taco truck glowed against her skin back when he was first beginning to suspect that maybe, just maybe, there was something there, it was always coffee that reminded him of her the most.

Reminded him that maybe life was good after all.

That maybe it wasn't bitter.

That maybe it was actually sweet.

It was why he'd chosen this city, and that spot.

Because this way, they would always have Paris—and the luxurious scent of coffee floating in the air.

Author's Note

The Rumi excerpt that Theo recites in chapter 23 is taken from *The Masnavi Book 1: Story 50,* sometimes known as "The Man with the Lion Tattoo." Most people in the West recognize Rumi's work from Coleman Barks's *The Essential Rumi,* which was responsible for almost single-handedly popularizing the thirteenth-century Sufi mystic and poet in the modern era.

The excerpt I chose was translated directly from the original Persian by Dr. A. Azfar Moin, professor of religious studies at the University of Texas at Austin. I worked with him to come up with an interpretation that captures the authentic spirit of the original text while still feeling fresh for a modern twenty-first-century audience. I've given the story a new title here.

Unless Dr. Moin decides to pen a brand-new volume of Rumi's poetry himself one day, this is the only publication of this exact translation in existence. If you try to Google it, you're not going to find it.

It's only here in *A Latte Like Love.*

To Suffer the Needle's Pain

Brother, bear the needle's pain
And draw out the poison from within.

Break free from the prison of your mind
And rise up, kill the self, master your fate.
If you do, you'll command the Heavens.
The sun can't touch you if you burn yourself.
Its light slips by those who hold fast to the radiance of suffering,
To the peace found through pain.
The thorn blooms into a rose.
The drop becomes the ocean.
The fragment of a soul unites with the infinite.

Who let me do this?

I've been asking myself that question every day (*pinch me*), and while the answer is "A lot of people, actually," chief among them is Cindy Hwang. I once begged the universe for an editor who really got me, who truly *understood* me at my core, and boy did it deliver. Working with you is a lifelong dream come true. Thank you for plucking me out of obscurity and taking me under your wing.

I also begged the universe for the agent of my dreams, and then Jessica Watterson came barreling into my inbox. You're the best damn publishing partner and cheerleader and hand-holder and book-titler I could ask for. I have no idea what I'm doing. I'm so glad you do.

Thank you to my amazing team at Berkley: Elizabeth Vinson, you're incredible. I know I can always rely on you to tell me exactly what's up and how best to get things done. Vikki Chu, this is the cover design of my dreams. I'll never be over that gorgeous hand-lettering. Lindsey Tulloch, my production editor, who worked with my copyeditor, Janine Barlow; proofreader, Daisy Flynn; and cold reader, Danielle Barthel, to make sure my manuscript read smoothly and clearly. My interior book designer, Alison Cnockaert, who took my notes and tendency to play with text and turned it into something crisp and clean with so much character. Jessica Plummer, my marketer, and Kristin Cipolla, my publicist, thank you for getting my name out there and making people actually want to read what I wrote. Again: I have no idea what I'm doing, and I wouldn't be anywhere without the intrepid group of publishing experts I have surrounding me. Thank you for having my back.

To my cover artist, Cindy Car: I never thought I would have a cover like this for any book, much less my very first. It's so beautiful. You're so, *so* talented. Thank you for coming with me on this journey.

Thank you to Katy, for being the first one to finish reading any of my books, for telling me to write fanfic, for spending every Monday night dopamine cycling with me, and for always, *always* being there for me when I've needed you. And to Jen, my college roommate and earliest reader. You've been there from the beginning, rushing to read my late-night roleplaying updates the second I posted them, and you've never stopped. You have no idea what that means to me. Thank you both for being my rocks.

Torrey and Gillian, my lovelies, my beloved group chat, my life changed when y'all slid into my DMs. Thank you for the unhinged voice notes, the sleepovers, the Kome dates. Katy B.P.: my god, thank you for grabbing me those extra play tickets and for screaming with me about everything. I'm so glad we're still friends after all these years—and you too, Matt. You're my oldest friend, and one of my greatest cheerleaders. Amber: your art is incredible. Lauren: I'm so thankful every day that we met at work and then became writing friends. I'm so proud of us. Anne: my work wife, my same brain, my eternal brunch date and platonic life partner, let's do this shit. Greg: thank you for being a fabulous CP, D&D and movie buddy, and friend. And Billy and Lydia: thank you for the writing retreats and for yelling at me when I refused to show anyone my work. Lydia, ripping the laptop out of my hands to forcibly read the first chapter of something I wrote did actually make all the difference.

Monica: for every blank document I long to draft in, there's a completed manuscript full of mistakes just waiting for your grabby hands to fix, and I love that you live for that while it makes me want to crawl out of my own skin (thankyouloveyoumissyoubye).

I have to shout out my day job coworkers for being so, so incredibly supportive. Not everyone is lucky to have bosses as fantastic as mine (Doug and Doreen, lookin' at you), but I'm especially thankful for Azfar, who casually jumped in over lunch to help me translate some thirteenth-century Persian because it sounded like fun. (It was.)

Thank you also to the community of all the other authors who have helped me along the way: Sarah, Shep, Jeeno, Thea, Ehi, Madge, Kat, and especially Ali, who is the best publishing mentor, role model, and author advocate out there.

I wouldn't be here at all without fandom and AO3. To all my Reylos, especially my fandom big sisters, Junk and Jenny, who adopted me early and changed my life for the better. To everyone who has ever read, given kudos to, commented on, shared, or done fanart for one of my fics, followed me on social media, yelled about my stories, cried in my DMs, laughed at my jokes, listened to my playlists—*thank you*. This is for you too. (And also you, Rian Johnson. You know what you did.)

Pippa, my Shiba, my babygirl, my heart dog, thank you for reminding me to touch grass. Often literally, but also by immediately demanding to play *every single time* I sit down at my desk to write. I know you can't read, but you're so wise: play is important.

And last but not least: to my parents. You get to choose your friends, but you don't get to choose your parents—and the universe deigned to give me the very best ones. They have spent my whole life trying to do so much better for me and my sister than what they ever had.

My parents have moved mountains—and states—to make sure that I could chase my dreams. They bought me so, so many books, introduced me to the magic that is the library, read to me at night well into my teens, didn't question when I chose to study French literature in college (twice) for some bizarre reason, packed me up and drove me home when I quit grad school, and fed me when I was far too tired to cook for myself while I worked full-time and wrote and edited this book. They also drove in from out of state just to babysit my senior dog that one time I booked a wild, last-minute trip to New York that ended up changing my life. My mom gave me my first romance and fantasy novels. They shaped who I am as a person.

Anything I have ever done has been because you were there supporting me more than anyone else, and you always have been.

Thank you.

I love you.

Photo courtesy of the author

MICHELLE C. HARRIS grew up deep in the heart of the Central Texas Hill Country, devouring as many books as she did tacos. By day, she wrangles academics at a university, and by night, she pens stories about love, magic, and men who yearn under the intense supervision of her Shiba Inu, Pippa. In her spare time, you can find her playing volleyball, buying more tea than she could ever possibly drink, and writing fan fiction about star-crossed space wizards on AO3.

VISIT MICHELLE C. HARRIS ONLINE

MichelleCHarris.com

Ready to find
your next great read?

Let us help.

Visit prh.com/nextread

Penguin
Random
House